PRIMAL

MICHELLE ROWEN

AVA GRAY

JORY STRONG

LORA LEIGH

BERKLEY SENSATION, NEW YORK

THE BERKLEY PUBLISHING GROUP
Published by the Penguin Group
Penguin Group (USA) Inc.
375 Hudson Street, New York, New York 10014, USA
Penguin Group (Canada), 90 Eglinton Avenue East, Suite 700, Toronto, Ontario M4P 2Y3, Canada
(a division of Pearson Penguin Canada Inc.)
Penguin Books Ltd., 80 Strand, London WC2R 0RL, England
Penguin Group Ireland, 25 St. Stephen's Green, Dublin 2, Ireland (a division of Penguin Books Ltd.)
Penguin Group (Australia), 250 Camberwell Road, Camberwell, Victoria 3124, Australia
(a division of Pearson Australia Group Pty. Ltd.)
Penguin Books India Pvt. Ltd., 11 Community Centre, Panchsheel Park, New Delhi—110 017, India
Penguin Group (NZ), 67 Apollo Drive, Rosedale, North Shore 0632, New Zealand
(a division of Pearson New Zealand Ltd.)
Penguin Books (South Africa) (Pty.) Ltd., 24 Sturdee Avenue, Rosebank, Johannesburg 2196,
South Africa

Penguin Books Ltd., Registered Offices: 80 Strand, London WC2R 0RL, England

This book is an original publication of The Berkley Publishing Group.

This is a work of fiction. Names, characters, places, and incidents either are the product of the authors' imagination or are used fictitiously, and any resemblance to actual persons, living or dead, business establishments, events, or locales is entirely coincidental. The publisher does not have any control over and does not assume any responsibility for author or third-party websites or their content.

Copyright © 2011 by Penguin Group (USA) Inc.
"Bleeding Heart" by Michelle Rowen copyright © by Michelle Rouillard.
"Skin & Bone" by Ava Gray copyright © by Ann Aguirre.
"Angel-Claimed" by Jory Strong copyright © by Valerie Christenson.
"Primal Kiss" by Lora Leigh copyright © by Christina Simmons.
Excerpt from *Nightshade* by Michelle Rowen copyright © by Michelle Rouillard.
Cover illustration by S. Miroque.
Cover design by Rita Frangie.
Interior text design by Kristin del Rosario.

All rights reserved.
No part of this book may be reproduced, scanned, or distributed in any printed or electronic form without permission. Please do not participate in or encourage piracy of copyrighted materials in violation of the authors' rights. Purchase only authorized editions.
BERKLEY® SENSATION and the "B" design are trademarks of Penguin Group (USA) Inc.

PRINTING HISTORY
Berkley Sensation trade paperback edition / February 2011

Library of Congress Cataloging-in-Publication Data

Primal / Lora Leigh . . . [et al.]. —Berkley Sensation trade paperback ed.
   p.   cm.
  ISBN 978-0-425-23905-6 (alk. paper)
  1. Occult fiction, American.   2. Love stories, American.   3. Paranormal romance stories,
American. I. Leigh, Lora.
  PS648.O33P75 2011
  813.087660806—dc22

                   2010046257

PRINTED IN THE UNITED STATES OF AMERICA

10 9 8 7 6 5 4 3 2 1

PRAISE FOR AUTHORS OF

PRIMAL

MICHELLE ROWEN

"Rowen never disappoints!"

—Gena Showalter, *New York Times* bestselling author

"Rowen's characteristic wit, infused with a dark edge. A great read!"

—Kelley Armstrong, *New York Times* bestselling author

"A high-octane thrill ride to a fresh, new, dark and sexy world."

—Eve Silver, national bestselling author

AVA GRAY

"Ava Gray is a must read!"

—Larissa Ione, *New York Times* bestselling author

"Sexy, clever, and tightly plotted."

—Lauren Dane, national bestselling author

"Riveting romantic suspense . . . [The] chemistry sizzles."

—*Publishers Weekly*

JORY STRONG

"Never a dull moment within this blazing read." —*Fallen Angel Reviews*

"The passion is going to blow your darn mind." —*Dark Angel Reviews*

"Jory Strong will leave you hooked." —*Romance Junkies*

LORA LEIGH

"Lora Leigh delivers on all counts." —*Romance Reviews Today*

"Erotic, fast-paced, funny, and hard-hitting." —*Fresh Fiction*

"The incredible Leigh pushes the traditional envelope."

—*Romantic Times*

CONTENTS

Bleeding Heart

MICHELLE ROWEN

WITHDRAWN

The events in *Bleeding Heart* take place a few days after those in *Nightshade*.

ONE

"She's the chick with the vamp-killing blood?"

The loud voice pulled me out of a thick cloud of nightmares about pale-skinned monsters with sharp teeth and claws. I opened my eyes wide and stared up at the peeling white paint on the motel room's ceiling.

"Yeah, her name's Jill," was the reply. Both voices—one familiar and one not—came from outside, and I could hear them clearly through the thin door.

"So, what are you? Like, her protector or something?"

"Something like that."

"Shit, man. You're not forgetting you're half vampire, right? What if you get a taste of her? Will it kill you, too?"

"I don't drink blood, so I'm not planning on finding out."

I slipped out of the lumpy bed and moved toward the window to the left of the door so I could peek outside. The view was the same as it had been for three days—a very unglamorous gray cement parking lot with a dying twenty-foot-tall palm tree blocking my view of the main street.

Declan Reyes stood with his back to the green door, his profile clearly visible to me. He'd lost his left eye a long time ago, and the damage was covered by a black eye patch. His face was scarred around that patch from old injuries, just like the rest of his body. Dhampyrs like Declan—half human and half vampire—healed fast, but scarred from every flesh wound they received. They also didn't have the benefits of immortality like a vampire did. Thanks to his human side, Declan was every bit as mortal as I was.

He had his arms crossed over his chest, and he faced a dark-haired man only a couple inches short of his six-four. The man looked tough, like a bouncer or a bodyguard.

Or, more likely, a vampire hunter.

Declan had said he was going to contact one of his old pals here in Los Angeles to see if he could help us out. This must have been the pal in question. Nice of him to make house calls.

The idea of anyone else getting involved with my problems didn't set my mind at ease, but I was trying not to complain. I'd recently become extremely guarded about my privacy. It was safer that way.

The man's lips parted to show straight white teeth as he grinned. "Wait. I think I get it. You're doing her, aren't you?"

"Doing her?" Declan replied dryly.

His smile widened. "Got to say, I'm surprised. Rumor had it that you were . . . uh, how do I put it?"

"What?"

"Neutered. Don't take it the wrong way, but that's what I heard. That serum you were on before—the shit that kept your vamp side at bay—I heard it fucked with your libido. Always wondered why you were never that interested in hitting the titty bars with me. I guess now I know, right?"

Declan glared at him without speaking, and I gripped the window ledge, worried that there would be a fight between them. This was one of Declan's friends? He sounded like a Grade-A asshole, enough to make my skin crawl.

I actually jumped when Declan laughed a second later. It was a humorless sound.

"My sex life is none of your fucking business, Jackson."

"I'll take that as an affirmative." Jackson was laughing, too. "What about the permanent drug you're on now? Does that—"

"It works the same as before. Actually, it feels even stronger than the other one. I'm with Jill to keep her safe until we find a way to get the Nightshade formula out of her blood." Declan's jaw tensed. "That's all."

"So you're not fucking her."

"It's none of your damn business either way. But no."

Jackson's shit-eating grin didn't waver. "But you have. No wonder you're so into this chick. Memories of a great lay can fuel a guy for a long damn time. I bet she's hot. When can I meet her?"

"She's sleeping."

I pushed open the door, leveling my gaze with the nosy hunter I'd already decided to dislike. "I'm awake now. Hard to have an afternoon nap when there's so much testosterone flying around."

"You heard all that?" Jackson scanned the length of me. I'd slept in jeans and a black tank top so I was already fully dressed.

"I heard enough."

He glanced into the room, his gaze stopping at a plastic baby bottle and pile of disposable diapers. "Did I wake the baby?"

"There's no baby," I said, with a sharp look at Declan.

Jackson frowned. "Just collecting kid paraphernalia in case one suddenly appears out of nowhere?"

"I was looking after a baby for someone, but Declan took her elsewhere yesterday and won't tell me where." I sounded as pissed as I felt. I had a hard time hiding my feelings, especially when it came to the things that were totally out of my control.

A vampire—a vampire *king*, actually—named Matthias had asked me to protect his newborn daughter. It was his last request he'd made just before he'd died from drinking my blood.

He was gone. But the promise I'd made remained.

The promise that Declan had taken out of my hands.

"Jill . . ." Declan looked at me out of the corner of his good eye. "Am I lying?"

"It's better this way."

"We'll have to agree to disagree on that."

I *did* agree that my current life was nowhere a baby should be, and I'd be the first to acknowledge I wasn't born with strong maternal instincts, but it bothered me that he'd made this choice alone and refused to tell me where she was—only that she was safe and being cared for. Declan believed the baby was in danger and that any vampire who wanted to find her could mentally influence my weak human mind to learn where she was. She was a dhampyr like Declan. Because of that, her infant blood was worth its weight in diamonds to vampires who believed the rumors that it imbued true immortality when consumed.

Maybe Declan was right to take her somewhere she'd be better looked after than with us, but it didn't mean I had to like it.

He was just damn lucky I'd come to trust his judgment about shit like this.

The vampire hunter extended his hand. "Jackson Gale. Great to meet you, Jill."

I glanced at Declan, but his expression was unreadable. Another one of his drug's side effects, apart from impotence, was keeping my dhampyr traveling companion virtually emotionless. It was a difficult thing to get used to.

Finally, I grasped Jackson's hand and shook it. "Charmed, I'm sure. So what's going on? Or would you like to continue talking about what a great lay I am?"

Jackson grinned. "Nice."

Declan's expression tensed. "I wish you hadn't overheard that."

"Doesn't matter."

For an emotion-free dhampyr, he now looked a little bit embarrassed.

"Declan's filled me in on the Nightshade formula in your blood." Jackson eyed me. "How do you feel?"

I paused for a moment, deciding how much I wanted to share with this stranger, then figured what the hell. "I've felt better. But I haven't had any side effects for a few days."

"What kind of side effects were you getting before?" He leaned against the wall next to the open motel door. I hadn't yet stepped outside. I glanced around to make sure nobody but the three of us was within hearing distance.

"After I was first injected, I got nausea from hell. And lots of pain. Those side effects have leveled off, but this poison will kill me unless I find a way to get it out."

"Damn." He watched me, his brow creased. "Then lucky for you I'm here. I've been looking into things, and I know where you need to go."

"Where?" I failed to keep the naked eagerness out of my voice.

"The parachemist who created the Nightshade formula in the first place—everyone thought he worked alone, but they were wrong."

Declan crossed his arms. "He didn't?"

Jackson shook his head. "He had a partner a couple years ago, Dr. Victor Reynolds. He works out of a covert research facility on the edge of the city. He wants to meet you—both of you—to see if he can do anything to fix this." His previously amused expression faded, and I was surprised to see concern now etched there. "Look, I don't know you, Jill, but I can see that you've been through a lot of bad shit. You're not a part of this world. You shouldn't have been dragged into it."

"You're right, she shouldn't have," Declan said, and we shared a look. I'd been in the wrong place at the wrong time and come between him, his gun, and a man who'd used me as a hostage before injecting me with Nightshade—the only sample of it there was.

Only a week ago I didn't know vampires were real. That there was a branch of science that specialized in the paranormal. That a formula could be developed that would make my scent irresistible to vampires, but one taste would turn them into fire and ash. I'd fallen head first down the rabbit hole, and I'd been looking for a way out ever since. Looked like Jackson just might have a map for me.

While I could never forget everything I'd seen and experienced, I was ready for this roller-coaster ride to be over once and for all.

"When can I meet Dr. Reynolds?" I asked.

Jackson looked at each of us in turn. "How does now sound?"

WE DROVE WITH Jackson forty minutes across Los Angeles to what looked like a small, run-down warehouse on the edge of the city. Declan parked about two hundred yards away from it, shielding the car behind a Dumpster.

"You're sure this is the right place?" I asked as I stepped out of the passenger side of the car and warily eyed the unfamiliar location.

Jackson slammed the rear car door behind him. "Yeah. It's a secret research facility. Emphasis on the *secret* part, which is why it doesn't look like much from up here. It's all underground. The place goes twenty stories down."

"What kind of research do they do here?" Declan asked.

"What kind do you think?"

Declan looked at the building. "They keep vampires here?"

Jackson nodded. "Locked up in the basement. If you're doing research, you gotta have some guinea pigs at the ready. A few days starved off blood and they make for better test subjects; their vampiric traits can't be hidden anymore. Saving mankind from the monsters is hard work." He grinned. "Come on. I promise nobody's going to get bit."

Funny guy. All his flippant comment did was give me second

thoughts about this. A shiver went down my arms, and my stomach began to churn. I had to remember that guys like Jackson were used to this sort of thing and could find the humor where I didn't. Still, things felt off. I didn't like the prospect of being anywhere where I knew vampires were hanging around, even if it was against their will.

However, my motivation for getting rid of the Nightshade was strong. I really wanted to live, so I summoned all the courage I could and followed him.

We walked around to the front of the building, and Jackson pushed open the large front door. There was a security camera mounted up to the left on a ledge to keep an eye on visitors.

I grabbed Declan's arm before he went inside. "Can I talk to you?"

He flicked a glance at Jackson. "Give us a minute."

"I'll wait inside." Jackson entered the warehouse and closed the door behind him.

Declan turned to me. "What is it?"

"You sure you trust this guy?"

"Yes. I've known him ten years—we trained together. He's always known I'm a dhampyr and he never held it against me like some of the others did. He's a good guy."

I could tell that he meant every word.

I was quiet for a moment. "You know, he kind of reminds me of somebody."

"Who?"

I raised an eyebrow. "You."

Declan snorted humorlessly "You mean, if I wasn't all scarred up and pumped full of drugs that make me into a robot."

I frowned. "Declan—"

"It's true, Jill. And I know it. Talking to him earlier—what you overheard. He knows me. He knows that you and I can't . . ." His jaw tensed. "Not anymore."

Declan and I had sex once when he'd briefly gone off his emotion-and-desire-repressing serum for the first time in his adult life. He'd never been with anyone before me, but he'd been a very quick learner.

I pressed my hands against the hard planes of his chest and looked up at him. "I am willing to give it a shot. You never know what might happen with a little experimentation."

He searched my face. "You're looking for a miracle."

I nodded. "Every damn day, actually."

"This isn't one of them. This serum's permanent."

"I don't believe anything's ever *completely* permanent."

I went up on my tiptoes and pressed my lips against his. He didn't push me away, but he didn't kiss me back, either. I could taste him, I could feel him, I could touch him. But I couldn't *be* with him—not really. It was so frustrating. Sometimes it was difficult not to remember how good it had been between us. It hurt to think it might never happen again.

For such a tough-looking man, one you might not want to run into in a dark alley, one who looked like he could kill someone with his bare hands—and Declan *could*—I literally ached for him. But it was an ache that would have to go untended. Like he said, he was like a robot right now—virtually emotionless and without the distraction of lust or desire. Too bad. They were very worthy distractions.

His gray eye held an edge of regret when I pulled back from him. "I'm sorry, Jill."

"Don't be sorry."

"It's good that we're here. I knew Jackson could find somebody to help us. Then you can go back to your normal life and forget all about this." He pushed open the warehouse door and walked through to join Jackson on the other side.

His message was clear. I could forget about *him*.

Because Declan Reyes, dhampyr vampire hunter, one with scars deeper than just physical, a man I couldn't make love to no matter how much I wanted to, thought he had no place in my regular human life.

The ache I already felt for him spread to my heart because I knew he was right.

TWO

"No guards?" I asked skeptically after entering the cavernous interior of the warehouse.

"Downstairs," Jackson replied. "There are security cameras everywhere. Very few people know this place exists, and everyone who works here is screened and background-checked. The elevator only works for those who know the code." He grinned. "Feel better?"

I scanned the seemingly empty space. "Not really."

"Just chill. It's fine. This place has been around for years. Follow me."

Jackson led us to an elevator that, after he punched in a code that he shared with Declan so he'd know what it was, took us deep below ground.

Dr. Reynolds was waiting for us at the end of a long hallway in a large white room. He was fiftyish, with fine features and dark hair that was salt-and-pepper at the temples. Wire-framed glasses perched on his nose. With the white coat over his clothes and a stethoscope hanging around his neck, he looked like a family doctor who'd graduated top of his class. This helped ease my mind a little.

He'd given me a brief medical examination—eyes, mouth, ears all got a check. Heart rate. Blood pressure. He scribbled his findings down on a clipboard before he finally looked up at me. "I can help you, Jill."

My heart leapt. It was exactly what I'd been waiting to hear. I wanted to pinch myself to prove this wasn't just a dream.

"How can you help her?" Declan asked. He didn't sound as relieved as I felt. Instead, he sounded wary, suspicious, and not the least bit friendly.

His query earned him a sharp look. "I believe I asked you to leave the room before I started my examination."

"I'm not leaving Jill's side." Declan stood just out of reach, his arms crossed over his chest. I saw a glint of the silver stake he kept in a sheath on his belt under the edge of his black jacket. He didn't look directly at me, despite his fierce and protective claim.

Jackson had left when he'd been asked to. Declan, however, had flatly refused, not budging a step when Dr. Reynolds made the original request. It was fine with me. More than fine. His presence helped to give me extra strength to face whatever the doctor had to say to me.

Dr. Reynolds's jaw tightened as he glared at the stubborn vampire hunter. "Declan Reyes. Your reputation precedes you."

"Oh yeah?"

"You're a dhampyr." It was said through clenched teeth.

Declan didn't reply to that, which was confirmation enough.

"Declan's with me," I said, not liking the tension that had been steadily rising in the room. "Whatever you have to say to me, I'm fine with him hearing it, too."

"Maybe I'm not fine with that."

"Let me guess," Declan said. "You have a problem with dhampyrs."

"Is it that obvious?"

"Yeah."

The doctor's narrowed eyes flicked to me. "You know dhampyrs are extremely dangerous to humans, don't you? Perhaps even more so than vampires."

I'd heard this song and dance before. I held the gaze of the doctor, whose face had flushed with anger. "Declan's different."

"Have you seen the *other* kind of dhampyr?" he asked sharply.

"Yes." A chill went down my spine. There were two types of dhampyrs, and Declan was the more human type. The other kind were referred to as *monster* dhampyrs because of their more monstrous appearance and appetites. They were as mindless as they were ravenous, like large, pale, humanoid piranha—sharp teeth, soulless black eyes, and an overwhelming need to feed.

The stuff of nightmares, actually. I had the sleepless nights to prove it.

I watched Dr. Reynolds, whose attention was now focused on Declan. There was something there that made me uncomfortable— a willingness to believe the worst. This is what Declan had been putting up with all of his life—people jumping to conclusions about what he was, based on half of his DNA.

I'd come face-to-face with several hungry vampires since I was first injected with Nightshade. I easily remembered what it felt like to be bit by one of them—the sharp pain as those razor-sharp teeth cut into my flesh. Just because every one of them who had tasted my blood had died a quick and fiery death didn't make the thought of getting attacked any more pleasant.

"Declan's with me," I said. "And I trust him completely. If you have a problem with that, then we're going to have to leave."

After a few more moments, Dr. Reynolds's unfriendly and tense expression faded and his brow furrowed. "I apologize for my unprofessional behavior." He removed his glasses and rubbed his eyes, then cleaned the glasses on his sleeve before putting them back on. "My wife, she—she was killed by a dhampyr. It's colored my objectivity."

Immediate empathy surged through me at the thought of anyone facing death at the hands of one of those nightmarish monsters. "Oh my God. I'm so sorry."

"So am I." His jaw tensed and his expression shadowed. "This is neither here nor there. I need to take some samples of your blood now so I can study it."

I rolled up my sleeve without argument, happy for the change of subject, and he set to work. He drew in a sharp breath when he first saw the color of my blood. It wasn't red. It was more of a dark, *very* dark, crimson.

"It's incredible," he mused aloud.

Seeing it only made it that much more real. I flicked a glance at Declan before returning my attention to the doctor. "What? Incredible that I'm still standing. Still breathing?"

A slight smile played at his lips. "I'd be lying if I said no. Yes, it's incredible that your body has withstood the poison for so long, especially with visible transformations like this. It's infused your entire being. If it was developed by regular chemistry, there's little doubt that you wouldn't have survived this long. However, parachemistry is different."

"So you can help her," Declan said. "For real?"

Declan's voice was enough to put a crack in Dr. Reynolds's pleasant expression. He really didn't like the dhampyr and wasn't making much of an effort to hide it. "Yes. I'll use these samples to create a new serum that will release the Nightshade from your cellular makeup."

"Sounds . . . encouraging?" I said, gripping the edges of the examination table. My heart pounded so hard and fast it was difficult to appear calm.

His expression darkened. "Once we separate the formula from your blood, I think we can cleanse the blood through intensive hemodialysis. Dialysis isn't normally a painful process, but I should warn you that the separation process likely will be . . . difficult for you."

The thought of more pain made me cringe. I'd experienced so much pain since first being injected that it had redefined agony for me. This wasn't something I'd choose if I had any other option. There weren't any other options.

I hadn't been expecting a magic, sugarcoated pill to cure me. It would have been nice, but this wasn't a fairy tale.

I nodded firmly. "Let's do it."

"You'll stay here during your treatment—the floor above us is where my patients stay. It will be quite comfortable for you."

I assumed that the vampire guinea pigs didn't get the same first-class treatment. "What do you want in return? I don't suppose this is covered by health insurance."

He placed his clipboard under his arm and moved to the other side of the examining table, giving Declan a wide berth. "If there's any way I can rediscover the formula, if I can extract it from your blood and re-create it—it'll be an invaluable weapon. Even though you'll no longer be a part of it, there's no reason why the Nightshade program needs to be discarded completely."

He was helping me so he could try to re-create Nightshade. Sounded reasonable to me.

I nodded again. "When do we start?"

"The moment I have the information I need from these samples. I'll be in touch as soon as I can."

I felt lightheaded from the blood donation as Declan and I left the examining room and rode the elevator back up to the warehouse level. Declan kept his hand at the small of my back in case I lost my balance.

We got off the elevator and walked through the empty warehouse until we emerged into the sunlight again.

He eyed me cautiously. "You okay?"

"I'll be fine." I pressed my hand to my forehead. "Must be all the blood he took. I'm feeling a bit drained."

"I'll go get the car," Declan said. "Wait here."

I nodded and leaned against the wall, just outside of the front door, and watched him disappear around the edge of the building. I eyed the camera that was trained on the front door. For something that was there for security reasons, it made me nervous.

"Did it go well?" Jackson asked. I started a little, since I hadn't seen him standing to the other side of me.

"I think so." I rubbed my fingertips over the Band-Aid at the crook of my arm. "Listen, thanks for pointing us in the right direction."

Jackson smiled. He was actually quite attractive in a biker-dude kind of way, and the expression helped soften up the rougher edges. "I'm usually a hard-ass when it comes to shit like this, but I'm really sorry for what you've been through."

That surprised me. "You don't strike me as the type who's sorry for much."

"I'm not."

I blew out a long breath and pressed back against the wall. The air was dry, hot, and smelled like dust and exhaust fumes. The meeting with Dr. Reynolds had tired me out. Hope was an exhausting emotion to entertain. "You've known Declan for ten years, have you?"

"Around that." He shook his head. "Seems strange seeing him with a woman like you."

I raised an eyebrow. "A woman like me?"

He shrugged a shoulder. "I can tell a lot just from meeting a person once. You're somebody who needs a man in her life who's able to show her a good time."

"Am I?"

"And I saw how you looked at him before."

"How's that?"

"Like he's on the menu."

I couldn't help but snort at that. This guy thought he knew it all. I wasn't a big fan of cocky. "Is that right?"

"Declan, he's . . . a good hunter. Loyal to a fault. I know you met the man who raised him."

"I did."

"Then you know Declan will stay with someone even when it's obvious to everyone else it's a bad idea."

I bristled at that. "That's how you think it is with him and me?"

"There's nothing there, Jill. Just a shell. He's a machine. A soldier. He kills rogue vampires. It's what he's done, 24/7, for as long as I've known him. He isn't somebody who's going to make a good boyfriend."

This conversation was beginning to make me uncomfortable, but if it was a means to get more information about Declan, I could tolerate Jackson for a while longer. "I'm not looking for a boyfriend right now. I'm a bit preoccupied with trying to stay alive with blood nearly the color of tar."

"Maybe so." Jackson drew close enough to me that I could smell his spicy aftershave. His gaze swept the length of me. "But you're a woman of passion. You have needs he's not able to fill." He reached forward and twisted a piece of my long black hair around his index finger before leaning closer to me. "I can fill them, Jill. If you want me to."

"Oh yeah?" It was warm outside—easily over ninety degrees— and Jackson's body heat only made it warmer. A trickle of perspiration slid down my spine. He was hitting on me. That didn't seem like something someone should do to a buddy's female companion, even in an unusual relationship like mine and Declan's.

"I can take you to places you've never been before. I'm not asking for a relationship here, just a bit of fun. A way to let off some steam."

A bit of fun—something I hadn't had in a very long time. Too bad it was Jackson doing the offering. "What about Declan?"

He shook his head. "Declan's like a eunuch. He can't satisfy you like I can, even if he wanted to. It won't be long before you start looking elsewhere. Despite all you've been through, I see that fire inside of you. And I know how to quench it."

"You want to fuck me." I stated it bluntly to make sure I understood him correctly—not that he was being subtle about it.

"Very much. And what do you want?" He leaned closer so

I could feel the line of his body, which included a very stiff erection that he wasn't shy about pressing against me.

"What do I want?" I put my hand on his chest and slid it down between us, over his rather impressive denim-clad hard-on. Then I grabbed it and twisted. "I want you to fuck off."

Pain registered on his face, but he let out a low, throaty laugh. "I guess I have my answer."

I let go of him, feeling that my point had been made rather succinctly. "No offense intended, of course."

"Of course not." His eyes flicked behind me as he cupped his hand over his assaulted groin and stepped away from me. "Declan. You're back."

I glanced to my left. Declan's emotionless gaze was narrow, and I wondered if he'd seen what just happened.

"Let's go," was all he said.

Very soon I'd start the painful process of cleaning my blood. Soon I'd be back to my normal life—the life that didn't include amorous—or rather, lecherous—vampire hunters who left me cold, or dhampyrs who made my blood hot and my body yearn for more than they were able to give me.

I'd never been a big fan of disappointment.

THREE

I had a shower back at the motel room to cool off. Declan went out to get us food. When I emerged with wet hair, after pulling on some clean leggings and a tank top, he was already back.

He held up the brown paper bag. "Burgers. And fries."

"Running for my life is fattening." I didn't really mean it. Since I'd been poisoned, I'd lost weight. I could actually count my ribs now, which was a bit disturbing, since I wasn't eating any less than I normally did. I figured the Nightshade revved up my metabolism. It was another side effect to add to the list.

I leaned my hip against the table and ran my fingers through my damp hair to get the tangles out. Declan sat at the small table and looked down at his hands. He seemed preoccupied about something.

"What's the problem?" I asked.

He looked at me. "Why do you think there's a problem?"

"You're quieter than normal. Not that you're usually a chatterbox, but—"

"I heard you talking with Jackson."

"What part?"

"All of it." He raised his gray gaze to mine, stroking his fingers over his eye patch to adjust it back into its proper place.

"He came on to me."

"I know."

"And I told him to fuck off."

His lips curved. "I know."

I felt concerned, since he still looked troubled. "What's really wrong, Declan?"

He shook his head. "If he'd forced himself on you any further, I would have ripped his head off. As it is, he took a simple *fuck off* as an answer. He's very popular with women. Your rejection must have come as a shock considering his track record."

"Do you think I was tempted?"

He blinked. "Were you?"

"No. Were you jealous?"

He gripped the edge of the table, his knuckles whitening. "I don't know. With the serum, all—all I feel is this emptiness inside of me. Where there should be emotion, there's . . . nothing, just an empty black hole. I know that's where all the shit I should be feeling belongs. I never felt it before—never *noticed* it, anyway—but I do now."

"Emptiness."

"Yeah."

I bit my bottom lip as my throat began to tighten. "I know how you feel. I have that, too."

"You do?"

I nodded. "It's hard to deal with that empty feeling, but sometimes we don't have any choice."

His expression darkened. "Jackson gave you a choice."

I couldn't resist rolling my eyes at that. "Yeah, he did. Since I can't be with you, he was more than willing to serve as a replacement. Really big of him."

His brows drew together. "Is that why you feel empty? Because we can't be together?"

We were treading on dangerous territory. I wasn't really prepared for this conversation about emotions and empty black holes with a man I couldn't really have. It felt like trouble, and I already had enough of that to begin with. "Look, Declan, let's just eat. It's been a long day. Maybe tomorrow Dr. Reynolds will get back to us."

"He will. I don't doubt it. He's a serious dick, but I really think he can help you. Then you won't have to deal with all of this, deal with me, with horny assholes like Jackson sniffing around you. You can go back to your regular life and normal men who can be with you when they want to be."

I reached across the table and grabbed his hand. It was currently clenched into a fist. "Normal guys are completely overrated, just so you know."

His hand relaxed in my grip. "I'm about as abnormal as they get."

"Feeling sorry for yourself tonight?"

He gave me a humorless smile. "That's just the problem. I'm not feeling anything. And yet . . ."

"What?"

"The thought of you with Jackson . . . I wouldn't call it jealousy, exactly. But it bothered me. I didn't like it."

That was interesting. Not jealousy, but something that triggered some sort of reaction in the emotion-free dhampyr.

I intertwined my fingers with his. "I'm not having a luxurious fast-food dinner like this with him, am I?"

"No." He leaned back in his chair, pulling his hand away from mine. I tried not to take it personally. "He was right about one thing."

"Which is?"

"That you're a woman of passion. You deserve more than this."

I glanced around the small room. "More than . . . burgers and fries at a seedy motel?"

"For starters." He wasn't smiling anymore. His jaw tightened. "You said something earlier. I think I want to take you up on it."

"What's that?"

"What you said about experimenting."

I remembered exactly what I'd been talking about. "Declan—"

"No. Jill, don't say anything."

This was coming totally out of left field. I was ready to question him, but I couldn't say anything because he stood up, pulled me against him . . . and kissed me.

I'd kissed him a couple of times since he'd been shot full of the permanent serum, searching for a response, and was disappointed when I didn't get one. This time he'd initiated it; he was kissing *me*. And I was responding. Earlier I'd decided on a cool shower, but the heat of Declan's kiss warmed me up immediately.

"Do you think . . . you can . . . ?" I whispered against his lips, not wanting to finish the sentence.

"This isn't about me, Jill. This is about you. That is . . . if you want this to happen." He held my face between his hands. "Say yes."

"Yes," I said, without thinking twice.

When he kissed me this time, he picked me up and carried me to the bed.

I locked my arms around his neck. "My hair's wet."

"Do you care?"

I grinned. "Not really."

He placed me gently down on the bed and began kissing down my throat, filling his hands with my breasts. I could barely believe this was happening. A potential solution to my Nightshade troubles earlier. An experimental Declan now. This could all be a dream.

It didn't feel like a dream. It felt real. And I didn't want to question it a second longer.

Grasping the edge of my tank top, he pulled it up, skimming it over my skin. I wasn't wearing a bra underneath, which saved some time. I gasped out loud as his mouth closed over my right nipple and he slid his tongue around it in a hot, wet circle.

He looked up at me. "Let me know if I'm doing this right."

I struggled to breathe normally, but it came out like a needy moan. "So far, so good."

He moved to the other side, making me shiver, goose bumps breaking out along my skin. I helped him to peel my top off over my head, then squeezed my eyes shut.

Experimenting with Declan was a very good idea. I was so very glad I'd thought of it.

When he kissed me again, sweeping his tongue against mine, I pulled at his black T-shirt, sliding my hands under to feel his skin beneath, down over his hard, rippled abdomen. I started to unbutton his jeans and slide the zipper down, but he grasped my wrist to stop me.

"No, Jill."

I looked up at him with surprise. "Why not?"

"I already told you, this isn't about me."

"I want to touch you."

He pulled my hands away from him and raised them up above my head. "If you can't play by the rules, then this game will have to end."

He was easily strong enough to keep me pinned, but his grip on me was loose enough that I could have broken it if I wanted to. "I'm not sure I like those rules."

He moved his mouth to my ear, and my bare breasts flattened against his T-shirt-covered chest. "I want to make you happy, Jill."

I believed him. His expression held no fire to match what I was feeling, but rather, endless sincerity. He couldn't make love to me, not completely—not the way I wanted—but he still wanted me to be happy after what he'd overheard Jackson say to me.

Jackson had offered me no-strings-attached sex.

I'd said no because I wasn't attracted to him. I didn't want a quick lay, and I didn't want Jackson. I wanted more than that, even though I knew that wanting more would only leave me frustrated.

Declan wanted to take away some of that frustration. Here. Now.

Which meant my clothes came off. But his stayed on.

"I can stop." His deep voice got raspy when he spoke quietly. "Or I can keep going. Your call."

My throat felt thick. It was a mix of cool disappointment and hot desire. I could have Declan, but not all of him.

"Do you want me?" he asked when I didn't answer right away.

I nodded wordlessly.

"Do you need me?"

"Yes."

"Then keep your hands like this." He pressed them up against the headboard, curling my fingers around the cool metal rails.

I drew in a breath. "So I can't touch you at all?"

"Those are the rules."

I gripped the headboard tighter. "Fine. Your move, dhampyr."

A shadow of a smile played at his lips, and he sat back on his heels, his feet still clad in his heavy-laced boots, and slid the palms of his hands down the front of me between my breasts. His hands were calloused and rough against my skin—it made my nipples tighten and I shivered. I arched my back off the bed unconsciously to meet his touch.

"You're beautiful," he said.

"So are you."

He chuckled deep in his throat. "You're lying. My scars—"

"Are part of you. And that makes them beautiful. I think we've had this conversation before."

"Jill—"

"I wouldn't be in a situation like this with somebody I found unappealing, Declan. Trust me on that. You make me so hot I can barely sit still."

He leaned over, his mouth only an inch from mine. "How hot?"

I inhaled sharply as I felt his hand slide under the waistband of my leggings and down between my legs where he'd easily feel the proof of just how much I wanted him. My grip on the headboard tightened.

"You're right," he whispered. "Very hot."

I gasped. "You're teasing me now."

"Maybe a little." He hooked a finger in either side of the elastic waistband of the leggings and slid them down my legs until they were off. I lay naked on the bed, my arms still above my head, while Declan, fully dressed, swept his gaze over me.

I had to admit, me being naked and vulnerable at the moment and him being fully dressed and totally in control was hotter than I thought it would be.

"How's the experiment going so far?" I asked, my voice breathy.

He raised an eyebrow. "Good, I think. You?"

"Excellent. A-plus."

He kissed me. My lips parted and he slid his tongue against mine, which made me groan low in my throat at the chance to taste him deeper. My breath caught as his hand returned between my legs and he stroked me there until I felt boneless with need.

He didn't say anything as he kissed his way down my body. I watched him, my hand now held against my mouth as he parted my legs and pressed his mouth against me there. I cried out and let go of the headboard completely so I could grip the back of his head when I felt his tongue slide over me.

"Declan—" But I couldn't form actual words anymore. His name was barely understandable.

Pleasure crashed over me, so intense it was close to pain. My body quaked against his mouth and hands, raising off the bed, but he held me in place until I came again. A scream escaped my lips then, despite my attempt to muffle it with the back of my hand.

He brought his face back to mine and kissed me hard and open-mouthed so I could taste myself on his tongue. By this time I was utterly ravenous for him.

"Please, Declan," I begged. "I need you inside of me. I want you so much."

I wrapped my legs around his fully clothed body and ground myself against him as if he were naked. I desperately needed him thrusting deep inside of me. I wanted him even more now than I had before. He'd given me two incredible orgasms, but I wasn't satisfied. A small taste had only intensified my hunger.

Slowly, very slowly, I regained control of myself until I found I was kissing him more than he was kissing me. I held his face between my hands and stared up at him, dismayed to see his expression held some regret.

Tears stung my eyes. "Please don't look at me like that."

He looked pained. "I'm sorry, Jill. I want to be more for you, but—but I can't be."

Every bit of hot, aching desire I'd just felt for him hadn't been matched. He felt nothing. The mind was willing, but the body couldn't comply. My skin felt electric, sensitive, as though if he touched me again, he might send me right back over the edge.

I sat up so we were face-to-face and hugged him against me. "It's okay."

"It's not."

"For now it is."

"The experiment . . ."

I pulled back so I could see his face. "Speaking for myself, the experiment was a complete success."

A smile touched his lips. "I'm glad to hear it."

"I am a fan of science."

I kissed him, sad that this time he only briefly returned it.

It had been a short detour, but we'd returned right back to square one.

At least there were some French fries waiting as my consolation prize.

FOUR

I'd had bad dreams every night since I was injected with Night-shade. This was the first time I had one about Declan.

It started off well enough.

We were having dinner, and it wasn't salty, greasy fast food scarfed down in a cheap motel room. We were at a restaurant—one of my favorites, a little Italian place that was just around the corner from my apartment in San Diego.

He placed his hand on top of mine, and I looked up at his face.

It *was* Declan, but it wasn't the Declan I'd come to know. The black eye patch was gone, and he had two beautiful green eyes instead of one gray one, which was a trait of a dhampyr or vampire. He didn't have any scars marring his handsome features. His hair was a bit longer than the short-cropped cut I was used to. And he had an easy grin on his face that was as unfamiliar as the dark blue suit he wore.

"You look like you've just seen a ghost," he said.

"Feels a bit like it." But I wasn't as shocked as I could have been at his appearance. It felt right, as though I was accustomed to seeing him like this. "You look really good."

"Better than normal?"

"Well . . . *different*. What happened?"

"Nothing happened. That's just the thing. I'm not a dhampyr. I'm not a hunter. I don't get a scar every time I get cut or shot.

I didn't lose my eye because I never fought with the vampire who clawed it out with his fingernails." He raised an eyebrow. "What do you think of that?"

"I'm speechless, that's what I think. You look—"

"Like I could be part of your real life."

"Actually, you do." I smiled and entwined my fingers with his. "No more vampires. No more running for our lives. We can be together. It's perfect."

His expression shadowed. "It's not perfect."

"What?"

"Your blood . . ." His brows drew together.

I felt something warm on my face and swiped my hand under my nose. I was bleeding, dark red blood that looked almost black. My heart sank at the sight of it. "I'm the one who doesn't fit in now, aren't I?"

"I wish I could help you." His gaze moved to the right and his expression tensed. "Maybe *he* can."

I turned my head to look. The sun was bright outside, and there was a man standing in the doorway staring at me so intently I couldn't believe I hadn't noticed him yet. It was Declan—the scarred version. One eye. Ragged from ten years of hunting vampires. Wearing a black leather jacket that had seen better days.

He wasn't smiling.

"Jill . . ." he said.

I immediately rose from the table and went toward him, but it felt as if the air had thickened, making it difficult to move. Panic snaked through me.

Declan jerked forward a step as if he'd been hit from behind. He gasped for breath, then clamped his scarred hand against his stomach and looked down at it. Bright red blood gushed through his fingers. When he looked up at me, I noticed his throat was now slit as well. Blood pumped out of him with every beat of his slowing heart.

I couldn't breathe. I tried desperately to fight through whatever this was that was holding me back.

"Declan!" I woke up screaming and clutching at the solid form in front of me.

"I'm here," Declan soothed, stroking my hair. "It was just a nightmare. It's okay, Jill. You're okay."

I pulled back from him and searched his face, my eyes wide. He was here. He was alive. "I thought that I . . . I thought that *you*—that you were—"

"Whatever it was, it wasn't real." He held my face between his hands and wiped my tears away. "I know all of this has been a struggle for you, but it's almost over. Try to be strong for just a little while longer. Can you do that?"

I nodded soundlessly.

"Jill . . ." Declan began after a few silent moments went by. He was frowning.

"What?"

"That experiment last night . . ."

I eyed him. "What about it?"

"Do you regret it? Do you wish we hadn't even tried?"

I hesitated. "You really want to know how I felt about it?"

"Yes."

"It was amazing, but . . ."

His brow furrowed. "But what?"

I looked directly in his gray eye and pressed my hands against his warm chest. "But I've been thinking about it. And as good as it was . . . I—I don't want you to touch me or kiss me like that again unless you really, really mean it and feel something in return. Understand?"

He held my gaze before nodding firmly. "I understand."

There was a ringing sound. Declan fished into his pocket for his cell phone and held it to his ear. "Yeah?"

He didn't take his attention off me for a moment. He stayed seated at the edge of the bed.

"Got it," he said, then ended the call, his jaw tightening. "That was fast. Reynolds is ready to see you again."

"The doctor is in," I said, my voice shaky.

"You ready?"

The dream troubled me. What did it mean? That I wanted Declan, but only if he was perfect and normal? But if he was normal, that meant I wasn't. The only thing I knew for sure was that when I saw the real Declan injured, dying, all I wanted was to get to him. To help him. To comfort him. But I couldn't.

And then it was too late.

I guess I didn't need to hunt too far to find the symbolism there. I nodded firmly. "I'm ready."

WE RETURNED TO the warehouse. I got the same strange feeling I'd had yesterday as we entered the main doors, unguarded apart from the security camera.

"What's wrong?" Declan asked.

"This place . . ." I shook my head. "It freaks me out knowing there are vampires downstairs that Dr. Reynolds is using as test subjects."

"This is how it's done, Jill. If you want to test ways to exterminate vampires, you need vampires to exterminate."

"So this is nothing new."

"No. And this isn't the only facility like this in the country— both government and privately funded. The vampires used in programs like this are the most messed up, the ones that can't keep their fangs out of humans. They're brought here instead of ending up on the wrong side of a stake."

I hesitated and looked at Declan. "You'll stay with me?"

"If you want me to," he said, holding my gaze.

I nodded, though my throat felt thick. He'd stay with me until all of this was over. Through the pain. Through the drama. When everything was pain free and drama free, he'd be gone. I guess I'd just take things an hour at a time. Hell, a minute at a time might be a better idea.

Jackson was waiting for us at the elevator. "Dr. Reynolds wants me to take care of a little matter downstairs. But first I'm supposed to take you down to his examining room so you can . . . do what you have to do."

His gaze flicked to Declan.

"Problem?" Declan asked as we got into the elevator and Jackson punched in the code.

"No. Nothing. Just business." He turned his attention to the digital floor numbers above the doors that showed our descent.

He seemed grumpy today, not that I was an expert on the varying moods of Jackson Gale, vampire hunter. Maybe he was pissed about my rejection yesterday. I doubted it. I didn't get the impression he was actually serious about me in a romantic way. He just wanted to get laid by a woman he perceived as horny enough to say yes. I wasn't quite there yet.

I thought about what had happened between me and Declan last night. While it had been rather . . . satisfying . . . it was also entirely unsatisfying, which is why I said what I had to him. Sex wasn't just the means to an orgasm for me—although it was a lovely gift with purchase. I needed to have the emotion to back it up. When I looked at Declan's face, I wanted to see the same desire that I felt reflected there—the same desire I had seen on his face in the past. Otherwise the one-sided sex experiment was fun and more than enough to get me off, but ultimately hollow.

Soon it might not be an issue at all. With me cured, my blood cleansed, and no reason to stay with Declan any longer, I figured it would be unlikely that I'd see him again. I'd go back to my regular life—my succession of unfulfilling jobs, socializing with friends and coworkers, visits with my sister and my nieces, random dating of entirely normal men, ones a lot like the unscarred, non-dhampyr version of Declan in my dream—and that would be that.

It would be strange to know he wasn't close by, watching over me. The thought made me feel something I could only describe as grief. Grief for a man who'd come into my life unexpectedly and disappeared just as quickly as he'd arrived.

I stayed close to Declan, nearly, but not quite, touching him. He was motivated by wanting to help me get better. So was I. I think I might have followed someone into the very depths of hell in order to get my blood cleaned out. The thought of the pain that was to come was an issue for me, but not enough to stop me from moving forward.

We got off the elevator and went down the hallway to Dr. Reynolds's examining room where we'd been yesterday. Other than the sparse furnishings of the stainless steel table and metal chair, there were cupboards on the walls, a sink, and a filing cabinet.

Jackson spoke briefly with Dr. Reynolds at the doorway, then nodded at us and took off down the hall.

"Come in," Dr. Reynolds said. He reserved his smile for me, an expression that froze at the edges when it became obvious that Declan was staying at my side. "My assistant's joining us in just a moment." His gaze moved toward the open door. "Here he comes now. Please, don't be alarmed."

I didn't have to wonder about what he meant by that for long. Another man entered the room—he had dark red hair and was wearing a white lab coat. His skin was very pale, his cheeks gaunt.

Declan tensed and pulled me back by the edge of my shirt so abruptly I let out a small shriek of surprise. He grabbed for his stake.

My stomach lurched and every muscle in my body stiffened the moment I saw the assistant's fangs.

He was a vampire.

He smiled uneasily, his gray eyes moving to Declan's sharp silver stake. "I guess Dr. Reynolds didn't mention me yet?"

Declan moved himself in front of me. "No. He sure the hell didn't."

"Please relax. I mean you no harm."

"Wish I could say the same," Declan growled.

Dr. Reynolds's face looked tight. "Lawrence is my assistant. I'm so accustomed to having him around that I sometimes neglect to let others know beforehand what he is. It's not an issue for me."

"What the hell is going on?" I demanded. This unexpected revelation had choked me and I struggled to breathe normally. It was one thing to think there were vampires downstairs, safely locked away. It was an entirely different thing to have one in the same room, wearing a lab coat just like Dr. Reynolds. A little warning would have been nice. A little warning and I wouldn't have shown up in the first place. "If he gets close enough to get a whiff of the Nightshade—"

"He won't." Dr. Reynolds moved to stand next to the redheaded vampire, protecting him in a near mirror image to what Declan was doing for me.

"I already know about you," Lawrence said. "And I'll be staying well back just in case."

I glared at them. "Nice that one of us had some warning."

Dr. Reynolds spread his hands. "Lawrence has been my research assistant for five years. He was turned against his will a year ago but retained his good sense and human morals, enough for me to trust him to stay on as my assistant. He believes as I do that most vampires are a threat that needs to be eliminated."

Lawrence stepped out from behind Dr. Reynolds, keeping a wary eye on Declan, who hadn't budged or said a word, but I could feel the menace coming off him in waves. He wasn't happy about this little unexpected turn of events. That made two of us.

"Many vampires keep their human personalities," Lawrence said evenly. "I'm one of them. I value my job here. Victor and I have a great deal in common."

I wasn't letting down my guard yet. "Like what?"

His expression shadowed, and I could see pain there. "He knows what it's like to lose a wife."

I shivered at his bleak tone. "What do you mean?"

His throat worked as he swallowed. "Susan accepted me after I was turned. But—she disappeared without a trace six months ago. I've been searching for her, desperate to find her."

"We think she was taken by another vampire," Dr. Reynolds said. "But I don't think anyone should give up hope yet."

Lawrence took a shaky breath and nodded. "I'm trying."

"I know."

"We should have been told about this up front." Declan's voice didn't hold a whole lot of empathy. He held on to me so tight I thought my arm might bruise—sometimes Declan didn't know his own dhampyr strength. But I didn't try to pull away. "You having a vampire assistant, no matter what the story is behind it, doesn't make me feel all warm and fuzzy about being here. It's fucked up."

"If I had told you, you might not have returned." Dr. Reynolds adjusted his glasses. The stiffness in his expression made me think he was having trouble speaking cordially to Declan. With his prejudices against dhampyrs, the two would never become best friends. "You might think I had ulterior motives in bringing you here, but you're not the only ones who were kept in the dark."

I watched him warily. "What are you talking about?"

"You, Jillian." Dr. Reynolds turned to look at me directly, his gaze sweeping over me from head to foot. "When I heard about the Nightshade formula, I had assumed it was a slow-moving poison that would weaken its victim over time, something that would lead eventually to death. But it's not like that at all, is it?"

I let out a shaky laugh. "No, it's a bit more immediate than that."

"It's amazing, is what it is."

I grimaced. "I have other words to describe it. *Amazing* isn't one of them."

"When a vampire bites you, only seconds need to pass before it dies."

"Pretty much. But it's still enough time for them to kill me if they want to."

His jaw tightened. "It's such a waste."

"Why?"

"I can't re-create it." His expression reflected his deep disappointment. "The original composition has changed too much since bonding with your blood. However, I discovered something I'd like to show you." He nodded at Lawrence. "Go get him."

Lawrence left the room without a word.

Declan finally tucked his stake away and let go of my arm. "We didn't come here for any more fucking experiments. We came here because we thought you had a solution for us. Do you or don't you?"

"Patience," Dr. Reynolds snapped, casting a fiery glare at him. But then he cleared his throat and took a deep breath. "I apologize for my rudeness. But as a hunter, you, I think, will appreciate how important this discovery is. Will you just give me a couple minutes to show you what I've found?"

Declan was silent for a moment but then nodded. "A couple minutes. That's it."

"Thank you."

Lawrence returned with another man whose gray eyes were glazed. With a push, he stumbled forward into the room.

"Sit," Dr. Reynolds said, and the man sat down heavily in the chair without being asked again.

Uneasiness moved through me. "What's wrong with him?"

Dr. Reynolds went over to the chair and walked a slow circle around it. "He's been chemically subdued so he won't cause us any problems."

A breath caught in my chest. "He's a vampire?"

"Yes." The doctor grasped the vampire's chin in his hands and squeezed. "Last week he killed a family whose car had broken down at the side of the road. Three children and two adults died to feed his hungers."

"I needed to feed." The vampire's voice was weak. "I couldn't stop myself."

"You're a murderer who killed five innocent humans. You'll get no sympathy from me." Dr. Reynolds let him go, and the vampire's chin dropped to his chest. The doctor wiped his hand on the front of his lab coat.

My stomach churned at the thought of it. At the moment he didn't look that dangerous. "You have him on drugs?"

"Yes. We have very powerful tranquilizers on hand here, but they still don't last long when it comes to monsters like this."

I eyed the other vampire in the room, the helpful one. If he didn't show his fangs, he looked as human as anyone else, apart from his pale gray eyes. He stayed on the other side of the room, a good twelve feet away from me. Most vampires didn't have a problem with the scent of the Nightshade as long as they kept their distance. I'd really rather not have any more problems today.

I crossed my arms tightly over my chest. "Look, I'm not letting him bite me, if that's what you want me to do."

"I don't want that."

"Then what sort of experiment is this?"

"It's to show you how your blood can be used when it's outside of your body."

I shook my head. "I suggested that to someone else, but if it hits oxygen, it's useless as a poison. Something about the air keeps it from working properly."

"Then it shouldn't come in contact with oxygen." Dr. Reynolds opened a case on the table to our left and removed what looked like a gun. It was small and silver, with a short, thick needle protruding from the end of it. "Inside this is a vial of your blood." He held the device in his right hand, just as he might a gun. He approached the vampire.

I tensed. "What are you going to—"

I didn't have the chance to finish my sentence. Dr. Reynolds pressed the device to the vampire's throat, jabbing the needle into his flesh, and squeezed the trigger.

FIVE

The vampire gasped as he was injected. He looked around as if seeing us for the first time.

"What did you—" He drew in a shaky breath, and his face
began to show strain. "Please, no—I need to—"

His words broke off, followed by a chilling moment of silence.
Then he screamed, raising himself up off the chair. Before he could
get fully to his feet, fire poured out of his mouth and quickly consumed his entire body. A moment later, just after the stench of burnt
flesh filled my nostrils, he exploded in a scattering of fiery ash. It
was the usual death of a vampire—one I'd seen several times before
this. Quick. Efficient. Scary as hell.

I stood frozen in place, my hand against my mouth, my eyes
wide with shock. I'd known what was coming, but that hadn't
made it any easier to see. It was exactly the same as what happened
when a vampire bit me. It was my poisonous blood—the take-out
version.

"Holy shit," I managed to say.

Dr. Reynolds smiled widely. "It's amazing. This is the third vampire we've tried it on."

Lawrence nodded. Considering he, too, was a vampire, I was
surprised he didn't look more disturbed. "It's worked perfectly every
time."

Declan stood stoically beside me as he watched the proceedings.

"The Nightshade formula alone was useless. It had to be bonded to a human's blood to work."

Dr. Reynolds's smile faded as if he'd forgotten the dhampyr was still in the room. "That's right."

"Then it's too bad you can't replicate it and find another volunteer to take Jill's place."

The doctor looked down at the silver gun. "That would make everything much simpler. The source is Jill's blood itself—and any new blood her body creates is immediately infused with the poison. Jill's blood is the beginning and the end of the Nightshade program."

This was one situation where it wasn't that great to be popular. It was too bad that the very thing that was killing me could be a huge help to others. Talk about a lose-lose situation.

A million possibilities sped through my mind. "Why don't we take a couple of days and you take all the blood samples you can from me before we start getting the Nightshade out of my system?"

Dr. Reynolds's expression held relief. "I'm glad you're willing to help."

I leaned against the examining table. "Of course I'm willing to help. This isn't my world, this isn't anything I want to be a part of for longer than I have to be, but I'm not naïve. I know that my blood can kill vampires and that this is a very good thing. If the Nightshade wasn't also killing me, I'd be all for making regular donations."

"But it *is* killing you."

Apart from the poison, I'd been bitten, bruised, and beaten nearly senseless. This roller-coaster ride sure as hell didn't come with a safety harness.

I nodded. "Yes. It is."

His jaw tensed. "I don't want to hurt a civilian, Jill. You're a civilian."

"It's time for this to be over," Declan said sharply. "You can either help or you can't. Which is it?"

I could tell he didn't approve of my blood donation suggestion. It wasn't on our current to-do list.

Dr. Reynolds glared at Declan, then back at me. "You care about your companion a great deal. I wasn't sure at first, but it's true, isn't it?"

"Her safety is my first priority."

Dr. Reynolds laughed under his breath. "My wife and I were opposites, too. Two different worlds, but we made it work."

I wasn't sure how we'd moved into this area of conversation without any warning. "Whatever Declan and I are to each other isn't exactly important right now."

"You care about him."

"Of course I do."

"Even though he's a dhampyr." He made the word sound more like an accusation than an observation.

I looked at the dhampyr in question. He had his eyebrow slightly raised, his gaze on me, as if waiting for my reply. "I'd be dead if it wasn't for Declan."

Not the most romantic of declarations, sure. But it was still true.

Dr. Reynolds pursed his lips. "I met my wife four years ago after I'd decided to accept my confirmed bachelor status. My days were spent with test tubes and chemical formulas. Parachemistry, parascience, it's an obsession for me. Always has been. But Clara . . . she made me see that there was more to life." His voice caught. Lawrence moved toward him and squeezed his shoulder.

I swallowed hard. Seeing other people in pain affected me. "She sounds like she was an amazing woman. I'm so sorry for your loss."

"So am I."

"You said a dhampyr killed her."

"Yes." His jaw tightened.

I shivered. "I—I haven't seen too many monster dhampyrs, but the ones I have seen have been scary as hell. It must have been horrible for you, but I'm sure there was nothing you could have done to save her."

He removed his glasses and pinched the bridge of his nose, squeezing his eyes shut. "You're wrong."

I was confused. I looked at Lawrence, whose gray eyes flicked to me.

"It wasn't a monster dhampyr," he said.

I was surprised. "It wasn't?"

"Lawrence . . ." Dr. Reynolds began.

Lawrence hissed out a breath. "It's time you faced this once and for all, as we discussed. Maybe then you can finally move on."

"I could say the same to you."

"You lost Clara two years ago. It's only been six months for me."

"It's different."

I watched them warily. Declan stood like a statue beside me, his hands clasped behind his back like a soldier at ease.

"No, it's so similar I'm surprised you can't see it." Lawrence wrung his hands and looked at me. "My wife is human—a human married to a vampire. Victor's wife—she was a vampire."

My mouth fell open. "A vampire?"

Reynolds put his glasses back on. His face was still. It looked as if he'd managed to put a lid on his grief for the moment. "She was already a vampire when I met her. It was difficult for her sometimes to control her hungers, but she maintained herself with class and dignity. Right up until she was murdered."

"Murdered by a dhampyr," I said.

"Yes." Dr. Reynolds's expression had rapidly turned from raw emotion to absolute ice. "The very dhampyr who stands with us in this room."

Shock slammed into me by the cold, blunt statement. My gaze

shot to Declan. He watched Dr. Reynolds carefully, no outward re-action showing at this accusation.

"You're saying that I killed your wife," he said.

"Yes." The word was a hiss.

I felt the tension in the room rise to a sickening level. I waited for Declan to deny it, to say it was impossible that he'd killed Dr. Reynolds's wife.

But he didn't.

Declan didn't move from where he stood, his expression didn't change, but his gaze grew more intense. Dr. Reynolds had gotten his full attention. "I don't kill innocents. I don't creep up behind them and slit their throats. I face them. They know who I am and why I'm there. That's when they usually attack."

The low-level hate I'd sensed previously from Dr. Reynolds now spilled over. I'd assumed he hated dhampyrs in general. I had no idea it was specifically focused on Declan. "I watched from the shadows when you staked her. Yes, she was defending herself. Of course she was. What other choice did she have?"

"To explain who she was. To deal with me on an intelligent level. If she'd done that, I might have given her the benefit of the doubt. I'm sent out after rogue vampires who cause damage and death, not loving wives of scientists. If I slayed her, it means that she was dangerous."

"You can justify it any way you want to. It doesn't change what happened."

Declan hissed a breath out between his clenched teeth. "Jill, we're out of here. This isn't a man who wants to help you. Not today anyway."

He was right. Dr. Reynolds didn't seem focused on the Night-shade anymore. While what he'd said was chilling and it turned my stomach, I also believed Declan. If he'd killed Clara, he'd done so because she was a serious threat.

I took his hand and he pulled me toward the door. Lawrence stepped back so he wouldn't come within smelling distance of me.

"You're not even willing to apologize to me for murdering my wife?" Dr. Reynolds said softly.

Declan froze and looked over his shoulder. He let go of my hand. "You yourself admit that your wife was a vampire. One who found it difficult not to give in to her hungers."

"And I feel her loss like a hole in my heart every day."

Declan faltered, just a little. If I hadn't been watching for it, I would never have seen it. A microscopic sliver of doubt slid behind his gaze, and his forehead furrowed. "To my knowledge, I've never killed a vampire that didn't deserve it. It's a war out there, one we need to protect humans from. Bad shit happens every day. But if I was the cause of your wife's death and she didn't truly deserve it, then yeah, I'm sorry as hell for that."

Dr. Reynolds stared at him for so long I wasn't sure if he'd ever speak again. A scattering of emotion played on his face—grief, sadness, doubt, pain.

I knew Declan's life was one filled with violence. His emotion-repressing serum was actually a bonus in that respect. It kept that part of him, the part deep inside that went past the scars, past the damage, relatively pure and untouched. For all the killing he'd done, that he'd have to do in the future, it hadn't broken him. For all the horror he'd had to face in his life, Declan's heart wasn't dark.

That's why that glimmer of doubt, of regret, in his otherwise emotionless expression troubled me. Just a couple of days off his original serum last week was enough for him to experience emotion—all kinds of it. Once you experienced something you'd never had to deal with before, was that something you could just forget?

"When Jackson contacted us to meet with you," I began, "you would have known Declan was with me, that he was protecting me. They're friends."

"Yes. I knew."

My chest felt tight. "So is that what this is? A lie saying you could help me just to get us here so you could drag an apology out of Declan for what happened to your wife?"

It wasn't that I didn't empathize with his pain—I did. But the relief I'd felt, the hope I'd allowed myself for my own solution, was fading with every second that passed. I hated being used, no matter what the motivation was.

Dr. Reynolds's face tensed. "I didn't lie to you. I had—I *have* every intention of helping you to the best of my ability. The fact that you're aligned with the dhampyr who murdered my wife is an unfortunate complication."

It was difficult to breathe. "So what now?"

"I need to make my peace with what has happened and find a way to move on." He glanced at Lawrence.

The vampire nodded. "You can do this."

"My research has always come first. If I would have had to choose between Clara and my work, I would have had a very hard time with that decision. In the end, I think I would have chosen the research over love. She knew this. She accepted how important it was to me. It's everything. My research *is* me."

I watched him, feeling a swell of pity. "Sounds lonely."

"It can be."

Declan crossed his arms. "I hope you can put your feelings about me aside, even if it's only long enough to help Jill."

"Like I said, my research is everything." Dr. Reynolds held his hand out to Declan. I was surprised that he seemed so ready to shake the hand of the man he held responsible for slaying his vampire wife.

Declan hesitated only a moment before he grabbed hold of Dr. Reynolds's hand and shook it. "If there's anything I can do for you . . ."

"There is. You can help in my research."

"I can?"

"Yes." Dr. Reynolds pulled a syringe out from his pocket and plunged it into Declan's chest. I watched in frozen shock as Declan batted his hand away and immediately ripped the needle out, glaring fiercely at it before casting it to the side.

"What the fuck do you think you're doing?" he snapped.

"Research," Dr. Reynolds said again, backing up a step.

Declan fell hard to his knees and braced his hands against the ground. It was a tranquilizer. He'd been injected with a tranquilizer.

I'd stopped breathing. "What's going on? Why are you doing this? Research? What does that mean?"

Lawrence grabbed the back of Declan's jacket and pulled him up to his feet. Declan's eyes were already glazed, and he now moved like a rag doll. Lawrence pushed him down into the chair. Around it was the scattering of gray ash—all that was left from the vampire, other than the lingering burning scent.

Dr. Reynolds moved closer to him, his gaze flicking to my stunned expression. "Stay where you are, Jill. Don't come closer to Lawrence, just in case he's affected by the Nightshade. We don't want any accidents here."

I ignored him and ran toward Declan, but Dr. Reynolds caught my arm. I tried to pull away, but his fingers dug into me painfully. I glared at him. "Explain to me what the fuck you're doing to Declan. Now!"

"I need him." There was a steely look of determination in his eyes. "I've seen what your blood can do to a vampire, but I don't know what it will do to a dhampyr." I noticed with horror that he had the silver gunlike device in his hand again, which he tossed to Lawrence. "And I want to find out."

Before I could say anything, before I could take a breath or even scream, Lawrence jabbed the needle into Declan's neck and pulled the trigger.

SIX

Now I screamed. But it was too late to stop this.

A gasp caught in Declan's throat. His face tensed, and his teeth clenched and then parted as a roar escaped from him.

"No!" I pushed away from Dr. Reynolds with all my strength, then ran directly to Declan and grabbed hold of his arm. The vampire stumbled back from me to keep his distance. Hot tears ran down my cheeks. "Declan, no! Please—"

When he looked at me, I could see the pain in his single gray eye. "Jill . . ."

My name sounded broken, jagged.

His head slumped forward.

"No!" I scrambled to touch him, fumbling to feel for a pulse at his throat, scared to death that there wouldn't be anything there. Scared to death that my blood had killed him.

It had been a big question up till now and we were about to learn the answer—what did my blood do to a dhampyr?

Declan was half vampire and because of this, he was affected by the scent of the Nightshade inside me—drawn to it. To *me*. He hid it well, but I knew it troubled him. He'd never drunk blood before, he had no need to. But just because there wasn't a need didn't mean his vampire side didn't still crave it.

For all I knew the Nightshade could kill a dhampyr as easily as a full-blooded vampire. It wasn't something I'd wanted to put to the test.

But here we were anyway.

His heart was still beating, too erratic and too fast, but it was strong beneath my touch. Fear was still a bitter taste in my mouth. I was afraid that the next moment his heart would stop and he'd be taken from me forever. He was unconscious, either from the pain my blood had caused him or from the tranquilizer, but he was still alive. I wanted to sob with relief, but I couldn't allow myself the luxury.

I turned to Dr. Reynolds and the look on my face must have showed every bit of the rage I felt. "You shouldn't have done that."

He actually took a step back from me, which was a surprise. I wasn't the scariest thing on the planet, not compared to somebody like Declan, but he reacted as if I might be a threat. "He's alive."

"And you're damn lucky he is."

"Or what would happen? Would you kill me in revenge?"

My hands clenched into fists at my sides. "Feeling the way I do right now? I just might."

"Then who would help you with your little problem, Jill? I'm not aware of another person alive in the world who has as much knowledge as I do when it comes to parachemistry."

"I guess I'd just have to deal. Because if you had killed Declan claiming it was for research when it's clear to me that it was vengeance, pure and simple"—I swallowed hard—"I would have taken his stake and plunged it into your throat."

His brows went up. "Violent. You struck me as a nice girl, Jill."

I glared at him. "Maybe I was once upon a time. Things have changed."

The phone on the wall started to ring. Keeping a wary eye on me, the doctor went to it and picked it up.

"Reynolds here. Yes . . . just a moment." He held the phone out to Lawrence. "He says it's important."

Eyeing me as he gave me a wide berth, Lawrence went to the phone.

Dr. Reynolds had used a horse-load of tranquilizer on Declan. He was strong—easily the strongest man I'd ever known in my life—but he was completely out of it right now.

I touched his face, stroking his eye patch back into place, since it had shifted a little. I traced down his deepest scar, the one that started on his forehead and ran down past his patch to his jawline. I leaned closer and brushed my lips against it.

Declan protected me ninety-nine percent of the time. I would protect him for the remaining one percent. And if Dr. Reynolds or his loyal vampire assistant wanted to get to him again, they'd have to go through me first. An empty threat normally, but at the moment I felt ready to tear someone's finger off with my teeth if they so much as pointed it in my direction.

I stroked his forehead. "Declan, please wake up."

His eyelid fluttered but didn't open.

"You're alive," I told him, just in case he needed the reminder. "My blood didn't kill you. I'm sure it hurt like hell, though, and I'm sorry for that. As soon as you wake up, we're getting the fuck out of here."

"Jill, it's time we got started," Dr. Reynolds said.

I glared at him. "With what? Fixing me?"

"No. I need more time to work on a viable serum. You said we could take more samples of your blood to keep in reserve."

"So we're here not because you were ready to start helping me, but because you wanted me to help you. *After* you tried to kill Declan. That makes a ton of sense, you bastard."

His jaw tightened. "Perhaps my personal feelings got in the way of what I should be focusing on."

"Wow, you're fucking brilliant. No wonder you're a scientist." My eyes narrowed. "Can't really say I'm in much of a mood at the moment to be all that cooperative. All I want to know is if Declan's going to be okay."

"If he's survived this long after being injected with your blood, I don't see why not." He looked openly disappointed about that.

"You don't honestly believe Declan set out to kill your wife just for the hell of it, do you? She must have—"

"Must have what? Deserved it?" he snapped, but then his expression softened again. "I—I don't know anymore. In a war, sometimes it's hard to tell which side is right. I myself have had to do many things outsiders might consider evil. But in order to learn, to grow, I had to find a way to—"

His voice broke off with a grunt of pain and he spun around. It took me a second to register with shock that there was now a knife sticking out of his back. He grappled to pull it from his flesh, and it clattered to the ground.

Lawrence stood behind him, his hands fisted at his sides. The look on his face left no question as to what he was feeling.

Rage.

My eyes widened with horror. "What the hell are you doing?"

Lawrence didn't take his attention off Dr. Reynolds. "I trusted you, you son of a bitch."

His eyes had turned to black—normally what a hungry vampire's did. Dark blue veins branched down along the sides of his face to his neck. That was another very bad sign.

The fact that Dr. Reynolds was still on his feet made me think that the knife hadn't been deep enough to kill him. Blood stained his white coat.

"What are you talking about?" he demanded.

"That phone call? That was somebody I had searching for Susan. They finally figured out where she is."

"You need to calm down, Lawrence. We need to talk about this."

"All of this time I've trusted you, Victor. You gave me a chance when everyone else wanted to have me staked. You saw that I still could be a help to you, despite what I am. I thought you and my wife—you were the only ones who gave me a chance." He let out a shaky breath. "And this is what you do to me? To us?"

I was listening, but I didn't understand. Something had broken in Lawrence; his voice had a pitchy quality that made me think he wasn't in complete control of his sanity at the moment. Whatever he'd heard on the phone had broken him.

"Lawrence—" Dr. Reynolds began, his voice filled with pain.

"She's been here all the time, hasn't she? In the rooms that are off limits to everyone but you. You son of a bitch. You stole her from me and have been using her in your goddamned experiments, haven't you? Haven't you?"

He came forward enough to grab the doctor by his coat and shook him hard enough to rattle anyone's brain.

I crouched next to Declan, holding on to his arm tightly. "Declan, wake up. You have to snap out of this now."

That feeling of dread I'd had in my gut ever since we arrived at this place—maybe I should have paid attention to it. But I never could have predicted this.

"I knew what you'd do if I told you the truth," Dr. Reynolds said, his voice strong but now with a naked edge of fear to it. "Lawrence, listen to me, you didn't know this, but—but Susan was pregnant. She was keeping it a secret from you."

The rage on Lawrence's face faded, replaced with shock. "Pregnant?"

"It was your child. A dhampyr was growing inside her."

"Jesus."

"She didn't want you to know—she knew you'd take it badly. She came to me to get an abortion."

A shiver went down my arms. Abortion was the normal way to deal with a human woman pregnant with a dhampyr. Since most of them turned out to be the monster kind, a birth that only happened when the dhampyr literally clawed its way out of its mother's womb, which inevitably led to the mother's horrific death, there really wasn't much choice. Births of the more human dhampyrs like Declan were the rarity.

"Did you abort the fetus?" Lawrence demanded.

Dr. Reynolds shook his head. "The fetus was to be kept alive, monitored."

"Another damn experiment."

"Yes."

"All this time I've been beside myself with worry and she's been here. The same place I come to every day, working by your side. And you never told me."

"There was no other way."

"It's always about research for you, isn't it Victor?" His expression twisted into something ugly, and he raked a hand through his red hair. "I have a secret, too, one I've kept so it wouldn't hurt you. Clara wanted to leave you before she was killed. She'd fallen in love with another vampire. She hated that you spent all your time here, working on ways to kill her kind. *Our* kind. If you hadn't been such a damn workaholic, then maybe she wouldn't have ended up on the wrong side of that hunter's stake."

"No, it can't be true." Dr. Reynolds's expression filled with sick shock. His lovely vampire wife hadn't been so lovely after all.

"Where is Susan?" Lawrence shook Dr. Reynolds. "Where? Tell me and maybe this can end well for you."

There was silence for a few very long moments.

"She's dead."

"No!" Lawrence's expression shattered, and he shoved the doctor back from him.

"The birth, it—it happened only yesterday. I did everything I could to find a way around it. To try to save her. It was impossible. The other woman we have up on the next floor—the one set to become our next test subject for dhampyr breeding—she tried to help. She held Susan's hand the whole time until it was . . . too late.

The dhampyr was killed immediately; it was too vicious to keep for further testing. I'm so sorry, Lawrence."

"She died yesterday." His voice was barely audible.

"Yes."

Lawrence looked down at the floor before slowly raising his tear-filled black eyes to Dr. Reynolds. "I'm going to kill you."

He surged forward with inhuman speed. I shrieked as the doctor grabbed hold of my arm and threw me toward the vampire. Lawrence caught me. I felt the strength in his grip; the vampire was strong enough to break me in half.

Lawrence inhaled sharply, and his lips drew back from his sharp teeth. It seemed impossible, but his already black eyes grew even darker, like shiny, soulless buttons.

Dr. Reynolds moved toward the door. "You can't resist the Nightshade inside of her. Take her. Bite her. Drink her blood. Give in to it."

My fear ratcheted up another level. "No—" I pushed at the vampire, but his grip on me only grew tighter. "You don't want to do this."

I knew from the crazed look in his eyes that if he bit me, he'd tear my throat out. It would kill him and me at the same time.

Lawrence's upper lip peeled back farther, and a growl sounded in the back of his throat. "It's so powerful."

I felt as if my bones were going to snap if I fought him any harder. "Bite me and you die."

There was barely any human intelligence left in his gaze—he was a grief-filled monster who needed to feed. "I want to die."

"No—"

"But first I want everyone else to die. Starting with him." His black-eyed gaze moved over my shoulder.

"Let go of me," I snapped.

He did what I asked, pushing me so hard I flew backward until my head slammed against the side of the examining table. I crashed to the floor. My vision blurred as the pain swept through me. Out of the corner of my eye I saw Declan rise shakily from the chair and reach toward the sharp silver stake at his belt.

"No . . ." I said, but it was too weak for anyone to hear.

Declan flicked a glance at me before training his fierce gaze on the vampire before him. Lawrence wasn't unarmed. He'd snatched the already bloody knife off the floor, and I saw a silver flash as it arched through the air toward Dr. Reynolds's throat and the spray of red as it met its mark.

It was like my dream—everything slowed down, and the air thickened. I couldn't move. Couldn't speak. Couldn't scream. The vampire turned his attention toward Declan and surged forward to attack just as I lost consciousness and the world all around me faded to black . . .

SEVEN

The alarm woke me.

When I forced my eyes open, my head screamed with pain. I lay on my side in an awkward position on the floor, staring straight into the glazed eyes of Dr. Reynolds. Blood oozed down his forehead.

Dr. Reynolds was supposed to help save my life. He was my beacon of hope. My beacon of hope was now dead as a doornail.

The ear-piercing alarm made it difficult to think, but I knew I had to get out of here. I pushed myself up to my feet and scanned the room. White walls, gray linoleum floor, empty metal chair, stainless steel examination table to my right.

My heart slammed against my rib cage when I saw Declan lying on the opposite side of the room. He was badly hurt and not moving. I couldn't tell if he was breathing. There was blood—a lot of it. Stumbling, I ran to his side and fell to my knees next to him.

"Declan, no!" I could barely hear my panicked voice above the sound of the alarm. "Please, *please* don't be dead!"

For a long, horrible moment there was no reaction. But then his chest hitched and he opened his gray right eye. He blinked. "Jill—" His deep, raspy voice sounded as weak as I'd ever heard it, and that worried the hell out of me. "You—you need to get out of here. Now. It's not safe. Get out and run as fast and as far as you can."

I nodded. "Sounds like a good plan. Come on"—I grabbed hold of his muscled arm—"get up!"

He shook his head, the movement barely noticeable. "Leave me. Save yourself."

Anger pushed its way forward. "Stop being a bad movie cliché and get on your feet. I'm not going anywhere without you."

His jaw clenched. "I'm hurt."

"You'll heal."

"I'll be slow. I'll try to catch up. Find Jackson. He'll help you get out of here, and then—"

"No, listen to me, Declan." I gulped a breath to help give me courage. "We got into this mess together and that's exactly how we're getting out."

He glared at me. "Jill—"

"No." My throat hurt from shouting over the alarm. "I'm not leaving without you. If you're going to just give up and die right here, that means I am, too. So if you really want me to live to see another day, then you're going to have to do the same damn thing. Do you understand me?"

The fire in his gaze, ignited thanks to my stubbornness, faded a bit around the edges.

"Well?" I touched his face, wiping the blood away from a cut on his forehead. "What'll it be, dhampyr?"

His eye narrowed before he finally answered. "Fine. Help me up."

"That's more like it."

I grabbed his arm and helped him to his feet as much as I could, considering I was a full foot shorter than him. He leaned his nearly six and a half feet of solid muscle against me. His gaze moved toward Dr. Reynolds and the growing pool of blood forming a wet, red halo around the dead man's head.

"Fuck," he said under his breath.

"Just what I was thinking."

"You know what this means."

"Yeah," I said, grimly. "It means I'm definitely going to die. But it won't be here. And it won't be now."

One look at Declan confirmed to me that he'd fought with Lawrence and lost. Several deep knife wounds were in the process of healing. I tried not to worry about that, but it was difficult. He wasn't dead, and for that I was very grateful.

"I'm still feeling the tranq effects," he growled, straining to be heard over the loud alarm. "That's going to make this harder. And I don't have my stake—Lawrence must have taken it."

"Let's try to stay positive."

"You go ahead and do that. I'm going to be a realist."

"And what does your realist self tell you?"

"It tells me that I'm in rough shape and healing slower than I'd like." His grip on me tightened. "My phone's set to vibrate— someone's calling. Grab it."

Without thinking twice, I slipped my hand into the inner pocket of Declan's jacket and took out his cell phone, stabbing at the answer button and holding it to my ear.

"Yeah?"

"Jill? Is that you?"

"Who the fuck is this?"

"It's Jackson. Glad to hear your voice, too."

My grip on the phone tightened as I shouted into it. "Where the hell are you?"

"A level down from you, I think. What the fuck happened?"

I hurriedly explained to him about the vampire on the rampage.

"Shit. That explains it. The vampires have been let out of their cells down here. At least a dozen of them, maybe more. You need to get out fast. Is—is Declan dead?"

"No. But he's wounded."

There was silence for a moment. "Find the nearest stairwell. Don't try to use the elevator, it's been knocked out. If you see a vampire, kill it. Just don't let them get too close or you won't have a—"

The line cut out.

"Jackson? Are you there? Shit." I shoved the phone back into Declan's coat and tried my best not to worry about what just happened to Declan's vampire-hunting pal. "We have to move. Lawrence must have gone completely batshit crazy because he released everybody from their cages and they're hungry. We have to get out of here."

He looked understandably grim. "It's daylight. They won't be able to come outside."

Sunlight didn't kill vampires. However, it did fry their eyes, making them blind and much easier to kill. Because of this, they much preferred the nightlife. Point for us.

But that was only if we could get outside.

I'd known this felt wrong from the moment we got here. I'd been so greedy to find a solution to my problem that it had blinded me to everything else.

"Come on." I pulled Declan with me toward the door before I froze. Something Dr. Reynolds said came back to me. "There's another woman, other than Lawrence's wife, who's being kept here for his dhampyr breeding research. She's in danger. We can't just leave her here."

His arm was tense, his expression flat and hard to read. "If we can get to her, then we will. If we can't, my first priority is to get you out of here in one piece."

"But Declan—"

"No, Jill. This isn't up for debate. We're out of here."

Faster than I thought he was currently able to move, he pulled me along with him to the door of the office. It was already open, the hinges broken as if Lawrence had taken out some of his rage on them.

Dr. Reynolds had chosen his research over friendship and loyalty. He tried to convince himself he was one of the good guys, but keeping a woman locked away until she gave birth to a monster that ripped her apart—that wasn't something a good guy would do.

I felt Lawrence's pain, but this wasn't right. I was just thankful he hadn't killed me or Declan yet. All we could do was try to get out of here before he found us again and finished what he'd started.

Declan leaned against me as we walked, and that worried me. He was also dripping blood from his more severe wounds. As a dhampyr, he'd heal quickly, but not quickly enough.

"You okay?" I asked.

"Never better."

Emotionless, yes. But not without the capacity for sarcasm.

We had to keep moving. The underground facility was huge, with mazelike hallways. The debilitated warehouse on the surface was only the proverbial tip of the iceberg to what lay beneath.

The lights flickered in the hallway. Suddenly the blare of the alarm cut out, and the resulting silence seemed as loud and as frightening as the noise had been. I strained my ears, trying to hear beyond the sound of our own steps, but there was nothing.

"It's not the wounds that are slowing me down like this," Declan said after a moment, cutting through the eerie silence. "It's something else."

"What is it?"

His grip at my waist tightened. "It's your blood. It didn't kill me, but it's messing me up. I feel it."

Shit. "What does that mean?"

He brought his hand to his temple and rubbed as if he had a headache. "I don't know. My head's all cloudy, and I don't think it's simply from the tranquilizer."

I was used to Declan being so strong and capable. Seeing him in this weakened condition scared me even more than I already was. And since my blood caused it, I felt that it was my fault.

My jaw set. "I'd rather not have to carry you up those stairs, but I will if I have to."

His lips curled. "You don't give up, do you?"

"I'll let you know when I do. I'm not quite there yet." I froze when I saw the outline of someone standing in our path. No, he wasn't standing; he was moving quickly toward us. It was a vampire, his glossy black eyes almost glowing, the veins throbbing on his pale face. He looked like a monster straight out of one of my nightmares.

He hissed, baring his fangs, and his chest hitched as he inhaled my scent. Declan had told me that vampires didn't actually need to breathe. They did it more out of habit from having once been human than out of true necessity. I wouldn't exactly call them undead—they were still a strange and unnatural form of the living—but they were no longer human.

And this particular nonhuman wanted a taste of me. I guess he hadn't gotten the memo about Jillian Conrad, Nightshade carrier. Tasty death on legs.

The vampire grabbed me and dove for my throat, no conversation, no explanation, just a need to feed. Jackson had said that the vampires were kept near starving so they'd make for better test subjects.

This one wanted blood, *my* blood. Buckets of it. And he wasn't taking no for an answer.

EIGHT

Before I felt more than his cool breath on my throat, Declan grabbed the vampire and threw him against the wall. I heard several bones crack with the impact, but he leapt to his feet immediately as if he felt no pain.

He hissed at me. "I . . . need . . . blood."

"Too bad." I staggered back as he drew closer again. I'd let the thing bite me so my blood would kill him, but then I'd run the risk that he'd kill me, not to mention that a loss of blood weakened me. I needed my strength.

He didn't get the chance to bite me. Declan grabbed the vampire's head and twisted it sharply to the side. There was a sickening crack. He fell to the ground in a heap only inches from my feet, his black eyes staring upward. Cold sweat slipped down my back.

"Is—is he—?" I stammered.

"No. He'd be ash by now if he was dead. It'll take him a few minutes to recover."

"Recover from a broken neck?"

"Yeah. So let's move." He grabbed my hand and pulled me along the hallway with him.

The fluorescent overhead lighting flickered out completely, plunging us into complete darkness. A couple of seconds later there was a whirring sound as the emergency system came on. There still wasn't much light, only enough to see the vague outline of where we were going.

We came to the elevator. Even though Jackson said not to use it, I jabbed at the up button anyway, hoping for a miracle. Not surprisingly, nothing happened. The stairway was another fifty feet down the hall. It was so quiet now. All I heard was our breathing, the sound of our feet against the floor, and my heartbeat pounding in my ears.

Fear was useless to me at the moment. It was an emotion that only worked to freeze one in their tracks, like a deer in the headlights. Easy prey to be picked off one at a time.

Paranoia was another thing. That was helpful—a survival instinct that kept me moving, kept me holding tightly on to Declan's hand as we walked swiftly to our only escape route.

"So this is your life," I said. "Danger and death around every corner."

He eyed me. "Enjoying yourself, are you?"

"I can barely contain my glee."

"And you thought I got all these scars from having a cushy desk job?"

"You might want to consider a change in careers."

He snorted. "That's doubtful."

"No interest in settling down?"

"Only when they lay me down in my coffin. That is, if there's anything left of me then."

I grimaced. "That's a charming thought."

"This is a regular day's work for me—maybe a bit more fucked up than normal—but fairly regular. You deserve a safe and happy life where your neck isn't constantly on the line."

I met his gaze. "So do you."

His jaw tightened. "This *is* my life."

"Says who?"

"Says me. I know where I belong."

"Two hundred feet underground with a dozen hungry vampires running amuck."

His humorless grin returned. "It pays well."

He could laugh it off—gallows humor, I supposed—but my heart still ached for him. He'd never been given the chance to have a normal life. Being what he was—a dhampyr—left him with few options.

I thought about the Declan in my dream, the untouched one, the unscarred one—the one who hadn't experienced violent battle like this Declan had. Dream Declan was somebody I could see myself making a life with. He was normal. He was handsome. He was as close to perfect as it got.

But he wasn't *really* Declan; he was just some guy who sort of looked like him. And that was enough to give me second thoughts about my previous ideas of perfection.

We reached the stairwell, and I was disturbed by the sounds I could now hear—screams and crashes—they were coming from the level lower than we were.

Declan looked at me. "Probably not a good idea to go down there."

"That's where Jackson is—if he's still alive."

His expression turned grim. "I need to get you out first. Then I'll come back for him."

Fear knifed through my gut. "Like hell you will. You're hurt."

"I can't leave him here."

"I feel the same way about that woman."

He eyed me. "The woman you don't know. That you've never met."

"I don't care. I have to help her." I stopped climbing at the next floor, the one above where we'd been. This was where she was being kept—at least, that was the impression I'd gotten. "Come on."

I pushed open the door. The hallway seemed identical to the floor we'd been on. It felt a bit like a hospital hallway, and it smelled hyperclean, as if it had been recently flushed with antiseptic.

It was dark here and very quiet—too quiet—as if everyone had already escaped. If there had been anyone here to begin with.

I stopped walking and listened hard . . . and heard something. A steady pounding noise. "That might be her."

"Might be."

"Worth checking." I picked up my pace and moved down the hall until I reached the door from which the sound was coming. I pressed my hand up against it. "Is somebody in there?"

The pounding stopped. There was silence for a moment and then, "Help! You have to get me out of here! I'm locked in!"

I tried the handle, but she was absolutely right. I looked at Declan.

He nodded. "Step aside."

"Stay back," I told the woman through the door. "We're going to break the door open."

Declan kicked the door hard. It only took a few good kicks with Declan's heavy boot—not to mention his dhampyr strength—before it flew inward.

The woman was dressed in a pink hospital gown, her face pale with fear as she stared out at us with wide eyes. "Who the fuck are you?"

"You're welcome," I said. "Now let's get the hell out of here. We can do the meet and greet later."

"I'm not going anywhere with you." She looked warily at Declan, and whatever she thought of his fearsome looks made her noticeably cringe. "Where's Dr. Reynolds?"

"He's dead." I said it bluntly, but it made me flash back to what happened in the examining room. I shuddered. "And so are we if we loiter around here for much longer."

"Dead?" Her voice broke.

"I'm surprised you care. He's the one who locked you up."

"No—" She looked confused. "He's paying me a lot of money

to help him with his research. I need the money. My parents—I'm supporting them. I'm all they have."

I stared at her with surprise. "You agreed to be here? Do you know what kind of experiments he was doing?"

"Reproductive studies. I know I was agreeing to be artificially inseminated. For the money I'm being paid, it's worth it. I already agreed to give up the child when it's born."

I felt sick at hearing her story, knowing what she didn't know. She might have signed up voluntarily, but it was unlikely that she knew the results—that being artificially inseminated by a vampire would likely leave her torn in at least two very bloody pieces.

"Are you pregnant right now?" I asked cautiously.

She shook her head. "We were going to officially start tomorrow."

I let out a shaky sigh of relief. "We need to get out of here."

"Why? What's going on?"

"You know there are vampires here, don't you?"

"Vampires?" she repeated, frowning hard. "Are you crazy or something?"

We didn't have time for this. "Yeah, I'm crazy. Now let's go." I grabbed her arm, happy that she didn't fight against me as I pulled her out of the room.

She looked over her shoulder at Declan. "He's scary as hell, isn't he?"

Despite everything, that almost made me grin. "He's an adorable puppy dog compared to what's downstairs. Come on."

"Just keep climbing until we get to the surface," Declan said. When we reached the stairwell again, Declan swung open the door. Before I had the chance to go through, pale hands grabbed the front of Declan's shirt and dragged him over the threshold. The door closed behind him with a click.

I felt as though the breath had been completely knocked out of me.

"No!" I let go of the woman and grappled for the door, pushing it open so hard it bruised my hands.

I saw Declan fly backward, down a flight of stairs, and he hit the cement wall hard at the landing before tumbling down a couple more steps. Blood streamed down his forehead.

"Declan!" I screamed.

His pain-filled gaze locked on mine, and he must have seen the terror in my eyes. "Go, Jill! Take the woman and get out of here! Now!"

The vampire—no, there were *two* of them—drew closer to him. Normally, I had no doubt Declan could take them. But my blood had weakened him. He could fight for a while, but it wouldn't be long before they tore him apart.

He wanted me to leave him, to save myself and the woman. And maybe I would have done just that—in a previous life.

I glared at the woman. "Stay right here. Don't move."

"What are you doing?"

"Whatever I have to."

"Leave him. Let's just go! He said we should!"

I shook my head. "He should know by now I rarely do what I'm told."

There wasn't any more time to explain, to figure out a plan, to think things through. I had only a few seconds to save Declan. And I had only one weapon at hand. The same weapon I always had at hand.

Myself.

I took the stairs two at a time until I landed between the vampires. Declan was down a few more steps, and he sent a fierce look my way. I noticed his leg was twisted in an awkward position, and a chill went down my spine. He'd broken it in the fall. It would heal just like the rest of him did—quickly. But that was only if he lived.

"What the fuck are you doing, Jill?" he snapped at me.

I didn't have time for a Q&A at the moment.

"Hey." I tapped the vampires on their backs. In unison, they turned to me, their nostrils flaring, their lips curling back from sharp white fangs. I tried to see past the monstrous veiny exterior, the sunken cheeks, the black eyes. These were human once—a man and a woman. For all I knew they could have been husband and wife; accountant and journalist; teacher and lawyer. Whatever. I didn't know where they came from or what their stories were. I didn't really care.

All I knew was that they were a threat—to Declan, to me, to the woman I'd committed myself to rescuing. And I knew they were drawn to the scent of the Nightshade inside of me. Since they weren't well fed like Lawrence was, they didn't have his control— the control that kept him from sinking his fangs into me to get a taste of my irresistible blood.

These nameless vampires had no control. That was my hope. And, frankly, that was also my worst fear.

"Jill!" Declan's pained cry echoed in my ears.

I staggered back a step as the vampires changed their direction and started moving toward me.

NINE

All I could do now was hope the vampires didn't rip me apart before they tasted my blood. Declan grabbed a step and pulled himself closer, but he wasn't fast enough to stop what was about to happen.

"Delicious, right?" I said. Fear wasn't something I could control at the moment, so I gave in to it, wrapping myself in it like a thick blanket. "You need to drink my blood."

"Yessss," the female hissed. She had hair so pale blond it was almost white. I think it was a bleach job, since nobody had that color hair naturally. Her skin seemed even paler in contrast to the dark veins that branched along her jawline, and her lips were deep red, as if she'd already been drinking her fill of blood before they got to this floor. I could barely see the whites of her eyes, her irises were so large and black. She looked like some sort of angel, actually. An angel of death.

She grabbed hold of my hair, fisting it so tightly that I let out an involuntary cry of pain. The male vampire drew closer. I shuddered as he slid his hand over my stomach and pressed me back against the wall.

He sniffed along my neck. "Smells so good. Never smelled anything so fucking good in my life."

My heart pounded so fast it made me dizzy. Out of the corner of my eye I could see that Declan was trying to get to me. I shuddered with fear and disgust as I felt the male vampire slide his cold hand down between my legs and I felt his erection hard against my hip. I'd expected it, but it didn't mean I was prepared.

For vampires, blood and sex went hand in hand. Lust for blood turned into a lust for other things. It was all I could do to not beg them to let go of me. The female had a tight hold of my hair and she wrenched my neck to the side. Her other hand grasped my chin and she nipped at my jaw, not quite hard enough to break the skin. Her fangs were as sharp as scalpels.

This was typically the part in the movies where the good guys would arrive, stakes in hand, and make mincemeat out of the monsters, saving the damsel in distress who'd been foolish enough to wander off into danger and get herself eaten. But my life wasn't a movie. And I'd chosen this distress with full knowledge of the potential consequences. I didn't have nightmares every night because my life was big fun.

Do it, I begged inwardly. *Bite me. What the hell are you waiting for?*

Maybe if they'd been kept elsewhere, fed well, this might have gone differently. Hell, it might have gone even worse. I could have first been brutally raped before they killed me. The male obviously had sex on the brain, judging by the way he was pawing me, but it wasn't first on his list. It was likely a close second, though.

I thought I had braced myself, but the pain was always a horrible shock. And they weren't taking turns. The female was at my throat, her razor-sharp fangs slicing into my flesh. The male was at my wrist and I winced, feeling hot tears splash down my cheeks as he pierced my skin so deeply I was sure he'd hit bone. It hurt like hell, but I couldn't move or struggle anymore. Something about a vampire's bite rendered the victim paralyzed while they were fed on. I could feel everything, see and smell everything. But I couldn't try to protect myself or fight back, which made it even more dangerous.

I looked past the woman's pale blond hair and met Declan's horrified gaze. Strange—I couldn't remember the last time I'd seen so much emotion on his face. His serum shouldn't allow it, even in a situation like this. Maybe it was only an illusion.

It felt like forever that they fed on me, but I knew it was only a few seconds.

The female gasped first, pulling back from me and touching the dark red blood on her lips. The male was next, his eyes wide, his brow furrowed.

She gasped. "What is this?"

I glared at her as the feeling came back to my limbs and I was able to speak again. "It's heartburn, bitch."

She opened her mouth to scream, and I could see the fire coming up from deep inside of her. Before she could make another sound, she exploded in a fiery, smelly, ashy cloud. I tried to pull back from it so I wouldn't be burned, but I was already up against the wall. All I could do was wave at the scattering ashes.

The other vampire turned his stunned gaze to mine, mouth dark with my blood. I saw fury in his eyes. The female meant something to him and now she was gone forever. He grabbed my throat, hard enough to crush me, but his hands had already begun to crumble. His growl of anger turned into a scream of pain as the fire consumed him. A moment later there was nothing left of either of them. I brought my hand to my throat, which was tender, raw, and bleeding. The phantom stench of burnt flesh hung in the air, and I wiped the fine coating of ash off the front of my tank top and arms.

So close. He would have killed me if he'd had more time. Luckily for me, he hadn't.

Declan was on his feet now, favoring his left leg. He pulled himself up the remaining stairs and grabbed my shoulders. I expected him to yell at me for being so careless, for nearly getting myself killed. He roughly pushed my face to the side and took my wrist in hand so he could inspect the bite wounds.

"Damn it, Jill." He held my face between his hands. "Are you okay?"

I smiled genuinely, so happy I was still alive, that *he* was still alive. When I'd seen the vampire grab him when he opened the door, I'd thought that was it. We were living on borrowed time anyway. I'd thought our meter had just expired.

I nodded. "I'll live."

He met my gaze. "You saved my life."

"I think I owe you a few of those."

His jaw set. "Don't let it happen again. When I tell you to move, I want you to move."

"Yes, sir."

His lips twitched, as if he wanted to smile, but he held it back. "Let's collect your new BFF and get the fuck out of here."

"Your leg—"

"It's healing as we speak. I reset it already. I'll be fine, just slow."

Declan had reset his own broken leg before it healed wrong. I wasn't sure if I should feel sorry for the pain that must have caused him or be impressed. He was a serious badass.

I pulled the door open, expecting to see that the woman had taken off, but she was still there, sitting on the ground in the hallway, pressed up against the wall with her legs pulled close to her chest.

She looked up at me with fear. "Vampires."

"Yeah."

"I didn't know they really existed."

"They do."

She let out a shuddery breath. "What's your name?"

I gathered my long black hair, pulling and twisting it to the side to keep it out of my face. "Jill. That's Declan. You?"

"Laura." Her gaze moved to my throat. Whatever damage she saw there made her gasp out loud.

"Well, Laura. Let's get the fuck out of here, shall we?"

"Good idea."

We went back to the stairwell and started climbing. We were deeper than I thought. I was in decent shape from being a bit of a gym rat back in my regular life, but this was rough going, especially after being knocked around and fed upon. Declan brought up the rear, but he kept pace with us, which was pretty impressive considering his injuries.

Finally, we reached the main level, which appeared to be nothing more than an abandoned warehouse. It was dark in here. A hundred feet ahead of me was the exit. I saw the line of light around the large door through which we'd entered.

"Leaving so soon?" The voice froze me in my tracks before I took another step.

Declan moved to stand in front of me and Laura. "Get out of our way."

Lawrence came far enough into the dim light for me to see him. His eyes were still black. The crazed look in those black eyes seemed worse now. Bigger. Scarier. Mostly because he was smiling, drawing my attention to his mouth stained with blood right down to his chin. "Can't do that."

He wasn't a bad guy. I'd seen him before he'd received that phone call. He was smart and reasonable. And, yes, obsessed with finding his wife. And willing to assist Dr. Reynolds with injecting Declan with my blood without a second thought.

Maybe he'd been crazy all along, just better at hiding it before.

But maybe he could still be reasoned with. "Lawrence, this can end here. You don't have to do anything else you're going to regret."

He laughed, and the sound sent a shiver down my spine. "I don't regret anything. This was meant to happen. I've been a pawn, a flunky. So eager to embrace my past that—do you see what I've been doing?" His voice broke and his bloody smile disappeared. "I've been betraying my kind. I've been offering up vampires just like me like lambs to the slaughter. Months now. So many have died here."

Declan wiped at the blood on his face with the sleeve of his coat. "Those vampires deserved to die."

He wasn't quite as good at negotiating.

Lawrence glared at him. "Are you God? Do you have the right to say who lives and who dies?" His expression grew pained. "You—you're just like Victor—taking other people's lives and using them for your own gain. It makes me sick."

I pressed my hands together to keep them from shaking. "Lawrence, please, listen to me. You're not thinking straight right now."

Lawrence laughed again and it sounded sharp, like breaking glass. "Wrong. Blood brings clarity, and I've drank my fill today for the first time in my new life. Why have I resisted for so long?"

I was wrong. He couldn't be reasoned with. I had no idea how many people he'd killed in the basement after he'd dealt with Dr. Reynolds. A lot. Enough to change him from a conflicted research assistant to a single-minded mass murderer. There was no coming back from that. At a glance, it didn't seem as if he wanted to.

I locked gazes with Declan, but I couldn't read his expression past his black eye patch. Mine, however, must have been clear. I was scared to death, but I wasn't ready to give up yet.

"Lawrence," I began. "Dr. Reynolds was wrong in what he did, but you need to think about—"

"Shut the fuck up." He took a step toward me, and Declan pushed me farther back.

"Don't come any closer," Declan snapped.

Lawrence's brows drew together, and his head cocked to the side. "You care what happens to her, don't you?"

Declan's expression was dark. "Yes."

"She's poison to my kind."

"Jill can't be blamed for what's in her blood. It wasn't her decision."

"Doesn't change anything. Blood is something that should never be tainted—it's a sacred communion. I've tasted blood today, felt it hot in my mouth while a heart ceased to beat beneath my touch. I've never felt anything so amazing in my life. It was primal. Incredible."

Declan's expression didn't change, although I'm sure mine paled, as did Laura's. She trembled next to me, her arms crossed over her chest.

"How many have you killed?" Declan asked. "Guards? Researchers?"

The eerie, wistful smiled returned. "All of them, I think. I lost count."

"What about Jackson?"

"You care about his life. How interesting. Do you know he's the reason behind all of this?"

He wasn't making any sense to me, not that I was surprised about that.

Declan's fists tightened at his sides. "What?"

"Jackson knew what happened to Victor's wife and who was responsible. He offered to bring you in. Kill two birds with one stone. Victor wanted you dead. It was all he could do to not kill you the moment he first saw you yesterday."

Declan's stony expression shifted a little to something more raw. "Jackson sold me out. Sold us out."

Lawrence nodded, his smile growing wider. "Don't trust friends with huge gambling debts. One of many lessons for the day."

The vampire hunter hadn't made a great first impression on me, even less when he hit on me yesterday, but I'd been convinced he was trustworthy. Declan had assured me of that and I'd believed him. He'd been wrong. Jackson knowingly brought him here to be killed or tortured—with my blood.

The thought made me see red. I wanted to tear Jackson apart with my bare hands for betraying Declan.

Declan was a bit more reserved than I was. "How do I know you're telling the truth?"

"You don't. And you won't ever know for sure. He's dead—four vampires were gnawing on his bones last time I saw. I would have joined in, but I was already full."

"Lawrence," I managed to say through clenched teeth, my anger helping to push away a bit of my fear. "Enough of this. You need to—"

Lawrence stormed toward me so fast I barely saw it. When Declan blocked me, the vampire instead grabbed hold of Laura. She screamed.

"Let her go," Declan snapped.

Lawrence searched her face as she cringed away from him. "You're the one, aren't you? You were with Susan when she died."

Laura sucked in a breath, her eyes were red from crying. "S-Susan . . . yes, I was. Yesterday. It was h-horrible. I didn't understand what was going on."

His expression held so much pain it was difficult not to look away. "She was my wife."

"She said your name. She whispered it . . . before—" A sob caught in Laura's throat. "Oh God. I tried to help her, but there was nothing I could do."

"Then it really is true." Lawrence blinked hard, his black eyes shone with tears. "The last of my hope is gone."

"No." She shook her head. "There's always hope for new beginnings. Everyone has to deal with horrible things in our lives, but we need to move past them and start again."

"Start again. Even for something like me?"

"Everyone deserves a second chance."

Lawrence exhaled deeply. "Leave now. Don't look back."

He let her go. She hesitated only a moment, looking at me and Declan, before she took off for the door, wrenching it open to give me a brief glimpse of the bright sunlight outside. It was painful to realize how close we were to safety.

Laura ran through the door, and it closed behind her. The light disappeared, leaving us again in shadows.

I was glad she was safe, but that hope she'd mentioned disappeared right along with her. I didn't chance looking at Declan again;

I kept my attention focused on the vampire who'd just surprised me by doing a kind thing, letting Laura safely escape.

It was a little bit encouraging.

"What about us?" I asked after a long moment of silence passed. "Can we leave, too?"

Lawrence studied the ground as if transfixed by it. "No."

My stomach twisted. "Why?"

He raised his gaze to mine, and he didn't look as rational as I'd hoped. "Because what's in your veins kills my kind. Before, I thought it was for the best—that vampires were monsters and that I was one of the few that deserved to live. Funny how things change."

When he pulled the silver stake he'd stolen earlier from Declan out of the back of his pants, every muscle in my body clenched with fear—for myself, for Declan.

This vampire wanted blood. He'd already consumed as much as he could drink, so now he just wanted to watch it spill.

"You need to stop this." Declan's voice was much more controlled than mine was. "It doesn't have to end like this."

"With death?" Lawrence studied the stake he clenched in his hand. "Everything ends with death. I would have done anything for my wife, but I wasn't given that choice. Victor chose my destiny. This is all his fault."

Declan looked at me, his expression tense. His eye moved to the door fifty yards away from where we stood. He was giving me a silent order. He wanted me to make a run for it while he held Lawrence back.

"Your wife wouldn't have wanted this," I said instead. "She loved you. She accepted you even when you changed. You tried to be human so you could stay together. She wouldn't want to know you became a cold-blooded murderer. There's still time to stop this."

His gaze tracked to me. "I'm not human. The more I kill, the better it feels. The more *right* it feels." He looked at Declan. "I'm sure you know how that is."

Declan shook his head. "I've never taken pleasure in what I have to do."

I'd tried to talk sense into Lawrence, but he wasn't seeing reason. He'd embraced the monster within him. And that monster was the only one in the general vicinity with a very sharp, very deadly weapon in hand.

Lawrence was silent for a long moment. "I've seen you protect this woman. You'd kill for her—anyone who'd threaten her life. Am I right?"

"Would I kill for her?" Declan glared at him. "In a heartbeat."

Lawrence didn't look away. "Would you also die for her?"

Declan didn't hesitate to answer. "Yes."

My breath caught. Despite the fact that he couldn't make love to me, I knew he put my life before his. I just hadn't heard it stated so bluntly before. He wasn't lying. This was the raw, honest truth. He'd kill for me. He'd die for me. In a way, it made things easier, since I felt the same way about him.

Lawrence nodded. "Then you know how I feel."

"There's a difference. Your wife is already dead. And nothing you do now will bring her back. The man responsible for her death is gone. You killed him. You had your revenge. It's over."

Lawrence was silent for so long I thought Declan had finally gotten through to him, shown him the futility of what he was doing here.

"You think this is over?" he finally said. "It's not. It's just begun."

He turned toward me, and whatever life, whatever hope, I'd seen in those black eyes was gone. This was a man who had nothing to live for. Just rage and pain that he wanted to share.

He came at me fast, and I stumbled back from him, twisting my ankle and falling to the ground. I screamed just as Declan caught his arm, stopping the sharp stake only a few inches from it being a death blow to my heart. Declan's expression was strained as he fought to pull Lawrence away from me.

"Get out of here now!" Declan snapped over his shoulder at me. "Get to the sunlight!"

If I left, he'd die. I felt the truth of it deep in my gut.

I shook off the fear and panic, knowing I had to do something to help. I scanned my surroundings. There wasn't much in the warehouse—nothing useful, anyway. Cement floors. Large wooden crates stacked against the wall by the door. The scent of sawdust. That was it. If there was another security camera in here, it was hidden. Not that it would do us any good. Whoever monitored that downstairs was likely dead. We were on our own.

I screamed when the stake arched through the air and stabbed into Declan, piercing his shoulder. Declan let out a sharp snarl of pain.

"First I kill you." Lawrence pulled out the bloody stake. "Then I kill the woman. I can resist the Nightshade enough to do it. You're both murderers. You both deserve to die."

He kicked Declan hard in the leg that had just been broken, and Declan went down hard, crashing to the ground. Blood gushed from the stake wound.

Lawrence turned toward me, moving so fast I didn't have a chance to take another step back. He grabbed my shirt and pulled me closer. I fought against him, slamming my fist into his face, my knee into his groin.

Bleeding and injured, Declan grabbed hold of Lawrence's ankle. The vampire kicked him hard in the face and Declan landed on his back. Lawrence crouched down over his prone form, his silver stake aimed for Declan's heart this time.

I launched myself at him. Normally my blood was my weapon. This time it was my entire body. Not quite as deadly, but effective enough as a diversion. I caught his shoulders and pulled him off Declan. We both hit the ground hard. The stake skittered away on the cement floor.

Lawrence snarled and rose up above me. He clamped his hands around my throat and squeezed hard enough to cut off my breath. I reached out for the stake, felt just the edge of it against my fingertips, but it was out of reach.

It was too late, anyway. I was going to die.

TEN

"Jill! No!" Declan yelled.

Black spots appeared before my eyes, and my hands dropped to my sides.

Lawrence's face blurred. "There's no other way this can end. The moment you were injected with the Nightshade, you had a death sentence. Victor couldn't help you, even if he wanted to. I think you already knew that."

He was right. I'd been grasping hold of sand with every solution I'd chased after, watching as it slipped through my fingers. I wasn't sure why I hadn't given up yet and accepted my impending death without wasting energy trying to fight it. The Nightshade was a lot like Lawrence. It wasn't letting go until I finally stopped breathing. Until my heart stopped beating. Until my poisoned black blood went still in my veins.

Something about being with Declan—it was enough to keep me going. He was a warrior, this kind of thing was his life. He didn't know any different.

The Declan in my dream—the glimpse I'd had of him if he'd never been touched by death and darkness and violence. He was clean and handsome and unscarred.

But I wouldn't choose him over the Declan I already knew.

It was my last thought before more darkness spread across my vision.

There was a loud bang. Lawrence jerked backward, and his grip on me loosened. I tried to focus enough to see that there was now a spot of red on his chest. He looked up.

"You're dead," Lawrence said, then he jerked again as another bullet hit him squarely in the chest.

Someone came into my peripheral vision—it was Jackson, with a gun held in his right hand. He was covered in blood; he was leaving a trail of it as he walked toward us. And there was something wrong with his left arm, which hung awkwardly at his side, as though no longer fully attached to his body.

"Nearly dead isn't really dead, asshole." Jackson pulled the trigger again, but the chamber rang empty. He fell to his knees, breathing hard.

Lawrence rose shakily to his feet. "Regular bullets don't kill vampires. As a hunter, you should know that by now."

"No, they don't." Declan had managed to drag himself up to his feet and come closer, despite the fact that he looked almost as injured as Jackson did. "But this does."

His hand was curled around the silver stake that had been lying just out of my reach, and he sliced it into Lawrence's chest.

Lawrence staggered back, staring down at the weapon. When he looked up, there was a peaceful look on his face, replacing the earlier rage. "Thank you."

And then he was gone, his fiery ashes scattered in a horrible cloud, some drifting down to land on my face. I squeezed my eyes shut.

Declan kneeled down next to me and grabbed for my hand. "No, Jill—please don't be dead."

I would have smiled if the expression was currently possible. It sounded exactly like what I'd said to him in the examination room downstairs.

"Not . . . quite yet," I managed to say. "But . . . almost."

"Vampires," Jackson muttered. "I fucking hate vampires. Jesus, look at my arm. I seriously need an ambulance."

Declan looked up at him. "How the hell did you escape? He said you were dead. That four vampires were feeding on you."

"Never underestimate the power of positive thinking." Jackson grinned shakily.

"He also told me you sold me out to Dr. Reynolds." His expression darkened. "I'm sure you'll deny that, right?"

His grin faded. "I can't deny it. I did it."

Declan's grip on my hand tightened. He was more surprised than I was at the confirmation. "I want to kill you."

"I'm a lowlife scum sucker. You already knew that. Hell, you were one of only a handful who could tolerate me before this. May as well burn all my bridges while I'm at it."

"At least you admit it."

Jackson's expression was bleak. "That I'm a lying, selfish sack of shit? You got it. Now let's get into the sunlight before the vamps I didn't kill decide to climb the rest of those stairs."

It wasn't a victory parade as we dragged ourselves to the exit, but it would do. The hot sun felt so good on my face I nearly cried with relief. My throat felt sore, I was woozy from the loss of blood, and it would take a good long while for me to get over the last half hour of horror I'd experienced.

But I was still alive. And so was Declan.

And so was Jackson. Total asshole—no argument there—but he'd saved our lives. We would have died if he hadn't intervened. I was sure that fact hadn't escaped Declan's attention. Maybe we didn't owe him for that, since he'd gotten us into this in the first place, but it helped to even the scales a little bit.

Jackson looked at the warehouse exterior. "I'll call for containment. Luckily those vamps aren't going anywhere in the middle of the day. I'll get some guys to come in and do a sweep, exterminate the rest of them. See if there are any human survivors. Hell, what a fucking mess." He patted the pocket of his jeans with his uninjured hand. "Can I borrow your phone? I think mine got eaten."

Declan threw him his cell phone.

"I'll just go bleed over there and leave you two alone." Jackson nodded at the parking lot before heading off in that direction.

"How's your leg?" I asked, placing my hand on Declan's knee as we sat side by side on the ground just outside the warehouse door. Laura was nowhere to be seen. She'd taken off running and hadn't stopped. I hoped she'd be okay and not sign up for any more research programs that required one to be locked in a room deep underground.

He raised an eyebrow. "Healing. How's your throat?"

"I need ice cream. And a couple Band-Aids."

His jaw tightened. "I'm sorry everything didn't work out, Jill."

I laughed a little at that. It hurt. "*Not working out* is a bit of an understatement."

He nodded. "You're right. I'm sorry that in our search for a solution to your problem we were nearly torn apart by bloodthirsty vampires."

"That's better." I grabbed his hand and squeezed it, tracing my thumb over an old scar that ran across his knuckles. "We're still alive, so I'd say the day was a success."

"Your blood—"

I cringed at the memory. "If it had killed you, I'm not really sure what I would have done. I think I might have gone ballistic on Dr. Reynolds long before Lawrence got to him." I searched his face. "Did the Nightshade do anything to you? Anything bad that you might not recover from?"

He shook his head. "I think its effects are fading."

"Your human side was enough to counteract the poison."

"Yeah, but—but it did something else to me. Something that really messed me up."

"What?"

"It threw off the serum I'm on. It messed up my emotions. Made it fucking hard to think straight."

I knew I'd seen emotion on his face before. This was the confirmation.

I grimaced. "How do you feel right now?"

"I thought it might be permanent, but I can feel it fading as we speak. I don't think it was a cure for the permanent serum, just a glitch. Besides, the pain I felt when I was injected—not really something I want to experience again if I can help it."

I studied his face. "So you're back to normal?"

"Almost." His brows drew together. "You said something earlier—about our experiment last night."

This wasn't a good time to talk about that. "Declan—"

"No, hear me out, Jill. You said that it wasn't unpleasant for you to let me . . . do that."

The memory of his mouth on me and his hands skimming my body played in my mind. "*Not unpleasant* is also a vast understatement for what I felt last night."

"Yeah, but you also said you didn't want me to touch you or kiss you again if I wasn't feeling something in return."

I swallowed. "That's right."

"That means I better do this now while I still have a window of opportunity."

"What?"

He took my face between his hands and kissed me. This wasn't a one-sided kiss, one that lacked true feeling on Declan's part. Even with the salty taste of sweat and the faint copper tang of blood, this was incredible, amazing. Passionate. Real. The feel of his mouth against mine trumped any suit-wearing, perfect Declan in any stupid dream. A shiver of pleasure coursed through me.

When he finally pulled away, my cheeks were flushed and my entire body tingled. I stared at him with surprise, and he rewarded me with a grin.

"Was that better?" he asked.

I smiled back at him. "It was . . . not bad."

His grin widened. "It was better than not bad."

"Practice makes perfect."

"Tell me something I don't know." The smile faded. "Shit, I can feel it. The effects of my serum . . . it's coming back fast. I'm sorry, Jill."

I shook my head. "Don't be sorry."

I kissed him again, quickly, and already I felt it wasn't the same as a moment ago. I'd have to keep that one passionate, incredible kiss firmly in my memory. If it had happened once, it could damn well happen again.

Laura was right about hope. Even after everything that had happened, I was surprised how much I still had in reserve.

Declan stood up and held out his hand to help me up. "Let's get out of here."

I felt shaky, my body ached, and my throat was tender. I'd lost a whole lot of blood. I hadn't found a solution to my Nightshade problem. The scientist who claimed he could help me was dead, an act of vengeance for the sins of his past. There was a nest of vampires beneath our feet that had an extermination to look forward to rather than a juicy, human jugular to snack on.

I'd nearly died, but I was still alive. I had a chance to heal and to figure out what my next step was going to be.

And surprisingly enough, I felt rather hopeful about that.

One amazing kiss from Declan had made me see that nothing was permanent—there were always loopholes . . . or glitches. If his so-called permanent serum could be brushed aside once, it could be again. And if he could be healed, then so could I.

It was far from perfect, but I was okay with that. I already knew perfection was highly overrated.

Turn the page for a preview
of Jill and Declan's first thrilling adventure
by Michelle Rowen . . .

Nightshade

Now available in paperback from Berkley Sensation!

Life as I knew it ended at half past eleven on a Tuesday morning.

There were currently thirty minutes left.

"What's your poison?" I asked my friend and co-worker Stacy on my way out of the office on a coffee break.

She looked up at me from a spreadsheet on her computer screen, her eyes practically crossed from crunching numbers all morning. "You're a serious lifesaver, Jill, you know that?"

"Well aware." I grinned at her, then shifted my purse to my other shoulder and took the five-dollar-bill she thrust at me.

"I'll take a latte, extra foam. And one of those white chocolate chunk cookies. My stomach's growling happily just thinking about it."

Stacy didn't normally go for the cookie action. "No diet today?"

"Fuck diets."

"Can I quote you?"

She laughed. "I'll have it printed on a T-shirt. Hey, Steve! Jill's headed to the coffee shop. You want anything?"

I groaned inwardly. I hadn't wanted to make a big production out of it, since I hated making change. Unlike Stacy, math was not my friend.

By the time I finally made it out of the office I had a yellow sticky note clenched in my fist scrawled with four different coffee orders.

Twenty minutes left.

The line-up at Starbucks was, as usual, ridiculous. I waited. I ordered. I waited some more. I juggled my wallet and my purse along with the bag of pastries and take-out tray of steaming caffeine and finally left the shop, passing an electronics store on my way back. It had a bunch of televisions in the window set to CNN. Some plane crash in Europe was blazing. No survivors. I shivered, despite the heat of the day, and continued walking.

Five minutes left.

I returned to my office building, which not only housed Lambert Capital, the investment and financial analysis company where I currently temped, but also a small pharmaceutical research company, a marketing firm, and a modeling agency.

"Hold the elevator," I called out as I crossed the lobby. My heels clicked against the shiny black marble floor. Despite my request, the elevator was *not* held. The doors closed when I was only a couple of steps away from it, a look of bemusement on the sole occupant's face who hadn't done me the honor of waiting.

One minute left.

I nudged the up button with my elbow and waited, watching as the number above the doors stopped at the tenth floor, ISB Pharmaceuticals, paused for what felt like an eternity, and then slowly descended back to the lobby. The other elevator seemed eternally stuck at the fifteenth. Another bank of elevators were located around the corner, but I chose to stay where I was and try my best to be patient.

Finally, the doors slid open to reveal a man who wore a white lab coat and a security badge that bore his name: Carl Anderson. His eyes were shifty and there was a noticeable sheen of sweat on his brow. My gaze dropped to his right hand in which he tightly held a syringe—the sharp needle uncapped.

That was a safety hazard I wasn't getting anywhere near. What the hell was he thinking, carrying something like that around?

Glaring at him, I waited for him to get out of the elevator so I could get on, but he didn't budge an inch.

Behind thick glasses, his eyes were steadily widening with what looked like fear, and totally focused on something behind me. Curious about what would earn this dramatic reaction, I turned to see another man enter the lobby. He was tall, had a black patch over his left eye, and wasn't smiling. Aside from that, I noticed the gun he held. The big gun. The one he now had trained on the man in the elevator.

"Leaving so soon, Anderson? Why am I not surprised?" the man with the gun growled. "No more fucking games. Give it to me right now."

I gasped as Carl Anderson clamped his arm around my neck. The tray of coffees went flying as I clawed at him, but my struggling did nothing. I couldn't even scream; he held me so tightly that it cut off my breath.

"Why are you here?" Anderson demanded. "*I* was supposed to be the one to make contact."

The gunman's icy gaze never wavered. "Let go of the woman."

My eyes watered. I couldn't breathe. My larynx was being crushed.

"But she's the only thing standing between me and your direct orders right now, isn't she?"

"And why would you think I care if you grab some random hostage?" the gunman growled.

Random hostage?

Panic swelled further inside of me. I scanned the lobby to see that this altercation hadn't gone unnoticed. Several people with shocked looks on their faces had cell phones pressed to their ears. Were they calling 911? Where was security? No guards approached with guns drawn.

Fear coursed through me, closing my throat. My hands, which gripped Anderson's arm, were shaking.

"We can talk about this," Anderson said.

"It's too late for negotiations. There's more at risk than the life of one civilian."

"I thought we were supposed to be working together."

"Sure. Until you decided to sell elsewhere. Hand over the formula."

"I destroyed the rest." Anderson's voice trembled. "One proto-type is all that's left."

"That was a mistake." The gunman's tone was flat.

"It was a mistake creating it in the first place. It's dangerous."

"Isn't that the whole point?"

"You'd defend something that would just as easily kill *you*, Declan? Even though you can walk in the sunlight, you're not much better than the other bloodsuckers." The man who held me prone sounded disgusted. And scared shitless—almost as scared as I felt.

Bloodsuckers? What the hell was he talking about? How did I get in the middle of this? I'd only gone out for coffee—coffee that was now splattered all over the clean lobby floor. It was just a nor-mal workday—a normal Tuesday.

More people had gathered around us, moving backward toward the walls and door, away from this unexpected stand-off, hands held to their mouths in shock at what they were witnessing. I spot-ted someone from the office to my left rounding the corner where the other elevators were located—it was Stacy with an armful of file folders, her eyes wide as saucers as she saw me. She took a step closer, mouthing my name.

No, please don't come any closer, I thought frantically. *Don't get hurt.*

Where the hell was security?

I shrieked when I felt a painful jab at my throat.

"Don't do that," the man with the gun, Declan, snapped.

"You know what will happen if I inject her with this, don't you?" Anderson's voice held an edge of something—panic, fear, desperation. I didn't have to be the helpless hostage in this situation to realize that was a really bad mix.

He had the syringe up against my throat, the sharp tip of the needle stabbing deep into my flesh. I stopped struggling and tried not to move, tried not to breathe. My vision blurred with tears as I waited for the man with the gun to do something to save me. He was my only hope.

"I don't give a shit about her," my only hope said evenly. "All I care about is that formula. Now hand it over and maybe you get to live."

The gunman's face was oddly emotionless considering this situation. He wore black jeans and a black T-shirt, which bared thick, sinewy biceps. His face didn't have an ounce of humanity to it. Around the black eye patch, scar tissue branched out like a spider web up over his forehead and down his left cheek, all the way to his neck. He was as scary-looking as he was ugly.

"I knew they'd send you to retrieve this, Declan." Anderson's mouth was so close to my ear that I could feel his hot breath. His shaky voice held a mocking edge. "Who better for this job?"

"I'll give you five seconds to release the woman and hand over that syringe with its contents intact," Declan said. "Or I'll kill both of you where you stand. Five . . . four . . ."

"Think about this, will you?" Anderson dug the needle farther into my flesh, prompting another wheeze of a shriek from me. "You need to open your fucking eyes and see the truth before it's too late. I'm trying to stop this the only way I can. It's wrong. All of it's wrong. You're just as brainwashed as the rest of them, aren't you?"

With his chest pressed against my back, I could feel his erratic heartbeat. He feared for his life. A mental flash of memories of my family, my friends, sped past my eyes. I didn't want to die—no, please, not like this.

"Three . . . two . . ." Declan continued, undeterred. The laser sighter from his gun fixed on my chest.

Several onlookers ran for the glass doors, and screams sounded out.

"You want the abomination I created that goddamned much?" Anderson yelled. "Here! You can have it!"

A second later, I felt a burning pain, hot as fire, as he injected me with the syringe's contents. It was a worse pain than the stabbing itself. Then he raggedly ripped the needle out and pushed me away hard enough that I went sprawling to the floor. I clamped my hand against the side of my neck and started to scream.

The sound of a gunshot, even louder than my screams, pierced my eardrums. I turned to look at the man who'd just injected me. He now lay sprawled out on the marble floor, his eyes open and glassy. There was a large hole in Anderson's forehead, red and wet and sickening. He had a gun in his left hand, which he must have pulled from his lab coat when he let go of me. The empty syringe lay next to him.

Declan went directly to him, gun still trained on the dead man for another moment before he tucked it away, squatted, and then silently and methodically began going through the pockets of the white coat.

My entire body shook, but otherwise I was frozen in place. There were more screams now from the others who'd witnessed the shooting as they scattered in all directions.

Declan swore under his breath and then turned to look directly at me for the very first time. The iris of his right eye was pale gray and soulless, and the look he gave me froze my insides.

My throat felt like it had been slit wide open, but I was still breathing. Still thinking. A quick, erratic scan of the lobby showed where I'd dropped my purse and the coffees and pastries six feet to my right. Most of the people in the lobby were now running for the doors to escape to the street outside. A security alarm finally began to wail, adding to the chaos.

"You—" Declan rose fluidly to his feet. He was easily a full foot taller than my five-four. "—come here."

Like hell I would.

The elevator to the left of me opened and a man pushing an empty mail cart got off. The murderer's attention went to it. I took it as the only chance I might ever get. I scrambled to my feet and ran.

"Jill!" I heard Stacy yell, but it didn't slow me down. I had to get away, far away from the office. My mind had switched into survival mode. Stacy couldn't get anywhere near me right now; it would only put her in danger, too.

I left my purse behind—the contents of my life scattered on the smooth, cold floor next to the spilled coffee and spreading pool of blood. I pushed through the front doors, fully expecting Declan to shoot me in my back. But he didn't.

Yanking my hand from my wounded neck, I saw that it was covered in blood. My stomach lurched and I almost vomited. What was in that syringe? It burned like lava sliding through my veins.

I was badly hurt. Jesus, I'd been stabbed in the throat with a needle by a stranger. If I wasn't in such pain, I'd think I was having a nightmare.

This *was* a nightmare—a waking one.

A look behind me confirmed that Declan, whoever the hell he was, had exited the office building. He scanned one side of the street before honing in on me.

I clutched at a few people's arms as I stumbled past them. They recoiled from me, faceless strangers who weren't willing to help a woman with a bleeding neck wound.

My heart slammed against my rib cage as I tried to run, but I couldn't manage more than a stagger. I wanted to pass out. The world was blurry and shifting around me.

The burning pain slowly began to spread from my neck down to my chest and along my arms and legs. I could feel it like a living thing, burrowing deeper and deeper inside me.

Only a few seconds later, I felt Declan's hand clamp around my upper arm. He nearly pulled me off my feet as he dragged me around the corner and into an alley.

"Let go of me," I snarled, attempting to hit him. He effortlessly grabbed my other arm. I blinked against my tears.

"Stay still."

"Go to hell." The next moment, the pain cut off any further words as I convulsed. Only his tight grip kept me from crumpling to the ground. He pushed me up against the wall and held my head firmly in place as he looked into my eyes. His scars were even uglier up close. A shudder of revulsion rippled through me at being this close to him.

He wrenched my head to the left and roughly pulled my long blond hair aside to inspect the neck wound. His expression never wavered. There was no pity or anger or disdain in his gaze—nothing but emptiness in his single gray eye as he looked me over.

Holding me with one hand tightly around my throat so I could barely breathe, he held a cell phone to his ear.

"It's me," he said. "There's been a complication."

A pause.

"Anderson administered the prototype to a civilian before he tried to shoot me and escape. I killed him." Another pause. "It's a woman. Should I kill her, too?"

I tried to fight against the choke hold he had me in, but it didn't help. He sounded so blasé, so emotionless, as if he was discussing bringing home a pizza after work rather than seeking permission for my murder.

His one-eyed gaze narrowed. While talking on the phone he hadn't looked anywhere but my face. "I know I was followed here. I don't have long." Then finally, "Understood."

He ended the call.

Finally he loosened his hold on me enough that I could try to speak in pained gasps. "What . . . are you going . . . to do with me?"

"That's not up to me." Declan's iron grip on me went a little more lax as he tucked the phone back into the pocket of his black jeans. It was enough to let me sink my teeth into his arm. He pushed me back so hard I whacked my head against the wall and fell to the ground. I'd managed to draw blood on his forearm, which was already riddled with other scars.

I scrambled up to my feet, adrenaline coursing through my body. I was ready to do whatever I had to in order to fight for my life, but another curtain of agony descended over me.

"What's happening to me?" I managed to say through clenched teeth. "What the hell was in that syringe?"

Declan grabbed me by the front of my shirt and brought me very close to his scarred face. "Poison."

My eyes widened. "Oh my God. What kind of poison?"

"The kind that will kill you," he said simply. "Which is why you have to come with me."

I shook my head erratically. "I have to get to a hospital."

"No." He grabbed me tighter. "Death now or death later. That's your only choice."

It was a choice I didn't want to make. It was one I wouldn't have to make. More pain erupted inside of me and the world went totally and completely black.

Skin & Bone

AVA GRAY

For those who loved, lost,
and had the courage to try again

ACKNOWLEDGMENTS

You first met Silas in *Skin Tight*; I hope you enjoy his story.

Thanks to Laura Bradford, Cindy Hwang, Lauren Dane, Bree Bridges, Larissa Ione, Donna Herren, Jenn Bennett, Courtney Milan, and Karen Erickson. You all supported this series from the beginning, and I value your encouragement.

Thanks to Stefanie Gostautas for her excellent proofreading.

And thanks, as ever, to my family. Their patience and understanding make all this possible.

Finally, I send profound appreciation to all my readers. Your e-mails mean the world to me, so please keep writing. That's ann.aguirre@gmail.com.

ONE

PUERTO LÓPEZ, ECUADOR

The whole world roared.

One minute, Silas had a bottle of beer in his hand; the next, the cantina roof threatened to crumble down on top of him. Nearby, rubble pinned a waitress to the floor; blood trickled from her mouth. With the ceiling collapsing around him, he levered the wreckage off her and felt for a pulse. Dead. *Shit*. Falling chunks of cement and plaster forced him to dive for the doorway. He crouched, arms over his head, and willed the framework to hold. He hadn't escaped from the Foundation—and put several thousand miles between him and their hunters—to die here.

The reel of his life spun into motion, full of sorrow and infinite regret. Things he'd done and wished he hadn't, all the faces of people he'd hurt. In particular, he could still see the blond woman, Olivia. She'd begged him to kill her, time and again. More than most, she'd gotten into his head—because that was her gift—and her curse. To this day, she still haunted his dreams, and he didn't know how to make her go away. Maybe he couldn't. Sometimes he thought it wasn't even her anymore, but that her thin face personified his guilt.

But to be fair, his dark history had *not* begun down in the lab. It started years before in a deserted parking garage, where a mugger demanded his wallet, and he'd broken the man's neck. Without so much as touching him. Nobody had ever been able to explain that death; it remained an open cold case in Michigan to this day. That was when he'd known his difference ran bone deep. He just hadn't known *why* until the Foundation took him.

The tremors went on for over five minutes while he sat listening to the screams; cries of pain and horror filled what had been a bright Thursday afternoon. For the first time in months, he'd felt safe, because nobody knew him. He was just another anonymous expat. How ironic.

At last, the shocks stopped. Covered in dust and debris, he staggered into the dirt street of the fishing village. The wreckage humbled him. No matter how strong or powerful you thought you were, Mother Nature delivered a crippling kick in the nuts. Most of the buildings had been constructed of lesser materials, and they lay in ruins. He had been lucky; he'd chosen the cantina for its shady interior, knowing cement and plaster kept the cool air better.

"*Por favor,*" a woman begged. "*Ayúdame!*"

It sounded like she was close by. God, he wished his gift had some useful secondary application, but it could be used for only one purpose—and that was why he had chosen to accept five years of abuse in lieu of revealing it to his captors. He could *never* allow them to learn what he could do. The price was simply too high.

Ignoring the shallow cuts and bruises on his arms, he located the woman by listening to her intermittent calls. A fuckton of rubble had fallen on top of her, and he hesitated to start digging. He might make it worse: unbalance the wreckage and kill her. He'd intentionally gone off the grid, but now that decision carried awful weight. Out here, there was no emergency infrastructure, and no telling how long it would take Ecuadoran authorities to mount any kind of rescue. In all honesty, Puerto López probably wouldn't rank high on their list. More populated areas required assistance first.

Therefore, this woman had him, and nobody else. As he contemplated that, she wept in tiny choking sobs.

Using the brute strength that accompanied his size, he pulled chunks of cement off the pile and tossed them behind him, careful not to let the load topple inward. It required great patience, but fortunately, life had taught him about timing and waiting for the right opportunity. That permitted him to be methodical: *shift this, pull that, don't let it collapse.* He listened to her whimpering breaths; they weakened as he worked.

"*No abandone,*" he said, knowing his accent was terrible. "*Casi soy terminado.*"

To his surprise, she responded in English. "You're American?"

"Yeah. I'm doing what I can for you. Nobody official's on scene yet."

She responded, her voice tight with pain, "Thank you."

Silas spoke of inconsequential things as he dug. He told her how he'd traveled from California to Mexico and meandered south on hot, dirty buses. Sometimes there were boats, but he didn't like them. Everything he owned had been in the duffel he'd left at his hostel, but it was probably long gone.

At last he uncovered her legs. Blood spattered her dusty skin, but he couldn't tell how badly she was injured. He might be able to pull her out this way, but he needed more information first.

"Where are you hurt? Upper body or spine? Are your arms or shoulders trapped?"

"No," she said. "Please, just get me out."

Brave. All right, then. He curled his hands around her calves and towed her out in increments. Each movement made the wreckage teeter, and he was afraid she'd be crushed before he saved her. It was a hot day, overcast, and dust in the air lingered on his dry lips, coating his tongue. Finally, he dragged her shoulders clear, and then it was quick work. As he lifted her into his arms, the whole pile caved, plaster and cement slamming down to fill the space she'd vacated.

Despite the heat, she trembled in his arms, her taut silence revealing a fear he shared and that she'd kept locked down until now.

Though they were strangers, he would've hated hearing her die. And if he hadn't intervened, she would have. That was an odd feeling. For once, he'd done something right. While the world wailed around them, she let him hold her for long moments, and he couldn't remember the last time he'd been so close to a woman. His tough exterior usually terrified them.

Dark, wild hair spilled to his shoulders, uncut for months. They'd demanded he shave it, so they could monitor the hardware in his head. Back then, he'd also cut his eyelashes off because it made him look strange and stupid, easier to maintain the necessary pretense. Since the escape, his hair had grown back, and he had a scar behind his ear where he'd dug out their chip in a shitty gas station bathroom and prayed against infection. So yeah, he knew how he looked—and most of the time, he didn't care. Better if people kept their distance.

But she still hadn't glanced up from his shoulder. He might scare her yet. Cradled against his chest, she seemed small, but then, almost everyone did. Few men could look him in the eyes. He was always conscious of taking up space, pulling his arms and legs in so he didn't intimidate other people. Not that it worked—most practiced snap judgments.

"I'm better," she said at last.

He took it as his cue to set her down. "Are you vacationing here?"

"No, I'm with an educational coalition, teaching English. You?"

"Just traveling. I was drinking a beer when it all went down."

"I was shopping for the school." Her eyes went wide. "Oh my God, the *kids*." She tried to run but fell before she'd gone five steps. Her knee buckled beneath her.

It took him all of ten seconds to make up his mind and then even fewer to reach her side and offer his hand. "Show me. I'll help you."

Nodding, she let him pull her up, left her hand in his, and shook his in a formal greeting. The woman studied the ink etching his wrists and the backs of his hands. Black and red, the pattern continued up his arms and onto his shoulders, not that she could see it all. The tatts combined with the rest to render him pretty fucking scary, which was a good thing, traveling as he did. He expected a comment or recoil. Instead, she smiled up at him, her face grimy and blood smeared.

He slid an arm around her shoulders to support her. "How far?"

"Four blocks that way." She pointed behind them.

The light brown of her hair showed even through the dust, worn loose, but with random braids and trinkets, streaks of blue and pink that didn't look likely to wash out. Girls did such styles on the beach. But it was more practical to plait all of it in this climate. Her refusal showed a hint of vanity and a refusal to conform, echoed in the unusual colors.

"It would be faster if I carried you," he said.

For a moment, he thought she would protest. To make it easier for her, less passive, he knelt, so she could climb onto his back. It gave her a role to play; if she didn't hang on, she'd fall, and it took some of the control away from him. He understood the importance of such distinctions.

Without further comment, she got on and he straightened. The damage, as they walked, proved incalculable. People staggered in the streets, bloody and disoriented. Others stood outside wrecked buildings, weeping. No structure had gone untouched, and the rubble spilled into the road, making passage difficult. In a town this size, nobody cared about safety codes.

"That's quality work," she said, surprising him with a touch to the patterns curling up his biceps.

An unexpected compliment, under the circumstances, and then he realized she wanted a distraction from the mess surrounding them. "Thanks."

"I have one on my shoulder." She leaned forward, so he could see the stylized star by glancing back. "I'm Juneau, by the way. Juneau Bright. I should've thanked you before now. You saved my life."

"Silas."

That's a first, he thought. He was all too experienced at causing pain and doing harm. The role of savior was entirely new. Silas found he rather liked it. But he couldn't think of anything to say to keep the conversation going, and she fell silent, her anxiety kicking in anew.

The school lay at the heart of town. Total devastation. As they approached, Juneau sobbed, just once, and then swallowed her grief. He felt the tension in her arms as she did.

"It's no use, is it?" But he could tell she already knew the answer. The damage was so profound that there was no way the two of them could perform search and rescue safely. This required a crew, medical supplies, and equipment, unlike the small store where she had been buried.

Still, he answered, "I don't think so."

"What should we do?"

Silas arched his brows. She was asking *him*? "Other countries will send help in time. Ecuador will mobilize as soon as it can."

Really, he knew shit about such situations, only what he'd seen on TV. But somehow he didn't think she would be content to sit around and be grateful for her survival, even with that bad leg.

"That's not enough," she said. "There has to be something we can do."

"Do you speak Spanish? Because I have just enough to get by."

"I'm fluent."

He thought for a moment. "Then we should head for the medical center. See if any first aid supplies survived the quake. You can organize other survivors. Get them to round up the available food and water before opportunists start hoarding."

"The medical center is this way." She tapped his right shoulder, giving him directions, and he didn't even mind that she took it for granted he'd help.

Apparently she didn't look at him and see a freak, someone she should fear. God knew it had been long enough for him to shed that skin, but he'd been playing that persona so long, it had come to feel real. He had been traveling ever since the escape, his destinations random in case anyone was hunting for him, and he never stayed in one place very long.

These days, it didn't take much to make him start feeling trapped. Five years was too much of your life to lose, but the consequences would've been dire and far-reaching, had he chosen otherwise. Regardless, he had a lot in common with men who'd done time. They often drank at the same bars, and they accepted him as one of them, even if he'd spent his sentence in a different kind of prison. They didn't need to know that—and it was the closest he came to friendship, those silent moments with an upturned beer.

But maybe he could play hero with her for a little while. Maybe. She didn't need to know the truth, if she couldn't see it inked into his skin.

TWO

He was strong, and he spoke English. That was all Juneau knew about her new partner. Under the circumstances, that was already more than she could've hoped for. He was doing most of the heavy lifting. She'd tried to help, but he gave her a dark look and invited her to "take a seat," though she suspected he'd enforce his will if she balked. And honestly, the flaring pain persuaded her more than his authority.

So she watched him work. The medical center had held up better than most of the buildings in town. Only one wall and part of the ceiling had collapsed. Now Silas labored to clear the place out while she used a sheet to paint a banner that read, *Refugio aquí.* When she finished, she limped toward the broken wall to hang it street side, and as soon as he saw her move, Silas dropped the heavy chunk of plaster in his hands. He hurried toward her as if she were permanently crippled.

I might be, if it wasn't for him. Hell, I'd probably be dead. She'd never known a bona fide hero before. So far she'd managed to be normal around him, but it was hard not to let gratitude color her responses. And the fact that he hadn't left her to fend for herself in the wake of the disaster—it reiterated what she'd known when he pulled her from the wreckage. He was something special.

"I'll do that," he said.

"So, what, you're going to have me sitting around, waiting for guests?"

Her leg wasn't broken. She'd taken a look earlier, and it appeared to her that she'd sustained deep bruising around her knee. Nothing would cure that but time. Until then, she'd swallow some painkillers, once they cleared this place a bit, and do the best she could.

He thought about that a moment. "Help me, then."

When he approached to take the sheet from her, she realized all over again just how enormous he was. He had to be close to seven feet tall, because at five foot nine, she wasn't petite, and he made her feel tiny and feminine. That was new. As she watched him, Silas gathered makeshift tools, a couple of metal shards, and a wedge of cement. From the gentle crow's feet and brackets at his mouth, he looked to be in his late thirties or early forties. He had an interesting face. In fact, most women would probably consider him ugly with his crooked nose and overly strong jaw.

She followed him outside, curious about his methods, and while she held one end, he used brute strength to spike the sign into place. It wasn't straight, but the message was clear. They could expect survivors to start filing in, which meant they needed to finish clearing the medical center, lay hands on any usable supplies, and locate food and water.

"One of us needs to stay here," he said as he finished the task. "Since you're fluent in Spanish, it should be you."

"You just don't want me walking around on this leg."

To her surprise, he acknowledged that. "True. But my point stands. I can also bring back more supplies in a single run, and I'm better suited to deal with trouble."

Juneau nodded. "Go on, then. I'll finish up here."

Each step hurt as she completed what he'd started. But her determined hope faltered when she finished clearing all the way to the stairs. She found the doctor, still and lifeless. How the hell was she supposed to deal with this? Intellectually, she knew the dead had to be moved. Otherwise they risked disease and infection among the survivors. But the phone lines were down, and there was no one to call.

With a murmured apology, she rolled him onto a sheet and towed him out through the broken wall. Stray dogs might get at him out here. But she couldn't leave him inside with the living. A quick look around revealed a storage shed so flimsy that it must've swayed with the quake instead of collapsing. It was a little further than she wanted to go, dragging such a burden, but she couldn't leave him in the street. Juneau opened the latch and shoved the body inside.

Her return to the medical center went a lot slower. She was afraid of what else she'd find. But fortunately, the doctor seemed to have been alone at the time of the quake. Thankfully, he'd run a small practice.

By the time Silas got back, she'd managed to set up a couple of tables and had covered one of them with bandages, tape, and other medical odds and ends. The painkillers, apart from OTC ones, she left locked up. Since she wasn't a doctor, that stuff shouldn't be in circulation anyway. Silas came in pushing a wheelbarrow full of bottled water and canned goods, his face red and sweaty from working in the afternoon heat.

"Did you dig out a whole store?"

His smile came and went, fleeting as a bird gliding over the ocean. "Pretty much."

Silas went back almost immediately, leaving her to do the setup. Good thing she stayed, too. People began to arrive with dusty faces and bloody hands. Some, she could tell by their injures, had dug themselves out of the wreckage. She gave out water and aspirin while trying not to panic.

How the hell did I think I could manage an aid effort like this? I've never even owned a cat.

"Are you a nurse?" a woman asked in Spanish.

"No. I teach English." *Or I did. Before this.* "But I've had basic first aid training. I can tend wounds."

That galvanized three or four people to queue up around her. *"Me duele."*

"Ayude a mi hijo, por favor."

And she tried. At least, everyone seemed grateful for the water, more shell-shocked than anything else. The survivors asked relatively few questions. Doubtless they knew she had no answers.

A couple of families huddled together. Juneau prowled through the supplies, looking for ready-to-eat food. She breathed a sigh of relief when she saw Silas had managed to save a few boxes of granola bars. They would be crushed inside the envelopes, but the packages could be slit open and the contents eaten anyway. Those she doled out, feeling helpless.

When Silas returned the second time, she was still bandaging wounds. As she helped people, more arrived. He had another load of food and water. Two men attempted to intercept him to take what they wanted, but he stilled them with a single look. Yeah, she was incredibly glad to see him. The mood could easily turn in situations like this, and as people became more desperate, they'd do things they would never otherwise consider.

Her knee felt better, thanks to a couple of ibuprofen and some water. He, on the other hand, looked exhausted. But he didn't speak, merely went to work beside her, wrapping wounds with a competence that made her think he had experience.

To her vast relief, the Red Cross arrived by nightfall. They had their own supplies to add to what had been gathered, trained personnel, and emergency lanterns. Those gave the shell of the medical center an almost festive air, if you could overlook the weariness and worry.

The brunette woman smiled and spoke in accented English.

"You did a great job. Gave us a fantastic start. You'd be surprised how often we arrive and there's nothing done at all."

"Thanks. We tried."

Silas didn't acknowledge his part in the endeavor. He merely continued what he was doing: wrapping a bandage around a little girl's head. She'd wanted to help, but God, she was so done. It was such a relief to have professionals on scene now. If things went badly from this point, she could be absolved of responsibility.

In exhaustion, she propped herself against the wall and considered what came next. Clearly her time in Ecuador was done. Everyone she knew had been in that building. *Huh.* Maybe it had been better when she didn't have time to think. Despite her best efforts at self-control, tears slid down her cheeks. *So much loss.*

Silas settled beside her. He smelled of sweat and dust, subtly underscored with hints of blood. It should have been alarming, just like his size, but it wasn't.

"They'll start digging first thing in the morning." She guessed he knew she was thinking about the school from her expression. His voice came low and soothing. "Sometimes they recover people alive up to eleven days after a quake, maybe more in some cases, under ideal circumstances. Try not to give up hope."

Exactly what I needed to hear. Juneau let out a slow breath, gradually regaining her composure. "Thanks. You didn't have to do all this, you know. You're a lot kinder than I deserve."

"You make it easy."

"Do I?"

Odd, she'd never heard that before. In general, men complained about her odd fashion sense, her wanderlust, and the fact that she often dumped them after sex. A few times, she'd been accused of using them for their bodies. She seldom took things seriously, so when a guy took offense to her breaking up with him after they slept together, she always imagined him clutching a sheet to his bare chest in maidenly modesty. But the fact was, she always wondered if something better waited just over the next horizon.

Sure, she could settle down, but . . . why? Which was why she was now thirty-three and completely unattached. She'd never owned a home or a pet. Never formed any lasting ties, apart from her family, and even they had a hard time understanding her. In fact, her brother had made a website for her called JUNEAU IS NOT IN ALASKA, which she updated sporadically with pictures of her travels.

He nodded, his gaze gone far away. She had never seen eyes that color before. Generally they were lit by some other hue, or ringed in a softer shade, but his were all shadow, apart from the whites. In the half-light, she couldn't tell the difference between pupil and iris; they were just black, fringed in sooty lashes. At least two days of beard bristled from his jaw, giving him a wild look. Combined with the untamed fall of his dark hair, he radiated savage, certain strength, and it was a relief to have him beside her, though she didn't make a habit of leaning on men.

"Most people fear me," he said, low.

"Because of the tatts?"

"Because of . . . so many things."

"You'll always be a hero in my eyes," she told him.

Silas laughed softly, but the sound lacked all amusement. "You're alone in that. To most, I'm a monster."

He probably thought she'd pry. Well, that wasn't her style. She respected other people's privacy. If he wanted to talk, she was here. Sometimes it was good to unburden yourself to a person you'd never see again—and sometimes that made you the woman at the bus stop everyone wanted to get away from.

"Plan on destroying Tokyo, do you?"

He cut her an appreciative look. "It's next on my agenda, now that I'm done with Ecuador."

"Long way between the two. How do you plan to get there?"

"I don't plan anything," he said. "Easier that way."

That startled her. "Me either. And you wouldn't believe how much shit I get over it. My great-aunt keeps telling me I'll never snag a man if I don't settle down. Then I ask why I'd want to catch him, if he doesn't want to be caught."

"You're not lonely?" he asked.

Juneau leaned her head back and considered. "There's a difference between being alone and lonely, a hair's breadth, granted, but most often, I'm the former, not the latter. I make friends pretty easily, but I'm not so much with the lifelong bonds."

"Well," he said. "I'm sorry about the circumstances, but glad I met you."

THREE

Mockingbird spun in his desk chair, shoved off with both feet, and sailed across the room to check the status of an operative in Guatemala. His operations center would make anyone think he was nuts, based on the sheer number of computers and the far wall totally covered in reports of bizarre incidents all over the world. The map with red circles and multicolored tacks added a nice touch, too, but he was in far too deep for doubts. When he'd discovered the truth about himself, he'd gone looking for those like him. Freaks. Weirdos. It took years of sifting through the dregs, separating the real from the psychotic, although sometimes in his world, the two weren't mutually exclusive.

Then he learned these abilities weren't just popping up randomly. It wasn't natural selection, not a shift due to evolution. No, the blame lay squarely with the Foundation. He'd dug deeper into their records than anyone before. Anyone still living, that was, and the shit went all the way back to the forties.

The first experiments had, in fact, taken place in Nuremberg. The Foundation trail led from there to Poland, until the fifties, when it bled onward to Russia, and then in the sixties, it made the leap to the United States. And no doubt there were countless tangents he hadn't been able to track because all records had been destroyed—and everyone involved, killed. When they blew up his parents' house in retaliation for his digging, he realized it wasn't merely an adversarial relationship. It was war.

For a while, he'd formed an extremely satisfying partnership with Shrike. They'd wreaked a *lot* of havoc. When Shrike went after somebody, he did it scorched-earth style. But Shrike had handed in his resignation, something about settling down. Man, he'd never thought that guy would get tired of the life. He'd secretly suspected they'd run out of bodies before the other man lost his taste for vengeance. But what the hell—love did crazy things to a dude. He'd married an accountant for Christ's sake, not that she was crunching numbers anymore. They'd set up some kind of agency, offering redress and justice for those whose problems fell outside the jurisdiction of local law enforcement.

But now the Foundation hunted people like them. Aggressively. Before the destruction of the Virginia facility, it had been quiet. Folks dropped off the grid all the time, usually the homeless or transient population. For a while, the Foundation had been culling their old test subjects, the crazy ones who failed to control their ability and couldn't function in society anyway. Therefore, nobody cared. But now, they were taking people out of their homes: goon squads in black masks, hauling middle-class citizens off in their black SUVs, shit right out of *The X-Files*. The cops were asking questions, particularly in DC.

He made a habit of monitoring the chatter, and the feds thought Mexican or Latin American kidnapping rings were spreading their wings and pushing into the U.S. Mockingbird snorted with laughter. Dumb fucks. They'd never figure this out. He sometimes wondered what it would be like to go out into the field to give them a hand, but he was realistic. His strengths lay in recruitment, coordination, and the gathering of intel. So he'd crouch like a spider, spinning webs.

Then he actually *read* the screen he was staring at.

MOCKINGBIRD, WHERE THE FUCK ARE YOU? MISSION COMPROMISED. THEY SET KESTREL ON ME. NEED EXIT NOW.

He tried typing, but the terminal connection was dead. Smart. Finch was on the move. That only left the cell, if his agent still had it with him. They swapped them often, prepaid ones only, to make them more difficult to track. Not that it mattered so much anymore. But still, the Foundation didn't accomplish all their bloodhound work through paranormal means, just the most surprising hits.

"Shit. Shit!" He scrambled for the headset, hit the voice-scrambling software, and dialed, routing the call through four different servers. He was piggybacked on an Internet calling service, not that they'd ever find him. "You still there?"

His man in Guatemala wasn't as good as Shrike had been. But then, who the hell was? Finch got the job done, though, and he'd just made contact with an expat with a most interesting ability. In a few days, a nudge from Mockingbird would bring the new guy on board, provided the Foundation bounty hunters didn't find him first. It was harder than it used to be.

"I'm about to ditch this phone."

"How close are they?" He typed furiously.

Dammit. If only those bastards hadn't gotten a hold of Kestrel. She was going to be the death of them. Literally.

"Ten minutes behind me. Maybe less. I already bugged out of the hostel."

With a sigh of relief, he finished the hack and confirmed the booking arrangements. "Here's your extra strategy: there will be a driver waiting for you at Avenida de la Reforma. He'll take you north to Mexico. Can you make it to the Obelisk on your own?"

"I think so. I'm not far."

"Use the crowds to lose them if they get within vis-ID range. And *whatever* you do, don't use your power or Kestrel will have an even easier time tracking you."

"I know," Finch said. "But the show-and-tell portion of the entertainment is built into the recruitment package, you know?"

It was. Which sucked. But there was no other way to get potential freedom fighters on board. They used code names and voice scramblers and encrypted software during fieldwork, so the Foundation couldn't use the mind-fucker from their experimental dungeons and take down their whole network in one strike. He knew the names of his agents, of course, but he never used them; he didn't even think them. The agents never met Mockingbird in the flesh. Nobody knew what he looked like.

"Yeah. Get in touch when you can."

He hated waiting. Damn if he didn't want to be out there, doing what he helped others do. But he'd long since made peace with his limitations and his power. There were better uses for his time, and so he went back to reviewing the files of those who had escaped from the Virginia facility. If he could close down four more holes like that one, then he'd feel like he was getting somewhere.

He'd crossed Zeke Noble off his list of potential recruits because the man had returned home and started looking to put down roots, almost as soon as he got his life back. That kind didn't seek after violence or vengeance. Plus, his ability would offer limited use to the operation. Better to scrub his records and keep the Foundation off his back. That much, Mockingbird could do.

He keyed up a file and studied the photos he'd downloaded from a traffic cam. Silas Gamble. *Hm. Maybe.* His travel patterns had been erratic, as if he suspected he might be hunted. *Wise man.* He had a family, but he hadn't tried to contact them. Another plus—it meant he wouldn't balk at some of the things he might be asked to do. But he came with a handicap. No power, at least as far as the Foundation knew, but if captured, Mockingbird himself would try to hide his ability to prevent them from using it. Maybe Gamble had done the same. In Mockingbird's mind, Silas remained a question mark. He shuffled Silas's photos to the back of the screen with a click.

Olivia Swift. Dreamwalker. Oh man, he'd love to get his hands on her. It would rock so hard to have a nocturnal mind-fucker working for him. Finch could alter memories and implant suggestions, but he had no power if he wasn't physically in contact with his target. That limited his usefulness. Getting Olivia on his team would make this a whole new ballgame.

But first, he had to find her. She had done better than Gamble about staying off camera. He hadn't found a trace of her from any of his contacts. *Unusual.* He supposed it was possible she'd offed herself. Her profile pegged her as the least stable psychologically.

T-89. He'd be an asset, too. Mega-power there. Mockingbird had made contact with him, and surprisingly, he was still with Gillie Flynn. When his agent had gotten in touch, T had told him to fuck off. Politely. He'd said he "didn't have time for this shit," whatever that meant. Gillie would come in less handy. *Who needs a healer when you work alone?* It was a shitty setup in some regards, but it was the best way.

For now.

Very rarely, he permitted limited partnerships, but the redhead didn't seem like she wanted an eye for an eye, and he knew healing hurt her. At this point, he chose not to get in touch with her.

Mockingbird tracked Finch's movements on screen. If the agent could reach his rendezvous at the Obelisk, they'd be home free. Finch wove, probably dodging pursuers. He'd said he wasn't far. Not in geographic terms.

Almost there. You can do it, man.

But then his signal light flickered and went out. Now there were fewer on the screen than there ever had been. Maybe he was kidding himself, fighting this guerilla war. Maybe it was like the war in Vietnam, ultimately unwinnable. At least that's what his dad had always said.

Mockingbird leaned forward and cradled his head in his hands. *Fuck.* What he wouldn't give for T-89's killing power. Just for one day.

FOUR

Two days later, the situation was dire. The Red Cross had run out of supplies, and survivors went hungry. That meant rioting. Silas was sorry for that, but he also knew it meant he'd tarried too long in Puerto López. There was no transportation yet, so he'd walk. It was time to go.

For the second time, he found himself starting over with nothing but the clothes on his back. Another man might find that disturbing, but he had lost so much over the years that retaining his freedom meant everything. *That* was the only thing he couldn't sacrifice.

So he took off without speaking to anyone. He'd look for water on his way out of town. If necessary, he could go awhile without eating. Footsteps quickened into a run behind him. When he turned, he saw her—Juneau—the woman he'd saved.

"You're leaving." It wasn't a question.

"Yeah. Take care."

"I want to come with you."

Of all possible words, none could have surprised him more, except *I want to have your babies*. He studied her for a moment. She had braided all her hair that first day, and neither of them had bathed recently. Like him, she was grubby and worse for the wear from sleeping in her clothes and working with the Red Cross.

"Why?"

"I can't stay here."

He almost asked about that, too—and then he realized he knew the answer. They'd dug out the school the day before. No survivors. Not the children, not her coworkers. And so she wanted to run from the memories, still raw and fresh. He understood that impulse, though it was doomed to fail. No matter where she went, when she closed her eyes, she'd see their faces and suffer the survivor's guilt.

"It may be rough," he warned.

"That's fine. I just want to get away from here. I can help. Translate for you, if you need it. And it seems like I'm safer traveling with you."

Silas could never have imagined a woman saying that to him, seeing his size and demeanor as *good* things. Protector, not jailor. Could he switch roles, this once? He could never make up for what he'd done, but maybe he could balance some of the weight. Late at night, in that awful place, he had read their files. He remembered all their names: everyone he'd hurt, everyone who died. There had been nothing else to do, apart from watch TV. He left old shows on for noise and company, but they didn't assuage the need for human contact.

But down there, he had been the enemy, a collaborator who inflicted endless torment. Often, he'd thought of ending it. That way, the Foundation could never learn the truth about him, and he could stop the pain. He'd tried, once. The chip overrode his nervous system and forced him to black out. After that, he accepted his fate, but resignation was a terrible mistress.

On the outside, Silas had only one goal now. He wanted to find the families of those who had perished at Dr. Rowan's hand and give them closure. He just didn't know how to go about it. For the past months, he'd kept moving, fearful of staying in one place too long. The fear of being hunted had driven him out of the country, in fact. Led him here, to this moment, with this gray-eyed woman, gazing up at him in hope he'd save her once again. How fucking unlikely.

And yet he heard himself say, "Sure. It would be good to have company."

She fell into step with him. He set a slow pace, mindful of her knee, though she was moving better now. Over the last two days, she hadn't complained, though her leg was black-and-blue below the cuff of her baggy cargo shorts. She ought to be worried about replacing her possessions, her identification, and finding a U.S. embassy that could get her out of the country before things got worse. As it stood, he had no idea of her intentions.

It took longer than it should to work their way out of town. Twice, he glared refugees away; they were armed with rusty pipe, bits of broken glass. God knew, the last thing he wanted to do was fight, and only the fact that they obviously had nothing discouraged the looters. People prowled through the wreckage of damaged buildings, not looking for survivors, but for anything they could carry away. It felt to him like crows devouring the dead before the corpses had cooled.

The day waned as they made it to the southern outskirts of town. Sunsets were spectacular here along the coast, all violence and blood, red sky dotted with black-purple clouds; they reminded him of pocket galaxies being born. If not for the devastation behind them, he could almost believe they were taking a low-budget vacation, as if choice—and not the lack of it—had brought them to this pass.

What kind of woman left everything behind like this? Went walking toward the horizon with a man she'd met two days ago? Her contradictions fascinated him.

"Where are we headed?" she asked eventually.

"Salango is six kilometers south of here. The infrastructure may be destroyed there, too, I don't know. If so, we'll keep moving. Puerto Rico, Ayampe." He lifted his shoulders in a shrug. "It's a longer hike to Olon. Sooner or later, we'll find someplace with working phones, and buses running to other parts of the country."

"I don't have any money." But she didn't sound concerned; it was more a statement of fact.

He smiled at that. "Nor do I. This should prove interesting."

"Surviving on our wits?"

"Exactly so."

"Mine are pretty sharp," she said, and her smile hit him like a magnetic field, as if he had been flung up and outward, and then landed hard. Breathless. Yeah. She rendered him fumbling and awkward, as he hadn't been since his undergrad days.

Full dark fell before they reached Salango. He didn't think they could get lost, sticking to the road, but her steps had slowed to the point that they were making almost no progress. So he called a halt.

"I'm thinking we make camp for the night."

She glanced around, brow raised. "Where?"

"What's left of that *palapa*, a few hundred meters down the beach. It'll keep any rain off us, if not the wind and the insects."

The structure had been built of palm fronds—withered dry now—and driftwood. It looked to him like a squatter's hut. Half of it had pitched down, doubtless because of the shocks from the quake, but it was such a simple structure that it wouldn't take him long to shore it up. They'd have to sleep on the sand, but compared to the lab, it would be heavenly. The sea air alone made up for any number of deficiencies.

"Hungry?" she asked.

He nodded as he went to work. There seemed no point in whining about it, though. Without another word, she went off down the beach, stooping to study the sand every now and then. For long moments, Silas watched her instead of repairing the hut. Pure distraction, she was.

Eventually, she returned with a couple of crabs, beaming in the moonlight. She dumped them in his hands and pulled out a pocketknife. Without visible fear or disgust, she took care of the cleaning, cutting away the inedible bits. She cut the meat and then pierced them with a sliver of driftwood.

"If you can find some more dry wood, I can build a fire."

She hadn't been kidding when she said she'd be a help. He'd resigned himself to privation during the long walk. Though Silas had traveled a lot, both before and after his incarceration, he'd never done so as a wilderness type. He'd preferred riding the bus—people watching; disconnecting from the high-stress university job for three full months, and staying in hostels. But he always had a duffel bag and money in his pocket. Not this time.

Nodding, he went down the beach to look for firewood.

The world had changed in five years, and he wasn't equipped to deal with it. Maybe some day he'd apply for a job at a college again. Hell if he knew what he'd put on his resume about his long disappearance off the grid. God knew it bespoke a certain instability. Some academic types were prone to that, vanishing to live in a trailer in the Arizona desert for ten years and then popping up with some new earthshaking theory that made the erratic behavior acceptable. He didn't have a new hypothesis. He couldn't chance working in that place, though it would've offered some solace. He couldn't risk giving away the fact that their experiments hadn't ruined his mind, as they thought. No, he had to maintain the façade at all times.

As long as Rowan believed he was broken, he had some hope of minimizing the collateral damage. If they'd managed to re-create their success in him for mass production, his ability would've been weaponized. Unthinkable. He'd had no choice but to keep the truth from them: he wasn't their biggest failure. In strictest terms, besides T-89, he was the most powerful subject they'd ever produced. He was also the only one who'd successfully prevented them from discovering what he could do.

The walk took him a far ways before he thought he had enough wood to cook on, not that he could be sure. He returned at a run, worried now about leaving her alone in the dark so long. Granted, she was more capable than most, but she'd come with him for protection. If nothing else, his size deterred trouble.

He found her waiting with makeshift crab skewers in each hand. Nothing to fear. The beach flowed empty in all directions, and the ocean sang to him in rhythmic cadence. Soothing. Restful.

"Build a tent with the wood, if you can. Kind up propped up at an angle? That lets the oxygen flow through better."

"Like this?"

Silas did as she asked and then took the skewers. With her lighter, dried palm fronds, and a lot of patience, she got it to catch. He watched with naked admiration, enjoying the sight of her bent over the flames. They glazed her skin, highlighting her curves. Juneau had long legs; he couldn't help but notice, though it had been so long since he'd been with a woman that he wouldn't know what to do with her even if she presented herself naked. But he could look. No harm in that.

Exhausted, he dropped onto the sand and listened to the night. Seabirds called. Insects chirruped. The crabmeat smelled so good, juices crackling in the fire, that he almost moaned.

"Here. Be careful. It's hot."

And he laughed. God, it had been so long. "I just watched you cook those. You don't think much of the wits I'm supposed to survive on, do you?"

To his surprise, she ducked her head, sheepish. "It's not that. I just thought you might be too hungry to remember to be careful. My stomach feels like it's eating my spine."

"Delightful image." But he took her warning to heart and blew on the seafood kebabs long enough not to sear his tongue.

It was sweet and a little gritty. Not nearly enough to sate his appetite, but it did take the edge off. They should reach Salango by midmorning, and then they'd figure out what to do next. Funny how he'd come to include her in his thoughts, even though he didn't make plans.

Later, they lay back to back on their sides. It gave him a strange feeling, nothing he could put a name to, but less alone, though as she'd said, alone was not always the same as lonely. For him, it always had been. Until now. Until tonight.

Until Juneau.

FIVE

Once again, she'd cut and run. It wasn't the first time Juneau had chosen the highway, just the occasion she felt guiltiest about. She always wanted to help . . . at first. Until she hit that personal wall and realized she couldn't take it anymore.

She could've stayed. Kept working for the Red Cross. But the worse things got in Puerto López, the more she wanted to get away. Sure, she knew terrible things happened in the world, but she didn't want to see them. She preferred her pocket universe, where she controlled the flow of information. *Head in the sand*, an old boyfriend had called her. Well, yeah. And she recognized the futility of it, but she'd never seen the point of moping over what she couldn't change. Just keep moving; keep looking for the next shiny thing. Maybe it wouldn't save the world, but she'd live a relatively happy life, at least.

Salango might've been a quaint fishing village, smaller than Puerto López—before the quake. Her hope that they would find normalcy here died as they came into town. Though the damage was somewhat less, away from the epicenter, she saw no signs they could find transportation or a functioning infrastructure. The bottled water wouldn't last much longer either, and she wanted a shower. Desperately.

The building materials were such that it hadn't taken much stress to topple the houses and business, and people were picking through the wreckage. And worse? Here, people had set up barricades, protecting their territory and the salvage that lay within it. Armed men stood ready to defend them. It seemed surreal that they would fight over piles of wood and cement, just for a chance at what might be buried there, but then she saw the dirty, big-eyed children peering around the roadblocks. *That*, she thought. *That's why.*

"It's no better here," she said softly.

Right now one of those chicken buses she'd bitched about earlier in the year sounded pretty damn good. Unfortunately, they had to keep walking south. *What town came next? Puerto Rico.* But she didn't know how far it was; she hoped Silas did.

"But we can't leave without finding supplies," he answered. "Let's cut around this street and see what the rest is like."

There was no official aid here—not yet—and nobody to manage hostilities. The military would be sending troops, but earthquakes could rock the world in up to a one-hundred-kilometer radius. It would take time to determine the areas most in need of pacification and deploy soldiers appropriately. Meanwhile, the folks in Salango were on their own. The gunmen stared after them, eyes cold and watchful, but they made no moves. Juneau felt that regard until they turned the corner.

In the distance, the rat-a-tat-tat of gunfire echoed, chilling her blood. "Somebody challenged them?"

"Maybe. Could be warning shots." But from his somber expression, he didn't think so.

That brought it home to her then. This wasn't an adventure. It wasn't a joke. She was stuck in ravaged Ecuador with no food, no money, and a stranger who had dug her out of a death pit. *Christ almighty.* Her breath went in a whoosh.

"I . . . need to sit down for a minute." Blindly, she put out her hands and found her way to the broken curb. The earth itself had buckled a short distance away. Across the street, two stray dogs were fighting—one black and one dun—over a hunk of meat. In this situation, it might even be human, and the thought was more than she could bear.

He knelt beside her and took her chin in his fingers, tilting her face up. "It's not the heat. Not dehydration?"

"No. It's just sinking in. How screwed we are." She laughed at her own stupidity. "I'm the original proponent for performing without a net, but this . . . shit. Even *I'm* scared now."

More gunfire. Screaming. *Real.* It was real. And the people she'd run away from? Also real. The children she'd taught and her co-workers in the coalition, all gone. Shaking set in. If she hadn't gone shopping, if he hadn't found her—

He hesitated and then spun to sit beside her. His arm went around her shoulders; for a giant, his touch felt delicate. But his body felt solid. Immovable. If she'd had to wind up in this mess, she could've done worse for a companion.

"Just breathe. Don't think about it. Sometimes the only way you stay sane is living in the now. No past. No future. Get through this minute. Then tackle the next."

Juneau relaxed by millimeters, despite her desperation. She remembered how he'd spoken to her while he worked to get her out. God, she'd been so scared. No air. His tone was the same now—soft and soothing, echoed by the slow stroke of his big hand up and down her biceps. And it felt good.

"I'm okay," she said eventually.

To her relief, he didn't ask questions. He just pulled her to her feet, and they continued on. Near the outskirts of town, they found the ruins of a small store. But before they could check it out, two men, both armed, came around the side of the building.

The shorter one glared and lofted his pistol. "*Vete a la chingada.*"

"He said—"

"I know what he said." Silas planted his feet, drawing up to his full height. "Tell him we need food and water and we can't leave without those provisions."

This so wasn't a good idea. But she translated nonetheless. Now the taller one scowled, bringing his gun up, but it wasn't bravado.

He removed the safety and aimed it at her heart. They were willing to kill over these odds and ends.

"We should leave," she whispered to Silas.

"This place is ours," the taller man said in Spanish. "Leave now, or I shoot your woman."

Silas slid in front of her. Despite the danger, he seemed fearless, as if he thought himself bulletproof. "Not happening."

He extended a hand, made a quick twist in the air, and the bigger one screamed, clutching his wrist. His weapon clattered to the pavement. Silas sucked in a pained breath and turned his gaze to the other, who gaped at his moaning friend. Then his expression hardened, and his finger tightened on the trigger. Silas repeated the gesture, and the second man howled in anguish. This time, she heard an audible snap, as if from a broken bone. They cowered before Silas, eyes filled with terror.

What the hell—

"Advise them to leave before I do worse."

Her voice shook as she relayed the message. The men fled without picking up their guns. Once they'd gone, before she could process what had happened or decide if she needed to run, too, he swayed hard and then caught himself with his left hand. His right, he cradled against his chest, his face bone white and sweaty.

"I don't understand what just happened . . . but you don't look so good."

"Take a look around," he bit out. "I'll be fine by the time we need to move."

So he wasn't going to explain. Against all logic, it really seemed like he'd broken their gun arms. With a flick of his wrist. And he'd said he could do worse. Was she *safe* with him? It seemed best to do as she was told, at least for now. Juneau hurried away to poke through the rubble, looking for usable supplies. Conveniently, the two men who'd arrived before them had gathered things into a pile.

When she came back to tell him, he was sitting in the shade with his head tilted back, his mouth still compressed into a pained line. He spoke without opening his eyes. "If you don't want to go further with me, I understand."

Do I? First instinct—hell no—but neither did she want to travel alone. If she had confronted those men without him, she might've ended up shot, raped, kidnapped, or some heinous combination of the three. Whatever his deal—and she wasn't convinced he hadn't hypnotized them all somehow—he offered more protection than she could afford to discard. And he seemed to be on her side, at least.

"This isn't the time to talk," she said, "but I'm going to have questions later."

He considered and then: "That's fair. I'll answer. Did you find anything?"

"I think we're set."

Silas pulled himself to his feet, still favoring his right arm. "If we follow the road, we should be fine."

"How far are we going?"

"Eight kilometers, give or take."

She did the conversion and came up with an answer of about five miles—in addition to the distance they'd already traveled—and with no guarantee of an end in sight. It might not be any better in Puerto Rico. *Damn.* Her feet already hurt. She was in decent shape, but hiking with an injured knee on inadequate food took a toll. Then again, staying here wasn't an option. Not with those guns going off and two inexplicably injured men who might be running for backup even now.

"I can make it. What about you?"

"My legs are fine."

As they set off, she noticed he set a slower pace. He could take three steps to each one of hers, if he wanted, effectively forcing her to run. But she couldn't tell if it was kindness or weakness. His face was still pale, still clammy with sweat, and he held his arm as if it were fractured, though she saw no swelling or injury.

The sun blazed down, reflecting off the broken pavement, and sweat poured down her back. She had been wearing these clothes for four or five days now. In fact, she'd lost count.

"So how did you end up here?" he asked eventually.

She recognized the tactic as a calculated move. He wanted her at ease again. But since she appreciated the gesture, she went along with the conversational gambit.

"After college, I did a stint in the Peace Corps. When I got out, I went for TEFL certification because I still wanted to travel, just with more freedom than I had in the Corps."

"That's Teaching English as a Foreign Language?" At her nod, he asked, "Do you have a regular degree in education as well, then?"

She laughed. "No. Sociology, actually. The pay isn't great in developing nations, but I don't like being locked into a two-year contract like many schools in Europe demand. Here, they're content with a handshake agreement that I'll stay for one school term."

"And it lets you see the world."

"Exactly." It was rare someone got it right without asking a hundred more questions about her motivations.

God knew, her loving, well-intentioned family never tired of telling her she could do so much more with her life. Her mother couldn't stand that her youngest taught English in Ecuador for the equivalent of three dollars an hour while her middle son had become a surgeon and her eldest son the partner in a law firm. It wasn't that Melva Bright didn't love her; she just wanted her to achieve great success and be happy. She didn't get that the two didn't go hand in hand, where Juneau was concerned.

"I used to teach theoretical physics."

Holy crap. He must be hella smart. Juneau glanced at him in surprise, although she ought to know better than to judge a man by his hair, which he'd caught up in a tail, or because he had a few tatts. "Not anymore?"

"No."

"How come?"

"I suppose you could say . . . I dropped out."

"You ever going back?"

He paused, black eyes gazing out over the long road unfurled before them. "I don't know for sure, but . . . I think not. I suspect that part of my life is over."

"You didn't enjoy it?" It wasn't like her to interrogate other people like this, but he fascinated her. Mostly because with his broad shoulders, broken nose, dark ponytail, and tribal tatts, he didn't resemble any college professor she'd ever known. If the physics professors had looked like him, she might've taken more interest in the hard sciences.

Then again, maybe that's why he quit.

Silas answered slowly, his voice deepening with notes that whispered of rue. "I did, once. Then everything changed. And I'm not the same person I was then. I can't stand and stare at a whiteboard for hours while pondering problems that have no real-world application. I have something else I must do now."

"Walk across Ecuador?"

His eyes crinkled in a surprisingly warm smile. "No. That's tangential to my true goal."

"And that is?" *Unforgivable. Nosy. Prying.* But she wasn't sorry she'd asked.

"To make amends."

That sounded like a twelve-step thing. She'd known her share of addicts. Guiltily, she flashed a look at his arms, but the ink made it impossible to tell if he had track marks. If he'd managed to kick the habit, though, more power to him.

The sun soon stole her desire to talk, however. They stopped for periodic water breaks, but the food had to last. Juneau welcomed the cooler weather when the sun sank away from the zenith, falling toward the horizon. She'd thought she was pretty tough, until now, but really, it was all she could do not to whine because there was no traffic on the road. Even if there had been, they shouldn't accept a ride anyway. Kidnapping was big business in this part of the world.

As they crested a hill, the most welcome vista unfurled. Three simple white vacation bungalows, built on a rise overlooking the ocean, sat off to their right. Two of them had been damaged to the point of being uninhabitable, but the third appeared to be more or less intact. She quickened her pace without even checking to see what he thought of the idea. Proper shelter, running water, a regular toilet . . . oh yes, *please*.

She ran up the path, framed by brick and stonework. Cracks lay in what had been a pretty pattern, but nothing dangerous. Juneau vaulted some chunks of the other casitas and kept going. On closer inspection, the third house hadn't escaped unscathed, but all four walls were standing, despite the fissures.

"Sound enough?" she asked Silas over one shoulder.

He studied the fracture running parallel to the door. "I think so."

"Can you get us in?"

In answer, he slammed his left shoulder into the door, and it popped like a champagne cork. "They'll never know it wasn't quake related."

Inside, it was beautifully cool and dim. A white and blue ceramic floor—some tiles now had cracks in them—led to a simple sitting room. This was a tiny vacation cottage, where the attraction lay in the landscape, the ocean, and the wildlife. Admittedly, it was gorgeous with spectacular sunsets, crystal clear water, unspoiled beaches, and the prospect of endless solitude. One didn't come here for the luxurious accommodations, Juneau reflected. Still, she could tell the place had been built well, or it wouldn't be standing. Simple worked when it came with running water.

"God bless the ecotourist," she said on a happy sigh. "Dibs on first shower."

"Go ahead. I'll get the generator running, if there's any fuel."

It stood to reason there would be. This was probably a latchkey place with an absentee owner who took bookings online. There might even be some food in the cupboards. Wouldn't that be wonderful? The few stale, crushed pastries and cans of soup they'd found in Salango would only go so far.

Juneau went down the hall and into the bathroom. God, it would be good to feel human again; she wouldn't think of children who had no more birthdays coming or coworkers' families who were praying to hear good news. *One minute at a time*, he'd said. Well, she could do that. In fact, she excelled at it. It was the longer stretches that gave her trouble.

SIX

A ping made Mockingbird turn to check it. So Silas was in Ecuador. He wondered if the Foundation tracked in the same way he did. Wait, they couldn't. They might have Kestrel now, but they lacked his unique talent. He studied the picture of the fugitive, working with the Red Cross in the aftermath of the quake. *Disaster relief, who would have guessed?*

He needed to get an agent to Ecuador. Warn Silas not to use his ability, if he had one. *If only I hadn't lost Finch in Guatemala*—but no use lamenting the irrevocable. If Finch wasn't dead, he'd soon be working for the enemy. They needed to find Olivia Swift, like, yesterday. Her ability to fight covert battles while their adversaries slept would prove invaluable.

But that was a pipe dream. He had no idea where she was; she'd gone ghost. Then it occurred to him: *Maybe she wipes our memories in our dreams.* Maybe he'd found her. At that, he prowled through all his files, but there was nothing. *Could she convince me to get up in my sleep and erase the records?* A cold chill went through him. If she was unbalanced, there was no telling what she might be doing out there.

Anyway, he had no proof that was the case or that she knew anything about him or his efforts to find her. Sitting in this room, surrounded by humming electronics, was making him paranoid. Better to focus on the mission.

Tanager was in Florida. She could hop a plane to Ecuador, but getting to Puerto López, where Silas had last been sighted, would be tricky. Fortunately, Tan specialized in persuading people to do impossible things. That made her a natural for this job.

She hated carrying a laptop, so he used the phone straightaway, engaging the voice scrambler. "Tan, I have a job for you."

"I'm on vacation." It was a halfhearted protest, and they both knew it.

"Maybe I should call someone else. It's bound to be dangerous."

"Now I'm interested."

He'd known she would be. "We have a possible recruit trapped in Ecuador."

"What's his X?"

In his opinion, Tanager had read too many X-men comics in her youth. "Uncertain. If he has an ability, he managed to keep it out of the Foundation records."

"So he could easily be a zero."

That was what they called *failure to evolve*, the term used by the lab geeks to describe all the corpses their experiments left behind and all the human detritus that wound up with tumors, lesions, and shattering mental illness. *Zeros*. Rage boiled through him.

"I think it's a risk we should take, in case he's viable. But if you don't think you can handle it—"

"No, I can," Tanager said. "Did you get my tickets?"

"You're going first class to Quito, but you'll be on your own from there. There's nothing I can hack that far off the grid."

"It's not a problem. I'll find and warn him. Am I recruiting?"

"I'll leave that up to you. Do so if you think it's safe and he'll be valuable."

"I live to thwart the Foundation. Over and out."

He knew she did, and that was only a small portion of Tanager's problems.

SEVEN

Getting the generator running didn't take long. Silas dreaded going back inside because sooner or later, she was going to ask. She'd seen what he could do, so there was no way she'd accept silence on the subject. He could put it off long enough to shower, but there would be a reckoning.

The agony in his right arm had dulled to a low throb. Apart from general human empathy and not wanting to cause harm, the resonant pain he suffered in using his ability offered strong deterrent. He could count the times he'd done so on one hand. And no matter the torment or provocation, he'd never shown the Foundation what he could do. Eventually, his handlers had stamped his file with a big red FAIL and put him to work. That was the only accomplishment he could take pride in for the last five years.

And now, now his secret was out.

"Bathroom's free," she called.

But when he passed the sitting room, he saw she wasn't dressed. Well, not exactly. She'd fashioned a makeshift toga from a bedsheet. He tried not to stare, but she had amazing skin, all smooth and golden, and it didn't look like she had any paler strips. Which meant—

No way. You can't start picturing that. She's already half a step from being terrified.

"You washed your clothes?"

She nodded. "There's a line out back, I'd guess for wet beach things."

He couldn't believe she was so casual with him, after what she'd seen. But when he studied her more closely, he glimpsed tension in the line of her shoulders and a hint of fear in how she clutched the white fabric. Like he might use his mind to tear it off her.

And no wonder, he thought bitterly. *It's too bad it doesn't because that might have a useful application.* But his so-called gift didn't work that way. He had dominion over the human body—over skin and bone—and the blood in between. It was the grimmest, darkest thing imaginable, and he had to control it. Fortunately, he'd learned to leash his anger long before this curse manifested . . . because he'd come into his full growth young.

Silas went on to the bathroom, gliding past the mirror without glancing at it. He hated his reflection, even now, because he still saw the empty-eyed monster he had pretended to be. In the middle of the night, he sometimes wondered if that wasn't the truest version of himself.

Fortunately, the previous renter had left some shampoo behind, and he found a sliver of bar soap in the dish in the shower. It was a small stall, commensurate with the rest of the bungalow, and he felt pretty trapped the whole time. But God, it was good to be clean. Afterward, he scrubbed his clothes and then went looking for his own sheet. There were spares in the hall closet. This arrangement filled him with misgivings—it was surely a bad idea to sit around with her, nearly naked—until their clothes dried, but neither of them had a change. Sometimes you just did what you could in the circumstances and hoped for the best.

By the time he finished hanging his shorts and T-shirt, she had a meal ready: tortilla soup and crumbled crackers. Since they hadn't eaten since the mouthful of crab the night before, it smelled divine. They devoured the food in silence, and then she sat back in her chair, regarding him with a determined expression.

"So I've been going over what happened in my head," she said. "Because I can't quite make myself believe it. I mean, it *did* happen, right?"

No question what she meant by *it*. "You didn't imagine the incident, if that's what you're asking."

"You broke their arms. With your mind." Her incredulity hit eleven on a scale of one to ten.

He put his spoon down and folded his hands in his lap, staring down into his white ceramic bowl. Patterns formed in the smears of soup: charged particles attracting others. As a child, he'd once imagined worlds existed on that scale.

"That's accurate."

"I don't even know what to say. Wait, yes I do. Are you going to hurt me?"

The question hit him like a lash, though he supposed it was reasonable. He felt utterly exposed. Silas might've said any number of things, but he could only manage to answer, "No."

But she noticed, and contrition flashed across her expressive face. "I shouldn't have asked that. Duh. You saved me . . . and you did again with your brain trick, even though it hurt you. You're a *hero*."

"I'm not."

"You are to me."

At that, he finally raised his head; it was the second time she'd said so. She'd propped her elbows on the table, and the way she'd leaned forward to make her point, it pulled the sheet dangerously low on her breasts. He looked—and he wanted her. Silas wished he didn't, because it reminded him of all he'd lost and everything he could never have again. But she was beautiful in the way of a sunset in the mountains or a black swan diving by night: haunting, memorable, but ultimately ephemeral. The memory might linger, but *she* would not.

Juneau went on. "I guess I just don't know how I'm supposed to feel, and really, I'm just numb, and tired, and I don't have any more shock to spare."

"Don't be afraid of me." He wanted to beg because he'd liked the easy way she treated him. It had been precious and new, and he hadn't known how much he needed it until the fear crept into her eyes.

"I'm not."

She seemed to sense his doubt and came around the table. To his astonishment, she planted herself on his knee. Oh, that was *not* a good idea. Though he didn't intend to hurt her, it didn't mean he lacked all male instincts. As she leaned into him, he noticed she smelled like him—the same soap, the same shampoo—but on her, it gained layers of sweetness. She'd taken her hair out of the braids, and it curled about her shoulders, brushing his bare skin in tantalizing sweeps as she breathed.

"I don't know how to put this," he said roughly, "so I'm just going to say it. I can't have you so close to me."

"Why not?"

Could she really be asking that? He found it hard to believe any woman could be so naïve. But he spelled it out anyway.

"Because we're nearly naked, and you're gorgeous."

Juneau surprised him by leaning in and running her fingertips up his bare arm, tracing the pattern of his tattoo. Christ, it felt good. His muscles tensed. Maybe she wanted to go where this led after all.

"It might not be smart," she said, "but I want you. I want sensation to dispel the pain and the exhaustion. I want to bang my heels on the bed until we both pass out and wake up feeling one hundred percent better, even though nothing has changed. I can tell you agree by the way you're trying to pierce my hip."

It was too much to hope she hadn't noticed. But it had nothing to do with survival and everything to do with her golden skin and long legs and the way she sparkled with life. He had been dead so long that he wanted to get inside her and feel her heat. Maybe she could revive him all the way.

"That's a natural physiological response to your warmth and proximity."

Juneau raised both brows. "So you're saying you don't want to?"

"It's more that I don't trust anything good coming so easy."

She grinned down at him. "I never said I'd come easy. I intend to make you work for it."

He didn't understand her lightness, especially under these circumstances, after everything they'd seen, and what she knew about him, for God's sake. He said so aloud. Her smile faded a bit.

"Are you going to judge me, too? Tell me I'm not serious enough? Answer this: how does that *help* anything? How does misery make things better? I learned a hell of a long time ago that it's better to decide to be happy—and pay attention here, Silas—make no mistake, happiness is a *choice*. If I choose to focus on all the terrible things in the world, then I might as well shoot myself because it's not getting better. Or I can take my pleasure where I find it. I refuse to live my life under a rain cloud, even if other people think I should."

"And what do you have to be happy about?"

"I'm alive. I'm clean and full, and I'm with you."

God, he found her all but incomprehensible. How could anyone think being stranded with him was a good thing? And yet some frozen, lonely part of him melted just a little. Just enough.

She added with an impish grin, "Look, if you're worried about your reputation, I'll tell everyone you put up a big fight."

Maybe all those years of playing dumb made him that way in truth. "What?"

She sealed her finger against his mouth. "Shh, don't talk. I just want to kiss and touch you a little. We won't do anything you don't want . . . and we'll stop as soon as you give the word."

Reluctant amusement curled through him, leavening the ache in his cock. Eighteen years ago, he'd said the same thing to some girl he desperately wanted to fuck. Juneau made it impossible to brood, and just as difficult to excoriate himself with old guilt. Silas fell into the moment with her, willing to let her lead for a little while.

He gave a lopsided smile. "Fine. As long as you don't tell."

Then her mouth took his in a way that he'd never known: demanding and authoritative. She took, her tongue gliding against his, owning the kiss. It should have been funny when her hand crept up his chest, circling furtively toward his nipple. Instead it aroused him fiercely. By the time she turned her attention to his neck, he was squirming in the chair.

She sat back, her breath coming in little gasps. "Are you seduced yet?"

"Completely."

His hands moved, almost of their own accord to where her makeshift sari knotted on her shoulder. She watched him, eyes shining. As he'd guessed, she sunbathed in the nude, so she was golden all over. Her body was finely made, almost too pretty for him to touch, and yet it sent a jolt of pure lust through him when he covered her breasts with his palms. She made a sweet sound in her throat, her head falling back. Juneau closed her eyes as he caressed her, sweeping his thumbs in delicately teasing circles. He turned her, so she straddled his lap, giving him better access.

"Your lips, now."

He had to be dreaming. But disbelief didn't stop him from leaning forward to nuzzle her breast in a soft, openmouthed kiss. She sank her hands into his hair, whimpering, and it gave him the courage to use his teeth a little. Oh, she liked that. Juneau responded with her hips, grinding on his cock.

"You're gentler than you look," she whispered.

"Is that all right?" He hardly knew what to do after all this time.

"I like it both ways. Depends on my mood."

Silas didn't think he'd ever dare to be rough with a woman. It mattered he succeed in giving pleasure, if she trusted him enough to allow him close. But he couldn't be sure what she wanted: tender and soft or wild and demanding. It had been five and a half years since he'd been with anyone like this.

"And now?"

"Gentle," she said dreamily. "Until I'm all over tingles."

Silas scooped her into his arms and strode out of the kitchen. There had to be a bed in this place.

EIGHT

Few men could manage this with her height, but Silas made it look easy. Juneau enjoyed the ride down the hall, but then he set her lightly on her feet outside the bathroom. The sheer size of him took her breath away. He carried the muscles of a man who had done manual labor: tight delts, broad shoulders, bulky arms. The ink on his biceps showed to advantage with every movement, and his dark hair had a tendency to curl. Juneau admired him as she watched him rummage through the medicine cabinet.

They were both adults; she knew what he was looking for, and she was grateful he'd remembered. It spoke to the kind of man he was, caring for his partner, even when she got a little carried away. Maybe he should take it as a compliment . . . because low-level arousal still simmered in her blood.

"Any luck?"

Please, give us a break, here. It's been a rough week.

He flashed an oddly shy smile. "Apparently. The previous renters left a few things behind, besides the soap and shampoo."

"Tell me you found some."

In answer, he held up a partial box of condoms. "Score."

"If the stars align, you will. Check the date?"

"They're good for a while yet." He paused. "Has this ruined the mood?"

"Look on it as an intermission. We'll get warmed up again.

Although from the looks of you—" Juneau admired the tent in the sheet still tied around his hips.

"Yeah. It's been a while."

"Really?" He looked like a guy who could tap some ass anytime he wanted. Maybe in a bar, not a Starbucks, but women who went for a certain type would eat him up. God knew she wanted to. "How long?"

"Five and a half years."

"Jesus, *why*? Were you locked up?"

Silas regarded her, his black eyes intense on her face. "Would that change your mind about me?"

It was a terrifying question, and her family would be horrified that she was actually thinking about her answer—that it wasn't an immediate *yes* and *where are my clothes?* Over the past week, they'd spent more time together than people who dated for weeks. She'd seen him caring for injured children with endless patience and comforting grieving women in his broken Spanish.

"No," she said at last. "But I'd want to know what you did."

His face stilled. "I wasn't incarcerated in the sense that you mean. But I've been . . . away."

"Like on sabbatical, living in the wilderness?"

"Not exactly." In a curt gesture, he sat the condom box on the edge of the sink. "Look, Juneau, I've hurt people. Killed with these hands." He stared at them with such loathing, as if they didn't belong to him, as if they did those things against his will. "And I understand if you want to walk away from this. I won't stop you. But I won't lie either. Not even for someone I want as much as you. I've promised I won't hurt you . . . and you either believe that, or you don't."

"Shit," she said. "Were you a soldier?"

"No more questions. Do you want to fuck or not?"

When he put it like that . . . well, yeah. Maybe he was dangerous. And she was definitely crazy, because she liked it. She wanted all his strength stretched out beneath her, wanted to drive him wild. A bolt of pure lust lanced through her. Juneau took two steps and leaped at him. He caught her, both arms wrapping around her.

Silas buried his face in the curve of her neck. Christ, he felt good. Nobody had ever held her this way, her thighs around his hips. But he wasn't content with that for long; his cock throbbed against the curve of her ass. She snagged the condoms as they left the bathroom. *Gonna need these.*

"You thought I'd back out on you."

He tossed her onto the bed. "I was afraid you might."

"You know why I didn't?"

"No clue."

One possible answer occurred to her as he untied the sheet from around his waist. A woman just didn't turn down a man like that, whatever the reason. He was built on . . . grandiose scales. As if he could read her mind, he glanced down and lifted his shoulders in an amused shrug that was part diffidence, part pride. Naked, he was every bit the gladiator: equal measures in sinew, ink, and scars.

"Because you hate yourself too much for somebody without a conscience. Your eyes are so fucking sad, and I want to take that look away, if only for a little while. I want to give you something good."

A shuddering breath escaped him. "It's been so long since anybody said anything like that to me."

She beckoned to him. "Then let's make up for lost time."

Silas lay down beside her, and he dominated the bed. She couldn't look without touching for long. Juneau ran her fingertips along his arm, tracing the lines of his tattoo.

"Does this have a meaning?"

"Each pattern represents a person."

People you loved? Or killed? Juneau liked the element of danger and mystery that clung to him, and she had no doubt he would protect her, even if it came to violence. It already had, in fact. A primitive part of her approved.

He rolled on his side, drinking her in. She had no hang-ups about her body, and such intense scrutiny pushed all her buttons. Beneath his gaze, she arched and stretched as if in satiation. Silas drew in a sharp breath, and then he cupped her head in his head and leaned in for a kiss. Even in this, he was maddeningly gentle. His lips brushed hers repeatedly, lightly, seducing rather than conquering. She dug her nails into his shoulders and threw a thigh over his hip.

Instead of being drawn, he nibbled a path down her jaw to her throat. Tingles sparked through her, furling her nipples, and her core went liquid. God, he could nuzzle her neck all day. A whimper escaped her, and he shuddered, as if her pleasure sounds connected to his. She sank her hands into his hair, tugging not so gently.

"I need to finish," she whispered. "The past few days have been . . . stressful."

In response, he kissed a path between her breasts and down her stomach. He hooked strong arms beneath her thighs, lifted her bodily off the bed, and brought her lips to his. *Dear lord.* How had she done without this? It was delicious. Silas kissed her first, all softness, sweetness, and she moaned. But he wasn't finished, thank God.

"Move for me. Show me how you like it."

A fierce haze filled her head, urging her hips into tight circles against his mouth. She used him quite shamelessly, conscious of nothing but how he could please her: lips, tongue, whisper of teeth. *Yes.* The pleasure went white hot, rioting along her nerve endings, and Juneau arched as an orgasm quaked through her. He licked until it almost tickled.

With shaking fingers, she pulled him away, drawing him up to give him a sweet, hot kiss. The taste of her on his lips sent a wicked thrill through her. He touched her breasts as if he wasn't sure he had the right, despite the fact that he'd just given her a luscious climax. *Time to return the favor.*

"That was lovely," she said huskily. "But here's the thing. I want a good, hard fucking, and it's been a while for you. How long do you think you'll last once you get inside me? I'm awfully hot and wet."

He groaned. "I've no idea. You're not helping by talking about it, though."

"Don't worry. I have a plan."

"Should I be alarmed?"

"Certainly not." She curled her fingers around his iron-hard erection. "I propose to take the edge off for you. Then you'll be good to go for the next round."

"You have a lot of faith in my resilience."

"Don't I, though?" Juneau pumped her fist, fingers flexing. "But you know yourself best. Want me to stop?"

His breath went ragged as he arched. "God, no."

"Good. Because I want to watch you come anyway. I need to see your face. There's nothing hotter than a man losing control."

Silas fell back against the pillows, hands fisting at his sides. "Enjoy the show, because I'm getting there."

"I know you are." She worked her hand faster, watching his expression and adjusting the rhythm and pressure according to his reactions. "Like this?"

"Harder," he gasped.

He bucked, helpless in her grasp, and she'd never been so turned on in her life. So big, so powerful . . . and at her mercy. She gave him the extra pressure, and he lost it, panting and moaning as he spiraled up.

"Look at me," she whispered. "You're mine when you come."

His body locked. The orgasm rolled through him in waves that left him trembling. He spurted on her hand, on his belly, and chest. With one fingertip, she touched and tasted. Shivers wracked him; Juneau didn't know if she'd ever seen anyone come that hard before. An odd tenderness suffused her. She picked the sheet up from the floor and used it to clean him off, and then she curled up against him.

It took him two tries to get his arm around her. "Damn."

"Feel better?"

"Better is a nap. This is . . . I don't know what this is."

She nestled her head against his shoulder. "I'll take that as a compliment. But I still want the sex, you know."

"Give me a few."

"If I must. Just remember you're on the clock, mister."

A startled laugh escaped him. "I seem to have lost my time card."

"Don't worry, I'm keeping track."

"*Are* you?" He brushed the hair away from her face, gazing with an expression that unsettled her.

"I was teasing."

"I know. It's just . . . people don't. Tease me, I mean. They look away. They hurry off. I'm not used to this kind of normal."

She jabbed her elbow into his side. "I think I'm offended. Nobody's ever called me normal before."

"I'm sorry. Let me make it up to you." Silas ran his hand down the curve of her hip and drew her atop him.

Juneau glanced down in mock surprise, admiring his erection. Damn, the man was big. "Has it been a few minutes already?"

"Looks that way."

"Then if you don't mind, I'll do the honors. I'm still humming." She reached for the condoms and drew out a foil packet.

He watched as she tore it open and then moaned when she rolled it down his cock. Huskily, he observed, "You're good at that."

"I'm not going to win any awards for abstinence, if that's what you're asking. But I've always been careful about it." Her answer sounded defensive, even to her.

But it wasn't as she'd feared. He didn't judge her for knowing what she wanted and going after it. Nor did he condemn her because she liked sex and didn't care whether it always occurred in the confines of a committed relationship.

Silas merely watched with silent, avid admiration as she rose up on her knees and guided him into her body. She worked slowly, stretching to accommodate him. He lay beneath her, stomach rippling with the effort of letting her set the pace. But despite his best attempts, his hands framed her hips and he pulled her down, hard.

She grinned. "Impatient?"

"Sorry. Did I hurt you?"

"No. It's . . . good." Supporting herself on his chest, she moved on him experimentally, watching his face.

As she rode, he licked his lips, eyelids drifting to half-mast. It seemed like he was in control, except his breath came in ragged gasps. Each time she pushed down, he arched to meet her, and they found a rising rhythm. *Oh God. So . . . hot. Yeah. Like that.* Need spiraled into pure and perfect tension.

"It's been so long," he gritted out.

That was the only warning before he flipped her beneath him and caught both her wrists above her head in one big hand. Then he set the pace, driving with long, deep thrusts. Juneau wrapped her legs around him and tilted her pelvis, moaning when his strokes became more powerful. For the first time, she felt almost overwhelmed by a lover, as if his intensity might break her wide open—and not in the physical sense.

Yet unable to resist, she tightened her thighs, working her hips faster against him.

Getting there. So close now.

She stared up into his dark, tormented eyes, the dark hair falling across his brow, and she drew him down. His lips took hers as he claimed her body, his tongue gliding against hers. God, he tasted good, equal measures fervor and desperation. She'd never had anyone kiss her as if he were starving for her, and it sent her over the edge. Her pussy tightened on his cock, making him moan into her mouth, and then he arched, grinding into her.

"Fuck. Oh, *fuck*, Juneau."

Recovering before he did, she held him and wouldn't let go, even when their heartbeats slowed. His tears dampened the side of her neck, and what the hell did she say now? Part of her wanted *never* to let him go.

"Wow," she said eventually.

Silas smiled down at her, dropped a kiss on her nose, and then went to dispose of the condom. *Mmm. Delicious.* She could barely remember feeling better than this. The world was crazy outside the bungalow, but she wouldn't think about it tonight.

When he came back, he lay down beside her, gentled somehow. "How'd you come by your name anyway? It's unusual, isn't it?"

At this point, she didn't even mind answering, though she'd told the story countless times. "I was conceived there. My mom always wanted to visit Alaska, and I guess she was *really* grateful my dad took her."

He laughed softly and drew her into his arms again. Listening to the slow, steady thud of his heartbeat, she decided, *Hell, yeah, the future can wait.*

NINE

"I'm clear," Finch said.

Mockingbird slumped in relief; he'd honestly never expected to hear from this agent again, after his signal went dead. But he must have ditched it in case the enemy was tracking it, too. "How?"

"I think a new power popped up on her radar. They lost me."

Kestrel's weakness offered their one saving grace. Sometimes he even planned for it and orchestrated a simultaneous firing of abilities among his agents to overwhelm her, so she couldn't track any of them. Unfortunately for Finch, he hadn't been able to coordinate anything on such short notice, so he'd been stuck, waiting and hoping. This was unexpectedly good news.

"Lie low for a while. I'm going to see what I can find out about what's going on in their organization."

"Roger that. No powers. I'm on vacation in Mexico."

"Enjoy the sun."

This part he loved. He didn't need the keyboard. Instead, he thought about the information he wanted and it filled the screens around him. Which was why he always knew more about the Foundation activities than they did. If he didn't work in a protected room, Kestrel would find him in a heartbeat. As it stood, she didn't know where he was, and he preferred to keep it that way. But he had to be careful. Unlike most hackers, since he used his brain, he was susceptible to viruses that translated as physical ailments. It had taken him years to devise firewalls for his mind, and they were still imperfect.

"Shit," he said.

Mockingbird read the lines a second time. *Ecuador*. According to the other data, that had to mean they were going after Silas after all, the sneaky bastard. *He must've saved Finch's ass, firing up . . . whatever he can do.* All the more reason to get Tanager to him quickly.

He memorized the coordinates Kestrel had sent to the extraction team, and then said, "Call Tanager." The computer complied, and in a moment, he heard Tanager's voice.

"This better be good. I just arrived in Puerto López."

"How? The region's unstable."

"I . . . persuaded a pilot to land a small plane nearby. Military base."

That was Tanager, all right. She could convince her mark to do damn near anything, even if it was stupid, dangerous, or completely counter to his best interests. She was a great asset in the field.

"I know where your target is. Or at least where the strike team's headed. You ready?"

"Always," she said.

Mockingbird gave coordinates. Tanager scrawled the location; he heard the pen scratching on paper. "I'll find someone to take me. Thanks for the info."

"That's my job."

TEN

Silas roused early, a habit born of living so long on someone else's timetable. He heard nothing now but the lap of the waves and the cry of seabirds. But something hid in that silence. A noise had woken him, but the sunrise kept its counsel. Still, his nerves prickled. Gently, he set Juneau away from him.

God, she was beautiful, but he didn't linger. He couldn't let her soft skin or pretty hair distract him. Something wasn't right.

He crept outside and pulled his clothes off the line. Fortunately, they were dry and permitted him to dress quickly in the half-light. Cocking his head, he listened again. Then he heard them. Footsteps. They were trying to be quiet, but rocks covered the path leading down from the road, and it was impossible not to make some noise. Lots of men, incoming. He snatched her shorts and tank top, and retreated, trying to think, to plan.

It has to be the Foundation. They know, somehow. Though it sounded paranoid, he didn't doubt his instincts, even if he didn't understand why or how. They'd take him and kill her because of what she knew, what she'd seen. That, he could never allow. He'd promised to protect her, and he would—whatever the cost.

"Juneau," he whispered. "Wake up. I need you to hide for me. There's going to be a fight."

She didn't wake up groggy, unlike most people. By the time she got her feet on the floor, she was already stepping into her shorts, eyes gummy but alert. She didn't even ask him any questions as she pulled the shirt over her head. Instead she cupped his face in her hands, laid a firm kiss on him, and said, "Be careful."

Silas caught glimpses of them as they surrounded the house, geared in black, wearing bulletproof vests and carrying tranq guns. He surprised the first one at the patio door, but he silenced any outcry with a gesture, cutting off his oxygen. Agony flared, though this couldn't kill him; it just made him *wish* he were dead. Blood vessels popped in his own eyes, sending jags of pain tearing through his skull.

He stayed away from inflicting wounds for a reason. Unlike other applications of his power, cutting people made him bleed as well. Though he could, in theory, skin someone alive, he'd take too much damage to walk away. Therefore, choking and broken bones offered the best solution, pain without actual injury.

The curse connected him with his victim, making Silas part of the hunter's skin and bone. He felt each thrash, each spasm; it wasn't empathy or telepathy, nothing so kind or clean. No, it was a death bond. When the other man breathed his last, the resultant reverb nearly knocked him on his ass.

"Fuck," he breathed.

If there were a lot of them, the mental echo might knock him out. *No. That can't happen.* If they took him, they'd terminate Juneau, and they'd never stop until they perfected his ability for use in black ops. Imagining a whole squadron of men killing in silence, without remorse, sent a cold chill through him. He just had to thresh through them, however many there were. He'd been fighting ever since he first discovered what he could do, fighting against what he might become.

Not anymore. He'd already killed to protect her. He'd do it again and again, however many times they required it of him.

Cold settled inside him as two more pushed through the back

door. Silas swung around the corner to avoid the tranqs. The darts slammed into the wall, and then he took them. Twin gestures, dual focus. He'd never done that before, and anguish streaked red-black across his field of vision. These men, he didn't choke out. He snapped their necks cleanly, as he'd sworn he'd never do again. The resultant blaze in his own spine made his eyes water, but it wouldn't last. No damage. No broken bones. Only blood drew blood. He just had to hold on and stay alert.

How many were left? He crouched and hugged the wall, edging down the hallway. They would be coming in the front, too. Surrounding a structure was protocol for these guys. He felt shaky and nauseated from the feedback, but he forced himself to keep moving. Juneau didn't make a sound in the closet, thank God. Silas didn't know if he could do this, if he had to worry about her, too.

Since it wasn't a big house, he reached the door fast. *No choice. Gotta end this.* He flung it open, expecting to dodge more tranqs. Instead, he found a small woman with white blond hair, cut in short, jagged strands, standing before three motionless men. They wore gear just like the others, but they'd forgotten their mission. Her voice rolled over him, sweeter than a nightingale's song.

"You don't want to hurt us," she was saying softly, irresistibly. "You're going to put down those guns, turn, and walk into the sea. Nice day for a swim, don't you think? Then you're going to swim until you can't see land anymore. Once you're out there, you'll check out the ocean floor."

Horror overwhelmed him. Even though she wasn't focused on him, he felt the siren call of her voice, and he almost wanted to go with them when they took their first somnambulant steps toward the sea. Silas planted his feet and watched them go, pain pinching at his temples.

"You're like me."

"Nuh-uh, pal. We're all special snowflakes . . . I've never seen the same ability manifest twice. Mockingbird thinks the abilities come from our unique genetic code. But if you mean I'm a former test subject, then . . ." She tapped her nose.

"Who are you?"

"Tanager will do. I'm here to extricate you, but we need to move fast, since we've both used our abilities at this site. Come on."

The bounty hunters were almost at the ocean now, still shuffling like sleepwalkers. "Do you have a vehicle?"

She nodded. "It's parked up on the road."

"Let me go get Juneau."

"Mockingbird didn't say I was supposed to rescue anyone else."

Silas spun. "It's nonnegotiable. You take both of us, or neither. I presume you have some use for me, or you wouldn't have come."

The woman sighed. Her makeup looked particularly heavy in the morning light, eyes ringed in dark kohl. Her lips, too, were painted black, offering sharp contrast to her spiked platinum hair. She ran tired fingers through it and then said, "Whatever. We need to make tracks."

He went inside at a run and found Juneau pressed up against the back of the closet. She reached for him first, letting him draw her out. But she was trembling, despite her silent bravery. He hugged her close for a moment and then stepped back.

"Come on. We've got a ride out of here."

"Are you going to tell me what the hell is going on?"

He shook his head. "Not now. If this woman is telling the truth, we can expect more hunters . . . and soon."

"Hunters? I thought they were looters, because of the quake. What—"

"Juneau. Do you trust me?"

"I—yeah. If you were going to hurt me, you've had more than one shot, and you've been nothing but kind."

Kind. Most men would be offended by that word, but it wrapped around his heart like barbwire. She saw something in him nobody had, at least not for years. Not since before he was taken.

"Then let's go. I promise you'll find out more after we get moving."

Wordless, Tanager led the way back to the road, where a driver waited in a battered Jeep. He looked military from his bearing to his haircut, but his eyes held that hypnotic shine as he turned to watch them cresting the rise. His hands still rested on the wheel, like he hadn't moved since she got out of the vehicle. *Creepy.*

"I found my friends," the woman said. "Now you need to drive us to Ayampe. There's nothing more important to you than our safety. Understand?"

"*Sí.*"

So her power works across language barriers. Interesting.

Tanager got in front, and he helped Juneau in back and then swung up himself. The Jeep jerked into motion. This early, the wind was cool. She laced her fingers through his. The trembling had stopped, but she still seemed spooked—and she hadn't even seen the bodies—or the lemming men drowning themselves.

"What happens once we get to Ayampe?" he asked Tanager.

"I find us a pilot and get us the hell out of Ecuador."

"Doesn't that mean using your ability? I thought you said we couldn't. Isn't it dangerous?"

"It would be for *you*, since you don't know how to block Kestrel. As long as we stay on the move and get back to base, which is built to conceal us, we'll be fine."

"Before today, I haven't done . . . that in more than five years."

"Well, you were detained, weren't you? And hiding your light under a bushel." She winked at him over her shoulder. "Clever boy."

Silas set his jaw. "Regardless, I'm not likely to recidivate if I have a choice. I'm more interested in making amends."

"Whatev. Talk to Mockingbird about that."

Juneau glanced between them, her eyes widening. "She's . . . like you."

"I wish people would stop saying that," Tanager muttered. "I'm starting to feel not special, and that makes me bitchy."

"What are you going to do with him?" Silas asked, indicating the driver. "Won't he tell the Foundation everything, if they find him?"

If she expects me to let her kill some random guy—

Tanager shrugged. "He'll remember exactly what I tell him. He won't say anything about us. As far as he knows, he decided to take a sudden vacation."

Damn powerful gift.

"Where are you taking us?" Juneau spoke in a low, firm voice, despite the fact that she had to be seriously freaked out.

"I didn't want *you*," Tanager told her. "The big guy insisted."

Silas sat forward. "That doesn't answer the question. I'd like to know, too."

"I'm not telling you where. I'll tell you what. You've been tapped to join the resistance. If you decline the invite, after speaking to Mockingbird, I'll give you the story I want you to remember, and leave you somewhere safe. After that, you're on your own. But the Foundation has your scent now, and they'll never stop looking. So you're better off with us."

"The Foundation?" Juneau frowned, glancing at Silas for explanation. "This sounds like an episode of *The X-Files* I saw once."

Shit. It's time I told her everything.

So there, in the breezy backseat of an old Jeep, he did.

ELEVEN

None of this seemed real. Several hours later, Juneau glanced around the "safe house" and wondered what the hell she was doing here. The safe house was more of a warehouse, all random junk, bare swinging bulbs, and echoing, cavernous space. This shit had nothing to do with her. She needed to call her family and let them know she was okay, maybe go visit before she took her next overseas job. She no longer kept a place in the U.S. because she didn't linger long enough stateside for it to be worth it, and her mother enjoyed when she came home, however brief it might be.

But she glanced across the table at the big man, nursing a cup of coffee, and her heart did a funny dance in her chest. Maybe it was stupid to think he needed her, even a little, but she'd noticed the way his onyx eyes sought her, as if reassuring himself she hadn't left. It wouldn't hurt to stay awhile, if they'd let her make a call.

"Tanager," she said. "Is there a phone I can use?"

"Sure. Back office. Dial nine first."

"Who pays for this place?" Silas asked.

"Not us. Mockingbird keeps the power and phone on, charges it to the parent company that owns the property."

Christ. Juneau stood and left what had likely been the break room, crossing the dark floor with its looming ceiling. Broken windows adorned the walls like sharp teeth, casting shadows from the swinging bulbs. She stifled a shiver as she passed into a darker hall-

way. There were no light fixtures back here, so she had to feel her
way along the walls. She slid her fingers through something tacky,
and she shuddered.

Inside the office, she found the switch. Radiance flickered overhead, highlighting the general wreckage of the room. The phone
was ancient, a rotary dial—the kind her grandmother had leased
from the phone company—and it sat on the floor, right beside the
jack. Whoever these people were, they didn't travel first class.

Juneau knelt and dialed; it took way longer when you had to
wait for the wheel to finish spinning to input the next number. But
the sound quality was good as the call went through. Her mother
picked up on the third ring; she sounded faintly out of breath. Maybe
she'd been outside in the yard or sitting on the porch.

"Hi, Mom. It's me."

"Junie!" Nobody but Melva Bright ever called her that. Right
now, she didn't mind. "God, we've been so worried about you, ever
since we heard about the quake. Your brother's been calling all over
Ecuador, trying to get news."

"Jack?" she guessed. He was the lawyer, better suited to getting
information out of people than Joseph, the surgeon.

"Who else? Where are you? Are you safe?"

"Honestly, I'm not sure." That much was true. "I got a lift with
some other survivors, and we're making our way out of the country.
I'll come home as soon as I can. Things are . . . unbelievable here."

"I can only imagine. But thank God you found a phone to let us
know you're all right."

"I have to go. There are others waiting to use it. Give my love
to Jack and Joe."

"Of course, sweetheart."

After she disconnected, she sat for long moments, holding the
phone as if she'd lost her lifeline. Her mother's voice lent the situation an illusion of normalcy, but clearly things weren't. Taking a
deep breath, she headed back to the others. She entered silently in

accordance with Tanager's gesture and propped herself against the wall. The other woman perched on the edge of a worktable, swinging her legs.

At first, she didn't know why she had to be quiet, and then the laptop crackled. A ray of energy shot from it—and holy *shit*—she'd never seen anything like it, outside the movies. A small, holographic image appeared, glowing blue. Surely this was fake; this thing couldn't actually talk. But the figure turned as if acclimating itself, and focused on Silas. It didn't have features—didn't look like any particular person—it was just an avatar.

"I see Tanager got you out." The voice was unquestionably male, but it came out with electronic interference, different than a voice scrambler. This was a new thing altogether.

"I always get my man." The blond woman grinned, showing straight, white teeth. She'd fit right in at clubs where Juneau had partied in college; everyone wore black and too much eyeliner. Leather and metal spikes, preferred attire.

"That's why I sent you," the hologram said to her and then added to Silas, "I imagine you have questions."

"To say the least. Who are you? For that matter, who's she?"

"I'm Mockingbird. You already know Tan. We don't use real names, even in private, in case one of us is captured. We're both part of a resistance movement, working covertly against the private organization that created us."

Whoa. To be honest, Juneau hadn't given full credit to the big guy's story. He'd seemed to want to unload, and it seemed churlish to deny him that opportunity, even if she didn't buy what he said. Although it was damned hard to explain what he could do otherwise, but her worldview didn't allow for secret labs and Mengele-style human experiments. That was way darker than she'd *wanted* to believe. However, now she'd watched Tanager Jedi-mind-trick two men, using the power of her voice alone. In conjunction with Silas breaking people with his brain, she had to admit the evidence was

compelling. The Chinese curse *May you live in interesting times* had
come true with a vengeance. Shit didn't get more interesting.

Which presented an interesting question. If they were a covert
operation, what did they do with normals? A cold chill surged
through her. She didn't want to die for the uber-cliché of *knowing*
too much. It might be her imagination, but Tanager watched her
with greater than necessary focus, given she wasn't doing anything.

Surely Silas wouldn't let them hurt her. *If he can stop it*, a small
voice said. *If Tanager works her siren mojo on him, he may not be
able to resist.* Come to think of it, she'd only seen the ability work
on men. Maybe it wouldn't work on Juneau, and if so, she could
defend herself. Die trying, anyway.

"And what do you want with me?" he asked.

"For you to come work for us."

Silas laughed, but the sound faded as he realized nobody else
shared his amusement. "You're serious?"

"Deadly. We could use a warrior to help us take out their
hunters."

His black eyes turned sharkish. "You mean set myself up as bait.
Use my ability to lure them in and then execute them when they
show up."

A shiver rolled through her. He didn't sound offended; he
sounded . . . intrigued. Silas studied his hands once more, as if he
saw blood on them—and maybe he thought he could mitigate that
with more. She didn't know if she agreed, but she couldn't imagine
what he'd gone through either, if what he'd told her was true.

"I wouldn't have put it that way, but essentially, yes. I coordinate all the agents from a secure location. Under most conditions,
you would be working alone, though if we locate another facility
like the one in Virginia, you would definitely be on the strike team
sent to clear it."

Silas froze. "There are others?"

"At least four. Two have been relocated since Shrike took out Dr.

Rowan, and the other two never pop up on my informational grid. It's possible those have shut down because they're old—they were established in the seventies—but I won't rest until I've liberated all the test subjects and shut down this program for good. If we make it too difficult and too expensive, the moneymen will cut off the research and close those divisions down. By yourself, you can go individually to each family and say you're sorry for their loss. That's *all*. With us, you can accomplish much more."

"I'd work with him again," Tanager said. "He's cool in a crisis. He was swatting those bloodhounds like flies when I arrived."

"How do you pay for all of this?" By Silas's expression, he didn't mean the rusty, abandoned warehouse.

"I won't lie to you. My talent is such that I can skim from corporations without leaving virtual fingerprints. I set up numbered accounts for our operatives and we're funded Robin Hood–style. But I target the parent companies behind the Foundation, if it makes you feel any better."

"I have a couple of conditions," Silas said. "If I work with you, I still need to visit those families. Otherwise, they'll never know what happened to their children, their mothers and fathers."

Juneau's heart gave another little twist; his passion moved her. So few people cared about *anything*, anymore. God, she loved a man with a mission.

Tanager dropped lightly to her feet. "You'll need some help with that, hoss. These people will have no reason to accept the truth from you."

"And you'll give them a reason?" Silas asked.

"It only works on men," she answered, confirming Juneau's hunch. "But chances are, we can find some male relative to convey the news. If I tell him we're cops and we have news about Sally Missing, he'll repeat it with one hundred percent conviction."

"Why would you help me? This is personal."

Her gaze went hard. "Because I want you onboard, and if this is

what it takes, so be it. You can teach the Foundation to fear us—
and what it feels like to be hunted."

"Could you give me a few minutes to talk to Juneau in private?"

"Of course," Mockingbird said. "Tanager, take the laptop to the
back office. I have some things to discuss with you anyway."

TWELVE

This was a new thing. Unlike most, his ability was constantly evolving. Two weeks ago, Mockingbird hadn't been able to do this. Unfortunately, such power came at a high cost. He wouldn't be able to do this forever, which meant he had to step up the recruitment and find someone who could take over for him. Which wouldn't be easy. As far as he knew, he was unique. But then, everyone was.

What he was doing now, he guessed, was some form of technically powered astral projection, impossible to say for sure. Science hadn't advanced anywhere near enough to try and chart the reasons why.

"You sure about this, Tan?" In this form, he could see her only in sparks of Tanager-shaped light.

God, he envied Silas. To be able to work out in the field, up close and personal with her? That sounded like a fucking dream come true. *Lucky bastard.* But the truth was, Mockingbird was far too vital—and too fragile—to survive outside his controlled environment. He hadn't always been so weak, but the stronger his ability became, the more his body deteriorated. *I am an imperfect adaptation*, he thought, while waiting for her answer.

"I'm positive," she said. "We need him. The combat abilities are rare, and even more rare for them to manifest in someone who isn't batshit crazy."

That much was certainly true. It seemed as though causing physical harm to others through paranormal means didn't do the human psyche any good. Part of that could be attributed to the experiments, of course, and long captivity. But they'd found some subjects who'd come into their powers on their own, and to a man, they'd turned to mass murder as a hobby. But Silas was different, and Tanager was right. They *had* to have him. Her short-term cooperation with his personal penance was a small price to pay.

"Very well."

He hated thinking of all the time she would spend with Silas in close proximity. Sometimes knowing an operative's background provided too much insight. But of all his agents, she was the only one he'd formed a personal attachment to, even though he shouldn't, even though it was stupid, and wrong, and pointless. She'd never even seen his face. Never would.

That's me, the ultimate untouchable.

"It won't be a big deal. I like him. And it'll be nice to have someone around that I can talk to about shit. Plus, he's had it worse than me, which takes some doing."

He wished he offered the warning for altruistic reasons. "I think he has some attachment to the regular who came in with him."

Her tone turned cold. "Yeah. I was going to ask—what do you want me to do about her?"

THIRTEEN

"You're going to do it." It wasn't a question.

Juneau had borne all the weirdness with an almost unreasonable calm. Not that Silas wanted a woman by his side who couldn't face the unexpected without melting down. But he didn't know how much more she could take.

"Yeah. But I don't know how it's going to work. You and me."

Juneau shrugged. "Hey, you're in demand. I'm just somebody you dug out of a rock pile. I appreciate you looking out for me while we were in Ecuador, but I gather we're stateside now. That means once I head out, I can take care of myself. I need to get new IDs made, replace my bank card, and go see my family. I'd really like to hug my mom."

He would, too. But after so long, he couldn't imagine what he'd tell her. *Sorry for six years of silence. It wasn't my fault, I swear.* Yeah, that'd go over well. But he had to address the fundamental misconception in what she'd said.

"You're not. In fact, you're the only person I've trusted with who I am in years." Since before he'd been taken. "I'm not ready to lose that. Maybe you'd rather walk away, I don't know. It hasn't been long enough to be sure what we feel isn't what they call emotional response to extremity."

"Any port in a storm?"

"Exactly."

She nodded like she agreed with him, and his heart clenched. Doing the right thing sucked. He wanted to beg her to stay with him and never leave, because he might never find anyone like her again.

"So what do you suggest, then?"

He took a deep breath, nearly unable to voice the words for the razors in his throat. "We should part ways, at least for a while. Get some perspective. And maybe you'll decide you want nothing more to do with me."

"I should go to Chicago anyway. That's where my family is."

How funny—and sad—that despite what they'd shared, he hadn't known that about her. "I'll open an email account."

Silas told her the name and service he'd use; she committed it to memory. Juneau pushed away from the wall. "I should bail before they get back. Something tells me they won't like how much I know about their organization."

"They don't know if they can trust you yet."

"Neither do you," she said softly. "You're taking a big risk on me. I might be able to parlay what I know into a big payout from these corporations."

He shook his head, smiling. "You teach English to impoverished children for a few dollars an hour. You don't own more than you can carry. If money motivates you, then you have an odd way of showing it, Juneau Bright."

Her eyes shone, as if she wanted to—but would not—weep. "I hate how well you know me already . . . and how hard this is. I know it's the right thing, but this is the first time a man has ever asked me to go before I was good and ready."

That hit him like a brick in the gut. "I'm trying to be noble here. You're not making it easy."

"Best quick and clean, then." She crossed to him, set her hands on his shoulders, and kissed him as he'd never been kissed in his life, as if she wanted to steal his breath and keep it, so she'd always have some of him with her. It made him feel . . . loved. Maybe it was the wrong word, but he clutched it close to his chest. "Good-bye, Silas."

Watching her leave hurt worse than killing with his hellish power. *Grant that it's not forever*, he thought. *Grant that she comes back to me.* In his mind's eye, he saw a painting his mother had owned— a tchotchke with a quote imprinted on it—something about loving something and setting it free. He suspected whoever wrote that down initially had never loved a woman like Juneau Bright.

This is best. She'd lived her whole life avoiding ties. *The last thing she'd want is a permanent arrangement with someone like me. I'm damaged goods. At least this way, she may remember me fondly. I'll always be a hero in her eyes.* Sadly, those thoughts offered scant comfort.

When Tanager returned with the laptop, she narrowed her eyes at him. "Where's the chick?"

"I cut her loose." He met her stare measure for measure. "Is that a problem?"

She smiled. "Not for me. Mox may disagree."

"Don't call me that. We can't have her in the wind, knowing what she knows." A pause. "She's got family in Naperville. I bet that's where she'll go. If she's not *with* you, as in your personal business," Mockingbird's tone made it clear what he meant, "then we need to take care of her."

"No. If she's harmed, I'll find you and make you sorry. I'm not working with people who think nothing of punishing innocents."

"MB means bringing in our resident mind-fucker, hoss." Tanager laughed softly. "She won't be injured. She just won't remember you."

"You have someone who can do that?" he asked.

"You'd be surprised what Mockingbird's turned up. He has an eye for talent."

Much as he hated to consider becoming a blank spot in her

memory, if she didn't get in touch with him, it might be best. He could start this new life with no ties. Silas just wished that didn't sound so fucking lonely. But at least he'd have purpose.

"Can you give me a window of opportunity?" he asked. "We're not . . . together, but we were. Briefly. It's up to her if we continue to be. She can't make that decision if you cut me from her brain too quick."

Mockingbird asked, "What sounds reasonable? If you trust her, I'm willing to give her a little time. I don't think she'll run right to the Foundation, and even if she did, it would take a while for her to find anyone who would believe her."

"I think she's solid," Tanager said, unexpectedly. "I don't think she'd sell him out. At least, not voluntarily."

Silas froze. "Will the Foundation go after her?"

"They might, if anyone had survived the strike in Ecuador. But since you ended three and I drowned the others, nobody will be talking."

He felt like ice water ran in his veins. "You're sure they all died?"

"Positive."

The Mockingbird holo cleared its throat. "How long, then?"

"A month?" Silas figured if she hadn't emailed him in that time, then she'd have decided it was best to leave things be.

"Done. I won't send Finch until I hear from you. And welcome aboard. Tanager has your first assignment."

The woman nodded. "Foundation bloodhounds are hunting some poor bastard here in Texas, and we're taking them out. It'll be safer if we use my ability as bait this time. That way, Kestrel won't know we're working together. We can plan more on the move. Ready?"

Despite the lingering pain of farewell, he preferred to stay busy. So, "Yeah. The sooner, the better."

"I like the way this guy thinks. Do you have anything else for us, MB?"

"The pharmacy on the corner of Fourth and Main has a prescription for you, Silas. It'll help with the pain after you use your ability."

"Tanager told you?"

She shrugged. "You were in bad shape when I showed up. Dealing with a few more guys would've put you on your ass. You need to countermand that."

"Does your siren voice have a drawback?"

"Siren voice." She laughed quietly. "I dig that. And yeah. But I'm not telling you what it is. It's . . . personal."

Shit. He was sorry he'd asked. "Thanks, Mockingbird. I appreciate the extrication. Not just for me either."

"Thank me by kicking some goon ass." The holo sounded almost . . . sad. But why would he?

"All set?" Tanager closed the laptop without a farewell and rolled into motion. "Then let's hit it."

FOURTEEN

The bus station in Houston was grungy. Not unusual in that regard.

When she'd emerged from the warehouse, Juneau hadn't even known where the hell she was. They'd flown in at night and then hopped a second plane. They'd worn blindfolds, too, all enough to set off her fear-o-meter. Fortunately, it had been daytime when she slipped out, and she'd felt safe enough to ask directions from a couple of milling teenagers.

"Bus station's about eight blocks that way," one kid said.

His friend added, "Can't miss it. It's right by the McDonald's."

Easy enough. She felt conspicuous in her wrinkled shorts and tank top. The weather didn't quite match her attire, but it was warm enough that she didn't look crazy, at least. Just maybe . . . overly optimistic. A fair number of people hung around in the fast-food restaurant parking lot. Others made their way by crossing an actual set of railroad tracks. *Doubtless the bus station's on the wrong side, too.*

But there was no help for it. She brushed past two seedy men who stood smoking by the front doors and found the pay phones. *Deep breath.* Her hand trembled as she reached for the handset. *It shouldn't be this complicated. Make the call. Leave all the crazy behind. And I have his email, if I decide I want to get in touch later.* Thus bolstered, she dialed zero for the operator and asked to make a collect call.

"What number?"

She gave her mother's and then spoke her name at the tone. Thirty seconds later, she had her mother on the other end of the line. "Where are you, honey? Can you talk more now?"

"I'm in Houston," she answered. "And yes. But my stuff got buried in the quake. I'm going to need a hand getting home."

"What can I do?"

Wiring money could be tricky, since she had no ID and no friends here. "Could you buy me a one-way ticket to Chicago, online, and then call to confirm my description with the ticket agent? I hope they'll give me a break if my mother vouches for me."

"Absolutely. I'll book you on the next bus and be waiting for you at the station on this end. Give me ten minutes to make the purchase and then call."

"Thanks, Mom. You're the best."

And she was. Juneau never minded the *live up to your potential* talks because her mother delivered them with warmth and concern, never nitpickery. But by this point, even her mom had accepted she would never fit the corporate mold. She went into the bathroom to wash her face and hands, and braid her hair. She used a thread unraveled from her tank top to tie it off. It was amazing what one could become accustomed to. In the mirror, her face looked thin and tired.

She left the bathroom and headed up to the front counter. The woman seemed to recognize her by the slight smile. "I just talked to your mom. That hair's unmistakable."

"I don't have ID. I lost everything in Ecuador. Now I'm just trying to get home."

"Oh man. You're a quake survivor." The agent looked as though she wondered how the hell Juneau had wound up in Houston, but she didn't ask. "It's not a problem. You have twenty minutes until your bus arrives."

"Good timing. Thank you so much for this."

"Anytime. Enjoy your trip."

Well, that would take some doing since she had no money. But fasting for twenty-four wouldn't do her any harm. Spiritual types did it all the time.

The bus ride seemed interminable. She transferred in Dallas and then passed through Garland and Greenville. Juneau spent fifteen glorious minutes, drinking from a water fountain in Texarkana, trying to fill up to drive away the ache in her belly. She was weary and heartsick, *so* ready to come home. Midnight found her in Little Rock, and by four a.m., she was sitting in Memphis, waiting for the driver. They spent an hour there. At last exhaustion took its toll, and she slept. The next thing she knew, it was two fifteen in the afternoon, and she'd arrived in Chicago.

As promised, her mother was waiting for her. She hugged Juneau and then stepped back to look at her. "So glad to have you home, safe and sound. Come on, let's get out of here."

If, going forward, she never spent another minute in a bus station, that'd be fine. To Juneau's vast delight, her mom had brought *food*. Praise the glorious midwestern obsession for feeding people in times of trouble. The nylon lunch bag held a chicken salad sandwich, an apple, and her favorite sweet: peanut butter cookies with chocolate chips. To cap it off, a bottle of sparkling water. She dug in while her mom drove, navigating the afternoon traffic. It was colder here than in Houston, so she was glad for the car's heater.

"There's a sweatshirt in back if you need it."

Juneau finished the apple and then snagged the hoodie. She wriggled into it with a sigh of satisfaction and then went back to her meal. Her mom knew enough to be patient, so she could enjoy the food. *She still makes the best chicken salad ever.*

"Thanks."

"It's what moms do. I hope you intend to stay awhile this time."

She thought about it. "Yeah. I think I've had enough traveling for a bit. You haven't turned my room into a home gym yet?"

"No. I keep it up for you, since you don't have your own place." But there was no disapproval in her voice, just statement of fact.

"I feel like I could sleep for a week. After I shower. Do you mind?"

"Not at all. It must've been pretty rough."

Juneau thought of her lost coworkers and the children, and the big, dark eyes of the survivors she'd left behind. Even she couldn't muster up a light reply, so she merely nodded and turned her head against the window, wondering where Silas was right now. It felt strange to be alone; he had been right to call their bond one formed in extremity. But she didn't feel whole without him nearby. Surely that would change in time. It wasn't love. It had been sex—and a memory she could treasure.

Naperville. Juneau couldn't believe she was here. It was all so . . . normal with the neighborhoods laid out in organized grids, streets planted with flowers, and trees standing stately in the yards. This time of year, everything was greening up. Springtime in the Midwest was beautiful. So different from the tropical climate she'd become accustomed to in Ecuador.

It took two days to prove her identity sufficiently to replace driver's license and passport, and then fill out the requisite forms. Her mother fussed over her, and she didn't mind. After everything, some TLC hit the spot.

For the rest of the week, Juneau tried not to think about Silas. She didn't think about the sharp curve of his nose, how good he was in bed, or the way his eyes crinkled when he smiled. Not about how he'd stepped between her and a bullet or how he'd protected her every step of the way.

That weekend, her brothers came from Chicago to check her out personally. They'd both called to make sure she was all right, but her mother insisted they should all be together her first weekend home. Not for the first time, she wondered how Jack and Joseph felt about being asked to drop everything just because she'd turned up like a bad penny. They never complained, though. Apart from the hideous teasing they'd forced her to endure as a tween, her brothers were pretty cool guys. Both were disgustingly successful—a credit to her mother, who'd raised them on her own. Juneau couldn't remember her father; he'd died when she was four.

It's a good thing I keep clothes in my old room, she thought, tugging on a pair of jeans. They fit loosely, even though they were at least ten years old. Juneau found a T-shirt and then went down to greet her brothers.

Jack was the oldest—and the tallest. He had dark hair and blue eyes; they all took after their father, leaning toward height. Growing up, Juneau had despaired of ever being as pretty as her mom. Even now, Melva Bright looked ten years younger than her actual age, and people were starting to mistake them for sisters—that could be depressing, if she let it. She didn't.

Joseph looked more like Juneau, sharing similar features, along with gray eyes and lighter brown hair. They'd always been closer as kids, and still were today. He had slender hands, and each time she saw him, she marveled that he saved lives on a daily basis. She hugged them each in turn and suffered through a prolonged scrutiny.

"Yep," Joe said at length. "She still has all her parts."

Jack laughed. "Is that your professional opinion?"

"Absolutely."

Her oldest brother kissed her forehead. "It's good to see you, Junie. You had us worried shitless."

"Don't call me that."

It was so good to see some things stayed the same, no matter how much everything else changed. They enjoyed a meal in her mother's kitchen, catching up and laughing. Her mother focused on why her brothers hadn't married yet.

"It's not like you aren't settled in your careers," Melva said, gesturing with her fork. "And I want grandchildren while I'm still young enough to enjoy them."

Jack choked on his antipasto. "Maybe you could let me *find* the right woman before you mentally impregnate her, Ma?"

Gazing around the table, Juneau knew she should be totally happy right now. No question. She'd survived an insane, incredible situation, but it was *all over*. By now, she ought to be thinking about her next job, checking lists online, and finding a new adventure. Instead, she felt stuck in a holding pattern, unable to make a choice.

She sat quiet while the others talked, and after dinner, she washed up the dishes, then grabbed a sweatshirt out of the hall closet and went out to the porch to sit on the swing. Over the years, she'd done a lot of thinking—and brooding—here. It wasn't quite warm enough, but she needed the push and sway to align her thoughts.

Joe followed her out eventually. "Mind if I sit?"

"Would it stop you if I did?" She grinned up at him.

"Nuh-uh. You have that *I need to talk* look."

"Maybe I do." She drew one knee up and wrapped her arms around it while still gently nudging the swing with the other. "I met a guy in Ecuador. In fact, he's the only reason I'm alive."

"Wow. That's major." Sometimes Joe still sounded like he was sixteen, and that always made her smile. But these days, he had a perspicacity he'd lacked in his younger years. "So you're into him, but you're wondering if the hero factor's coloring your opinion."

"Exactly. He was the one who suggested we cool it for a while. Give us time to get perspective and see how we feel down the line."

"Sounds like he has his head on right. I appreciate that he didn't take advantage." Her brother mock-scowled. "He didn't, did he?"

She laughed softly. "None of your business."

"Do I have to kill him?"

"Please. I'm thirty-three, Joe. Your list would be pretty long, at this point."

"I *so* don't need to hear that." He ruffled her hair gently. "What are you going to do, then?"

"I don't know. That's what I'm trying to figure out."

Later that night, she went up to her room and flicked on the ancient computer. It still ran, but her mother only had dial-up; she used email, but she didn't figure the Internet machine was good for anything else. Instead of checking her messages, Juneau went to the website Jack had designed for her and scrolled through the old picture galleries. These shots shared one commonality: they featured her and a group of strangers with whom she'd lost contact as soon as she left the country. She didn't have many close friends, just a series of friendly acquaintances. Nobody stayed in her life because she didn't let them. She always had to keep moving.

So was it at all possible that she wanted to keep the one man who'd told her to walk away? Maybe it was just sheer mental perversity making her think so. As requested, she'd give it time. It couldn't be love, anyway; she'd decided long ago she just wasn't wired to stay with one man.

But how will you know if you never try?

By day eight, she had to admit it: Silas was a hard man to forget. No matter *how* many days passed, she couldn't forget him. No amount of conversation made her stop longing to hear him laugh again. Nothing she did drove him out of her mind. Juneau woke with the sound of his voice in her head and the memory of his touch lingering on her skin. She played the Blink 182 song "I Miss You" repeatedly, until her mother asked her what the heck was wrong.

So at the end of the month, she emailed him.

FIFTEEN

It was done, then.

It was just as well Silas had work with Tanager; otherwise he would've had too much time to focus on the pain. He missed Juneau more than he could've imagined. Some bonds couldn't be broken, but maybe she was better off without him. He checked his email obsessively. The month passed in interminable agony, and on that last day, he woke up feeling dark as a moonless night.

Tanager was gone from their shared flat. She'd be headed to Chicago now. To find Finch and make sure he put Silas from Juneau's mind. She'd made her choice and so couldn't be trusted with their secrets. Soon she would recall nothing of their time together, but at least he would remember that he'd had something beautiful for a little while.

His partner's absence meant they wouldn't be working today. In the last month, he'd learned how to manage the pain associated with his ability with a judicious combination of meditation and meds, but he didn't mind the break. It gave him time to make peace with the inevitable. Silas couldn't honestly say he was surprised. Yet he couldn't stop himself from checking the account he'd set up just for Juneau one last time.

And there it was in black and white. Hope. Salvation. The potential for all future joy.

Silas, I can't get you out of my head. I don't know if you're the one, but I want to find out. I can't do that if I'm not with you. Call me. J.

He started to dial her number, and then he paused with his fingers on the dial. *Shit. Fuck.* He had to stop Tanager. With trembling hands, he punched in her cell, but it went to voice mail. She might already have some guy in the air in his personal plane. For obvious reasons, Tan never flew commercial.

He sat down at the computer, calling to book tickets while he worked online; successful multitasking had never mattered so much. *If the number's listed, yeah. Here we go.* Silas scrawled the address. *Thanks, reverse lookup.* Then he did try to call Juneau, intending to tell her to stay the hell away from Tanager, but she didn't answer. *Fuck. Maybe it's already too late.*

"First available flight to Chicago. Yeah. Thanks."

Every second the ticket agent delayed, chatting away, made him want to reach through the phone and throttle her. At last they wrapped up and he sprinted for the door. He had no idea where Tanager was, whether she'd already left the city. If only he had some clue—he scared the shit out of his cabbie with his muttering and growling. For once, Silas didn't care at all, as it motivated the man to drive faster.

He leaped out at the airport and vaulted over a trolley full of suitcases. The delays seemed endless. First he used a self-service terminal to print out boarding passes, since he'd memorized his confirmation code, then he had to wait in an endless security line. Shit had changed a lot while he was locked up. Fortunately, he had nothing to search, which made the agents glare at him, because it meant he was breaking some travelers' algorithm. He didn't care about that either.

Finally, he took his seat on the plane, and the whole time he was in the air, he found it hard to sit still. The only thing in the world that mattered was finding Juneau before Tanager had Finch mind-fuck her. *Don't let me lose her*, he thought, and his desperation carried the weight of a prayer.

He hired a driver at the airport, since an hour in a town car cost about the same as paying for a grubby cab. On the way, he called Tanager four more times, but she didn't pick up. He left six messages and then texted her for good measure. *Don't mess with her.* Juneau still wasn't answering either, and maybe when she did, she wouldn't know who he was.

"Do you want me to wait?" the driver asked as they pulled up in front of a good-sized house with white siding and a brick walkway. "That'll be another hour."

"No. It'll be fine." He hoped.

Silas slid out of the car and sprinted up the drive to the porch. Inside, he could hear voices. He rang the bell, and in the seconds it took for someone to answer, he died a thousand deaths. A small woman who looked to be anywhere from forty to sixty answered the door; she had Juneau's stormy eyes.

"Ah, you must be Junie's young man." To her credit, she didn't bat an eye at his appearance.

Relief left him weak . . . and uncertain how to proceed, now. He followed her into a living room decorated in warm, inviting shades of peach and brown. Tanager sat sprawled on the couch, drinking a Coke. She aimed a daggered grin at him.

"You didn't answer your phone," he said, low.

Finch was nowhere to be found. Which meant he'd made it in time.

"I know. I'm not a nice person." Her expression said *I like to fuck with you.*

Before he could decide whether to hug her or bitch her out, Juneau came out of the kitchen. Her step faltered when she saw him, surprise lighting her features, then she came at a run and threw herself at him. He'd never been greeted like that in his life, not even when he was normal. He wrapped his arms around her and buried his face in her hair.

"Missed you," he whispered, for he had no explanation why he was here, otherwise. "And I thought this would be better than a call. Surprise."

"Someone turned the ringer off on the phone anyway," she answered, her voice muffled by his chest.

He cut a look at Tanager, who smirked. *Guilty*, she mouthed. Clearly she enjoyed driving people crazy. But now that fear had receded, he didn't even care. Her fuckery had gotten him here faster. Without her interference, they might've screwed around with phone calls and tentative plans that dwindled into doubt. She'd prodded him until he came charging in like a rabid bull. And Juneau didn't seem to mind.

"Let's go in the kitchen." Mrs. Bright beckoned to Tanager. "I suspect these two have some talking to do."

Tan shook her head. "I gotta bail. I just wanted to see his face when he walked in."

Juneau and her mom seemed puzzled by her words and her swagger as she left. Silas couldn't stop smiling. He rather liked the little bitch—and he was certainly grateful to her.

He didn't let go of Juneau, even as he maneuvered them to the couch. Tucking her against his side, he said, "I was worried you'd write us off."

"I tried," she admitted. "But I kept thinking about you. And doubting myself. Why the hell would I ever go looking for greener pastures when I already had somebody willing to die for me? And you just *met* me. I'm guessing it only gets better from here, though relationships are a new thing for me."

"Me, too. We'll find our way together if that's what you want."

"It is."

"I'm not going to have a normal job, you know. It will mean

traveling a lot and doing dangerous things. And I'll be partnered with Tanager for a while yet."

"That works for me. I didn't say I wanted to settle down, only that I want to be with you. I'm sure I have some skill they can use." She canted her head, her voice dropping to a whisper. "They don't just hire people with powers, do they? Because I think that's discrimination."

For the first time that month, he laughed. Only she had ever been able to bring out the lightness in him like this; he'd always been serious, even as a kid, focused on string theory, particle physics, and shit that puzzled the rest of the world. He'd wanted to make a difference—and he would, just not in the way he'd originally intended. But as John Lennon said, *Life is what happens to you while you're busy making other plans.*

Silas kissed her temple. "I tried so hard to give you space and distance, so you could be sure this is what you want. But without you, I was so much nothing. Just skin and bone, going through the motions."

Juneau exhaled in a shuddering breath, and then her mouth found his in a kiss that broke him and reshaped him with its heat and sweetness. Even though she hadn't said the words, he felt it in her lips with each brush, each tease. *I love you. I love you.* Afterward, she framed his face in her hands and rubbed her forehead against his. With her fingertips, she traced the patterns on his arms. He still remembered all the names of the people he'd hurt, but he no longer felt quite so doomed or displaced. Working with the resistance, he could make amends in a tangible way.

"This is a kind of madness, but I don't want it to stop."

"Our life together won't be safe or settled, but I *promise* it'll be extraordinary. If you come away with me, I'll dedicate the rest of my days to making you happy."

"That's exactly what a mother wants to hear," Mrs. Bright called from the kitchen.

The oh-so-beloved woman in his arms gazed into his eyes and laughed. "Sold. But I think you'd better come meet my mother properly."

"I'd love to."

And that was the last normal thing they ever did.

Don't miss

Skin Heat

by Ava Gray,
now available from Berkley Sensation!

Angel-Claimed

JORY STRONG

ACKNOWLEDGMENT

Thanks to my critique partner, Sue-Ellen Gower. Your insight and support are greatly appreciated!

ONE

Sajia woke to the acrid stink of fear. Her nightgown clung to her body, wet with sweat. Or perhaps from the fog creeping in off the San Francisco Bay as night battled with day, streaking the sky with hints of color.

The chill she felt at seeing the drapes pulled back and the window open pebbled her skin in a way the cold didn't. Though she now lived in a mansion guarded by vampires and their servants, old habits remained, as did a human's inherent fear of the night and predators that roamed it.

She'd shut drapes and window alike before going to bed. It was a habit drilled into children from the moment they were old enough, mobile enough, to unlock a window and die as a result of it.

Sajia rubbed her chest as though she could slow the thundering beat of her heart. She tried to shake off the fear-smell, but it clung like a heavy shroud, making her think it belonged to her until movement, a nervous fluttering at the doorway, jerked her from a terror that had only recently crept its way into her life with each awakening.

She saw the blood-slave then, and dread descended, as thick and heavy as the fog outside. The girl was pale, wringing her hands, frightened that she would lose her life because of something others had done.

There was only one reason a blood-slave would come for her,

and it jerked Sajia from the bed. "Corinne?" she asked, naming the scion she'd only recently become companion to.

"It's not my place to say," the girl whispered. "The Master demands your presence."

There were many masters in the Tucci household, but only one by that name.

The blood-slave continued to hover in the doorway, trembling like a field mouse. Afraid to be in the presence of anyone who might draw The Master's ire, afraid too that when the audience was done, she'd be the one called to The Master's bed and bled dry.

Sajia offered no reassurance. Anything she said in an effort to comfort the girl would be a lie.

She stripped the damp nightgown from her body, tossing it onto the bed and dressing quickly. Supple black pants molded to her legs. A sleeveless shirt in swirling earth tones of yellow and brown and green left her arms bare, revealing the marks carved into her upper arm, pale, freshly healed symbols identifying her position and indicating she served the Tucci family.

She pulled soft, short boots on last, and the blood-slave turned without a word, scurrying down the hallway as if wanting to put as much distance as possible between her fate and Sajia's.

Sajia followed. Despite the worry for Corinne that tied her stomach in knots, her steps sounded confident against the tile floor. Her footfalls echoed off the unadorned walls, their stark white surfaces a reminder of a servant's place where the rest of the estate was lavishly decorated. A manifestation of power and wealth, though compared to the Tassone and many of the other vampire families, the Tucci were paupers.

The moment Sajia passed from the servants' living area, two vampires positioned themselves behind her, trailing her to The Master's parlor like deadly shadows.

Additional vampires waited outside that room. And more inside, a mix of inner-circle guards and family members.

No one spoke. No one moved. Yet Sajia felt their presence against her skin in a frigid blast, like a grave opened to reveal icy horror.

The Master sat behind his desk, caught forever at the age of thirty-five, his pockmarked face a testament to a time when vaccines didn't exist and bleeding by leeches was a common treatment.

Whatever name he'd gone by then, at his death and rebirth he'd shed it like a snake does its skin. What the vampires called him privately, beyond *Sire*, she didn't know. The humans knew only one word for him. *Master*.

Even fearing something had happened to Corinne, Sajia didn't blurt out a question. She bowed her head and waited for The Master to speak first, forced any hint of rebellion deep inside herself at the required subservience.

She knew her place. It was well defined in a world forever changed by a long-ago war that decimated human populations and crushed nations, then was thrust into years of violent anarchy after the supernaturals made their existence known.

Peace, of a sort, had finally come with the carving up of territories. In San Francisco, vampires ruled. Absolutely.

They were apex predators. And humans, little more than cattle to be counted by the head instead of as individuals.

And I am one of those cattle, Sajia told herself, resisting the urge to touch the small gold scorpion at the base of her throat—a talisman and the only thing she possessed that belonged to parents she had no memory of, a reminder that she'd chosen to remain in servitude rather than leave San Francisco. No human beyond their childhood was allowed to live in the city unless they were found to be useful to the vampires. She didn't want to move away from the aunt and uncle who'd raised her after her mother and father perished in a fire in the San Joaquin, or from the cousins who were like brothers and sisters.

Becoming *bajaran*, confidant to the still-human scion of a vampire family, not only allowed her to remain in San Francisco but also put her in a position to intercede on behalf of her own family if they needed help. It came with significant risks to them and to her, though even from the start it had been more than a role taken for benefit.

She'd liked Corinne from the moment they met by chance on the pier, and had come to worry for her future. But then that was the point of providing scions with *bajaran*, so there would be a trusted human in place should they survive their transition to vampire.

Finally The Master broke the silence, perhaps convinced she harbored no guilt, since she hadn't gone to her knees and confessed in an effort to save herself. "Did Corinne tell you arrangements have been finalized for her to be sent to Los Angeles?"

An ache seized Sajia with the thought of being torn from her family. "No, she didn't tell me."

"She is to produce children with a Gairden scion."

Fear on Corinne's behalf tightened the knot of worry in Sajia's belly. The Tucci blood was weak, though it would be suicide for her to speak those words out loud.

Not all families produced readily viable scions, genetically related children who would survive their transition. The Master decided when it was time to attempt it. Corinne's biological mother and father both died in their transition, as did two older brothers and a couple of cousins.

Given that there were other still-human scions of the Tucci family and that The Master valued male children far more than he valued female ones, it was easy to imagine the worst, that the Gairden blood was so much weaker that they'd paid well to infuse their line with Tucci blood.

Sajia kept her head bowed, knowing there had to be more or she wouldn't be standing before The Master in a roomful of vampires.

"Corinne has a boyfriend? A lover?"

Caution fanned into existence. "I don't know of one."

She suspected a budding romance. Corinne was at the age to

dream of love and a future of her own making rather than accepting the reality of a fate orchestrated for her by The Master.

Let her have this time, Sajia had thought, not pushing for answers these past weeks, and now barely suppressing a shiver at how quickly secrets could turn deadly.

Being *bajaran* meant walking a fine line between loyalty to the individual and loyalty to the family. Betrayal meant death. Or worse. And with vampires, there were so many things worse than death.

Honor, in the style of *omerta*, from the days when humans ruled and mafia families held power, was a thing the vampires embraced as if they'd created the concept.

Perhaps they had. They'd been around since the dawn of creation. Or so she'd been told, though she'd never been allowed into the private libraries. Never read the histories where they were central figures.

"Recently you've spent a great deal of time at the occult shop," The Master said. "Why?"

"Corinne has an interest in such things. I've accompanied her there."

"And taken note of what she's studied?"

"There's been nothing in particular."

"She has not been interested in charms or spells that might conceal her whereabouts?"

Sajia knew then, though she wouldn't have thought there was a spell or charm powerful enough to hide a scion from being tracked by the vampire family she belonged to.

"Corinne is missing," she said, daring to lift her head and meet The Master's eyes because only by doing so could she convey that she was unafraid of what he would find if he seized her mind.

It was a boldness born of desperation. If he answered her challenge and discovered the periods where she blacked out, coming back to herself sometimes in locations she had no memory of going to, she'd die tonight, in this room.

The scorpion-shaped charm at Sajia's neck felt warm against the cold of the moment and the icy precipice she stood on. Her shirt clung to her skin as her nightgown had earlier. And her heart beat furiously against her chest.

They would smell her fear, hear the thundering race of her pulse, but they would also expect it. Though she had nothing to do with Corinne's disappearance, she wouldn't escape punishment because of it. As *bajaran* she was responsible for Corinne's well-being. It remained her duty to know Corinne well enough to anticipate her actions and keep her safe from the impulses and ill-conceived plans of youth.

Like prey transfixed by a serpent's stare, Sajia continued to meet The Master's gaze. A subtle shift, perception rather than true movement, told her the danger of having her mind invaded had passed. Taking a *bajaran*'s oath protected her from it unless there was reason to suspect betrayal. But he was The Master and no one would challenge his actions.

He steepled his hands and rested them on his chest, letting the tension build until it once again became evident that guilt or fear wouldn't compel her to offer additional information. Finally he acknowledged, "Corinne is missing. She was taken to Oakland, though all that remained in the memory of the fisherman who piloted the boat is Corinne's face and a vague recollection of a charm he passed to her before she hid herself under his nets."

At the flexing of The Master's fingers, the wall of vampires near the doorway parted to reveal the naked form of a man. The skin on his face and hands was deeply tanned from spending his days on the water.

It took only a glance for Sajia to know he was dead, drained of blood. The bite marks on his flesh were ragged and unhealed.

He'd been questioned and killed elsewhere. His body washed to rid it of the urine and feces that had come at death, if not before, so as not to offend The Master when the corpse was brought into his presence.

Sajia allowed no pity to show, though she felt a glimmer of it. Only a man driven to desperation would come to San Francisco on business not sanctioned by the vampires. Or a greedy fool.

She looked away from the corpse. Understanding it for the message it was, that it could just as easily be her, or one of her family members.

"With your permission," she said, "I'll leave to begin searching for Corinne."

ADDAI STOOD NAKED on a snowy ledge high in the Sierras. White wings spread out on either side of him as if to catch the howling, frigid wind and use it to lift upward in glorious flight. Long black hair streamed and whipped at his back like a satin cape.

He was impervious to the temperature, uncaring of air traveling fast enough to become a multitude of icy needles. What was cold to a being with origins in the dark of endless space and unfathomable universe? To a being who was the essence of light, born of the essence of power? A favored creation until the one humans named a god decided to breathe life into mud and lay claim to this planet.

And so it had begun.

The defeat of the Djinn who'd called this world theirs.

The birth of envy and betrayal. Of temptation, and lust grown into love.

Lucifer's challenge and the casting out of his followers.

A second angelic fall.

The slaughter of mortal and Djinn wives, of angel-sired children.

Followed by the deluge, a flood to further cleanse the world, though such a cleansing proved an impossible feat.

All of it spanning his existence, though in thousands of years he had become something different than he once was, the reason for the change embodied in a name.

Sajia.

Djinn. Long-ago enemy.

He'd found her drawing water from a village well, her family in the distance, loading trade goods onto camels. He'd meant to kill her first and move on to the others, but instead it was his own sense of purpose that had died in the face of her fear, in the mirror she became as she backed away, water jugs shattering as they fell from trembling fingers, her soul calling to his, weeping and making his own cry at the thought of her loss.

In the desert they'd become lovers, husband and wife. His fear of becoming Fallen had kept him from tying his fate to hers and irrevocably making this world his own.

A fist of pain formed around his heart as he remembered sharing a last, lingering kiss before lifting her onto a camel's back, and how he'd fought the urge to go after her as she rode away with her family, all of them answering the summons of The Prince who ruled them.

He'd turned away, not yet ready to bind himself so thoroughly to her that the gathered Djinn would accept him among them as ally and not enemy. But some part of her spirit already lived in him. He'd felt the moment of her death in a searing blaze of agony that opened a chasm of emptiness in his soul. One that filled with terrible rage and hate when he went to the place where the Djinn had gathered and found Sajia's lifeless body among those of her family members.

With a sweep of snowy wings he shook off the nightmares of the past, forging the emotion they brought with them into formidable determination. After thousands of years she was reborn, and soon she would be returned to him.

Iyar en Batrael, the most powerful Djinn of the Raven House, had gone to the fiery birthplace of his kind and called Sajia's name. Though she would hold no memories of her previous life, it didn't matter to Addai. She was his to love and possess, to forever protect from harm and keep safe even as a new war loomed—one heralding the return of the Djinn from their prison-paradise deep in the ghostlands.

Addai looked down at the chalet built when humans still possessed the technology to achieve such a feat, in the time before what they called The Last War. Then beyond it, at a sweeping vista of desolation.

Not the ruins caused by bombs, but the harsh lands given birth by Earth itself. Rugged, barren mountains covered in snow. And at their base, flatlands where water was scarce and survival a challenge, even in the days when humans ruled the world.

He would bring her here first. He, who could allow a millennium to pass without clothing himself in flesh, who could close his eyes in rest and wake to the dawning of a new era, now counted the hours, the days. Chafed in impatience at the demands of heart and soul to be reunited with Sajia, at the demands of the body to have her beneath him, legs splayed and arms clasping him to her as she welcomed him deep inside her.

His eyelids lowered as images of the past returned. Despite bearing the mark of the Scorpion House on her skin, she'd been so very, very submissive. He had but to walk into the tent and she would kneel before him, naked as he'd demanded she be in the privacy of their quarters.

Head bowed and long tresses a silky curtain flowing over her breasts, she'd been the picture of perfection. She'd enticed him with the feminine line of her spine and the sweet curve of her buttocks, her thighs parted slightly in subtle invitation, in subtle defiance. The sight of her that way never failed to harden him instantly, even when it was one held only in his memory.

Desire coursed through Addai and he took himself in hand. He would bring her here first and tend to her every need himself.

In the future, after they were bound by the incantations of his kind and the spirit-sharing of hers, then if she desired it he would surround her with servants to do her bidding, except in the most private part of their home. There she would wear nothing against her skin and be seen only by him.

He would guard her as he'd been unable to do in their previous life together. Perhaps insist that outside the home she wear *abaya* and *niqāb* so no man could look on her figure or her face and see what was his alone.

Addai's hand tightened around his hardened cock with thoughts of covering Sajia's body with his own. Desire burned through him, fire in veins of ice, scorching heat in a being capable of delivering merciless punishment and eternal agony.

There would be no physical release until Sajia was returned to him. Not with a woman and not by his own hand. Only she would satisfy him. No other.

He let himself imagine their first meeting. It was a favorite fantasy of his.

There'd be fear when she saw him, as there had been before. Instinctual on her part, especially if she'd been raised in this world instead of the Djinn kingdom and hadn't been told she was his reward, the price for his doing the things he'd done on behalf of her kind.

Some part of her would recognize him as her natural enemy even with his wings hidden and his essence wrapped in the flesh of a mortal. But that fear would soon become an erotic one. And the desire to flee would yield to an addiction to the forbidden, to a craving for carnal punishment and complete surrender.

She would soon hasten into his presence, growing wet and ready as she went to her knees before him, hands clasped behind her back, long black hair caressing smooth buttocks as she looked up at him, offering a silent pleading for him to allow her to worship him with her mouth.

A shudder of need went through Addai, a measure of control was lost. The fingers wrapped around his cock moved up and down, delivering pleasure until the psychic touch of the creation bond announced the imminent arrival of one of his brothers.

With a thought Addai clothed himself in black pants, leaving his feet and torso bare. He leapt from the precipice, wings slicing through the wind as though it didn't exist, allowing the cold air to do what his will could not, subdue the hard evidence of desire and hide the nature of his contemplations.

He landed on a snow-covered balcony. An instant later Tir appeared and the reason for his presence became obvious when the Djinn, Irial, materialized next to him. Though they were allied, without Tir to serve as guide, Irial wouldn't easily have found the chalet.

Addai's heart pounded in anticipation at seeing the eldest son and favored messenger of Iyar en Batrael. Every muscle tightened as pride warred with the desperate desire to ask the question never far from his mind. *Where is she?*

Irial wore the mark of the Raven House on his cheek like a stylized tattoo. Wings and talons outstretched, the bird was a symbol of what Irial and those like him were capable of—guiding a Djinn soul back for rebirth.

The snow melted beneath Irial's feet in a slowly widening circle, a showy reminder that the Djinn were creatures of fire. Wicked amusement danced in the Raven prince's eyes like a wild flame set in the midst of a green forest, setting Addai's teeth on edge and making him struggle against lifting his hand and calling his sword from its sheath of air and hidden reality.

Irial's teeth flashed white in his deeply tanned face, goading Addai, daring him to break the silence and ask what message he'd brought.

"Tell me," Addai said, willing to cede that much of a victory to Irial, satisfied in knowing the prince of the Raven House would one day be brought to his knees by a match arranged for him to serve the purpose of seeing the Djinn returned to Earth.

"My father sends word. He wants you to know the reward promised is now yours to claim. He says you will recognize it when you see it, but cautions you to remember all things are part of the weave, including this."

"Where?" Addai asked, refusing to name Sajia *it* or to reveal her existence to either Irial or Tir.

"Your prize is in San Francisco. Or will be shortly. In the occult shop protected by the Tassone sigil."

TWO

Sajia girded herself to approach the threshold of the occult shop. No other description of the effort fit as well.

It'd been like this from the very first visit she'd made with Corinne. Not just a sensitivity to magic, but a deep aversion to it.

Sweat ran down her back. And already her stomach roiled, leaving her fighting to suppress a violent spew of vomit, as if her soul would flee any way it could.

She smoothed slick palms over her pants and forced herself forward.

A step.

Two.

Her lungs constricted, as if squeezed by a giant fist to force the air out. She barely stifled a gasp. Another step and the Tassone mark was clearly visible, etched in the glass next to the door: a serpent with an apple in its mouth, the three segments of its S-shaped body impaled by an arrow that ran from a point behind the head to just before the tip of its tail.

Unlike in Oakland, the city across the bay, there were no bars covering the glass, no shutters of solid wood or steel to keep someone from breaking in during the day, or guard against the things that roamed the night. The Tassone symbol alone was enough protection.

Sajia resisted the urge to touch the knives she wore at her hips. Except in practice she'd never had to pull them since becoming *bajaran*. The recently carved symbols on her arm served as a deterrent to trouble.

She wondered if that would remain true when she crossed to Oakland. Unlike San Francisco, that city was controlled by humans, many of whom would gladly rid the world of anything touched by the supernatural.

Those humans with gifts were required to live in a certain area of town, outside of the one patrolled by guardsmen and police. Their houses were marked, identifying the nature of their talents.

Beyond the area set aside for them lay the red zone, a place where vice thrived and the lords who controlled it enforced their own set of laws. Brothels lined the streets, human as well as the ones housing shapeshifters not welcome in the lands controlled by the Were. Gambling clubs and opium dens were common, as were private gathering places where humans could indulge in whatever amused them.

Oakland was a port city. But even without the visiting sailors and merchants, there was plenty of business for the red zone. And that's where Sajia feared she'd find Corinne. She couldn't imagine one of the gifted sheltering a vampire scion, or one of the law-abiding.

Given the fisherman's corpse, she didn't think she'd find Corinne's trail by going to the docks. Which left the occult shop as a starting point.

Forcing air into lungs that fought against expanding sent a spasm of pain through Sajia's chest as she opened the door and stepped into the shop. It smelled of books and incense, scents she usually found pleasing, relaxing.

Not today. And never here.

She made her way to the counter. The man behind it looked up at her approach.

He was a stranger to her, gray-skinned and balding, cadaverous in appearance. His fingertips and lips blackened from ink.

Choice stood in front of her. Honor played a role in vampire society, and with it came the concept of saving face.

She could ask about Corinne directly, inquiring as to what, if anything, he might have seen while her charge was in the shop. The scarring on her arm gave her the right to those answers. Or she could ask about the token, hoping that finding its source might lead to where Corinne was hiding. She couldn't do both.

If she survived this and found Corinne unharmed from her adventure, she'd prefer not to suffer additional punishment because she'd confirmed, by use of a name, that a scion had slipped away from the Tucci estate, in all likelihood because of a betrothal.

Sajia chose the latter, and though she'd been raised in a vampire-controlled city, the word *master* still tasted vile on her tongue. She forced herself to use it anyway, to evoke what courtesy might be extended to the Tucci family.

"I'm inquiring on behalf of one of my masters," she said, "trying to find out the name of someone skilled enough in the use of magic to create a token allowing a human with blood obligations to hide."

The clerk's lips pulled back. Smile or grimace or show of distaste, it tightened his skin and accentuated the shape of his skull. "Visit the Wainwright witches for that answer. You'll find them in Oakland. But be prepared to pay for the information. Nothing comes without cost where they're concerned."

Sajia thanked him and turned away from the counter just as a man entered the shop. At the sight of him her heart flip-flopped in her chest, seeming to stop and then race forward in wild abandon, torn between fear and desire.

He was mesmerizing. The face of a god—

Or a fallen angel like those painted on canvas, created in the imaginations of artists who'd lived well before mankind developed the technology to destroy the world.

Black hair and equally black irises. Carved perfection and carnal sin.

She wet her lips without being aware of it until his gaze dropped to them, hungry and fierce and commanding.

"Sajia," he said, her name turned into a caress, into images of naked bodies stretched out on silky sheets, lips and hands exploring without inhibition, mesmerizing her until she forced the erotic pictures from her mind.

How he knew her name, she didn't know. But unless he'd been sent by The Master to assist her, she had no time for him.

He blocked her exit, leaving her no choice other than to approach him. Sajia stepped forward, fear and desire both trying to cloud her thoughts and narrow her reality until it contained only him.

The rush of emotion nearly drove Addai to his knees. Thousands of years hadn't prepared him for the reality of this moment.

Sajia. It was as though she'd stepped out of the past, her form and face exactly as he remembered them, her soul calling to his in haunting song and the promise of ecstasy.

How the Djinn had managed it, he didn't know and didn't care. All that mattered was that she'd been returned to him.

Despite his fantasies of their first meeting, he felt no disappointment at the quick pass of fear from her eyes. The desire he saw in her expression, and sensed like a heated stroke along the length of his body, more than satisfied him.

His thoughts flashed ahead, mentally enfolding her in arms and wings and willing them to the mountain home he'd prepared for her. He reached out, expecting her to take his hand. "Come."

Denial flashed through her eyes, exciting him until fantasy and reality collided with a single question. "Did The Master send you?"

A blink. A full opening of his senses and Addai recoiled in horror. She was human. Worse if the purposeful scarring of her arm read true. A servant bound to vampires.

Rage whipped through him at the betrayal—the same black abyss of fury that had once led him to send his brother into a slavery lasting thousands of years. And yet even in his fury, desire overrode revulsion and the call of her spirit to his had him grabbing her bare wrist and jerking her closer.

She reacted instantly, drawing a knife he hadn't bothered noting and pressing it to his belly as if she'd gut him where he stood. His cock responded with a hard throb. His body accepting, craving her even as his mind rebelled.

The blade tip slid through the thin shirt he'd willed into existence, breaking skin. And the release of his blood undid a masking spell, revealed the ice blue sigils scrawled across her forehead like a thorn crown, and around her wrists like manacles. Angelic symbols of binding not visible to any mortal. A script placed there by one of his kind, the power necessary to turn flesh into a living prison the telltale signature of only one ally working with the Djinn.

Addai's heart sang. She wasn't human as he'd thought seconds before, but Djinn trapped in a human form, returned to him as promised.

His eyes noted it then, the thin, tight chain worn around her neck like a collar. Sigils etched into the gold and holding knowledge he could only guess at, the pendant, scorpion shaped. The mark of her Djinn House and symbol of a protector. The identification of her soul's nature.

"Release me," she said.

Never. But he held the words and complied only so he could better take her measure.

"Did The Master send you?" she asked again.

He fought the pulling back of his lips in a savage smile promising retribution. She would call no one else *master*. Only him.

Addai glanced at the scarring on her arm and recognized the sigil as a farmer recognizes a dung beetle before stepping on it. Tucci.

Not allies.

Yet, the voice of reason managing to suppress his urge to kill.

If he was to achieve his goal, seeing the return of the Djinn and the control of this world taken so he could live openly with Sajia and know their children would be safe, then he couldn't afford war on another front, especially with vampires.

Addai suppressed a curse as the message delivered by Irial, the reminder from Iyar en Batrael that all things were part of the weave, took on new meaning.

Sajia would be a foundling placed in the world. Delivered into the hands of humans and her reality shaped by them, her loyalty given to them—and worse, to a vampire scion.

"I'm here for you," he said, an ambiguous answer.

She frowned in response but drew the knife away from his skin. His testicles pulled tight in protest at the loss of contact, in anticipation of reclaiming it.

Once fear had served as challenge and erotic excitement. But now he found implied violence had the same effect.

She would submit. She would find pleasure in calling him master.

"Shall we go?" he asked, eyes flicking in the direction of the counter and the man behind it.

She sheathed the knife. "Yes."

They left the shop and though she tried to hide her weakness, he was so finely attuned to her that he caught the sigh of relief and the subtle relaxing of her body. Magic of the kind found in the occult shop was anathema to the Djinn. Few could work it, and many found it sickening to be in its presence.

A few steps away she stopped and turned to him, hands resting on the hilts of her knives.

He smiled in challenge, daring her to pull them from their sheaths.

"Has Corinne been found?"

Addai made the connection immediately, between the question and Sajia's position as *bajaran*. His smile faded to a frown, and his amusement flashed to irritation at seeing an inevitable delay before he could take her to his bed.

"No."

"Then why am I being summoned back to the estate?"

"Did I say as much? I said only that I am here for you. And I am. Did you discover anything useful at the shop?"

"I've never seen you before."

He shrugged. "I am Addai."

"I don't know that name. Prove you serve the Tuccis."

His smile returned, as sharp as one of her knives. He'd spent no time among the Tucci, but it was his business to know the lineage of all the vampire families in San Francisco. Even without the prospect of alliance, he would have gathered the information. Like the Djinn, vampires were natural enemies, but unlike the Djinn, the origin of their conflict began elsewhere, on a long-dead planet light-years away.

Dismissing the threat of Sajia's weapons, Addai placed his hands on her waist to prevent her from taking a step backward. It was torment and paradise at the same time to feel her beneath his palms.

He leaned forward, mouth drawing close to hers as if to share a secret, though his intent was to claim a taste of what belonged to him. "Sajia," he whispered, touching his lips to hers, sharing breath and life and spirit, as was the Djinn way, as had been their way so many thousands of years ago.

She resisted, clamping her jaw shut and firming her mouth against his invasion. Had she remembered him, she would have known denying him was a dangerous game.

One of his hands settled on her back and forced her forward, flush against his body. The other slid upward, covering her breast possessively.

"Fight all you want," he murmured against her mouth, the hand at her breast leaving to grasp her long braid, wrapping it around fingers and wrist, a taut leash preventing her from moving her head. "It will only make my victory sweeter and your surrender more satisfying."

She started to pull her knives and he laughed, the hand on her back sliding lower, caressing her buttocks, holding her in place as he ground against her mound, against the clit he knew would be swollen and erect given the heady scent of feminine arousal that filled his nostrils.

A small moan signaled her yielding and he took advantage of it, thrusting his tongue into her mouth in an unbridled claiming.

Desire nearly overrode restraint as she responded, twining her tongue with his, rubbing. Meeting thrust for thrust in a challenge that could only end one way, with his cock deep in her body, stretching her, filling her in shared pleasure and the release of seed.

The air around them shimmered. The will keeping him human in appearance threatened to give way in the spread of wings and radiance.

Only a small sliver of rational thought kept him from doing it. There were too many people present on the street and no way to strip the memory of what they'd seen from all of their minds, when leaving it risked that one of his kind would stumble upon the image and know of Sajia.

It was agony to end the kiss. Addai managed it only by telling himself that soon she'd be home, naked in the place he'd had built for them.

She would know the truth of what she was to him then. Wife. Mate.

His in every way.

Only his.

"You want proof," he said, forced to pragmatism by the presence of so many witnesses. Returning to her earlier question so they could get done with this business of looking for her missing charge rather than waste time doing battle over it. "Ask me something about the Tucci, something only a human well acquainted with them would know."

"Name the youngest, and the most recently transformed vampire of the Tucci line."

Addai laughed. "Ah, a trick question given the majority of scions die during their transformation and a great number of those passed off as Tucci descendants are favored humans with no genetic link. To hedge my bets I'll give you three names to prove I know the different ways your question might be answered. Demas is the most recent addition to the Tucci family, though he is not a true descendant regardless of claims to the contrary. Euan is related by blood and the youngest if measured in total years of existence, while Ilario, who survived the change five years ago, is older chronologically but the most recently transformed vampire bearing Tucci genes. Satisfied?"

"Yes."

"Good. Then let's be on our way. What did you intend after leaving here?"

"To go to Oakland. That's where I believe Corinne is. If I can find out who made the token hiding her from the Tuccis, it might lead me to her. The clerk suggested I visit the Wainwright witches for answers. They're my first stop."

"Excellent," Addai said, pleasure purring through him at the mention of an ally powerful enough to speed this nuisance business of a missing vampire scion to its conclusion.

Sajia escaped Addai's arms and hurried toward the car she'd taken from the Tucci estate, and Mario, the driver who was both friend and family member. With each step she told herself she couldn't afford to be distracted or delayed. But even as she hastened to put as much distance as possible between herself and Addai, traitorous heat curled through her with the remembered imprint of his body to hers and the intensity of the desire that had poured into her with his touch.

Mario stood next to the back door, waiting to open it for her. He was stiffly formal in his uniform, the lines of his face smooth in an attempt to avoid any expression, though she saw the worry in his eyes. Guessed he recognized Addai and wanted to warn her against involvement with him—not just for her sake, but for all of theirs.

If not for Addai, she would have opened the door for herself and climbed into the front seat. Mario's sister was married to one of her cousins, and expecting a child.

Sajia got into the back, Addai sliding in next to her, crowding her, making it difficult to think about anything else but him. Any lingering doubt about his belonging to the Tuccis was banished by how quickly Mario obeyed Addai's command, delivering them to the area set aside for the gifted then departing afterward rather than wait.

At first sight of the witches' home Sajia nearly balked at going any farther. It sat squat and dark, windows glistening as the sunlight struck them, like malevolent eyes looking out on the world. The hair rose on her arms and neck, and she wondered if she'd feel the same nearly unbearable sensations that she had experienced when she entered the occult shop.

Her mouth went dry. The clerk's words about the cost of dealing with the witches whispered through her mind in ominous warning.

Looking at their house, the sigil-inscribed doorway with its gargoyle-head knocker, the wrought iron fence with its etched warnings, she could well believe anything to be found here entailed a great deal of peril. Danger not just in the form of death, but to the soul.

She glanced at the man next to her. Addai. His name resonated through her in a way that made no sense, as if some part of her recognized him and was determined to have him, regardless of the turmoil, the uncertainty caused by Corinne's disappearance.

A shiver slid through Sajia, and it had nothing to do with the prospect of entering a place where magic was practiced. Her nipples pressed against the thin material of her shirt, and her channel clenched in hungry need.

She was no virgin, but she'd never had a lover like him. A man who would make the most physically attractive of the vampires appear plain, and the most powerful of them seem less than equal.

Confidence poured off Addai along with waves of heated sensuality. It seemed inconceivable that another vampire family, especially the Tassone, hadn't claimed him first with promises of immense power and wealth and immortality.

She shied away from thinking about him risking the transition and not surviving it. He turned then, sensing her eyes on him. His smile sent her heart tripping. His gaze as it moved over her face in slow appreciation then downward to her breasts, had her struggling to breathe normally.

He laughed, a husky erotic sound that wound its way through her. Leaning in, he said, "There is nothing about you that escapes my notice. It pleases me to know you are as aroused in my presence as I am in yours."

Sajia forced her attention back to the witches' house, angry at herself for being distracted by him, for thinking about anything other than finding Corinne. For all she knew Addai had been sent to test both her resolve and her loyalty to her charge, to report back how diligently she carried out her responsibility, perhaps even to suggest to what extent she should suffer for her failures.

She took a step forward, determined to succeed. Closed her mind to worries about what the witches might ask in return for their aid.

Addai's hand curled possessively around her upper arm. "No harm will come to you here," he said, swinging open the gate and ushering her through the opening.

Stepping into the witches' territory was like pushing through an unseen curtain of gossamer. It left the impression of clinging, invisible strands and made Sajia want to brush herself off.

At the door, Addai lifted the knocker, a brass ring held in the mouth of a gargoyle. Only a moment passed before his summons was answered by a handsome woman with a streak of silver along the part of black hair.

"Addai," the witch said, and Sajia felt a surge of hope and relief. She wondered then if he'd been sent because The Master guessed this search would ultimately involve the Wainwright witches, and saved face by sending aid without the others knowing of it, since she had no power to negotiate on behalf of the Tuccis.

"I'm sure our appearance here is no surprise, Annalise," Addai said, pitching his voice to hold a warning the witch couldn't fail to hear in her mind and feel in her soul. Whatever power she held here on Earth, she was still human, and he, a being whose reach extended into the spiritlands. He'd played his part toward the return of the Djinn and the battle for control of this world that loomed, and would continue to play it, but there would be no interference, no further payment, not where Sajia was concerned.

He had no intention of allowing either witches or Djinn to draw Sajia into their web of intrigue and destiny. He was her destiny. She needed no other.

The witch showed no signs of fear. He didn't expect it.

"This way," Annalise said, turning and preceding them down the hallway. "You are correct. The matriarch anticipated your visit. It is fortuitous you came here sooner rather than later."

Sajia's curiosity brushed against Addai's senses. And though this delay irritated him, it wasn't without its compensations. He found himself enjoying the heated glances she cast in his direction when she thought he wasn't looking, savoring the build of heat and anticipation, the exquisite agony of being near her but not yet inside her.

The matriarch waited in the parlor, a shrunken hull of flesh and bones dressed in black. An abomination of spirit that had him fighting the urge to call his sword even knowing that delivering physical death would free neither the Djinn nor the human soul now entangled and tethered to this life in a single frail body.

He guided Sajia to a small couch across from the matriarch. Filmy, opaque eyes settled on them as they sat, sightless from cataracts, though the witch hadn't needed them to see in a long time.

"What do you know of Sajia's missing charge?" he asked.

The witch's attention shifted to Sajia. "So the rumors of the missing Tucci scion are true."

"Yes," Sajia answered. "Corinne was last seen getting on a boat. The fisherman piloting it brought her to Oakland after first giving her a charm capable of hiding her trail from The Master. But the man had no memory of who hired him or what happened afterward."

"And now he is dead, drained of information and blood," the matriarch said matter-of-factly. "Beyond your reach unless you ask the shamaness Aisling to bargain in the ghostlands. Though someone capable of creating such a token, and leaving no memory of themselves, probably has allies in the spiritlands and the ability to ensure nothing useful would be learned from the fisherman."

"Do you know who would be capable of crafting such a spell and attaching it to a token?" Sajia asked.

"Besides those of my family? Yes. Maliq. He makes his home in the red zone and is known for his willingness to work even the darkest of magic if his price is met."

The white-moon eyes returned to Addai, craterless orbs bringing a sense of foreboding. "It wouldn't surprise me in the least to learn Maliq created the token, but if you're successful in finding him, I think it's likely you'll discover he's the pawn of another. I've heard your brother has turned his attention to the vampires and amuses himself by trying to set one family against another."

Every muscle in Addai's body went taut at the mention of his brother. He had scores of them, some allies and some enemies. But like a bored human schoolboy left alone on the playground and desperate to draw a favored companion back, only one brother passed his time with games in the way the matriarch alluded to.

Caphriel. Angel of the final apocalypse, as he himself had once been. Sharing purpose though their ways of delivering it differed, sharing a name that regardless of translation was always the same: Death.

Addai rose to his feet in a fluid movement of suppressed violence. Resolve pounded through him with each heartbeat, beginning and ending with one word. *Sajia*. With one thought. *Take her to the chalet and keep her there, away from games involving vampires and safe from discovery by Caphriel.*

He pulled Sajia from the couch, arms locking her to him.

She struggled, pushing and squirming, but against his strength she had no chance of escape.

"Cast a circle," he told the matriarch. "Let one of the others engage Caphriel if this Tucci scion is of any importance. Sajia's involvement with vampires is ended."

A word from the old witch and a circle flared into existence, a writhing ring of power that would mask the unleashing of his own.

Addai relaxed his will and all semblance of being human fell away.

White wings spread out behind him, glorious light shimmering and bent into a physical form.

He enfolded Sajia in them, a brush of feathers against cloth and skin. And with a thought, he took her home.

THREE

Shocked disbelief held Sajia motionless. Her mind argued against the reality of Addai being an angel, a creature of myth and imagination, of his taking her from the witches' house between one heartbeat and the next. She trembled, imprisoned and unresisting in steely arms and feathered wings until his last words, and the witch's, arrowed their way into her consciousness, slicing through all other emotion and bringing with them a terrible fear, not just at the fate awaiting her family if she abandoned her oath, but that Corinne might be in danger instead of hiding.

Sajia struggled, pushing against Addai's now-bare chest and trying desperately to get her hands free so she could grasp her knives.

His lips against her hair, he held her easily, as if her fight to get free barely registered and required little of his strength to subdue. "You have nothing to fear from me."

"Then let me go," she said, the words a repeat of what she'd told him in the occult shop.

His laugh was dark, possessive. "Never. But I will free you to look at your new home."

She chilled as soft feathers fell away and he stepped back, leaving her standing in cool air and elegant splendor, in a room housing treasures older than any she'd seen in the Tucci estate.

Floor-to-ceiling windows defied the elements, daring them to rail against a structure that shouldn't exist. Allowing for a view that drew her forward with its majesty, its harsh testament to the power of nature, snow-covered mountains and the near desert at their feet.

The sight made her breath catch, not just at the beauty but at how far they must be from San Francisco. "Where are we?"

"In the Sierras."

Panic seized her. It was a fist around her heart that squeezed mercilessly, spearing pain through her chest and making her breathing erratic. "Take me back."

"No."

He prowled forward, a sensual menace reflected in the windows. She pulled her knives then, whirling to meet him.

"Why?" she asked, the question meant to encompass the entirety of his actions.

"Because you belong to me."

It was said with complete belief. And though it galled her to consider herself property that could be passed on to another, she denied his claim. "The Master didn't give me to you. He wouldn't as long as Corinne is missing."

Addai's smile held the promise of death. "Think of any other male as your master and I will slay him."

He lifted his hand and it was as if a tear appeared in reality, a sheath of air and light from which he drew a sword.

Cold menace radiated from both man and blade. In reaction her fists tightened around the hilts of her knives as she prepared to duck and lunge.

His smile became a snarl. "Do not fear that I will use my sword on you, Sajia. I would die before I let any harm come to you."

His voice rang with truth, stunning her. Confusing her even as an insidious warmth spiraled through her. Desire reawakened. Awe that he could want her, care about her to such an extreme.

With the flick of his wrist the sword disappeared. He stepped forward, uncaring and unafraid of the blades she held. She stepped back, unwilling and unable to attack until he answered her.

His wings spread out behind him, bars of a feather-soft cage. His hands reached, but rather than try to disarm her, they settled against the glass behind her, trapping her at the expense of leaving himself vulnerable.

A dare? No. The arrogant curve of his lips spoke of utter confidence.

For a split second she was tempted to draw blood as she had in the occult shop. "Why me?" Sajia repeated.

Addai wanted to dismiss the question as easily as he'd dismissed the fate of the Tucci scion. Desire rode him and restraint threatened to fall away now that he had Sajia alone.

His earlier pragmatism and willingness to linger in Oakland were gone, washed away by hot lust and insatiable craving. Thousands of years of waiting had him nearly shaking with the need to have her lying beneath him, her bare skin and curves pressed to him, her legs open and her body welcoming his.

His gaze flicked to the scorpion-shaped pendant and he decided to answer the question, to tell her the truth, though not all of it. There would be time to tell her she wasn't human. To unravel the angelic spell glowing in ice blue script on her flesh, to free her from it so she would be fully Djinn.

Once she'd been *mārdazmā*, able to change into another shape, though without a non-corporeal form. The need to bind her to a human form suggested that reborn she could shapeshift, though she might well have a higher caste's ability to become little more than unseen particles.

Until he had her heart, her loyalty, her love, he couldn't risk her knowing she had the ability to leave him, perhaps escape his reach altogether by discovering how to cross from this world to the Djinn kingdom deep in the ghostlands.

He dropped his hand from the window to cup her cheek, marveling at the heat of her skin, the features so perfectly re-created, so well loved and so often dreamed of. He stroked his thumb over soft, trembling lips. "I would die before I let any harm come to you because once you were my lover, my wife. I failed you in that life, and because of it you were killed, slain by my kind. I won't fail you in this life, Sajia."

Denial screamed through Sajia. What he claimed was impossible.

Yet on the heels of that came doubt. Before mankind had nearly destroyed the world, vampires and Weres were a thing of fiction and dark fantasy, and the ghostlands called Purgatory or Sheol, or something else depending on culture and belief. From the moment she'd first encountered Addai his name had resonated through her in a way that made no sense, as if some part of her recognized him and was determined to have him, regardless of the urgent need to find Corinne.

Corinne's name was like a knife paring away everything unimportant. The past had no relevance, not now or in the immediate future.

"It doesn't matter," she said, ill-conceived words she regretted the instant she saw Addai's features tighten into a ruthless expression.

Hurriedly she tried to undo the damage and steer him toward reason. "I have no memories of our life together. Without them I'm not the same woman you knew."

He crowded closer, wings pulling in and forward so they touched her arms in an erotic, feathery caress, a cocoon of sensual heat. His thumb brushed over her bottom lip again, sending a fresh wave of tingling desire downward through her body.

"We will make new memories, Sajia."

Heat pooled in her belly and breasts. She couldn't deny the desire she felt, doubted she could resist the temptation he posed, the allure of becoming his lover. But neither could she turn her back on her responsibilities, knowing what the cost of it would be.

"Then let the new memories begin with our finding Corinne."

"No. One of the others will see to the task."

His face lowered and she turned her head, avoiding the touch of his lips to hers. "Any help you're willing to give or can arrange is appreciated, but I need to search as well. The Mas—"

Addai's teeth closed on her earlobe in warning, a sharp bite that aroused rather than frightened, though the words following it were whispered menace. "I won't issue another warning. Think of yourself as belonging to anyone else and you sign their death warrant. Your days of being around vampires are over. The marks on your arm will soon be gone and nothing will remain of your time with them."

"No," she said, fear making her pulse beat wildly in her throat, freeing her from the sexual thrall his presence evoked. "No. Even if Corinne is found by someone else, I took an oath. If I fail in my duties, then the punishment is mine alone. But if I betray the Tuccis or run away, then my family will pay for my transgressions."

"I will see that your family is taken to another city and given everything they need to survive in it."

"They have ties in San Francisco, lives there. Obligations to the vampires that aren't easily set aside. And even if they did leave, can you guarantee their safety if I break my oath?"

She knew he couldn't. Vampires were capable of pursuing vengeance over centuries. Some said their reach extended into the afterlife itself.

"As much as any human life can be safeguarded," Addai said. "A blink of an eye in the span of eternity and millions of them are born, grow old, and pass from this world. Those you call family will die, Sajia, regardless of where they live. I won't allow any chance of death taking you, not again. You are mine. You will remain here, out of danger."

Cold truth and implacable will, his voice held no compassion, nothing other than resolve delivering a fate she couldn't accept. A part of her wept even as she used the knives still in her hands, stabbed him in desperate reaction.

He danced backward rather than subduing and disarming her.

Eyes glittered as blood streamed downward over perfect flesh. "If you remembered me, Sajia, then you would know this will only serve as foreplay."

She crouched and moved sideways, away from the window, adrenaline spiking through her. Rational thought dominating in spite of the panic and fear.

Her only hope lay in changing his mind, not in defeating him physically. Only by demonstrating her determination and taking advantage of his earlier confession could she achieve it.

I would die before I let any harm come to you.

He came after her, arms held loosely at his sides and expression arrogant. Telling her without words that he didn't need to call the sword he'd shown her earlier in order to defeat her.

"Surrender now, Sajia, and the penalty will be minimal. An early lesson in submission rather than the freedom to explore your new home I thought to allow while we became reacquainted."

She didn't respond to the taunt, didn't back down when he lunged. She swung and missed, but the force of it conveyed the seriousness of her intent.

He laughed then feinted, playing with her, maneuvering her around the room. The wounds she'd inflicted with her knives had already healed, leaving only smears of blood over smooth skin.

She used the time to study her surroundings, looking for weapons and ways to escape.

Foreplay, he'd said, and she could see the truth of it. The front of his pants was tented by his hardened cock. His voice held no less evidence of arousal as he regaled her with what her lesson in submission would entail.

Kneeling naked and head bowed.

Remaining motionless and waiting for his touches as he spread them out, teaching her to crave them.

Hurrying to the bed when he finally ordered it and eagerly positioning herself so he could bind her wrists and ankles to the posts. in symbolic acknowledgment of her total surrender.

Sajia found it too easy to imagine. He was sculpted perfection, a dark angel of carnal sin.

She couldn't tell whether her traitorous heart beat more rapidly in anticipation of it or in fear of not being able to convince him of the need to return to Oakland.

He was in no hurry to catch her. If anything, he seemed to delight in the flex of his muscles, the folding and unfolding of his wings until she was driven to say, "You remind me of a male peacock."

"An apt though perhaps unflattering description, for you are definitely the mate I intend to impress with my prowess. Put down your puny knives and after a suitable length of punishment I'll let you handle something far more interesting."

It was impossible not to laugh. She had no personal fear of him. How could she when desire coursed through her and she knew he would never hurt her?

But that didn't diminish the tightness in her chest when her thoughts went to the fate of her family and her need to find Corinne. It didn't lessen her resolve to return to Oakland.

Arrogant confidence made Addai careless. On their fourth circling pass around the living room, Sajia drifted backward, toward a door leading to a railless balcony she imagined served as a landing place when Addai chose to use his wings to fly rather than preen. As he'd stalked her, she'd been able to catch glimpses of what lay beneath and on either side of it, had discovered the house wasn't perched on a sheer cliff, though the terrain below the balcony was steep and covered in rock and snow.

She'd mentally rehearsed her movements like a well-choreographed fight. There would be only one chance at victory.

A feint, as if she intended to make a running attack, had Addai backing up, hands beckoning, a come-and-get-me expression in place. If the stakes hadn't been so high, she might well have answered him, determined to wipe the smug confidence from his face. Instead, she reached around her, opening the door and escaping the room.

The cold took her breath. It bit into her skin, battering against her in icy blasts until the urgency of her situation allowed her to block it out.

She moved to the balcony's edge. Positioning herself close enough to jump and stand a chance of managing a handhold instead of hurtling downward in a bone-breaking rush that would only be interrupted if Addai took flight.

Addai followed, the amusement gone from his face and replaced by a terrible beauty. *Enough*, he said, lips that could call for adoration or herald damnation remaining closed as he spoke into her mind, demanded, *Come to me.*

Every cell in her body responded, trying to force her forward. His will was a cold lash of a whip across her soul, a thing of finely honed edges, carving away her own.

Come to me, he repeated, exerting more of his power.

She fought summons with summons, calling up the faces of her family members and seeing them being drained of blood, their bodies hung from the walls of the Tucci estate as a reminder to every human in San Francisco of the price to be paid for betraying an oath given to vampires. Calling up the image of Corinne and knowing she'd failed her.

The pendant Sajia wore grew hot, as if unseen, the parents who'd died in a fire aided her. Her skin burned where the scorpion lay against it, and the pain helped achieve what horrific imaginings alone couldn't; it drove the sound of Addai's voice from her mind.

He moved forward then, his expression ruthless, very nearly cruel. "Enough, Sajia. You won't escape. Even if you are so foolish as to jump, I'll merely retrieve you. What injuries you sustain can be easily healed. And tied to my bed you will soon forget why you ever wanted to leave."

"If forgetting my family and my charge and my oath were that easy, I would be in your arms now."

She took a small step backward, so she stood like a swimmer at the end of a diving board, with only the balls of her feet and toes keeping her on solid ground. "You might stop me this time, but what about the next? And the one after that? I would rather die attempting to get back to Oakland than live knowing I lay with you, finding pleasure while my family experienced only fear and suffering and death. Will you keep me a prisoner for all eternity, or end up killing me yourself when I grow to loathe you as much as I will myself?"

Her words encased Addai in ice. How well he knew the power hate and rage could wield. Standing among carnage and seeing her lifeless body had once filled him with those emotions. And what he'd done in the wake of her death made a vampire's retribution seem merciful in comparison.

His gaze went to the pendant and he cursed it, guessing that it and it alone had thwarted his attempts to use his mind and his voice to bend her to his will. She was human in form, human in belief, and with that first breath forced into clay at the dawn of their creation, they'd inhaled a susceptibility to angelic influence.

Addai's soul and body, heart and mind all screamed in protest at the thought of giving in to her demands. He would slaughter every Tucci, the scion Corinne included, if it meant Sajia would come to his bed willingly and accept the sheltered life he intended for her.

A primal scream welled up inside him, male frustration and the anguish of conflicting needs—to keep her safe from danger, yet find the scion and bargain with the Tuccis for Sajia's release from her oath so they'd never again return to this argument.

The muscles of his arms stood out as he kept himself from lifting them. Were he not standing on the balcony of the home he'd had built for her, he would have raised a hand to the sky and brought forth a sword of retribution, using it to call down lightning and reduce the chalet to rubble and smoldering ash.

He would not leave Sajia here unguarded. Nor did he want to leave her with anyone else. She was too precious, too long away from him to bear parting from again, even temporarily.

"Promise you will not leave me to go off hunting on your own," he said, as close to an admission of defeat as he was willing to give.

"Promise that you will obey if danger arises and I give you a command." A salve to his pride.

The capitulation cost him. It wasn't visible in his face or his voice or in the lines of his rigidly held body, but Sajia knew it regardless.

She moved from her precarious position at the balcony edge before a gust of wind could take her over. Closed the distance between them, willing to lessen the torment her victory caused him. *Needing to* with a depth that hinted at what they'd once been to each other, husband and wife.

It seemed natural to step into his arms, to spear her fingers into black hair as she lifted her face for his kiss. She welcomed the press of his body to hers and thrilled at the feel of his thick erection, the security of steel-muscled arms and feather-soft wings as he wrapped her in a sensual embrace.

"Promise," he said, a command ringing in her ears and mind.

"I do."

He claimed victory in defeat, his lips taking hers aggressively, his tongue thrusting into her mouth, giving no quarter as he overwhelmed her with sensation. *Mine*, his kiss claimed, and in that instant she couldn't fight it, couldn't deny it.

Heat poured into her, the clash of wills forgotten as lust coursed through her veins like lava running down a mountainside, scorching and consuming everything in its path.

Need didn't accurately define what she felt. Even *lust* was too tame a word.

A moan escaped and the sound fed his hunger. Arms and wings tightened around her. Carnal images flooded her mind, scenes of them together, his memories or her own pulled from the depths of her subconscious, she couldn't be sure, only that they made her shiver and crave the feel of naked skin to naked skin, hunger to have his body joined to hers.

She whimpered when his lips left hers, a protest against the loss of them. His eyes glittered, his features once again arrogant and commanding. "Do you still wish to leave our home, Sajia?"

"Yes," she said, despite the desperate ache of desire.

"Then we will go to the red zone. But rather than looking for the man who made the charm and trying to bargain with him for his client's name, there's a better way to locate the scion."

"How?"

She wouldn't have thought Addai could appear more dangerous than she'd already seen him, more hardened and ruthless and forbidding, but whatever he had in mind made it so.

After a long pause, he said, "I know of a Finder, but getting access to her will require dealing with the vice lord Rimmon. He's not quite my enemy, though neither is he an ally."

Addai's hand once again cupped her cheek, his thumb rubbing over lips swollen from their kiss. "We'll go to him, but only if you let me handle the negotiations, Sajia."

His voice held no possibility of compromise. She acquiesced with a nod. "Where will he be?"

"His club." Addai's sharp smile returned. "He calls it Temptation."

FOUR

Temptation. The club stood with the other Victorians on a street lined with them. Sajia knew of them, of course. But even if she hadn't, their nature and the kinds of people drawn to them were revealed in names like *Sinners* and *Greed* and *Envy.*

Bouncers guarded their entrances. Some of the clubs were member-only, reserved for the elite and wealthy, while others served a broader public. The vices they catered to varied, but all of them closed at dark, locking their patrons in for the night.

Vampires hunted these streets after the sun set. As did Weres and feral dogs, ghouls and any number of supernatural beings.

Her attention returned to the immaculately restored home in front of her. Even in the days before The Last War, this would have belonged to someone wealthy, someone with the money and inclination to preserve a historical building designed by a famous architect.

Unlike the thick-necked men in leather or jeans who guarded the entrances of the other clubs, the men on either side of the door-way here wore expensive suits. They looked like elegant gentlemen, though Sajia didn't doubt for a moment that they were armed and very, very deadly.

"Will we be able to get in to see Rimmon?" she asked.

Addai laughed, his hand moving from its possessive grip on her upper arm to settle at the center of her back like a heated brand. "Of course."

He urged her forward with a stroke to her spine. "Don't forget your promise, beloved. Allow me to handle things here, and regardless of any perceived danger, keep your knives sheathed. A threat of harm to you and it would be nothing for me to slaughter everyone in the club if that's what it took to assure myself you were safe."

Heat flowed through her, mixed equally with icy fear. She glanced at his face with its stunning beauty, savored the endearment and the depth of his feelings even as spikes of primal terror skittered through her at having such a ruthless, powerful being lay claim to her.

The bouncers remained on either side of the doors until she and Addai were nearly at the entrance. Then they each took a step, as though they would block them from entering rather than admit them.

"We will pass unchallenged," Addai said in a tone that slid through Sajia's mind like a faint echo.

The men turned simultaneously. In a synchronized movement, they opened the doors, saying nothing as Addai and Sajia stepped into the club.

Hashish and burning opium scented the air. A beautiful woman in an elegant gown and wearing gloves that reached her elbows left her place on a spiraling staircase. "Take us to Rimmon," Addai told her, and like the bouncers outside the club, she obeyed without protest.

Sajia shivered, glad she was immune to his command. Glad he wasn't able to enthrall her with his voice.

The woman's dress left her back bare. A slit in the skirt revealed glimpses of her labia with each step she took.

Temptation, Sajia thought, unable to keep from glancing at Addai to see if his attention was riveted to the part of the woman's skirt and the flash of her nether lips.

His eyes met hers, and he laughed before visually caressing her, scorching her as his gaze traveled the length of her body. *I have not waited thousands of years for your return to settle for transitory pleasure now*, he said, the words as clear in her mind as if he'd spoken them out loud.

"How are you able to do that?"

"We are all born with gifts." *And you are my wife.*

Denial sprang to her lips. He prevented it from taking form in the spoken word by halting and covering her mouth with his, his tongue thrusting, his hunger stealing her breath, stealing her will, her very soul.

Carnal images slid into her mind, serving as temptation and enticement. Not memories of a past she couldn't remember, but of the future he intended, where the distinction between the worshipped and the one who did so was blurred and indistinct.

Her breasts swelled and nipples tightened. Arousal flowed from her slit, wetting her inner thighs as her cunt clenched and unclenched.

The sound of clapping brought her back to reality with a jolt. She wanted to blame her loss of awareness on the decadent environment, the insidious lure of air scented with opium and sex. But she wasn't an accomplished liar, and she'd never practiced it on herself.

Addai released Sajia, reluctantly, regretting the impulse to silence her with passion. It would prove to be a mistake on his part, of that he was positive as he turned toward one of the Fallen, acknowledging the man's presence with the use of his name, "Rimmon."

"*Lord* Rimmon."

Addai laughed. With a sweeping gesture of his arm to encompass the humans lingering in the hallway and visible through the doorways of the rooms lining it, he said, "Perhaps to those who come here to worship in your temple."

"Are you not one of them, Addai?" The single emerald green eye in the Fallen's burn-scarred face settled on Sajia, though nothing of his gaze revealed whether or not he could see the angelic script written on her skin. "She is quite lovely. Do you intend to join me in my sin, or did you bring her as a gift and then think to make me hunger to take possession of her?"

Rimmon's smile became sly. "I am not averse to sharing her with you if you don't want to give up your prize completely. It would be like the days of old, though if my memory serves, you preferred to wield a sword of a different kind than I, and the screams arising from your presence stemmed from terror instead of ecstasy."

Addai fought against issuing a threat he couldn't deliver on. There were repercussions for killing his kind, even one of the Fallen. "Did your burning plunge from grace lead to this?" he asked, taking the offensive, once again indicating the mass of humans with a sweep of his arm. "Do you now conduct all your business with an audience present? If so, I'm happy to accommodate you. Saril is the reason I'm here."

All amusement left Rimmon. In a blink the look in his eye was as cold as his origins, the light glinting off it providing a glimpse of the power he'd once commanded. "Come," he said, turning his back and walking away.

He led them past rooms where men and women engaged in sexual acts while others watched, past those with rail-thin humans who favored the touch of an opium pipe against their lips to flesh or food, and still more where the occupants crowded around gaming tables.

They passed through an area serving drink and vicarious violence via television before entering a private room, a parlor decorated in furniture to match the age of the Victorian, though Addai doubted the view through the glassed wall would have been common in any house save a brothel.

"Your private dungeon?" he asked.

"Ecstasy achieved through the redemptive power of punishment—surely you can understand how such a thing might appeal to me."

Addai guided Sajia to a couch upholstered in French silk moiré, urging her to sit and taking up a position next to her. He draped his arm along the couch back in a casual gesture, though he felt far from calm at having Sajia with him in this place and this company.

Rimmon claimed the chair across from her, pulling it closer and making Addai ball his hand into a fist against the urge to call his sword to him. With privacy restored, Rimmon probably intended to taunt with a slow visual study of Sajia, but his eye settled on her arm and the vampire scarring there, then lifted to meet Addai's. "You keep interesting company."

Addai didn't rise to the bait. Instead he said, "What's your price for access to Saril? I have need of a Finder."

The emerald green eye narrowed, pulling on the scar tissue around it before the sly smile returned. "Seeing you makes me think of another of my recent visitors. Tir, he called himself. There's a certain similarity in look."

Rimmon's eye flicked to Sajia. "And situation. A brother of yours, perhaps? Though it could be argued we are all brothers even if some of us have so much further to fall and become forgotten. When last I saw him, he wore a collar of enslavement. I wonder if you believe his punishment fits his crime."

"He is free of it now."

"Ah. That explains how you know of Saril. He healed her in exchange for something I could provide. And now you want something from her. Divine intervention, I wonder? Or the vagaries of fate?"

Rimmon lifted a hand to his scarred face. "Had my daughter's life not hung in the balance between life and death, I might have asked Tir to restore me to my former glory. But from you . . . I have never heard it said that you offer anything but death."

His good eye returned to Sajia, this time undressing her, clearly imagining her in his bed.

Addai wasn't able to stop himself. He opened clenched fingers and his sword was there, hungry for the blood of the Fallen. "Death is still mine to offer."

Rimmon's smile was victorious, as if goading Addai into acting had been part of his price. "So she is aware of your nature. Good. Then let us discuss terms."

He paused, a silent command for Addai to put away his weapon before they continued. Addai complied, jaw clenched.

"One search," Rimmon said. "Assuming of course that Saril agrees to perform it for you. Done in my presence. And in return, I will give you a choice of payments."

He gestured to the room on the other side of the glass. "If death is still yours to deliver, then show me one given with pleasure and survived in ecstasy. Strip your companion and bind her to any piece of equipment, then attend her until her screams cease and she falls silent in *la petite morte*."

Addai's cock throbbed at the images Rimmon's words created. Desire burned through him, and he fought against revealing just how much he longed to join his body to hers. What Rimmon described was tame compared to the fantasies he harbored, the things he wanted to do with Sajia.

Next to him she sat ramrod straight, bristling with resistance and rebellion, seething in her silence but managing to keep her promise to allow him to negotiate with the vice lord. Had Rimmon's terms allowed for privacy . . .

She was safe from this particular bargain. He would never allow another to look at her naked form or witness her in pleasure and live to dream about it.

"And the second choice?"

"If you don't prefer pleasure, then there is only one other. Pain. The terms for access to Saril are the same, only it will be you who is bound, and your companion who selects which of my toys will be applied to your back."

Sajia jerked in denial, a small sound of distress escaping. Addai's hand moved from the back of the couch to her arm, his fingers lightly tracing the vampire marks, reminding her of what there was to lose if something happened to the scion, or if he decided to end their truce and risk her hatred by taking her back to the chalet and holding her there.

"How many strikes?" Addai asked. Compared to the agony of Sajia's death so long ago, physical pain was easily endured.

"As many as it takes for your back to resemble the bloody mess of mine when flesh and wings were burned away." Rimmon leaned forward abruptly, the cold eye alight with fire. "You are no less guilty than I was judged to be, and I would argue that your transgressions are greater."

"True enough," Addai said, following it by restating the terms, modifying them. "And for this, there will be one search, done before sunset on this day, in your presence *and* accompanied by your vow not to use what you learn in any way, or reveal it to another."

"Agreed."

Addai stood, and with a thought his shirt disappeared. "Let us begin then."

No! Sajia silently screamed as Addai tugged her to her feet. But she couldn't force herself to give voice to it, not with the lives of her family, and possibly Corinne's, at stake.

Rimmon touched a place on the wall, and it slid open to reveal a doorway into the dungeon. He didn't bother to close it after they entered.

She hadn't been able to see it from her seat in his parlor, but one wall was done fully in mirrors, and anchored to it was a saltire. Though she had never been bound spread-eagle for punishment, carnal or otherwise, she was well familiar with its use. No vampire estate housing servants or progeny was without one. In private or in public, in play or in deadly seriousness, vampires enjoyed torment and drawing blood.

"Perhaps you'd like me to assist you in choosing the best tool for the task," Rimmon said as he led them to a wall where whips and floggers and paddles hung from hooks, while canes and switches lay in narrow, ornate cradles.

Sajia shuddered at the thought of applying any of them to Addai. Of willfully cutting his skin and making him bleed.

Her reaction didn't go unnoticed. Rimmon laughed and said, "It's not too late to choose pleasure over pain."

Addai reached out, plucking a cat-o'-nines from the wall. Sajia's heart cried out at the sight of the thin strips of leather, the tails braided to form sharp edges.

"Use this one," he said. "It will make our stay here shorter."

Rimmon laughed again. "But far more painful. I'm not sure whether to feel pleased or cheated by your choice. But if you've made it, then we'll adjourn to the *crux decussata*."

He preceded them to the St. Andrew's Cross. The single eye shone like a multifaceted gem as he turned it on Sajia. "You'll have to do the honors of binding him."

Sajia's heart pounded in her chest, horror building there as Addai faced the mirrored wall. At the chalet, she'd claimed the past had no relevance, but as he lifted his arms and allowed her to place a manacle around his wrist, the first tender shoots of love took root in her soul. It humbled her that he would subject himself to such torment all because they'd once lived as man and wife.

She secured the buckles with trembling fingers. He turned his head and their eyes met, his holding a depth of commitment almost beyond her imagining.

Emotions flooded her, joy and tenderness and hope—all overlaid by a rising despair at what this bargain demanded. She knelt at his feet and a glimmer of the future they might have together once Corinne was found worked its way into her thoughts. Yet even as images of home and children came, part of her feared that one day he would decide he loved a memory, not her.

"The rest of it or our agreement is null," Rimmon said.

Addai's pants slid into nonexistence, and she bound his ankles. Regardless of the pose and the restraints, there was no diminishment of his innate arrogance and pride.

Looking up the line of his body, Sajia swallowed tears at the thought of marring perfection, of using the flogger to cut his skin and make him bleed when in that moment, all she wanted was to give him pleasure, to press kisses to his flesh and stroke him with her hands.

She forced herself to pick up the cat-o'-nines he'd dropped to the floor before placing his arms against the smooth wood and steel of the saltire. Rimmon moved a short distance away, taking a seat on what looked like a throne.

Sajia stepped back. She couldn't suppress the tears then, or the whimper, as she raised her arm and delivered the first strike.

Pain streaked through Addai. Wrapped in flesh, he felt it as a human might, though unlike a human, all he had to do was give up any pretense of mortality to be free of it.

A second blow followed the first, and then a third. He didn't bother to count beyond that. It would take more than what a human could survive for Rimmon's price to be met.

He watched Sajia in the mirror. His heart both wept and rejoiced at the sight of her tears.

Again and again she raised her arm and brought the cat-o'-nines down in punishing strikes. Flaying his skin so the muscles in his arms stood out in rigid relief as he fought to remain constrained by flesh.

The present dominated until blood flowed down his back. Then he gave himself over to memories.

Physical agony took the place of emotions he'd carried for thousands of years. Guilt and regret. Rage and hate.

There was catharsis in the pain and the bleeding. He embraced it, letting it wash the past away.

Endorphins rose. Where once fury had filled the abyss created by emotional agony, now desire filled the one carved out by physical pain.

Addai felt Sajia's anguish, and even more sublime, the strengthening of the bond between them as her tears continued to flow and her arm shook with fatigue and reluctance.

Her whimpers of protest were a serenade to his heart. He hardened and remained that way, each additional lash becoming another thread weaving their souls together.

Finally she threw the cat-o'-nines to the floor in a signal that payment had been made. Rimmon rose from his throne and touched one of the lions carved into the wood. Curtains closed over the glass separating dungeon from office. "It seems you made the better bargain. I'll be back in a little while to take you to Saril."

Sajia went to Addai on a shuddering sob, freeing him of the manacles around his wrists before Rimmon left the room. She knelt, undoing those around his ankles with fingers that trembled and a soul that ached.

He turned and her eyes traveled upward, soaking in the beauty of him, the unmarred skin. Felt the shock of remorse pushed aside by the sight of testicles hanging beneath a potent display of hardened masculinity.

She licked her lips in unconscious reaction, only aware of having done it when his penis bobbed, pulling away from his abdomen as if it would come to her mouth. She lifted her eyes to meet his and pushed words through a throat clogged with emotions that shouldn't be able to coexist. "Can you heal yourself?"

"Of course," he said, arrogance in his voice and something she wouldn't have thought possible except for the evidence of it only inches away from her face. Hunger. Dark and dangerous. Commanding and all-encompassing.

FIVE

The air shimmered, and Sajia felt the caress of it against her face like a faint icy breeze. In the mirror his back became whole, unblemished, as if the terrible damage, the pain she'd inflicted because of her oath, her family, had never been.

It wasn't compulsion as the vampires were capable of, but it was equally compelling. She could no more resist the pull of desire, the need to deliver pleasure after having delivered so much pain, than a blood-slave could a master's command.

Her hands settled on Addai's thighs. His muscles flexed beneath her palms, vibrated with tension though his lips remained sealed, his face austere, challenging her to coax an expression from him, a cry where he'd remained mute under the lashes of the cat-o'-nines.

She laughed softly, something she would have thought impossible moments earlier. He wouldn't be able to hold against the torment of her tongue, the teasing prelude to taking him in her mouth, sucking until he was once again at her mercy. In this his immense power didn't matter, he was still male.

Sajia leaned forward as her hands slid upward on his thighs. In the mirror there was the subtle flexing of his buttocks as he braced himself for the instant she would touch his cock.

She'd wielded the flogger without stopping, wanting to get it over with quickly, to hurry through it rather than commit each strike to memory. And now she found herself at risk of going quickly once again, but for far different reasons.

Her hands settled on either side of his thick erection, and she had to force them to remain there, just as she had to force herself not to press kisses along his hardened length. Where she'd hastened through the pain, she wanted to linger in pleasure.

She rubbed her cheek against his cock, soft skin against soft skin. It jerked at the contact, and he wrapped her braid around a hand, using it in a silent command to turn her face.

She complied, lips touching heated flesh, tongue darting out for a first taste. Savoring it.

A shudder went through Addai, a wave of such pleasure he only barely managed to remain standing. He'd been without a woman since her death.

The angels sent to this world weren't inherently carnal or emotional. It's what had made them good at watching impassively, patrolling, killing. But the longer they were here, the more they had free will, the more the temptations of the flesh assailed them.

Some of them succumbed. *He* had succumbed.

In that first moment he'd laid eyes on Sajia drawing water from the well, desire had consumed him and then love had followed it. To settle for another when he knew one day she'd be returned to him would have been a betrayal.

His hand tightened on her braid. When they were truly alone, he'd unbind her hair so the silky strands of it fanned out over her back and buttocks. He'd spear his fingers through it, an intimate act among the Djinn, one allowed only with those well loved and well trusted.

Now, Sajia, he commanded, accompanying the order with an image of her encircling his cock with her hand and guiding its head to her mouth.

Her sultry laugh had his buttocks clenching, his eyes closing briefly as he shored up his defenses, ordered himself not to beg, not to show any weakness.

There will be retribution, he warned.

I look forward to it.

She measured his length with a string of kisses, with a hot trail left by her tongue.

Fire engulfed him. Lust that caused him to thrust.

The only weapon he could use against her was his mind, his imagination and his memory of what they'd once done together. He wielded both ruthlessly, showing her the punishment she was earning by teasing him. A punishment he would deliver when they got home, when she was totally at his mercy.

Sajia grew wet at seeing herself draped naked over his thighs, her legs parted just enough to reveal her swollen folds and glistening slit. She'd never played sexual games, never had any interest in them despite their prevalence in the vampires' world.

She would never have imagined she'd allow a man to bend her over his thighs and deliver a spanking. But with Addai she discovered she wanted it, craved it, as if the images he projected into her mind found a deep longing to submit and coaxed it out of hiding.

On a murmur of pleasure she gave him what he demanded from her. Her hands left his thighs, one cupping the smooth, heavy sac between his legs, fondling and weighing and caressing, the other forming a fist around a cock that felt like satin over steel, like heated marble though so much more malleable than cool stone.

She guided him to her mouth, explored his penis with her tongue before taking his cock head between her lips and holding it there, his scent and taste making her think of icy peaks and desolate places, of harsh winter winds.

A small measure of victory came with the moan he couldn't suppress, the closing of his eyes as he gave himself over to sensation.

Thick, sooty black lashes should have made him look feminine, but his beauty had no gender; it was otherworldly, terrifying power given form.

And somehow he'd come to be hers. Somehow he'd moved heaven and earth so she was reborn and returned to him.

There was a fluttering in her chest, her heart destabilized by the enormity of what he'd done—not just in the past, but here, in the present, allowing himself to be bound, hurt, to become entertainment. Looking up the line of his body, seeing the pleasure in his face, she *wanted* to believe that she would always satisfy him.

She had a moment to wonder if Rimmon watched, if the curtains closing over glass gave only the illusion of privacy. Then banished the thought as she drew Addai deeper into her mouth, working him with her lips and tongue. Restraining him with the tight close of her fingers around his cock so he couldn't thrust any deeper. Keeping ecstasy out of reach, denied until he was panting, quivering, his hands no longer still but roaming, caressing, his words no longer contained, but her name turned into a litany.

He didn't beg. They'd have to be truly alone for that to happen. But she grew wetter at seeing a measure of the power she had over him, at knowing one day she might hear him plead to be allowed to come.

Her channel clenched and unclenched, the desperate need to feel him inside her intensifying as his lust grew and his breathing became ragged. She sucked, taking him deeper, swallowing on him repeatedly, no longer caring about staving off his orgasm.

Addai nearly came as her throat closed around him. Every fiber of his being screamed for him to abandon the last measure of control and allow himself release in a primitive, earthy claiming.

He might have if he hadn't sensed Rimmon's imminent return, if he hadn't so desperately wanted his first release to be in the tight, hot depths of her channel. Searing ecstasy joined to an image burned into Sajia's consciousness, not fantasy or memory, but shared reality.

It took incredible strength of will to pull from her heated mouth, to part from her long enough to remove her clothing.

As he knelt in front of her, his hands closed briefly around her ankles, where angelic script circled as it did her wrists.

Rising, he caressed that written above her heart, pressing his lips to her flesh as satisfaction of a different kind arrived along with the heightened need to get her back to the chalet quickly. With a word, he could release her from the bindings holding her in a human form, but there were also places where the containment spell had faded into nothing.

He pushed worry over it away. Resolve and the desperate need to claim her left no room for it.

He took her mouth, sharing breath and heat, his arm around her waist, holding her bare mound against his throbbing cock, thrusting and rubbing his rigid length against her stiffened, swollen clit as his tongue battled hers.

Her whimpers were a roar of pleasure through his mind. Her hands caressing him as her skin burned against his, a sweet torment he'd pay any price to endure.

I need you, she said into his mind, an intimate contact that had his testicles tightening in warning and enabled him to pull from her embrace, to turn her so she faced the mirrored wall, her palms pressed to it for support.

Then have me, wife, he said, white wings manifested behind him, spreading out in proud display, trapping the mirrored image of them together as with one thrust, he entered her.

Sajia cried out, nearly consumed by the intense pleasure of having his cock filling her, by the eroticism of his possession. She couldn't close her eyes to the sight of him, of *them* together.

The hard lines of his face showed arrogant control, but the throbbing of his penis, the sheen of sweat on his heated skin told a different story. She moved against him and his features tightened, awarding her a small victory. One she paid for as his hand cupped her breast while the other stroked her belly before settling on her clit.

Her channel clenched on his length, hungry for movement, for the feel of him thrusting. For a release that would come with the hot spill of seed deep inside her.

"Please, Addai," she whispered, hearing the sound of submission in her own voice.

His eyes flared hot in the mirror, and then he began moving in and out of her, the fingers on her breast and clit squeezing, twisting, delivering pain to blend with pleasure until finally there was only the sweet oblivion of orgasm and the soul-deep satisfaction that came from feeling him shuddering in release, of seeing his wings outstretched, trembling as ecstasy took him.

Addai nearly surrendered to the need to wrap Sajia in arms and wings and take her home. Emotion, intense and unquantifiable, surged through him with the pounding of his heart. Nothing could be allowed to happen to her.

His hands took possession of her breasts, weighing them as she'd done his testicles. Her arched back and soft cry were his reward, the fisting of her channel on his cock his sensual punishment.

Temptation and torment. If he thought she would forgive him for making her abandon the search—

"Dress," he told her, forcing himself to pull from her heated depths and step backward. His wings shielded her from view as the sound of a curtain opening announced Rimmon's return.

Retracing their steps through the club, Addai couldn't miss the presence of so many of the Fallen. They glided through the rooms like sleek sharks among hapless prey, the humans drawn to them, mesmerized in spite of what they'd become.

Where the phantom presence of wings would once have brushed against his senses, now there was nothing. And where so many of his kind in the same place usually created a symphony of sound, the sweet notes of power in a choir heard only by angels, now he heard only jangling discord, a grating pressure that scraped over his skin and had him grinding his teeth and fighting not to call his sword.

The Fallen gave him wide berth, though they didn't bother hiding their curiosity, or the sly hungry smiles that had as much to do with anticipating his ultimate downfall as desiring the woman he so clearly considered his.

There was no help for it. He could no more force his hand away from Sajia than he could let her out of sight now that she'd been returned to him.

He knew why the Fallen were here. Knew too what they couldn't. They were part of a larger plan involving Saril, Rimmon's sole living descendant. In the end those not considered Djinn allies would be named enemies.

Rimmon led them to the elegant staircase near the front doors, pausing after taking only a few upward steps. He murmured to one of the women who waited there, ready to descend and serve as hostess to those entering the club and desiring it.

Her face flushed with pleasure, and she left her position to climb the stairs. Envious looks from the other woman followed her, the skirt she wore parting with each step, her folds glistening, revealing her excitement at having been chosen.

At the top of the staircase she left them, moving down a hallway carpeted by handwoven rugs from what the humans had once called the Holy Land. Priceless artwork hung on the walls. And unlike the lower stories of the Victorian, this floor had the hushed feel of a private, inviolate sanctuary.

Rimmon stopped in front of a closed door. A peremptory knock announced his arrival, though he didn't wait to be invited inside. He entered the room.

Addai let Sajia precede him, then closed the door behind them as a precaution. Saril looked up from the book she was reading, eyes the same green as her father's, but wary and soft rather than anticipatory and hardened.

"I have a task for you," Rimmon said without preamble. He crossed to a table where an arrangement of wildflowers sat clustered in a squat vase.

Panic flared in Saril's face when he unceremoniously plucked the purple and yellow blossoms out of the water, tossing them carelessly on a table that had survived The Last War—when the furniture and books marking man's passing from ignorant ape to more refined creation became fuel for fires in caves built of crushed buildings and twisted steel.

He turned, the vase seeming more delicate in his hands. His lips curved upward in a twisted parody of mirth. "Did you think I was ignorant of your gift, Saril? It was once mine, as was this scrying bowl you so cleverly hide in plain sight by using it for your flowers."

He closed the distance to his daughter and put the bowl down on a reading stand next to her. Addai urged Sajia forward, halting her several feet away from the Finder when he spotted the weapon lying on the floor next to Saril's chair, no doubt left there in case one of the Fallen below grew foolishly impatient and tried to claim her.

The sword might be blackened, given permanent physical form and cast into this world in the same lightning strike of retribution that melted Rimmon's flesh and stripped him of wings, but angelic script remained etched into blade and hilt, words of power that coupled with will were capable of killing his kind, Fallen or not.

The inside rim of the bowl was also marked by angelic writing. And whether Saril guessed at the full truth or not, Rimmon's words held it.

Once *sight*, the gift to *Find*, had been his. But like so many of the grigori, the early angelic watchers, he became tempted by the mortal, led by carnal desire to share knowledge beyond what the humans were supposed to be given, and fell as a result of it.

Like pearls scattered among swine, Addai had thought on learning of it so many thousands of years ago. *The bowl and others like it troughs for the creatures of mud to drink from.*

But that was before Sajia. Before he himself gave in to the temptations of the flesh and lay down with one of the mortal—worse—with an enemy. For that crime and all the others following as a result of it, being judged Fallen would seem a merciful punishment should his transgressions become known and those allied with the Djinn fail to take possession of this world.

Rimmon took his daughter's chin in his hand. "I won't pretend that you'll use your gift because I ask it of you. What boon do you want? And don't bother saying your freedom. Too many know of your existence now."

"Because you've made me a prize," Saril said, anger vibrating in the words. "A prisoner you intend to hand over to another jailor."

"I do what is best for the both of us. You have always been a prize, Saril, one at risk of being discovered and taken at any time. If you view the luxury and safety I've surrounded you with as a prison, then so be it. Name your price."

Her lips firmed and her chin jutted forward in silent refusal. Addai silently cursed at finding his own happiness tied to this girl on the brink of discovering the fate arranged for her by the Djinn and their allies.

One search. Assuming of course that Saril agrees to perform it for you.

As the flaw woven into the negotiations with Rimmon showed itself, Sajia pulled from Addai's grasp, refusing to let his suffering be for nothing.

She went to Saril and crouched next to her chair, prepared to

beg. "Please put aside your differences with your father long enough
to hear what brought us here. We wouldn't have come if the need
wasn't urgent. Corinne—my charge—is missing and because of it,
everyone I love is at risk."

Saril's gaze went to the freshly healed scarring on Sajia's upper
arm. "You serve vampires?"

"Yes. I was orphaned in the San Joaquin soon after I was born.
My aunt and uncle brought me to San Francisco and raised me with
the same love they gave their own children. I took an oath to serve
the Tucci because I liked Corinne, and in becoming her companion
I would also be able to give back to my family."

"How old is Corinne?"

Sajia felt some of the tension inside her dissolve as hope returned
with the question. "Sixteen and still entirely human. She's not what
you'd expect of a vampire scion. Corinne is shy, some would say
mousy, though I think her forgettable appearance stems from lack
of confidence and the knowledge that among the Tucci, female off-
spring aren't valued until they survive the transition."

Saril's features softened further, and Addai spoke up, saying, "If
it has any weight with you, Tir is my brother."

The last of Saril's earlier resistance melted at the mention of Tir.
"I was dying and he healed me."

"Yes. That's his gift."

"Did he find what he was looking for?"

"He found it. And more. He's happily bound to a woman who
loves him."

A small sigh of pleasure escaped Saril at hearing of a romantic
ending. "I'll help you."

Her expression firmed again as she looked at her father. "I want
a day to explore the outer harbor, and your promise that any treasure I discover while doing it is mine to keep."

The single emerald eye narrowed as he contemplated what she

might be looking for, or what she might find. But apparently he decided that whatever it was, he could successfully deal with it. "Granted."

She took the bowl off the table and placed it on her lap, then reached out, halting when her fingertips were inches away from the marks on Sajia's arm. "May I? It might help me find Corinne."

Sajia nodded and Saril quickly traced the scars. When she was done, she placed both hands on the bowl and stared into the water.

One moment dragged into a second, and then a third. Sajia caught herself holding her breath and exhaled, the sound of it loud in the hushed quiet of the room. She wanted to stand, to look into the bowl, aware with the light coming in through the window of how late in the day it was.

Her palms grew damp waiting. Her heart beat erratically.

Finally Saril blinked and looked up, her expression deeply troubled. "She's being held prisoner on a fishing boat. The boat is moving. It doesn't seem too far away, but I can't tell if it's still in the bay or if it's reached open waters. There's no name on its side and nothing distinctive about it except that there's an old red lantern hanging on the right side of the cabin doorway and a blue on the left."

Fear settled around Sajia, squeezing like a merciless fist. The Tucci didn't own fishing fleets or container ships. If the bay and open ocean were to be searched for Corinne, The Master would have to negotiate with other families, and that would mean a delay and a loss of face.

Given how little he valued female scions, there was every possibility he'd decide to leave Corinne to whatever fate befell her, while placing the public blame for the failed betrothal on Sajia, claiming she'd betrayed her oath and ordering her killed to satisfy honor and the Gairden family.

Addai would never allow it. At the first hint of threat he'd take her away or he'd wage war on the Tucci, either of which would lead to the very thing that terrified her, the death of her family because of her. She glanced at him in panic, but some of it eased when he told Rimmon, "Sajia and I will take Araña's boat in order to look for the scion."

"As you wish. But the moment the *Constellation* leaves the outer harbor, the agreement I made with Tir for its protection ends. Bring it back into the waters I control and it'll find a resting place among the other sunken ships."

SIX

Though Sajia's trips to Oakland had been limited, like anyone serving a scion she'd been given lessons in geography and human politics. She knew the general direction of the outer harbor controlled by Rimmon, though not how long it would take to reach it.

"We'll have to hurry if we hope to get the boat into the bay by nightfall," she said as they left Temptation, matching actions to words—only to be halted within steps by a manacle of fingers.

"We'll continue our search for the scion tomorrow," Addai said, swinging her around to face him. "Tonight we return home."

The familiar arrogance was back. Deadly purpose returned to eyes as black as any abyss.

"No and no again," she said, her hand going to the knife at her waist, thoughts flashing first to their battle at the chalet and the blood she'd drawn there, then to his back coated with it as she'd wielded the cat-o'-nines.

The fight left her, though her determination didn't. She abandoned the blade in favor of stepping into him, close enough to share breath and heat.

She touched her hand to his chest and felt his heart beat against her palm. Steady strokes that made her think of home and safety, of a love so deep it defied even death. Of passion found in firm touches and feathery caresses, of desire all-consuming and eternal. Addai.

"Please," she said, knowing she couldn't allow herself to waver in her resolve. "This is important to me. Surely the boat has a cabin. We can take shelter there. It should be safe enough in open water, and if danger comes, I'll go willingly. A blink and we can be in your home, your bed."

"*Our* home. *Our* bed," Addai said, resolve melting with her entreaty and the soft pleading in her eyes as she looked up at him.

He was glad none of the brothers allied with the Djinn were here to witness his defeat. He conceded it only because he could tell himself that traveling to and from the chalet with Sajia posed a greater danger than taking possession of the *Constellation* for the night. With the sigils on her skin weakening, her Djinn nature might reveal itself as they traveled. His own passing through the metaphysical plane created little more than a ripple, but a Djinn breaching it left a trail of sound that would summon angelic enemies if they were near.

They would arrive with the intention of killing her. They would die in the attempt. But there was risk even in that, and victory over them wouldn't come without a cost.

He couldn't capitulate without giving her fair warning. He leaned in, lips touching hers, the image of her bound to the bed arriving in his thoughts as he issued his threat. *Don't think to control me with your body, Sajia. Soon enough you'll discover that I am the master of it.*

She shivered. Not fear, her scent and the hardening of her nipples spoke only of arousal. He smiled as he contemplated turning defeat into a chance to give her the first of her lessons in submission. No boat left the dock without a multitude of ropes onboard it.

"Let's go," he said, denying them both the kiss they craved, the exploration of wet heat and the thrust of tongue against tongue, the sharing of breath that bound their spirits together more tightly each time it happened. Her whimper at the loss of his lips against hers was a soothing balm laid over the turbulent, intense emotions her presence created in him.

The farther they got from the Victorian-lined street with its clubs serving human vice, the more deserted the red zone became. Shops gave way to clusters of homes where the poor lived, and then, as the air took on the smell of the ocean, to twisted steel and rusted ruin, what remained of cranes and shipping containers from the days of the humans' Last War.

Beyond the jungle of ruin, the exposed hulls and sunken debris of ships turned the harbor into a treacherous, watery graveyard. As they boarded the *Constellation*, Addai said, "Throw off the ropes. I'll start the engines."

He was unconcerned about navigating the dangerous outer harbor. Tir's memories were his. His brother had been the one to recover the *Constellation* for Araña and guide it through the minefield of wrecked ships.

To ease Sajia's mind, they searched for the fishing boat Saril had described until darkness crowded into dusk. Then Addai insisted they stop, and, as the anchor dropped, a hot swirl of desert-scented wind blew across the deck, announcing the arrival of a Djinn.

Irial's eyes lingered appreciatively over Sajia's form, settling briefly on the scorpion pendant at her throat before meeting Addai's. "So this is the reward my father spoke of. Now I understand why I was sent with food . . . and bedding. Perhaps I'll remain and aid you in the latter."

Addai took a threatening step forward before he could stop himself. With a laugh, Irial set down the basket he carried, then disappeared as suddenly as he'd arrived, choosing to take no form rather than become the raven of his House.

"Your brother?"

"No."

"He called me your reward." There was no anger in her voice, just the hesitant question, *Your reward for doing what?*

For traveling down the path your death set me on, Addai said, choosing to answer intimately, in a reminder of what they were to each other. *There is nothing I've done that I wouldn't do a thousand times again if that's what it took to get you back, or if doing it would rewrite the past so you were never lost to me in the first place.*

Sajia's heart turned over in her chest at his pronouncement. "I'm not the same person," she forced herself to say, silently confronting the fear she harbored, that one day he'd realize he loved the memory of who she had been in the past more than who she was in this life.

He crossed the distance, arms enclosing her. His expression harsh as his lips descended, claiming hers in a taking that left no room for resistance.

In all the ways that matter, you are the same, he said, his hardened cock an exclamation mark against her mound and belly. *Never doubt it, Sajia.*

As the last of the light faded, she pulled from his arms and picked up the basket left by their visitor. "I'll set out the food and make the bed."

She couldn't bring herself to ask him to keep searching for Corinne during the night, not when the risk existed that he could be pulled from the sky by a bioengineered sea creature or a supernatural one, hindered and drowned because of his wings. It didn't stop worry from gnawing at her, but deep down she accepted they'd done what they could for Corinne today, and she had to believe tomorrow they'd find and free her.

They ate at the small table in the cabin. Had Addai not been driven by thoughts of binding Sajia to the bed, he would have fed her by hand on the mattress. He would have dribbled honey over her naked breasts and watched as it slid over her curves, then along her flat stomach, filling the well of her navel before coating her sweet mound in an irresistible invitation for his tongue to follow.

His cock was hard again, a near-constant state since he'd first learned Sajia would soon be returned to him. Her flushed cheeks

and heated glances told him she was equally aroused, their time together at Temptation wetting a carnal appetite for pleasure rather
than appeasing the hunger of it.

He finished eating before she did and leaned back, drinking in
the sight of her, his heart aching as he visually caressed the face that
had haunted him for thousands of years. With a thought, he rid himself of clothing, then curled his fingers around his hardened length,
making no attempt to hide his actions as he moved his fisted hand
up and down on his organ.

Her heightened flush and the small catch of her breath served as
reward. The dart of her tongue as she licked honey from her fingers
a sensual punishment.

When she didn't reach for more of the bread or the cheese and
fruit that had accompanied it, he pitched his voice in a demand
no mortal would have been able to deny. "Remove your clothing,
Sajia."

A small smile played over her lips in answer. Her eyelashes lowered as she contemplated defying him, letting him know by her response that if she agreed to his demands, it would be because she
chose to. "Is this how it was before between us?"

"You've seen my memories of it."

"And if I don't want to play the slave to your master?"

"Disrobe, Sajia," he said in answer, pressing more of his will on
her, taking pleasure in the fact that he couldn't truly bend her to it.
Desire intensifying at the erotic fear he caught glimpses of when her
gaze strayed to the soft lengths of rope he'd casually thrown onto
the bed upon entering the cabin.

Long moments passed, the sexual tension building as she made
him wait, drawing out the game until he tightened his grip on his
cock rather than stroke it. She knew what would come if she accepted the first of his commands.

His heart thundered in his chest. Anticipation built along with
a craving that surpassed even the desires of his flesh, for her to trust

him, to demonstrate it by allowing herself to be bound as he'd allowed himself to be manacled.

He only barely suppressed a moan when she rose gracefully from her seat and stepped away from the table, providing him an unhindered view. The shirt was the first garment to hit the floor, her breasts drawing his attention and holding it.

Dark, dark nipples pouted in sultry beckoning, urging him to kneel before her and take them into his mouth. To bite and suck and lick until the evidence of her arousal flowed freely down her inner thighs, until the scent of it forced him to place his lips on her smooth, heated mound, to lap and thrust with his tongue before taking her with his cock.

Seeing the hunger in him, she cupped her breasts, rubbed the hardened peaks with her thumbs until only the pain of his hand around his cock kept him from taking her to the floor like a ravenous beast and fucking her.

He forced his gaze away from her beautiful breasts. "No transgression ever goes unpunished," he said, a warning he suspected would become a refrain in their lives together. "Take the rest of it off."

Her hands swept downward in a sensuous glide he was only too eager to follow with his lips. She paused, once again lingering, taking her time in obeying, fingers slowly loosening the pants, then pushing them off her hips, down sleekly muscled legs.

She bent with their descent, affording him the view of a delicate length of spine, the dusky curve of her buttocks as she removed her short boots before stepping out of the pants.

He could no more stop himself from closing the distance between them than he could force himself to leave her.

The feel of her skin against his was very nearly his undoing. It'd be so easy to lift her in his arms, to join his body to hers where they stood. One thrust. Two. And he could savor a quick release before carrying her to bed for a lengthier one.

He resisted, tormented them both by wrapping his arms around her, holding her heated mound against his hot, rigid length. His wings manifested, further enfolding her as he lowered his lips to hers, plunging his tongue into the hot depths of her mouth and shuddering when she welcomed it, rubbed her own against it before sucking him deeper, reminding him of the ecstasy he'd experienced when it was his cock thrusting between her lips.

My spirit to yours. The same formal words had a variety of uses among the Djinn, and though he longed to hear her speak them, between lovers they were unnecessary. To place her soul fully into his keeping, she had only to *will* it so and accompany it with the sharing of breath. He had only to speak the forbidden incantation to tie himself to this world and to her.

He craved the binding of their lives and spirits with the same desperate need he felt to join their bodies together. But where the latter required only that he push his cock into her slick, heated channel, the former required him to free her of the angelic script confining her to human form. And the moment he did so the knowledge of her Djinn nature separated and held in the scorpion pendant would flow into her.

He couldn't risk it. Not yet. Not until he was sure of her.

He shuddered, fighting the urge to place his cock head at her wet opening and enter her. It was all he could do to release Sajia rather than carry her to the mattress and immediately come down on top of her.

As if sensing his weakness, she said, *Make love to me*, projecting it into his mind and reinforcing it with the grinding of her mound and belly against his erection.

The deep craving for her willing submission gave him the strength to take a step backward and say, "You know what I want. Lie down and position yourself so I can tether your wrists and ankles to the bed."

A shiver went through Sajia. Her channel clenched violently.

She was so wet, so needy that tears nearly leaked from the corners of her eyes. He overpowered her with his beauty, with the depth of his desire for her.

Never would she have imagined complying so readily, so easily. She felt his eyes on her back, on her buttocks, on the glimpses of her swollen folds as she walked away from him.

Sajia got on the bed as he'd ordered, lifting her arms above her head and spreading her legs, loving what it did to him, hardening his face as he fought to master his lust, hardening his cock in defiance of the stranglehold he had on it.

He stood over her. Breathing barely controlled. The arrogant mask smoothing into place, bringing with it a visceral fear, a forbidden thrill that had her canting her hips.

His lips curved in a dangerous smile. His eyes were molten onyx as he freed his cock in favor of picking up the short lengths of rope and using them to hold her open, helpless.

He knelt between her thighs, wings visible but no longer a physical reality. His cock leaving a wet trail across his belly, his testicles on proud display as his eyes roamed possessively, hungrily, scorching her with his visual caress.

She didn't know what to expect, only that she craved his attention. Needed his touch as desperately as she needed air to live.

"Please," she said, bound, willing to beg for mercy where he hadn't been when he chose pain over pleasure rather than allow the vice lord to see her naked.

"No transgression ever goes unpunished," Addai reminded her, delivering a sharp slap to her bare mound.

The shock of it made her gasp even as the spike of heated lust that flashed through her clit and cunt had her lifting her hips off the mattress in a silent plea for another.

A flush spread across his cheeks as he delivered a second spank, and a third, heating skin that already felt as though it were on fire, making her cry out. Then cry out again when he braced his hands on the mattress, following the lash of masculine fingers and palm with carnal strokes of his tongue.

She fought the bindings then. Writhed against them, not to escape and flee, but to find release of a different kind.

As she'd enjoyed her power over him when she knelt, tormenting him with her mouth, he returned the favor, his wicked lips latching onto her clit, sucking mercilessly.

He took her to the edge of orgasm repeatedly, denying her each time it was only a rough stroke of his tongue away, when a hard pull of sensuous lips would have sent her spiraling into ecstasy.

Tears streamed from her eyes. Her nipples ached, and her breasts felt tight and full, her nether lips unbearably swollen.

She was breathless from pleading. From fighting against the ropes holding her open and helpless.

Shiver after shiver raced through her. Need as she'd never known before.

A swirling of his tongue over her clit had her sobbing, the thrust of it into her slit had her arching upward, driving it deeper into her channel. "Please," she begged again. "Please, Addai."

He rose above her, phantom wings spread, a dark angel embodying the purely carnal. The tip of his penis lodging against her opening.

True damnation was being denied this, Addai thought as he pushed his thick length through swollen folds. Buried his cock in her snug sheath only to retreat then force his way in again in the sheer bliss of being joined with her.

He made love to her until she screamed in release. Paused only long enough to untie her wrists and ankles so she could wrap arms and legs around him as he took her again, this time allowing himself the ecstasy that came with the heated rush of semen and the touching of his mind to hers, pleasure doubled then doubled again as she orgasmed when he did and slipped into satiated sleep.

Addai rose onto an elbow, lifting away from her only far enough so he could watch her as she slept and trace her lips with his fingertip as his cock softened in her channel. He didn't need to see the angelic script written above her heart to know where the incantation had weakened, where parts of it had faded and disappeared, leaving openings, like cracks in a vase, allowing what it contained to leak out. He could feel the breaks against his skin, the fiery core of her Djinn nature burning away the icy angelic sigils.

Wielding what the humans called spell magic wasn't his gift. He was thankful he wasn't faced with the choice of whether or not to restore the bindings. It was hard enough knowing that with a word he could free her of them.

He didn't dare. Though satisfaction and joy pulsed through him at how much ground he'd gained with her on their first day together, he couldn't allow her to be unrestrained by form, couldn't trust her to remain with him instead of searching for the scion during the night.

There were places he couldn't follow her should she choose to leave him behind. The water held only death for him. It was a place of darkness, with impenetrable depths that defied the light. Long before the humans added nightmare creatures to it, the kraken and leviathan called it home, and still did.

Freed of human form, she'd soon draw the attention of one of his kind. He couldn't allow that to happen.

He leaned down, brushing his lips against her forehead, her skin warm despite the ocean air. He doubted she felt the cold very often, wondered if she'd noticed the change in herself. The Djinn were creatures of fire.

The night deepened. Time to a being whose existence spanned eternity was meaningless, but because of Sajia, he marked the minutes and hours. She anchored him to them, filled them with intense emotion and sweet sensation.

Dawn was hours away when he felt the change in her. Her skin grew more heated, becoming so hot he was forced away from her.

He rolled to his feet just as her Djinn spirit escaped its prison of human flesh. In a shimmer, like heat rising from the desert, she became a nighthawk and took flight, going to the door and beating ineffectively against it in an attempt to escape.

Addai gave up his physical form, turning his will, his essence into a cage made of light and power. A gift rarely used but one he was glad to possess in that instant.

She threw herself against the unseen barrier, growing more agitated with each attempt until finally choosing another form. Feathers morphed to hard golden carapace as she became a scorpion and struck at the walls of her prison with a poison-charged tail.

When that didn't work, she changed again, and again, morphing from one shape into another until exhaustion claimed her and she collapsed, feathered once again, the dove she'd so often chosen when they lived as man and wife.

Addai took form then, freeing her from the cage. A step took him to her, and once again the air shimmered.

Feathers gave way to tanned skin and sleek female curves, the vampire scars restored like camouflage, preserved by the strength of the angelic spell placed on her. He lifted Sajia and returned her to the bed, settling down next to her for what remained of the night.

SEVEN

Dawn arrived with the cry of seagulls and the slap of water against the sides of the boat. Though Sajia was cocooned in warmth, held securely against a hard masculine body, she woke chilled and clammy, as if crawling from some dark, cold oubliette.

Her heart began racing and panic set in. She had the sense of having been awake for a long stretch of night, yet her last memories were of sexual satisfaction.

The blackouts were getting worse, lasting longer if she was right about spending most of the night awake but unaware. If she'd managed to get out of the cabin—

A hard shiver went through her at remembering the times she'd come to in a different room or outside the Tucci estate, the times she'd found herself close to a cousin's home, as if in thinking about them just before blacking out, she'd set a course for unconscious travel.

Had this happened to her in the past? Was this somehow related to the rebirth of her spirit?

The answer might lie behind her, his lips delivering soft kisses along her shoulder and neck as his cock grew hard against her buttocks. "Easy, beloved," he murmured. "I'm here with you."

A shiver of a different sort moved through her when the hand splayed across her stomach stroked upward to cup her breast. "I will never allow any harm to come to you."

He took the tender nipple between his fingers, squeezing as he placed a love bite where her neck met her shoulder. She moaned in reaction, maneuvered so her opening was pressed against his cock head in wanton invitation.

Her questions and fears melted away as he entered her, filled her in a slow slide of hot, hard flesh. His penis throbbed inside her like a second heartbeat, offering a different type of reassurance, a different type of comfort.

"That feels so good," she whispered, closing her eyes, laughing softly when it occurred to her that given his innate arrogance, she probably shouldn't stroke his ego too often.

"I heard that," he said, biting her shoulder in teasing rebuke.

Whether he meant her laughter or her thoughts, she didn't know. Didn't care as his hand abandoned her nipple to smooth over her belly and settle on her clit.

He stroked the underside of it with his fingers. Grasped and tugged. Tormented her with the back-and-forth rub of his thumb over the tiny naked head, the sharp spikes of pleasure streaking downward to make her toes curl.

She pushed backward, pressed swollen folds against his skin. "I could make you beg again," he said, his voice purring in threat.

The impulse to engage in sensual battle rose and fell with a thrust. "Please," she said, giving him victory with the needy sound of her voice uttering a single word.

It was his turn to laugh softly, in masculine satisfaction. "You are mine," he murmured, lips delivering kisses and sucking bites to her skin, cock moving in and out in a slow, intimate show of possession.

He said her name, whispered for her ears though she heard it in her mind as well. One word, and yet it translated to so much more, expanded only to condense into *Lover. Wife. Mine.*

Sajia closed her eyes, surrendering to the pleasure as he brought her to an orgasm that left her wanting to stay in bed all day and engage in nothing but lovemaking. For long moments she was able to linger in contentment, but reality wouldn't be held off.

The cry of seagulls and slap of water were a call to get up, to continue the search for Corinne, bringing Sajia full cycle to her waking fear. "Did I try to leave the cabin last night?"

The sudden tension in Addai's body answered her question. "What do you remember?"

She turned in his arms, the motion making him sigh in protest as his cock left her channel. "Nothing. I never do."

His expression didn't change. And that was yet another answer, though it begged the question. "Do you know what's happening to me?"

Trust. It had never been one of Addai's strong points.

The one glaring example of not trusting in the love they shared, not fully committing to it had ended in indescribable pain and thousands of years of loss.

Tell her. Free her, an internal voice urged.

His gaze dropped to the scorpion pendant against her skin, sigils inscribed into it, holding information about the Djinn. From there his focus shifted to the vampire marks on her arm. In her true form she would be free of the scars, but their loss wouldn't undo the chains binding her to the human family she'd been willing to die for. It wouldn't rid her of whatever loyalty she felt to the Tucci scion.

"Does it have something to do with my being reincarnated?" she asked, unknowingly providing him a way to escape the turmoil of choice.

"It has everything to do with it."

Anticipating her next question, heading it off, he said, "The periods of blacking out and not remembering what happened will pass."

The script on her skin glowed like an accusation. *Coward!*

Addai denied the charge. It was too soon to free her, too risky right now, when she might choose to hunt for Corinne on her own if the situation became dangerous and he decided to end her participation in it.

"We should get up and begin searching for the boat," she said.

"When this is over, promise you'll go willingly to our home."

She leaned forward, touching her lips to his, fingers stroking where his wing merged with his back and sending a shudder of pleasure through him. "I have obligations to the Tucci."

Her answer convinced him of the rightness of his decision to hold off releasing her from the angelic bindings keeping her human. "The Tuccis won't stand in the way of my desire to have you."

It was the wrong thing to say. In implying threat to the vampires, he'd reminded her of the repercussions to her family. Sajia grew still.

Not wanting to lose what he already had with her, he said, "They'll free you from your oath in a bargain that will satisfy all of us. You're my wife. Your place is with me."

Her eyes flashed with fire. She sat, taking the heat of her skin and her soft curves from him. "Maybe the woman you once knew was content to let you order her life as you saw fit, but I am *not* that woman. If you think otherwise, then you love a memory, not who I am. My place is wherever I *choose* it to be."

Pride and masculine arrogance demanded he prove the truth of his claim. He acted on it, tumbling her backward and lying on top of her, pinning her to the mattress. A quick thrust and he was inside her. "Tell me you'd choose to be apart from me. Tell me your soul calls out for any other but mine."

The soft yielding of her body and the heated, tight clasp of her channel on his cock made it impossible for her to lie. His wings settled against her thighs, brushed in sensuous reminder of how erotic she found them when they made love.

Sajia shivered. Her eyes closed as she gathered strength. Opened as she said, "I won't exchange one type of servitude for another, despite our games of dominance and submission. Despite what we once had. If I'm to love you as deeply as I did then, it will be because you treat me as an equal in our relationship. Not as your prize or your reward, but as a wife who is both joined to you and separate from you."

He wanted to rail against her demands, against hearing her say out loud what he already knew, that she didn't yet love him in the way he so desperately craved. He wanted to tie her to the bed again until she was mindless with pleasure, her will bent so thoroughly to his that they were one person, bound so intimately together that they wouldn't exist apart. But some small, rational part of him accepted an irrevocable truth: she wasn't the same woman he'd loved before, though he loved her no less for it. Her soul was more thoroughly Scorpion, honed in the fiery birthplace of the Djinn so she could survive in a world that had been changed forever by what the humans had done to it.

He could put none of his thoughts into words. Could do nothing to change their immediate future. That left him with only the moment, and the pervasive need to have her clinging to him, crying out his name in sobbed release.

If anything could ease him, it was how readily she gave him those things, even as she wrung out his surrender in equal measure. Making his buttocks clench and his breathing become labored, his skin grow slick and his thoughts scatter as he came in a lava-hot rush of semen.

They left the bed a short time later, remaining in the cabin only long enough to wash and eat a breakfast of bread and fruit. Then they resumed their search, using the *Constellation*'s powerful engines instead of its sails.

Lunch was eaten on the deck, with the vastness of the ocean spread out around them. In the distance several cargo ships were visible, two leaving the bay and three heading toward it.

Dotting the blue were fishing boats, large and small, populated with men working their nets or using poles and lines. It had been time-consuming getting close enough to each of them in order to eliminate it from their search.

Sunset was approaching when Sajia spotted a boat with a red lantern to the right of the cabin doorway and a blue on the left. Addai slowed the *Constellation*. He'd not thought it possible to feel what a human would feel, the knotting of his stomach that came with fear.

He couldn't be in two places at once. Couldn't will himself to the boat and guard her at the same time.

Free her from the bindings, the internal voice advised. And he denied it once again.

"Get in the cabin, Sajia, while I take the *Constellation* closer."

Resistance flared in her. A refusal he saw her fight to suppress as she remembered her earlier promise. She obeyed, though she left the door open and hovered just out of sight beyond it.

Three men were visible. All three rested their hands on their knives when he changed the *Constellation*'s course and headed directly toward them.

He kept the speed steady, calculating the distance and the point at which he would be close enough to use his voice as a weapon. And when it arrived, he said, "Lie down on the deck and you will be spared."

They lay down as ordered, docile in the promise of death and damnation he carried with him.

Truth or trap?

The doorway leading to the cabin was open. Addai reached beyond the three men and found terror and hope in the cabin, entreaties for rescue, not from only one human, but from two.

He sensed none of his kind. Sensed nothing other than the five humans onboard.

"I believe the scion is here," he said, drawing Sajia out with his words.

It took only a few moments to guide the *Constellation* alongside the other boat and secure them so they couldn't drift apart. Addai kept himself positioned between Sajia and the prone men, looking away from them only long enough to glance in and see the cabin's occupants: a homely girl, her wrists bleeding from the ropes securing them, and a boy, perhaps only a year older than the girl, his face badly bruised and his clothing dirty and torn.

Sajia drew her knives and entered to free the scions. A moment later, Addai heard Corinne's heartfelt sob, then her babbled apologies for not confiding in Sajia, followed by her identifying the boy as Sebastian, a scion of the Tassone family.

Satisfaction surged through Addai at learning who the boy was. Wariness followed as he thought of the message that accompanied the one sending him to Sajia. This had all the markings of something arranged by the Djinn. He wondered if the witch lied about Caphriel's involvement, then shook off his misgivings, telling himself that regardless of intent, finding Sebastian Tassone here gave him a bargaining tool to free Sajia from her oath and ensure her family could be made safe.

"Let's go," he said, moving as it became unbearable to have Sajia out of his sight, suddenly anxious to be done with vampire business and begin their life together.

"We need to get Corinne and Sebastian home," Sajia said, guessing at his intention to let the scions take the *Constellation*. "I need to speak with the Tucci master about my oath and my family."

He chafed at the necessary delay, but said to the Tassone scion, "Take off the charm hiding you from your family so they'll come for you."

The boy's Adam's apple bobbed up and down before he gathered his courage and stood taller. "I won't let Corinne be sent to Los Angeles." A blush crept up his face. "She might already carry a Tassone scion."

Sajia was torn between laughing and crying and raging. "Was that your plan? To run away and hide until she got pregnant?"

Sebastian's chin lifted. "If Corinne is sent to the Gairdens, she'll die. Their scions survive the transition less often than the Tucci do."

Tears spilled down Corinne's cheeks. "It was the only way we could think of to be together."

Sajia felt herself soften with pity and sympathy. She didn't need to ask why the teens hadn't petitioned Draven Tassone. There was nothing the Tucci could offer that would be worth weakening the Tassone bloodline for, no reason to form an alliance with a family so far beneath the Tassone in power.

"Take off the token," Addai told Sebastian again. "And when your family arrives to collect you, allow me to bargain on your behalf."

Sebastian's eyes met Corinne's in silent communication first, then he nodded, accepting Addai's offer, though he fumbled as he removed a coinlike token from his pocket and handed it to Corinne for safekeeping. She did the same, handing him the token she carried.

Sajia smiled at that. They might be scions, but they were still teens who thought they'd somehow manage to use the tokens to sneak away again.

"Where did you get them?" she asked.

"Maliq," Sebastian answered, naming the man the Wainwright witch had. "I met him in the occult shop. It's one of the places I visit every day as part of my schooling."

And probably how he'd met Corinne, Sajia guessed, or at least how they managed to slip messages back and forth without anyone becoming aware of the relationship.

"And the fishermen?" she asked, thinking not just of the ones who lay in peaceful surrender onboard the boat, but of the one who'd been drained of blood by the Tucci.

Sebastian looked out through the cabin door, and his expression hardened beyond his years. "Maliq arranged for a man to take us to Oakland and for a hiding place, but he must have sold us out. These three jumped us in the red zone."

Impatience rubbed over Addai's skin like an unpleasant breeze. The ocean grated on his nerves with its endless lap of water and its ever-present danger.

"Come out on deck," he said, anticipating the swift arrival of the Tassone and wanting them to see that their scion was safe.

Sajia left the cabin first. Corinne next.

The Tassone scion came last, and as he stepped through the doorway, Addai felt the release of a spell. *Trap!*

In an instant the men lying on the deck were freed from their fear. They rose, drawing their knives and rushing forward.

A thought and Addai's sword came to him. With the sweep of his arm, it sliced through the first of the men, measuring the darkness of his soul. Drinking in memories of rape, and the intention to do the same to the scions before delivering them to someone else.

The second and third men died just as quickly. Their evil measured as their spirits were cast into the ghostlands to be enjoyed by those who hunted and tormented there.

Pawns, Addai thought, anticipating the appearance of his brother.

Caphriel didn't disappoint. He arrived in a flash of glory, his wings the same snowy white of Addai's.

His attention went immediately to Sajia, and his smile held equal measures of amusement and cruelty. "When last we met, I wondered what drew you to lost causes, brother. Now it seems I've found your motivation, and a way to save you from yourself. Shall we keep this fight between us, or should we summon others and add to the fun?"

"Does your most recent defeat in the Were lands leave you needing to call for reinforcements?"

Caphriel laughed, slicing through the air with his sword in a playful manner. "She is sweet, but knowing you grieve her loss will be sweeter."

"I'll kill you first."

Caphriel smiled an instant before he lunged, his sword connecting with Addai's in a series of blows meant to drive Addai to the right and leave an opening to Sajia.

One touch, one bite of the blade could deliver death, instant to her human form and slow, like an icy poison, to her Djinn one.

In a fury of desperation Addai thrust and parried, wielding his sword like a fencer's blade. He scored a hit on Caphriel and received one in return across his belly.

Blood escaped in streams and pain streaked through him. Unlike punishment delivered by an earthly weapon, the damage done by Caphriel's couldn't be healed instantly by will alone. Wouldn't be healed at all if they fought to true death.

Fear drenched Addai, choice arriving once again. If he set Sajia free, then she would know he'd kept her imprisoned in form when she might have found Corinne earlier. She'd know he could have eased her mind, eradicated the terror of what happened in those times when she blacked out.

Learning the truth would crush the love just starting to blossom in her heart, leaving distrust and hate in its place—forever if he defeated Caphriel, or for the last moments of her life if he failed her once again.

He'd loved her once but not been willing to risk everything. A moment of indecision had led to thousands of years of regret.

Trust in what was beyond his control didn't come easily to him. But arrogance did.

He'd win her heart again if necessary.

Addai spoke the word to unravel the spell written in angelic script on her body.

Behind him Sajia gasped, but he couldn't afford to turn his attention from his brother, because in that instant, Caphriel launched an attack meant to make good on his threat to end Sajia's life.

Sajia remained standing by force of will alone as the scorpion-shaped pendant she'd worn all her life burned against her flesh, delivering knowledge in a molten pour that scorched through her like melted rock and creation fire, revealing a heritage nearly beyond comprehension. Djinn.

Daughter of Earth. Scorpion-souled. Protector of her people and the world that gave birth to her. Enemy to those not of this world: the angels who battled in front of her as well as the vampires the scions behind her would one day become.

The need to slay her enemies blossomed like a black rose in her chest, thorns of hate piercing her, as if they'd anchor themselves in her soul. But almost immediately came thoughts of Addai, the memories they'd created in the short time they were together. Tenderness and sacrifice. Pleasure and pain.

Those memories were followed by equally powerful ones. Of the humans who'd made her part of their family, though now she understood there was no true genetic link to them. Of the still-human Corinne, in ways like a younger sister.

The thorns of hate found no place to reside in Sajia's spirit. Fiery, elemental passion filled her, hot and intense, like a sandstorm sweeping across the desert and bringing with it the need to protect, to love, to live.

She thought to turn long enough to place the knives in the scions' hands so they could protect themselves and she could change form and join Addai. But before she could do it, he cut his brother so deeply that Caphriel's sword hand hung from cleaved muscle and severed bone, blood gushing as his free hand gripped the near stump, fingers clamping down like a tourniquet.

The tip of Addai's sword lodged itself in Caphriel's chest, piercing skin but not yet ending life. And even then, Caphriel laughed, taunted, "Do you dare, brother? My death might just turn our father's gaze back to this forsaken world. Will you risk it? Are you ready for his wrath? Are your allies ready? Peace, brother. For today. And tomorrow. For thirty days and then we will begin our games again."

Sajia went to Addai's side, her own blades sheathed. With the illusion of being human stripped away, her doubts about him fled. For a being whose existence spanned eternity, only the essence of who someone was mattered, the soul without regard to form, and hers called out to his just as his did to hers.

She placed her hand on Addai's arm. "Let him go."

"And have him make a game of trying to kill you?"

In his voice she heard a willingness to damn them all because of his love for her. And despite the threat of it, tenderness welled inside her, bringing with it an understanding that delivering death came far easier to him than trusting in life.

Stroking her hand along the edge of Addai's wing, she said, "I believe I've told you several times now that I am not the same woman I once was. I won't be so easy to kill this time."

Emotion clogged Addai's throat. So intense it would have taken him to his knees had they been alone.

The desire to return to the chalet with Sajia overpowered him, pushing him to hurry and be done with Caphriel and his games. "Ninety days," he said, bargaining as he had with Rimmon.

"Sixty. Beyond that, death would be a sweet release from the ennui."

"Sixty," Addai agreed, pulling his sword from Caphriel's chest.

Caphriel's form faded away in a weak shimmer, but his voice was strong in Addai's mind. *Enjoy her for the time she's yours. The next victory will be mine, brother.*

Addai sheathed his sword, and with its disappearance his wings also vanished. He turned, hardly daring to believe what he saw in Sajia's eyes, what he'd heard in her voice moments earlier. Acceptance rather than repudiation. Love rather than hate.

I have never desired another as I do you. There has been no other for me since that day we first met. "I feared—"

She touched her fingertips to his lips, silencing him. "You should if you intend to keep secrets from me or treat me as a prisoner."

His heart was light, filled with such joy that he smiled against her fingers, teased, *Not a prisoner, but a love slave.*

He accompanied the words with an image projected into her mind, the recent past overlaid onto a far more distant one, of her naked on her knees before him, eyes pleading and hands placed in supplication on his thighs as she both waited for his command to pleasure him and pleaded for him to give it.

Sajia laughed, a sultry sound that had him hardening regardless of the blood pouring from his wounds. But then she grew somber, "You're not healing."

"I will with our return to the chalet."

In her need to get to Addai's side, concern for the teens had fled Sajia's thoughts completely. They remained near the cabin doorway.

Neither seemed shocked or awed at having witnessed a battle between angels. They knew of the existence of such beings, she realized, guessing it was part of the history lessons reserved for scions.

The vampires of this world are the pale remains of beings fought elsewhere by my kind, Addai said, a shadow in her mind or anticipating her thoughts.

The noise of fast, powerful engines had them all looking toward San Francisco. And within minutes a swarm of speedboats had surrounded them.

Guards armed with machine guns boarded, efficiently clearing it of danger, their last duties to search the dead men then flip the bodies into the water.

A man who could only be a Tassone High Servant joined them on the deck of the fishing boat then. He was lethal beauty and deadly charm, his graceful movements making Sajia think of a cobra.

She suppressed a shiver when storm gray eyes became smooth steel, the change in them pronounced, arriving with the alien presence of the Tassone master as he took possession of his servant's body. This was a vampire's ultimate escape—if they were willing to

sacrifice power for continued life—to be able to completely abandon their own body, leaving it behind to burn or rot or sink to the
depths of the ocean while they lived on in another's.

His gaze flickered over her, taking note of the Tucci marks on
her arm before settling on Addai. "Apparently I am in your debt.
What do you require to discharge it?"

"It can be accomplished easily enough. Arrange a betrothal between Sebastian and Corinne, and as part of your terms to the Tucci,
Sajia is to be freed from her oath."

"And why would I want to do that, when apparently her service
would also bring me yours?"

A *trap neatly laid and neatly sprung*, Addai thought, the message Irial carried, reminding him that Sajia's return was part of the
weave creating alliance, now just another part of the pattern. And
yet with Sajia beside him, he could muster no rage at the maneuver-
ings that would result in him being tethered to vampires.

"For you to call on me as an ally, then you would also have
to offer protection to Sajia's family and safe harbor for the *Constellation*."

"Done. Thane will see to matters until sunset, then I'll send for
the Tucci master and make arrangements."

A blink and the vampire's presence vanished, allowing his servant's soul to escape whatever dark prison it'd been banished to.

Addai led Sajia into the cabin and closed the door. The wings
he'd hidden after defeating Caphriel materialized as he took her
into his arms.

"Home now," he said, willing his clothes away in the same
thought that took them to the chalet.

He unbound her hair as she stood in his embrace. Its silky length
trailed down her back and the enticing curve of her buttocks.

"I could command you to disrobe," he murmured. "And return
to your lessons of submission."

"Or you could make love to me," she countered. "And we could continue creating new memories together."

He laughed and quickly tugged her clothing from her body, a flash of possessiveness making him say, "Shift. Rid yourself of the Tucci marks."

Sajia changed, taking the scorpion's form in reminder and warning that he'd feel the sting of her ire if he thought to make her into something she wasn't. Returning to his arms when she became woman again, her skin free of scarring.

Be mine, he said, giving her a choice.

I already am.

Say the words.

She touched her lips to his, sharing breath and soul. *My spirit to yours.*

Always, beloved. And as Djinn fire coursed through Addai's veins and a tattoolike scorpion appeared above his heart, he lifted her, joining their bodies, evoking the incantation and forever binding his existence to hers.

Primal Kiss

LORA LEIGH

They draw us in.
They fire our blood, make us dream.
They give us comfort when the world turns dark.
They warm us when we're cold.
They begin our fantasies, they end them,
and when we dream, when we reach for the perfect
fantasy, they're always there.
This book is for that ideal, that comfort, that
fantasy, and that dream.
This book is for,
that perfect kiss.

PROLOGUE

FELINE BREED HOME BASE
SANCTUARY
BUFFALO GAP, VIRGINIA

The secured communications and defense bunker sat inside the base of a mountain less than a quarter of a mile from the main family residence in the valley now known as Sanctuary.

The main level was mission control, outfitted with the most technologically advanced electronics, satellite tracking equipment, and mission communications available.

The main level was also the entry level, with the first entrance winding through the various workstations from which orders were transmitted and Breed missions tracked throughout the world.

Sanctuary was the main mission base that the Breeds, the ultimate fighting machine, the balance between man and beast, were hired from and sent around the world to fight in the wars the non-Breeds began.

They were extraction experts, the perfect spies, assassins, trainers, commanders, and the best logistics experts in the world, and they were in high demand.

Mission control was never silent.

The second entrance was further around the side of the mountain, hidden from the main house and sheltered by a thick grove of trees. It opened into a serene lobby that could have graced the most expensive, most exclusive resort but was actually the site of the single most state-of-the art security system ever created. Breed guards manned the entrance both inside and out, while advanced surveillance apparatus scanned, identified, and logged even the stray insects that managed to breech the glass and metal doors.

The lobbylike setting was in fact the entrance to the Breed labs, and thus the security employed was even greater than that for mission control. In the past six months, the entrance had been all but welded closed and buried in an attempt to ensure an impenetrable defense against unauthorized access or exit by any Breed daring to betray the community fighting to save Breedkind.

Breed traitors weren't unheard of. There had been more than one in the fourteen years since the feline pride leader, Callan Lyons, had announced to the non-Breed world the existence of the Breeds.

He was both cursed and revered for his decision. There were days he wondered if he had made a mistake that would eventually destroy them all, or if history would see him as a visionary who had taken the only path the Genetics Council had left him.

Now, as he swiped the security card through the reader, then laid his palm on the electronic identification plate, he cursed himself.

Leaning closer for the retinal scan, he waited.

"Hello, Pride Leader Lyons, may I have your passcode?"

"Lyons, alpha, niner six, point seven three eight."

"Thank you, Alpha Lyons. I detect you have guests. Please pass alone. Each guest must pass verification before being allowed access into the inner lobby."

The electronic security couldn't be ordered, manipulated, or bribed. It could be programmed, but even that programming had so many damned safeguards that just setting the passcodes for today's meeting had taken more than thirty-six hours. He almost grimaced at the necessity of it.

As the doors slid open, he passed into the lobby, stood back, and waited as each of his "guests" went through the same security. Standing in the lobby, he could feel the faintest wash of heat over his flesh, a warmth most humans wouldn't detect but any Breed would sense.

To complete its verification function, the bio-scan system would compare his blood type, any unique internal anomalies, and the scan of his brain to the ones on file for him, just as it would for each of those coming behind him.

Taking this entrance into the labs wasn't the quickest way in, but it was the quietest. If they entered through the main house, family, Breeds, the human soldiers assigned to Sanctuary, and most especially any Breed spies still left within the base would be aware of it. Going through mission control held the same lack of discretion. And a few of those meeting today were men and women the feline, wolf, and coyote Breeds had gone to great lengths to hide.

They were there for a job, to make decisions that none of them were truly prepared to make and the additional security allowed for this meeting, and would give the participants the ability to make the decisions needed based on a live scrutiny of the situation at hand.

Feline Pride Leader Callan Lyons was certain that those with him today were, like him, unsure how to handle what they were about to face. The director of Breed affairs, Jonas Wyatt; the wolf Breed alpha, Wolfe Gunnar; and the coyote Breed alpha, Del-Rey Delgado, were accompanied by the scientist Jeffrey Amburg, a human Jonas had managed to capture nearly two years before. Others that must remain hidden included a human geneticist known for her advanced research in genetic anomalies, Amelia Trace. Alexi Chernov and Katya Sobolov, coyote genetic and physiological experts, stood next to her. Behind them stood Dr. Nikki Armani, council trained and human and one of the foremost experts on wolf biological, genetic, and physiological attributes. One by one they moved to the scanners, gave their passcodes, and stepped inside.

The feline Breed genetic expert, Elyianna Morrey, waited in the labs below with Jonas Wyatt's latest captive and the scourge of the Breeds.

The arrival of the other alphas and scientists was a closely guarded secret. The heli-jet that had flown them in was listed as delivering medical supplies and had landed in the secure area outside the labs to offload the fictional medical supplies.

Every precaution had been taken, but Callan had no doubt rumors of the visit were already swirling. No matter their attempts, it still seemed Sanctuary was plagued by too many eyes and ears that reported to either the Council fighting to destroy them, the pureblood groups determined to imprison them, or simply a host of other enemies that believed the Breeds were a sign of the destruction of humanity.

The fact that there were Breeds still betraying their own was an acid eating at his soul. The cruelty the Breeds had suffered in the labs hadn't been enough for some, it seemed. Compelled by bald-faced greed, the Breed traitors would send their fellow Breeds back to the labs and see them destroyed.

Once the final member of the group had passed the entrance, Callan led everyone to the lobby's large elevator and entered first. He stood at the back of the cubicle, his eyes narrowed, his gaze touching on each scientist as he prayed, God how he prayed, that despite the horror of what they were facing below, that some hope for the Breeds would come of it.

His gaze lifted as the elevator lights dimmed and a hovering blue light began to swirl around each individual. Unlike the bio-scan upon entry into the lobby, this DNA scan was unconcealed, overt. This final scan would identify the members of the party once again and ensure each person matched the criteria and identity the computers had been given.

Along with the automated check, a Breed enforcer of each pack as well as a feline would watch the monitors and compare the identities to known individuals before the elevator opened ten floors below the base of the mountain.

"Welcome to Sanctuary's labs, Alpha Lyons," the wolf Breed on duty spoke through the intercom. "All identities have been verified and access granted."

The double doors to the elevator slid soundlessly open, revealing a silent, steel-lined hallway.

Sanctuary had once been an unnamed lab in the control of the Genetics Council. The labs below ground had seen the countless births, tortures, and deaths of Breeds. Now, it was home to the hope-filled research that could possibly save them all.

At least, that had been their hope when they had taken the compound after arguing successfully that the Genetics Council owed it to them. A small partial payment for the horrors they had suffered. Breed financial accounts were still being contributed to by the countries and financial empires that had been found to have contributed to the Genetics Council's work.

But who could they sue now for the horrors they were still suffering and the extreme prejudice building around them?

"How is Ely doing, Callan?" Jonas asked, his voice quiet as they walked down the hall, scanners quietly humming as they did a final check for weapons, weapon components, or any conceivable manner of threat to the facility.

"She's doing better," Callan stated. "The past year has been hard on her, but she's coming out of it."

She had been used against the very Breeds who trusted her to ensure their health and well-being. A mind-control drug had been slipped into her system, creating in her an addiction and an inability to refuse the orders of those who had initiated the reprogramming of her delicate mind.

She had almost died as a result. And she had almost taken Jonas and one of their best enforcers with her, and Callan knew she still suffered the guilt of it, a guilt that might torment her for the rest of her life.

"The past year has been hard on us all." Jonas sighed.

For the past month, it had been especially hard on Jonas and his mate, Rachel, as they watched the changes in the child a monster had managed to get his hands on.

Callan felt his chest tighten, felt the ever-present fury that rumbled just below the surface and the animal genetics that roared out in rage.

Amber Broen Wyatt, the child Jonas had adopted after his mating to her mother, had been injected with a serum that was presently destroying the monster who had attempted to use Amber against Jonas.

That serum was eroding Phillip Brandenmore's mind, destroying it a cell at a time as it forced his body, his organs, his very cellular structure to change.

The monster, Phillip Brandenmore. For decades he had conspired with the Council. He had destroyed Breeds, spilled their blood, filled them with such agony that they had begged to die, that they had bled out, howling with the need to escape.

The same monster the Breeds were now fighting to save. That they were risking their own secrets to attempt to end his agony when he had never had a moment's mercy for the agony he had caused.

"Can she handle this?" Nikki Armani paused to glance at them, the long black braids she wore in her hair flowing around her as the dark chocolate brown of her eyes gleamed in concern. "Brandenmore is her own personal nightmare."

"She's handling it." Callan kept his expression calm, his gaze, if not serene, then at least, composed.

What else could he say? Ely no longer talked to him as she once had. Hell, she no longer talked to anyone about anything but the most mundane topics these days. She was more reserved than ever, more focused on her research and, it seemed, more determined to cut herself off from everyone who cared for her.

As they neared the end of the hall, the double doors there clicked open, and the stoic faces of the Breeds behind the heavy clear shield at the side of the doors watched them carefully.

Wolf, lion, and coyote Breed enforcers worked together here as they did nowhere else except perhaps the labs in the wolf Breed base of Haven in Colorado. The enforcers, who were charged with the protection of the labs, the research, and their futures, were specially selected and rigorously tested before being assigned to the most sensitive areas of the Breed strongholds.

Callan and his group passed through yet another sensor before heading down a shorter hallway to the observation room where Ely awaited them.

It was a journey that seemed to take a lifetime. Each step of the way Callan was too aware of the fact that what they were doing here was a slap in the face of every Breed living and dead. Because the assignment charged to the scientists moving ahead of him was to save the life of a man who had taken so many Breed lives.

As another enforcer stepped from his post in the hall and opened the doors to the observation room, Callan nodded back at him. This enforcer was human. The only human allowed into the compound, and this one only at Jonas's insistence.

Jackal had been a part of a specially trained Special Forces group when the Breeds had first revealed themselves. His loyalty to the Breeds stemmed from his commanders, Callan's brother-in-law, Kane Tyler, the man who had saved Jackal's life and the life of his sister.

He was Ely's personal guard, whether she liked it or not. And the fact that she didn't like it was voiced by her often.

Entering the meeting room, Callan moved to the far end and stood at the head of a long conference table. Chairs were placed around it, but no one sat. Instead, they turned and stared through

the window that looked down on the padded cell Phillip Brandenmore had been confined to for more than a month now.

What they saw was shocking, horrifying.

He was a seventy-five-year-old man, but he now had the appearance of a man in his fifties. His hair had grown back; his skin had
lost that dry, parchmentlike appearance. The dark age spots that
had once covered his face had almost disappeared, and he wasn't
stooped as he had been the night he was taken captive after Jonas's
attack on his mountain cabin retreat.

He sat against the wall, his head tilted back, staring up at the
deceptive appearance of a mirror, a sneer on his face.

He knew the mirror was more than a one-way reflection, that
eyes watched from the other side. Someone was always watching,
both from this room as well as from the room that the video cameras fed into.

"My God, he looks ten years younger than he did the last time
I saw him," Dr. Armani breathed out roughly.

Ely stepped from the shadowed corner of the room then. "As
indeed, physically, he's nearly thirteen years younger than he was
the night Jonas brought him in," she stated. "And the metabolic and
cellular changes are only increasing. As is the degeneration of his
brain. As his youth returns, we're seeing parts of his brain actually
dying off, and any sense of morality or right and wrong deteriorat-
ing. At the same time, his sense of cunning and self-preservation
seems to be growing."

Drs. Chernov and Sobolov moved closer to the window, their
expressions still and silent as they stared down at the deceptively
unassuming man that stared back at them with hatred and demonic
rage.

"He came several times to the Chernov labs," Katya Sobolov
whispered, her gaze somber and filled with shadows. "We often
had to hide our girls there for weeks to ensure he did not see them.

The Council would have given him whatever, whoever he requested for his research." Coyote females, one of the least created species of the Breeds. They were incredibly rare, and when found, usually killed.

Breeds. Phillip Brandenmore's research had been on Breeds.

"True evil filled this one long before he took whatever serum he created from the mates he destroyed," Chernov said then. "Better to let him die, to study him as he has studied those he tortured and killed. I would say it is no more, perhaps much less, than he would have done."

"But we're not monsters, nor are we evil." Ely stepped closer, her gaze tormented, large brown eyes so saddened they had the power to break Callan's heart. "And Jonas's daughter Amber isn't a monster. If we don't figure out what's causing this, and how to reverse it before he dies, then Amber could potentially suffer the hell Phillip Brandenmore is suffering now."

Only Callan saw Jonas's expression shift, saw the agony that pierced his icy, silver gray eyes. The infant was a sore point with Jonas. Greatly loved, treasured, and experiencing a subtle change within her own cellular makeup.

"What do you need from us, Dr. Morrey?" It was Dr. Sobolov who finally spoke, her pretty face tightening, becoming cool and composed as the scientist emerged, dedicated and willing to find the answers she needed.

Beside her, Alexi Chernov gave a tight nod, his expression less determined, but his gaze hardening as he too began to slip into the skin of the scientist he was.

"We have weeks perhaps." Ely sighed as she turned back to the sight of Phillip Brandenmore sneering up at them. "If we don't have the rest of the puzzle by then, we face losing not only Amber but also the opportunity to find the answers we need to continue hiding mating heat. It's our opinion the information has been contained so far. It's better to contain the truth as long as possible." To ensure world opinion and prejudice didn't turn against them. Their positions, as well as their safety, were still in a precarious state where fickle human fears were concerned.

"And his accomplice?" Chernov questioned. "This Horace Engalls the press has spoken of? What information might he have?"

"Engalls has been able to avoid us so far," Jonas drawled, and the look on his face had Callan making a mental note to press Jonas on whatever plans he might have with regard to Engalls. He had a feeling this was going to be one of those stories that would leave him with a very bad taste in his mouth.

"Phillip claims Horace only has the results of the tests and the drugs the research arm developed," Ely stated. "But, when he's not as lucid, he's very smug about the fact that Engalls is involved." Ely gave a shake of her head. "It's too hard to determine truth from lie with him, and even if we could, we can't reveal he's ever been here or use anything he's said to prosecute Engalls."

"If he will not be leaving here, then why save him?" Chernov asked cynically. "Merely study his dead body for the answers."

Jeffrey Amburg gave a little snort. "Because, like me, the bastard is of more use alive to Wyatt than he is dead. We have an expertise, you see. An ability, information, or contacts that Director Wyatt would like to make use of."

Amburg had been one of the Genetic Council's leading genetic scientists in regards to cellular and genetic mutations and manipulations. And he had practiced his craft well on the Breeds he created as well as those he was ordered to experiment upon.

Jonas turned, his dark brow arching arrogantly as his gaze raked over the other man. "After three decades of creating and torturing Breeds, you owe us at least that much," Jonas drawled as though amused. "And it seemed to me a better alternative than death." Then Jonas smiled, all teeth, canines flashing dangerously. "Or worse."

"Worse" being a volcano on a remote Pacific island that was rumored to have already tasted the flesh of others whom Jonas had deemed critical threats to Breed society. What more would he do to save the daughter that the animal inside him had accepted as its own?

Jeffrey stared back at him for long moments, in no way cowed by the look. Finally, though, he gave a small nod, realization seeming to cross his face. "I never considered the alternative perhaps." His lips almost quirked. "But, I have considered what I owe the Breeds, Mr. Wyatt. I rather doubt Brandenmore or Engalls will see the subject in the same light, though."

"I guess it's all according to the threats required to convince them to look at it from my perspective," Jonas answered mockingly.

Oh yes, Callan thought, he was definitely going to have to have a little chat with his little brother.

"Dr. Morrey, could you give us a clearer timeline for completing our agenda of re-creating the serum and reversing it, should Engalls not cooperate?" Amelia Trace stepped forward, her exquisite, gamine features so void of human emotion that Callan could well imagine a robot existing beneath the living flesh.

Ely breathed out roughly. "Best case scenario, perhaps a month," she stated. "Worse case, less than fourteen days." She gave her head a hard shake. "I can't get any closer than that."

"Then we should begin, yes?" Amelia asked with a slow, uncaring blink of her eyes. "We have a child to save."

And Callan was certain the others missed it. That flicker in her eyes. That betraying spark in a wash of brilliant, explosive blue.

For the first time, he saw emotion, and he sensed something more, something that was there, then gone, so quickly he couldn't analyze it or decipher it.

But still, it was emotion.

"And I have Engalls to deal with." Jonas turned to Callan,

his lips quirking with cool mockery. "I need to discuss that with you."

Which meant the plan was already in motion.

Better to apologize than to be told no. That was Jonas's philosophy. Callan hoped it didn't end up biting his brother on the ass. Better yet, he prayed it didn't end up biting *him* on the ass.

ONE

Every good girl loved a bad boy. It was a fact of life, a quirk of nature. Opposites attract, and the badder the boy, the more attractive he was to that good girl who couldn't help but be drawn to him.

Kita Claire Engalls had to admit that despite the fact that he was obviously a well-respected security specialist, Creed Raines was a definite bad boy. A wolf posing as a lamb, and that so wasn't working for him.

Six-four, cloudy gray eyes, thick black hair, and an oh-my-God body packed with muscle and covered with rich, darkly tanned flesh. At least, the flesh Kita had seen was rich and darkly tanned. She liked to fantasize the rest of it was too.

Sensuality curved his lips, edged at his thickly lashed eyes, and sometimes, just sometimes, lit the dark gray irises of his eyes with a wicked hunger. A hunger she glimpsed when she had turned fast enough to catch it in that instant before it was gone.

Brushing back a wisp of dark blonde hair as it fell over her shoulder, Kita couldn't help but wonder at the attraction.

He'd been with them far longer than any other security specialist. A few weeks past a year. She remembered marking the day, almost as though it were some inane anniversary. And it was all his fault. It was the bad boy corrupting the good girl she was.

She had been a good girl all her life, but that didn't mean she didn't recognize that glint in a man's eye. Just because she was a good girl didn't mean she was stupid, and it sure as hell didn't mean she wasn't well aware of what the sensations spiking through her body meant.

When her nipples hardened and throbbed and her clit swelled, aching for touch, she didn't just know what it meant, but sometimes she was even smart enough to know how to take care of it. When her flesh felt too sensitive and she was so aware of the need for pressure against her lips that she was forced to press her teeth against the lower curve, she knew it was a hunger for his kiss.

That didn't mean he knew how to kiss. She had assumed any number of men knew how to kiss and had been sorely disappointed. No doubt he would disappoint her as well.

She gave a small sigh as she pushed the sunglasses down her nose and watched as he stood at the other end of the pool. His hands clasped in front of him, the white shirt he wore bright beneath the brilliance of the afternoon sun.

She noticed the other two security specialists, as they called themselves—they were nothing more than hired guns, really—appeared to be sweltering beneath the bright, late-spring sun.

Creed Raines was anything but sweltering.

From where she lay against the lounge chair, she couldn't detect even a hint of sweat on his brow.

She stared into the dark lenses of his glasses, wondering if he was even awake. He hadn't changed position in an hour. He had to be asleep.

Could a man actually sleep standing on his feet?

Tilting her head, she watched him carefully.

She had heard of it happening during times of war.

Smiling, she mimicked a kiss toward him, then gave her lips a little flick with her tongue. And there wasn't so much as a smile or a change of expression.

So much for amusing herself by teasing him. It had become her favorite pastime over the past few years. Well, not teasing her body-guards, but definitely torturing them in one way or another.

"Kita, isn't it a little cool yet for sunbathing?"

Well, there went her fun for the day.

Sitting up, she readjusted the chair before pulling on the thin wrap at her side and then glancing up at her father.

"You didn't bring the iced tea, Daddy," she chided him with a smile as she curled her legs close to her body and allowed him to sit at the bottom of the chair.

For a man nearing sixty, he was still in reasonably good shape. His hair was still thick, though it was more gray than brown now. Laugh lines were slowly being replaced by worry lines, and his once laughing brown eyes were somber and tired.

The death of her mother last year had destroyed them both, but her father wasn't recovering.

"You should come in out of the sun." He cleared his throat uneasily. "It's still rather cool. You could become ill."

"I'm not a baby anymore, Daddy," she told him gently. "I don't get sick at the drop of a hat."

For a while she had, when she was younger. She was no stranger to pneumonia and no stranger to hospitals. Thankfully, she had grown out of it. But her father hadn't grown out of his habit of worrying about her.

"You're getting restless." His gaze sharpened on her. "Creed informed me he caught you trying to slip out of the estate last night."

She turned and stared back at the bodyguard. He had promised not to tell. The damned liar.

She turned back to her father just as slowly. "I'm not twelve any longer," she stated carefully. "I wasn't trying to slip from the estate. I believe I calmly got into my vehicle and tried to drive away."

"From the back entrance?" His brow lifted.

Kita wanted to roll her eyes; instead, she gave a little shrug.

"I wasn't allowed to leave, Daddy. I'm your daughter, not your prisoner . . ."

"My daughter who is now in danger." His voice tightened, the anger simmering behind his eyes coming through in his tone. "Your uncle is missing now, Kita. Phillip's body has never been found since the bodies of his guards were discovered in that cabin."

Kita dropped her gaze to her lap. Twining her fingers together, she tried to think of a way to change the subject.

She and her father didn't see eye to eye on her uncle anymore than they saw eye to eye on her confinement.

"Kita, stay close to the house." His voice hardened. It wasn't a request, it was an order.

She tried, she truly tried to keep her head down, to pretend to acquiesce to his wishes. But there was this part of her that just couldn't do it.

She lifted her head. "It's been two years, Daddy, since you and Uncle Phillip decided it was a good idea to attempt to walk into Sanctuary and abuse the Breeds' hospitality by trying to collect your ill-gotten research. I'm tired of putting my life on hold."

She hadn't agreed with them. She had remained silent over the years, she had tried to give her father the time he needed to fix the situation, but it was only growing worse.

"You don't know what the hell you're talking about." Surprisingly, his hand jerked out, his fingers curving around her arm as though he wanted to shake her.

Shocked, Kita's gaze flicked to where his fingers gripped her tightly before she turned and stared back at him. He too was staring at his hand as though it belonged to someone else.

"Dad?" The quiver in her voice wasn't fear. It was a reflection of the strike of betrayal she felt tightening her chest.

In response, Horace Engalls uncurled his fingers and pulled his hand back, but the surprise on his face disappeared as the expression of anger returned.

"What happened was beyond both our control." His jaw clenched, flexed. "What's done is done. It can't be undone. But I won't allow you to be used against me by the Breeds, Kita. I won't allow you to be turned against me."

What an interesting turn of phrase.

"No one could turn me against you, except you," she assured him as she slowly swung her legs over the side of the lounge chair and rose. "I think I will go in now. It's suddenly not as pleasant as it once was."

Her father rose as well, his hand gentler but no less firm as he once again gripped her arm and held her in place.

"The Breeds are moving against us, Kita," he bit out harshly, his once kind, gentle brown eyes now flinty with determination. "Phillip is missing, your mother is dead, your aunt Cara is under arrest, and there are rumors of Breeds targeting Phillip's entire family. I won't have them taking you."

"What are you so frightened of?" Kita could feel the nervousness, the sense of impending disaster suddenly tightening her stomach. "What have you done in the past two years? You swore." Her breathing hitched. "You swore to me and Mom that you would never help Uncle Phillip in his schemes again."

Her mother was gone, but she had believed he would honor the promise he made to her, that he would ensure he did nothing further to enrage the Breeds.

"Do you think I had to do more?" This time, he did shake her, just enough to shock her, to send a spurt of wariness pulsing through her. "Do you think, Kita, they wouldn't use you if they could? That they wouldn't take you?"

"Why would they want me?" This time she jerked her arm out of his grip, the hurt and anger rising inside her as she fought to hold on to it. She didn't want to argue with her father. She didn't want to fight with him, but God help her, what had he done that he was now so frightened?

It was enough to have fear edging past weariness. He had promised, and she had trusted him to keep that promise.

"God, Kita, they want you as a bargaining tool; they believe that by threatening to harm you, they can force something from your uncle. Or that I know something I don't and they can force it from me." He raked his hands through his hair, a grimace twisting his face. "They have Phillip. They'll come for me next."

"Only if they have a reason to," she whispered painfully as she stared up at him, desperate to understand where her beloved father had gone. "What have you done, Daddy?"

He shook his head slowly. "It isn't what I've done, Kee," he whispered then. "It's what your uncle's done. And it will destroy us all."

"No." She knew better. "It's not, Father. The only way I would be in danger is if you were involved."

His lips parted as though to speak, but no words came. It was in his gaze, though. It was in the guilt, the shame, and the pain in his eyes.

What had he done?

He had broken his promise to her and to her mother.

"I'm glad Momma isn't here," she whispered tearfully. "I'm glad she didn't live to see you betray her."

The blow against the side of her face caught her off guard. The shock of the burning pain, but even more, the horrible sense of betrayal was like a dagger shoved into her soul.

"Mr. Engalls." The voice was dark, low, and warning.

Kita's gaze jerked up to meet the dark lenses of Creed Raines's sunglasses and the tight expression behind them.

"What the hell do you want?" Her father turned on him then, enraged.

"I think you want to back off," Creed drawled. "I didn't sign on to watch a father that supposedly loves his daughter suddenly begin abusing her. Now did I?"

"Supposedly love," Kita choked out as she backed away from both of them. "That's a fairly apt description for a liar."

She didn't wait for her father to turn back to her or to see Creed's response. Kita all but ran from the two of them, the anger and the pain converging inside her to tear at her heart until she felt as though it were nothing but shreds.

Rushing into the house, she moved quickly through the first floor, up the stairs, and into her bedroom where she slammed the door closed and locked it.

Laying her head against the door, Kita blinked back her tears and knew the decision she had been on the verge of making for the past months had been made the second her father's large hand had connected with her cheek.

It was time to leave, no matter what it took.

CREED HADN'T EXPECTED this. Staring into Horace Engalls's eyes, he had to admit that even though he had sensed the tension and the anger building in Kita's father, he never imagined Engalls would strike his daughter.

Hell. Had he realized what was about to happen, he'd have stepped in sooner. The girl loved her father. She called him "Daddy" with that soft voice that bespoke a soul-deep affection.

He never would have allowed Engalls to do anything to threaten that affection or damage the precious emotion his daughter felt for him.

"Did I ask you to interfere?" The fear lay about Engalls like a particular stink, rancid to the senses.

Creed inhaled slowly, his senses amplified for some odd reason, the animal genetics that shared his body rising to the fore as though a true animal paced within his soul.

"You didn't have to ask," he assured the other man with the subtle Texas drawl that went with the identity he had stolen for this little adventure. "I offered. Do you really want to make her hate you? I'd say you're riding that line with that slap to her delicate face."

He could see the imprint of her father's hand on her creamy flesh, and he'd never had such trouble holding back the primal growl that edged at his throat.

In that second he watched Horace Engalls's lips tremble as emotion, a father's love, overrode anger and fear.

Engalls lowered his head, gave it a brief shake, then turned and stomped into the house, leaving Creed staring after his retreating back.

Creed almost smiled; definitely he felt a flare of satisfaction. For the past year he'd been working as one of Engalls's security specialists, slowly replacing the men that had originally come in with him with men he trusted himself. Men who would stand aside and ensure that when the time came, Creed would have a clear path to his objective.

To Kita Claire Engalls, the reigning, mostly spoiled princess of what was left of the Engalls empire.

He had been with her when her mother had died, just after he came to the estate. He'd been here each time she'd tried to slip from the estate for a bit of harmless feminine fun.

Sometimes shopping. Sometimes a late dinner with friends. A few times a bit of dancing at the exclusive nightclubs she and her friends enjoyed.

He knew her.

He knew her habits, he knew her expressions, her scents, and her flirtatiousness.

And he knew his dick was rock hard when she blew him those mocking kisses or watched him over the rim off her glasses as though he were a sensual treat and she wanted to lick him up a drop at a time.

Blowing out a hard breath, he strode to the house and entered as well. Hell, he'd be more than happy to let her have a lick or two, then he'd have his turn.

And he could well imagine the pleasure to be had there. A soft, delicate woman as heated as the hottest fire. Silken flesh. Sharp little nails.

His dick was vicious hard as he moved up the steps. The scent of her reached out to him, drew him. Hell, it was all he could do to keep his senses intact at the scent of her fear and her pain.

Betrayal was a bitter seed, and it was festering inside her. A father who had betrayed so many others surely would have no problem betraying one tender, trusting daughter.

And when he betrayed her, Creed Raines would be there. To deliver the final betrayal.

At that thought, he paused on the final step.

A feeling of reluctance stirred within his chest. Suddenly, fleetingly, the idea of betraying her seemed so very wrong.

Forcibly shaking the thought away, he took that last step, determination steeling him against these other emotions. He'd made a vow. He was a part of something far greater than a twinge of conscience.

Moving to the closed bedroom door, he rapped his knuckles softly against the heavy wood and waited. She was in there. He could smell her tears, her pain. The delicate scent of a woman who had reached a limit.

TWO

Kita swung the door open, expecting to find her father. Instead, she saw Creed Raines standing on the other side.

He'd witnessed her humiliation, witnessed her running. God, she hated that.

"What do you want?" For some unknown reason, she wanted to throw herself against him, to release the tears she was holding inside and feel his arms surround her.

Comfort. She wanted his comfort, and she had never wanted or needed that with the same strength as she did now.

He stepped inside, moving around her as though it was a foregone conclusion that he was welcome.

As though he belonged there.

"Close the door."

She turned and stared at him in mocking amazement.

"Did someone call and inform you that you were in charge or something?" She gave the door a hard push, though, before turning to face him.

Damn, she was just fucking pretty.

Creed watched her brush back a stray strand of hair, tucking it into the rest of her shoulder-length, dark blonde waves as she glared back at him with soft, doe brown eyes.

Damn, he loved her eyes. He also loved the way she pulled her lower lip between her teeth and pressed down, just a little bit. Just enough pressure to make his body tighten, his dick throb harder.

She hadn't changed out of the miniscule bikini she had worn by the pool, though it was somewhat obscured by the thin violet wrap she'd put on over it.

She looked good in that dark purple color. Good enough to eat and come back for seconds.

"Would you like to get away for a while?" Where the hell had that offer come from?

She blinked back at him before her gaze narrowed. "Where?"

"Does it matter?" he asked, crossing his arms over his chest. "Let me surprise you."

There was a part of him standing back in amazement and simply shaking his head in amused resignation. But the part of him inviting her out, that was standing there with his cock throbbing in anticipation, and his blood pounding in unusual excitement sent a sense of life burning through him.

There were times when he had felt like a robot, like a man without a course. But that was before he had stepped into the Engalls's home and met the princess he was to stay close to, close enough to gain her trust, her father's trust, so he could turn her over to Jonas Wyatt if needed.

"You'll surprise me?" He watched those dark, doe brown eyes suddenly gleam with anticipation. "What if I don't like your surprise?"

Oh, that wasn't happening. He knew her. He thought perhaps he knew her better than he knew himself.

"You'll love my surprise." His voice dropped, became rougher, a growl barely hidden now.

He moved toward her, the scent of her drawing him, the awareness of her feminine moisture gathering between her thighs, the subtle scent of it teasing his senses, intoxicating him.

She wasn't moving away from him either. She stared up at him, her breasts rising and falling heavily beneath the soft material of the wrap, her nipples pressing hard and tight beneath it.

The top of her head barely came to his shoulder, and as she tilted her head back farther, the fragile line of her throat was revealed. Beneath the cosmetic dental work that had been done to hide his canines, Creed swore he could feel a hollow ache, a need to clench into her flesh, to hold her in place. To dominate her.

His hand lifted, his fingers cupping the fragile curve of her neck, feeling the blood beating hard and heavy beneath the silken flesh.

"Why are you doing this?"

He almost smiled. No one could say Kita was stupid. She was flushed, aroused, and ready to fuck, but she was smart enough to realize he was acting out of character.

"Because, you need to get out." He stepped back, putting distance between them. "I don't want you slipping out, Kita. I can't protect you if I'm not with you."

Disappointment filled her eyes as she slowly shook her head. "I don't need your pity, Creed. And I'm not a child to need a treat to obey the rules."

She turned back to the door, opened it, and stood aside in silent invitation.

"Don't try to slip away," he warned her. "Your father is focused on the Breeds right now, but there are a lot scarier things in the world." And he had been there, seen them.

"What could be scarier than a Breed?" Doubt filled her tone. Like many non-Breeds, she had no true idea of the evil that could be found in the world.

"The pureblood societies who believe your father is holding the research your uncle is rumored to have done on several drugs that they believe could destroy the Breeds," he told her. "Those societies would take you if they had the chance, Kita. They would take you and use you against your father. If he doesn't have what they want, they would punish you, Kita, in ways you can never imagine."

And he knew the horrors of it. He had seen the results of it.

She didn't speak. As she stared back at him, he saw the flicker in her gaze, and he knew she would do exactly as he suspected she was preparing to do.

Kita was going to run.

"Don't do it." Before he realized his intent, he was leaning forward, almost nose to nose with her, the dominance rising inside him and nearly overwhelming him.

Creed was a perfect covert enforcer for a reason. He always kept his cool. He never gave in to his impulses. He kept them bottled, kept them hidden, only releasing the tension during sex. And he had partners for that. Women who didn't mind the rough foreplay, women who didn't mind fucking a Breed.

But never had it risen so rampantly, so quickly as it did now.

"Don't do what, Creed? Don't have a life?" she whispered bitterly. "Don't have a desire to live or a desire to be more than Daddy's little princess? Sorry, but the glitter wore off the princess act when I learned my father and my uncle had spent their adult lives torturing the Breeds."

"Don't run." He wasn't going to touch the rest of it. Not here and not now. "If you run, Kita, I promise, I'll find you. I'll find you and I will ensure that you never fucking run again."

Her eyes widened incredulously. "Are you threatening me, Creed?"

"Oh baby, I never threaten. I promise. And I promise you, you run from me, and you may end up regretting it."

It was all according to how she felt about fucking a Breed, he decided.

He could have her. And he would have her.

"I don't like threats or your heavy-handed promises." Her nose touched his as she all but went to her toes to glare back at him. "And you are not my keeper, Creed. You're my father's hired gun, nothing more and, I'm certain, most days, a hell of a lot worse."

Anger was driving her words. Anger and pain. Disillusionment was a hell of a journey to make, and she was making it in one of the most painful ways.

"I'm worse than you'll ever imagine," he growled back at her. "Your worst fucking nightmare, sweetheart, if you run. Trust me on that. Because you don't want to push me."

Because he was figuring something out himself, something he hadn't thought possible. In the past hour, he had begun to suspect that Kita Claire Engalls, the willful, stubborn little princess to a pharmaceutical empire, was actually his mate.

She eased back, her gaze still locked with his, eyes narrowed, her body almost trembling with anger. Anger and arousal. Hell, the subtle sweet scent of her pussy was making him crazed with the need to have her. To taste her.

"This conversation is finished," she informed him imperiously as her delicate little nose lifted, nostrils flaring in feminine offense. "You can leave now."

Oh, could he now? As though he were a dog to be ordered outside for disobeying its mistress? It so didn't work that way for a feline Breed. At least, not for long.

He knew her. He knew her expressions, her moods, her laughter, and her teasing. Until now, he hadn't really known her anger, and he couldn't say he was comfortable with it, but he could handle it.

"Don't push me, sweetheart," he warned her softly. "Don't force me into something we'll both regret."

He had no doubt in his mind she wouldn't hate him for life if he forced her into the mating heat, and he sure as hell couldn't warn her about it first.

Turning on his heel, he stalked from the bedroom without saying more. The problem was, he was so damned close to tasting her he couldn't trust himself. He wanted nothing more than to jerk her into his arms and take her lips in a kiss he knew would only fan the flames burning between them.

Hell, he hadn't expected to find his mate here, of all places.

The Engalls princess? Heir to a pharmaceutical company that had worked with Phillip Brandenmore to create a line of drugs potentially fatal to Breeds?

Brandenmore's scent blocker had made its way into the hands of pureblood societies and the Council-loyal coyote Breed soldiers still desperate to capture the mates of high-ranking Breeds or, God forbid, one of the hybrid children that had been born.

Especially the hybrids born of the wolves. The hybrid wolf-coyote Cassie Sinclair, as well as the child of Aiden and Charity Chance and the son of Dash and Elizabeth Sinclair. Children were so rare within the wolf Breeds that the Council scientists still operating would take any risk to acquire one.

Added to that was the drug therapy created to control a Breed mind. Horrific, destructive, it had nearly driven Elyianna Morrey insane even as it allowed her traitorous lab techs to steal and manipulate valuable mating heat data in an attempt to sell it, to Phillip Brandenmore and Horace Engalls.

Making his way back downstairs, Creed began moving to protect the delicate woman he suspected was his mate, especially from herself. She was in more danger than she knew.

In past weeks Creed had found signs of someone watching the house, but he could detect no unusual scents. Her father was acting strangely out of character, and there were rumors that the pureblood societies were looking to Kita to force Engalls to turn over information he had on the drugs his brother-in-law had given him to manufacturer. Those sample drugs and the ability to produce them on a large scale had been destroyed in an as-yet unexplained explosion at Engalls's manufacturing facility.

The Breeds hadn't done it. The information they had gathered said the pureblood societies hadn't done it either. That left but a few suspect paramilitary groups, but the Breeds had no sources within those organizations who could help them reliably finger those responsible for the explosion.

One thing was for certain: there were too many people looking to use Kita as leverage against her father. Get the girl, and the research could be theirs.

The Breeds desperately needed that research to go along with information provided just weeks before by the daughter of a Breed scientist. Storme Montague had hidden certain research on mates, primal fever, and a vaccine created in a little known lab in the Andes before the Breed rescues had reach that area. The vaccine mimicked one created in Russia for the coyotes and the men and women who worked with them. The vaccine, originally intended as an anti-body against a feared contagion associated with feral fever, was now revealing itself as a much-needed component in the mating and ability to conceive within the Breed community.

Piece by piece they were gaining answers to their questions about their own biology and the mysteries surrounding their creation and their abilities to procreate. They couldn't afford to lose what little research hadn't been destroyed because they hadn't realized the danger it could later represent.

And Creed couldn't afford to lose the only woman who had made him *feel*. Who made him realize he was more than just a Breed. She made him realize there might be a chance, however small, that he could be a man as well.

THREE

She managed to slip away from him.

A growl slipped past his throat as one of his human partners gave a loud, exaggerated cough before turning to stare at him in shock. They were standing in the center of Kita's bedroom as her father braced his arms on her opened balcony door.

"I paid you to keep this from happening." Horace Engalls turned on them as though it were their fault she had escaped. "You were to protect her."

"We were hired to keep anyone from getting to her. You didn't inform us she would end up running away," Creed pointed out.

"She's always slipping out," Horace snarled back at him, his brown eyes flickering with red rage. "You knew that."

"And we've always been aware of the nights that was happening," Creed replied with far more calm than he felt. "She's obviously far quieter than her friends have been when they've picked her up."

When it came to stealth, those women were like children in a candy store. All big eyes, giggles, and feminine charm.

"She's been taken then." A tremor vibrated through Horace's voice as he wiped his hands over his face. "God, they've taken her." He lifted his head, his eyes damp now with a father's tears. "Who could have taken her?"

To feel pity for this man went against everything Creed knew of him. Yet, the pity was there. In Horace Engalls's face, his eyes, his scent, there was only love and fear for his child.

"We'll find out," he promised, knowing she hadn't been taken. She had run.

The slap to her face the day before, two years of seclusion and fear, and she had had enough.

It would no doubt relieve Horace's mind to know this, but Creed had a far different agenda than bringing her home.

"How will you find out?" Horace swallowed tightly, visibly shaking now as the fear began to coalesce inside him. "There's no ransom note. There's nothing."

"But there will be," Creed assured him. He turned to the two men working with him. "Stay here, put a tap on the phone. I'll see what I can find out and report back." Turning back to Horace, he hardened his expression and his voice. "Stay here by the phones. Someone will call, and I doubt it will take long. The moment you hear something, one of my men will contact me."

He turned his back on the father and moved quickly down the hall to his own small suite and the leather bag he kept packed for emergencies.

A change of clothes, weapons, ammo, and a small medical kit were included. Pulling leather riding pants, a black long-sleeve shirt, and a leather jacket out of the closet, he tossed them on the bed before reaching for the black riding boots.

He was dressed and moving down the steps in five minutes flat. He ignored the three men walking into the study: Horace and the two human enforcers assigned to Covert Operations with the Bureau of Breed Affairs.

The lethal black, specially designed motorcycle sat innocently in the drive. Its frame was based on one of the less powerful touring cycles, but every aspect of its functionality had been adapted with Breed technology. Straddling it quickly, Creed pulled the full-face helmet over his head, strapped it beneath his chin, then started the ignition with a flick of his fingers.

Before pulling from the drive, he set the helmet to full security mode and then spoke into the voice-activated controls.

"Activate Engalls, Kita, tracking protocol on all tags."

The digital display came up on the inside of the visor as the computer answered. "All vehicles presently accounted for, and all but one deactivated and located in the main garage. Vehicle three is being tracked through both automotive tracking as well as electronic tag detected in Engalls, Kita wallet. Location currently identified and highlighted on your screen."

The digital display reconfigured to show the small red dot identified as Kita's vehicle at approximately five hours ahead of him.

"Computer, display routes to intersect in quickest possible time."

The map reconfigured once again. He could shave two hours off his time and catch up with her well before evening.

"Onboard navigation detected in vehicle," the computer spoke unexpectedly. "GPS programmed and displaying onboard directions to destination."

God love her heart, Creed almost smiled. Kita liked to say she was directionally challenged. She loved that GPS, which was the reason he had tied the trackers into the navigation on each vehicle her father owned.

The computer came back seconds later with the address of her destination, and this time, he couldn't help but smile. She was driving right into the thick of Breed territory and didn't even know it.

He loved it. He couldn't have asked for a better destination himself.

"Call Wyatt," he ordered the computer as he turned onto the interstate and began heading out of New York toward Virginia. The coordinates the computer laid out would have him arriving at her location before she did. A small Tennessee community that barely numbered in the hundreds during the tourist off season. And it was definitely not tourist season for that area right now.

"Wyatt is currently unavailable," the computer replied.

"Call Wyatt. Verification pass, tango, seven."

The computer paused for long seconds before replying. "Verification pass approved, Enforcer Raines. Director Wyatt will be on the line momentarily."

He didn't have to wait long.

"Wyatt," Jonas answered shortly.

"She's on the run," Creed informed him immediately.

"The Engalls brat?" Jonas growled. "Do we have a situation?"

"We can make it a situation," Creed replied before quickly launching into his explanation. He could almost hear Jonas thinking hard and fast on the other line.

"I'll have him contacted," the director finally stated thoughtfully. "Keep her incommunicado until further notice. I'll put the plan in effect and see if we can get Engalls to cooperate."

Which meant Brandenmore wasn't cooperating. The deranged CEO of Brandenmore Research had become so twisted, so pure evil and cunning that even as his mind was being eaten away, he was still scheming to destroy the Breeds.

The only hope left was the chance that Engalls could figure out where that research had been hidden. The Breeds had exhaustively searched every known location associated with Brandenmore and Engalls—corporate offices, research sites, private residences—but had found no trace of the research the Breeds knew Brandenmore had developed with Engalls's help.

"Do you know where she's headed?" Jonas questioned.

"I have her navigation system tagged as well as her wallet," Creed answered. "Her location was punched into the nav, and I have it now."

"Excellent." The satisfaction in Jonas's voice had Creed's lips tightening for a moment. "Keep her out of sight and out of communication, Creed. And pray." For a moment, the agony Creed knew the other man was going through slipped into his voice. "Pray Engalls cooperates when he suspects the Genetics Council has kidnapped his daughter."

And he was praying. But, Creed admitted, he had been praying since he learned what Brandenmore had done to the three-month-old infant: injected with the same serum he had injected into himself. The serum that was quickly killing him. And he refused to give the information on it, refused to do more than give them the original serum and demand they learn why it was destroying him and not the child. As though he feared giving the Breeds his research would result in whatever was needed to save Amber only.

Creed couldn't swear that wouldn't be the direction the Breeds took.

Let him die, and Amber would die. By refusing to turn over the research, Brandenmore was ensuring they dug deeper into the ailment destroying his brain. Unfortunately, they weren't going to find the answers in time to save him from death. And with him dead, the serum he had used, Ely had assured them, would no longer be of use without Brakenmore's living body to test any cure on.

A double-edged sword that Creed knew was putting not just the child at risk, but the entire Breed community as well.

Jonas had known the only weakness in the Brandenmore and Engalls families was Kita, Horace Engalls's daughter. He also knew other groups would be aware of that as well. Creed had been sent in to ensure she was safe, and to ensure that when the time was right, the Breeds would have possession of her.

Simply kidnapping her wouldn't convince her to transfer her loyalty from her father to them, though. Creed had been waiting, waiting, determined to take advantage of the slightest weakness where she was concerned.

If the Breeds had Kita on their side, then they would have Horace.

And Creed now had an ace.

Mating heat.

That twinge of guilt was only growing, though, tightening his chest and pricking at his soul. Because now, he knew her. And he knew, if she ever learned he had deceived her, she might end up being the only woman capable of turning her back on the phenomena.

Now wouldn't that just suck!

SHE WAS HOME.

Kita stepped into the small house, closed and carefully locked the door behind her, then let out a weary breath. The drive from New York wasn't overly long, but this time it had seemed to take forever.

Of course, if she had refrained from watching the rearview mirror, it might not have taken near as long, nor seemed so tiring. But she kept expecting to see Creed and that wicked black motorcycle of his riding behind her.

She felt stalked. Like prey. Like a hare running from the wolf and unable to find a hole deep enough to hide within.

She was safe now. She had to be. This hole had to be deep enough, because it was the only place she had left to escape to, the only place no one knew of.

Deep in the mountains of Tennessee, hidden outside a tiny little community of only a few hundred. The house wasn't in her name; it wasn't tied to anyone or anything she was associated with.

Her eyes closed, she ignored the sense that she had left something behind, or perhaps that something had followed her. She had been careful, and she had learned how to be careful.

Creed had taught her that over the past year.

She had watched him, she had listened and taken notes, and when she ran, she had remembered everything he'd told her about how to escape a possible enemy.

He wasn't the enemy, but he might as well be at the moment.

"Did you have a nice drive?"

A screech erupted from her throat as her eyes flew open, her hands jerking, scrambling for the doorknob and managing to do no more than turn before he was suddenly there.

Kita cried out in shock as his hand flattened against the door, pushing it closed and pressing her against it.

Full body contact.

In the year he had been in her father's employ, she had never felt the full effect of his hard, muscular body, or the heated warmth it generated.

Her head jerked back, pressing against the wood, her gaze connecting with his as she breathed in a shocked gasp. Against her stomach, hard and engorged, his cock pressed into her.

"Did you really think I'd let you get away so easily?"

Dark, rough, so sexy she swore her knees weakened.

Kita swallowed tightly. "How did you find me?"

"Maybe I'm just smarter than your average hired gun," he drawled.

Kita felt her lips. She hated it when that happened around him. That need to be kissed. It was so intense, an ache that quickly struck to other, much more sensitive areas.

"I'm sure you are," she retorted, but her tone wasn't snappish or shrewish as she would have wished. It was soft. It was a come-on and she knew it even if it was involuntary. She only wished she could sound like that on demand. "Now, tell me how you managed it."

The smile that quirked the corner of his lips suddenly had her heart racing, the blood pounding furiously through her veins. It was such a wicked look. Such an extreme bad-boy look.

Her thighs clenched, her clit became hot, swollen, and achy as she pulled her lower lip between her teeth and pressed.

"I could do that better. Every time I see that pretty lip clenched between your teeth, you make me want to take a bite too."

She felt herself melt. Her juices eased from her pussy, saturating the folds between her thighs as she barely, only barely managed to hold back a whimper.

"You haven't even nibbled," she whispered. "And I offered."

"Did you now?" His hand slid from where it was braced over her head, touched her shoulder, caressed to her elbow, then slid over the thin material of the sweater sleeve and gripped her wrist.

Before Kita could grasp the meaning of what he was doing, he'd gripped both her wrists, pulled them quickly over her head, and secured them in one large hand.

"Creed." It was a protest. She was certain it was.

It had to be a protest, she told herself. Dominance games really didn't turn her on. She liked slow, easy touches. Foreplay that lasted forever. Or at least longer than three minutes.

But she couldn't help but realize her cunt was suddenly so sensitive that even the feel of her moisture easing from it was a caress.

"Are you wet, Kita?" The dark male growl in his voice sent a shiver chasing up her spine.

She realized then why she loved his voice. It was strong, fierce. A dark, heavy sound, like a great jungle cat prowling around her.

Except Creed had a way of making her feel a hell of a lot more than that edge of fear she felt around the big cats. And so much more than the wariness she had felt around several of the Breeds she had come in contact with over the past years.

He made her feel alive. He made her realize she was more sensual, and more alone, than she had ever realized before.

"You're not answering me." His head lowered, his lips brushing against her cheek. "Are you wet?"

She shook her head as she fought the mesmerizing cadence of his voice.

"No?" The edge of amusement in his voice had her heart skipping a beat. "So, if I can manage to get my hand inside those snug jeans of yours, I won't find you slick and hot for me?"

His free hand moved to her waist, then to her hips before his fingers found the snap of her jeans and played with it teasingly.

The backs of his fingers brushed against the bare flesh of her stomach beneath the short hem of her light sweater. The warm caress, as delicate as it was, had her nipples tightening, throbbing as she felt her lashes becoming heavy, a sensual drowsiness stealing over her.

"Why are you doing this?" She needed to think right now. She had decisions to make, a life to build. "Why did you follow me?"

"Why did you run from me?" His head lowered until his cheek was beside hers, his lips at her ear, the warmth of his breath caressing the delicate shell. "Didn't I warn you not to run from me, Kita?"

He had, she remembered it.

"You're dangerous to me," she whimpered. "We both know it, Creed. I can't handle you."

He would break her heart. She wasn't the casual sex type; she'd learned that in college. She needed the commitment, the monogamy. She needed to feel as though she belonged, and she hadn't found that yet. Or at least, she hadn't felt it until Creed. From the moment she'd met him, something inside her had clicked, had opened a part of her sensuality that she hadn't known existed.

"How do you know you can't handle me?" A gentle, heated nip at her ear caused her to jerk against him, a breathy little moan leaving her lips as she stared at the wall across from them and fought to steal back just a few of her senses.

But it wasn't happening. He wasn't going to let it happen. In the next instant, the snap of her jeans parted.

FOUR

Creed watched her eyes and felt that irritating itch just beneath his tongue as the snap of her jeans parted under his fingertips. His palm flattened against her lower belly, his fingers tucked just above the warm pad of her pussy.

Sweet, feminine heat wafted to his nostrils, intoxicated his senses. She made him almost drunk on the scent of her arousal, on the knowledge of the sweet, feminine hunger that assailed her.

He'd never experienced anything like this. Mating heat was still a relatively mysterious phenomenon to those Breeds who hadn't yet mated. They recognized the altered scents of mates. There was an awareness of certain unnatural changes, a lack of aging, or at the very least a slowing of the aging process. But the unusually heated scent of mates' arousal was infused with something so deep, so emotional, the unmated found it impossible to process.

Mated couples made the unmated highly uncomfortable because they exuded a sense of emotion wholly unknown to unmated Breeds, a sentiment that went far beyond loyalty or brotherhood.

As Creed let his fingertips caress the soft flesh of Kita's stomach, felt her heavy breathing, scented the sweet heat of her pussy, he now understood the deep emotion of the mated.

Over the past year, he had come to know Kita, to sense her, growing ever closer to her, never realizing he was falling in love with her. Until now.

Now, staring into her big brown eyes as his fingers moved slowly lower, aching to touch her slick head, Creed realized that in the past months, he had been placing Kita even above Jonas's orders.

"Creed." The whispered plea on her lips tore through his senses as his lashes drifted to half-mast, her features flushing with a delicate pink of needy hunger.

A second later he found the soft, delicate curls just above her clit. They were warm, and lower, God, lower, he swore he could already feel the moisture he knew was gathering on the soft folds.

God, he wanted to kiss her.

His gaze dropped to her soft lips, the way her tongue peeked out and flicked over them. He wanted to take her, taste her hunger and her need. Taste the delicacy of her mouth before running his tongue down her neck, along her breasts, her tight nipples, before finding the luscious heat awaiting him there.

"Kita." He pressed his forehead against hers, swallowing and tasting the hint of cinnamon that eased from the swollen glands beneath his tongue. "We need to go a little more slowly."

Yet his fingers were just a breath from her clit, pausing, aching to stroke the tight knot of nerves that hid within the soft curls and tender folds of the woman he held against him.

"Okay," she breathed, but she didn't try to pull away. Instead, she pushed against him, her hands tightening on the material of his shirt as though to hold him to her.

She had no idea who he was. She had no idea what he was. A Breed, an enemy of her father, and once he kissed her, there would be no way to hide it.

His fingers slipped farther, touched the hot kernel of her clit, and he lost it.

He was a Breed, he wasn't a robot. He couldn't touch her, couldn't want her with such hunger and not take what was being offered to him so enticingly, so willingly.

"Creed, kiss me." The plea slipped from her lips and tore past what little control he had left.

"Kita, you don't know who I am." He fought to breathe in something more than the hot scent of her.

She moved against him, her clit stroking over his fingertips as he told himself he had to reveal the truth to her. Ordered himself.

"I dream of you," she whispered then. "Do you know how I fantasize about you, Creed? I touch myself and try to pretend it's you. I'm tired of pretending. I know you're the man I hurt for."

His head turned, his lips lowering to her ear where he nipped at it in sensual retaliation or in approval, he wasn't certain which.

"It may hurt worse," he groaned, "if I kiss you."

"Nothing can hurt worse."

Her head tipped back as his moved. He told himself he had only wanted to see her face, to move from the too rich scent of her arousal where his had rested, too close to the heavy vein pounding at her neck.

Her lips were there, brushing against his, sending a surge of lust tearing through him and a pulse of the hot, rich elixir held in the glands of his tongue.

Jerking his head to the side, Creed lifted his free hand and quickly jerked the cosmetic disguise from the canines at the sides of his mouth.

If she noticed what he had done, she didn't give a sign of it. When he returned, his lips covering hers, she gave to him. Her lips parted, a soft moan passed her lips, and Creed took full advantage.

The animal inside, repressed from far too many years of covert work, rose inside him with a savage, internal growl, and he gave her the kiss that a male Breed can only give to his mate.

A dark, wicked, primal kiss intent on binding her, holding her, on mating her in the most savage sense.

KITA HAD NEVER been given a kiss that made her hungrier. She could be aroused. She had been aroused many times, by several men.

Until this kiss.

She hadn't believed a kiss could be sexy, that it could fire the senses and pull her deeper into her arousal.

Until this kiss.

Creed's head lowered, the thunderous gray of his eyes ensnaring her gaze as she felt a heavy, sensual lassitude overtake her. Her lips parted involuntarily, her lashes fluttered as she fought to keep them open, and her heart began to race in heavy, erotic excitement as the finger at her clit exerted just the slightest pressure at the moment his lips brushed against hers.

The touch, though oh so subtle, was like heat lightning. A small gasp escaped her lips, giving him the perfect invitation to more fully lower his head and take possession in a way no other man ever had.

Confidently, teasingly.

With his tongue, he traced the curve of her lower lip, then drew it between his teeth, worrying it with sensual precision; after one last small nip, he bestowed a flicking lick that had her lifting closer to him.

Between her thighs his index finger stroked, pressed, subtle in its destruction and sexual favors.

Kita could feel herself shaking, trembling. There was such a sense of need, of hunger rising inside her, she wondered she wasn't crying out from it.

She wanted his kiss.

A full, seductive, melting, lust-arousing kiss that would burn her to the tips of her toes.

She had read about it.

She had dreamed about it.

She had sensed it had to be out there. After all, where there was smoke, there was surely fire, and even teenagers swore they had experienced the perfect kiss.

One that was primal.

One filled with hunger.

A kiss they couldn't resist.

In that second, his lips covered hers. Parting the desperate curves, his tongue slipped inside in a teasing kiss against hers, retreated and came back, as her arms lifted to twine around his neck and hold him to her.

His kiss became deeper still, and as a hungry growl vibrated against her lips and the arm slipping around her back tightened, Kita finally found that kiss she could lose herself within.

A subtle hint of cinnamon met her taste buds as his tongue licked at hers once again, his lips stealing her senses and her control. This time, this kiss, was that intimate stroke of fire and ice, lightning flaring through her senses, heat wrapping around her body. It was everything she had ever heard a kiss should be.

His arm wrapped around her, strong and warm, so strong. There was no breaking that grip. There was no way she wanted it broken.

Tightening her arms around his neck, she tilted her hips, pressing the hardened bud of her clit more firmly into his fingers as she felt him pushing her tighter against the door.

This should have happened sooner, she thought distantly. She would have never run if she had known she was running away from this.

The deep drugging kisses burned like fire in her soul, obliterating any thought of protest, any need to protest. Sensation traveled through her nerve endings, exciting them as nothing in her life had before. Before Kita realized she was moving, she was rubbing against him, desperate to get his fingers lower, to fill the emptiness inside her.

Nothing mattered but getting closer to him, to fulfilling the promises he made with his lips, with his tongue, with the hungry inhuman rumble of a growl that vibrated in his chest.

That sound was a warning, and one she chose not to heed. To heed it would be to pull herself away from him. It would mean re-

linquishing the warmth and the tidal wave of sensations he'd un-
leashed within her.

"Kita." Marked. Hungry. That sound sent a shiver racing through
her nerve endings.

Digging her nails into the material of his shirt, she was on her
tiptoes, arching into him. Feeling his cock pressing against her abdomen, she tried to get ever closer, his fingers curving, pressing
lower, rimming the clenched opening of her pussy as she gasped
and tried to draw more of the luscious, rich taste of his kiss to his
tongue.

"Kita." The hard, dark groan as he pulled back from the kiss
drew a protesting cry from her lips.

Struggling to open her eyes, she stared up at him, her breathing
hard and rough as she swore she could still taste him. She ran her
tongue over the lower curve of his lip, almost moaning at the heated
taste of cinnamon and spice to be found there.

Then the breath whooshed from her lips. Her back arched. Pleasure became sharp, all-consuming, as she felt two, hard, broad fingers pierce the clenched, tightened opening of her pussy.

Ecstasy began to build in her bloodstream, whipping through
her system and spasming through the inner muscles of her vagina
as it gripped his fingers in reflexive response.

Hard fingers slid up her back, tangled in her hair, and dragged
her head back as he stared down at her savagely.

"Do you have any idea what I could do to you?" His voice was
so dark, filled with the same hunger that gleamed in his eyes. "I
could take you, Kita. I am going to take you. Every sweet, soft inch
of that tight pussy."

Oh hell, she was going to come. Sensation slammed into her
womb, through her pussy, tightening it further as she felt her juices
surge between his fingers and her vaginal walls.

"Why wait?"

She'd managed to surprise him. She could see the surprise in his eyes.

Then Kita got the surprise of her life.

His lips pulled back in a grimace, flashing the very defined, wicked, animalistic canines at the side of his mouth that proclaimed his animal genetics.

He was a Breed.

Her eyes widened. His narrowed.

A growl rumbled in his throat as his fingers surged deep inside her, curved, and pressed against a hidden, too sensitive spot with one, two little rubs that destroyed her senses.

She was already primed for him.

She was already ready to go over that edge into oblivion.

She hadn't expected this. Considering all she had heard about the Breeds, she shouldn't have been anything but terrified. So terrified that fear should have been her only possible response.

Instead, she felt ecstasy.

Rapture.

A hard, guttural cry tore from her lips as an orgasm tore through her body.

It exploded in her clit, her pussy, then whipped through her womb and drew the rest of her body bow tight.

The wailing, desperate cry that fell from her was a sound she had never made before. It came from the very core of her being, as though the pleasure, a pleasure like none she had ever experienced before, had taken control of her senses.

Clamping her thighs around his hand, she tightened her pussy on the fingers that still caressed, still rubbed that primal spot inside her. Starburst radiated through her brain.

"Creed." His name was a sound of agonized pleasure as she felt the breath still in her chest for long, precious moments.

She wanted to feel every sensation. She wanted to know it, to memorize it. She wanted to lock it inside her and keep it with her for the rest of her life.

Because there was no way she could keep Creed. There was no way the Breed holding her could be the man she had longed for, the man she had ached for all these months. There were was no way her father's enemy could ever love her.

As the pleasure began to dim, reality took its place, forcing back the fantasy as she slowly regained her senses.

His fingers eased from the grip she had on them.

His cock still pressed against her hip, hard and fierce, the heat of his flesh seeming to radiate through the leather of his pants.

Thunderous gray eyes were nearly black, perspiration dotted his forehead, and his chest rose and fell with his harsh breathing.

And only one question could resonate through her mind.

Why?

FIVE

"Don't try to run again. You won't make it far."

Kita stared at Creed, her father's security specialist for the past year, and oh so obviously no more than a plant by the Bureau of Breed Affairs.

Sitting in the chair across from him, she crossed her legs, propped her elbow on the padded arm, rested her head against her palm, and just stared at him as he sat on the couch across from her, leaning forward, forearms braced on his knees, his eyes locked on hers.

"Now don't you just look like the disgruntled kitty," she drawled mockingly. "Or is that pooch? Feline, wolf, or coyote?"

His eyes narrowed. "Feline. Lion."

Her lips pursed in a vague imitation of thoughtfulness. "I must be top priority if the director of the Bureau of Breed Affairs sent one of his lion enforcers to play babysitter for the past year."

His lips thinned. "I wasn't your babysitter."

Her brows lifted. "Well, you weren't parked on my father's ass, so I rather doubt Jonas Wyatt had you babysitting him. So tell me, Creed, why were you there? Information? To simply keep tabs on us? Or were you there to kill one of us when the time was right?"

He sat back slowly, his arms crossing over his chest as his expression became set in cool, unemotional lines.

He wasn't there to kill her, and he wasn't there to kill her father.

"Information." She sighed. "That's why you're there, isn't it?"

"Then why am I here instead?"

"Dad sent you?"

"You were calling him 'Daddy' before," he pointed out, and in the shadows that crossed his face, she could have sworn she saw a hint of anger in his gaze.

He had no right to be angry with her. If anyone had a right to be angry, she did.

"What I call him is none of your business," she informed him with a mocking roll of her eyes. "He sent you?"

He shrugged at the question, and she took that for a yes. It was the only reason he would have followed her.

"When are we driving back? I can't leave my car here."

"We're not going back just yet."

How interesting.

Kita continued to stare back at him, wondering at that feeling of heated moisture between her thighs.

Damn him, he kissed like a fucking sex god. Like her greatest fantasy. He had done what others had failed to do. His kiss had only fueled her need. Then he had done what two other lovers hadn't even managed to come close to. He'd sent her into orgasm. And he had managed it with only his kiss and his fingers. Other men hadn't even been able to do it, no matter the grunting efforts they'd put into it.

SHE WAS GLARING at him.

Creed narrowed his eyes as he tried to read her expression.

It was impossible.

For the first time since he had become her bodyguard, Creed could not tell, by her expression alone, what she was thinking. But there was enough emotion rolling off her for him to guess by scent alone. And there wasn't enough anger to save her.

She should be furious. Ahead of the subtle scent of arousal still coursing through her, she should be raging at him. Which would only make the arousal hotter, build higher.

Instead, she was, first and foremost, aroused; behind that, he sensed irritation and confusion.

The confused part, he shared. Because all things considered, she was truly rather rational. Especially considering the fact that she was now in mating heat.

Just as he was. He'd had her kiss, he'd had her orgasm, but he was still vicious hard, his dick throbbing with furious hunger. It was the most intense need he had ever known. Since the moment his lips had touched her, since he had felt the warmth of her inner lips, the mating hormone had begun to build in the glands beneath his tongue.

It was more than an itch now. It was a burn, an arousal far deeper than it had been before the mating heat had kicked in.

"I don't like that look on your face," she muttered as he continued to watch her silently, to draw in the unique scents of her.

He arched his brow, unwilling to allow her into his thoughts just yet. To give her a chance to learn how deep his need for her went when he was beginning to grow very concerned over what the next few days would bring.

"And what do you mean, we're not going back just yet? That's why Dad sent you after me, correct?"

She wasn't calling her father "Daddy" any longer. And each time she said "Dad" instead, the scent of disillusionment drifted toward him.

Every emotion had a scent, and to the Breed senses, they were easily detectable.

Disillusionment was a scent that clashed with her innocence, her compassion. It was a dark scent of sulfur subtly underlying the sweetest, softest scent of a spring rain, the scent of her arousal. It was there, though, and it pissed him off.

"Cabin fever does crazy things to a person." He shrugged as he watched her carefully. "It's my opinion that perhaps you need a few days' vacation. A chance to relieve some tension."

It wasn't exactly a lie, but it wasn't exactly the truth either. But he wasn't about to tell her that he and his boss were leading her father to believe she'd been kidnapped.

"He doesn't know you're a Breed, does he?" Her lips pursed mockingly.

Amusement joined the other scents, just the slightest hint of it.

"No, he wasn't aware of it."

"What about the men you were working with?"

His brow arched. "I didn't tell them."

He hadn't had to tell them. They were part of the Bureau of Breed Affairs; Jonas had likely told them. If not, then it wouldn't have been hard for them to guess simply because Creed had been working with them for so damned long.

Kita shook her head in amusement, an amusement he could easily read on her expression this time.

"You don't hate Breeds," he commented.

She rose from her chair and moved languidly across the room before turning and leaning against the door frame and staring back at him. "I never hated Breeds, Creed. They didn't ask for what was done to them. They were born into it."

Created into it, Creed corrected her silently. They had been created into this world, and trained rather than raised, to be killers.

He nodded slowly. Over the year he'd been in her home, he had seen that in her. She'd been waiting, watching, neither trusting nor distrusting the Breeds. She had paid careful attention to news stories and discussions, and at odd times had seemed to be studying her father, essentially observing him in the act of just being a father.

"And now you've kissed one," he said softly. "Come in the arms of one. What do you think now?"

"I think you're just as savage and as determined as every report I've ever read says you are. And I highly doubt you've been in my home to protect me, no matter the danger. So why not tell me exactly why you were there."

"That was why I was there, Kita." It just wasn't the only reason he was there.

She nodded again, her expression, her gaze thoughtful. It was then the scent of her reached him. The increased feminine heat. The arousal burning hotter, burning brighter inside her.

"Time will tell why you're here then, won't it?" she whispered, breathing out deeply.

"Will it?" He rose to his feet himself then, moving toward her slowly, feeling the hunger rising inside him as well. "Perhaps it's an answer we should find now, Kita."

Her heat wasn't as intense as it would be once he'd spilled his seed inside her, but the arousal was high enough to slowly become uncomfortable.

Advances into the mating phenomena were coming in slowly, being researched to damned death, and only then was certain information being shared with the Breeds.

It was still a subject considered NTK, Need To Know. And only Breeds showing visible signs of mating, or those involved in highly sensitive operations, were given the information.

Creed had been given the information. He knew the suppositions, the small advances that had been made, the research the Breed scientists had done. And he knew the heat hadn't reach its full pitch yet. And it wouldn't until he released his seed inside her.

Until then, the hormone he had released so far would irritate more than anything else.

Unless he kissed her again.

It was a one-kiss gig unless he wanted her to hate him.

Condoms required.

There were still the tiny hairs along his visibly hairless body that carried the hormone, but the quantities were so minute that as long as he didn't kiss her again, then he could control it.

As long as he didn't fuck her without a condom, it would be a while before the ramifications were apparent.

At least, to Kita. He, on the other hand, was already feeling the ramifications. He'd kissed her, and so the hormone was now infused with the genetic impulse to increase the heat and torture their bodies until conception occurred. To mutate the genetics in his sperm to be more compatible with her ova even as any hormone shared with her would make her likewise more compatible with him.

Stopping in front of her, his hand reached out and gently lifted a heavy lock of hair. He felt almost mesmerized by that hair. So many shades of natural blonde shimmering against his fingers.

He could feel the rumble of a growl in his throat.

He could smell her arousal, her interest. He could smell emotion, tenderness, and yet a rising need for confrontation. A scent reminiscent of that detected within both mates and human couples alike. A scent that came close to love.

Forcing his gaze from the heavy lock of hair he held, he took in the slumberous passion outlining Kita's face.

"You've entranced me, Kita Claire," he whispered as he turned his head slightly, the need to kiss her barely held in restraint by the knowledge of the consequences.

"Have I really?" A trace of breathlessness infused her tone. "Maybe you've done the same to me, Creed, even if you are being rather arrogant about it."

"It's part of our genetics." His gaze centered on her lips.

No kiss, he told himself. He couldn't kiss her, he couldn't lick her, he couldn't bite her. His eyes closed as he leaned his forehead against hers. He couldn't taste the silken, saturated folds of her pussy no matter how his mouth watered for it.

He had to keep his tongue in his mouth, his lips closed.

He had to protect her, at least until he could tell her the truth.

But that didn't mean there weren't other ways to play.

There were many ways to play. Ways that would leave them both gasping, their bodies perspiring in release.

He would make certain she didn't miss the kiss. But he would. God help him, he would miss the taste of her wicked little tongue, the feel of her lips beneath his. And the taste of her soft pussy. That he was truly going to regret missing out on.

"Promise me something, Creed," she said.

His lashes lifted to stare down at her as the hunger ate at him.

"If I can," he answered.

"Promise me you aren't doing this for some sort of Breed revenge. That you're not sleeping with me in some attempt to make my father pay for whatever he and Uncle Phillip have done."

Uncle Phillip. Phillip Brandenmore was her uncle through Horace's marriage to Phillip's younger sister.

"I can swear to you that I'm not going to sleep with you to make your father or your uncle pay for whatever crimes they committed against the Breeds." That was easy enough. It was the truth.

Her hand lifted, the tips of her fingers smoothing over his cheek as he watched her soft brown eyes melt with emotion.

He'd encouraged emotion in her from that first day, from the first itch he'd felt beneath his tongue. He'd teased, flirted.

"Kiss me, Creed," she whispered the one plea he couldn't satisfy. "Like you did earlier."

His head lowered. A little. God help him, let him be able to stop when he needed to.

As his closed lips smoothed across her forehead to her temple, he let his hands drift up her hips, pushing beneath her light sweater to find her breasts.

Smooth, firm globes fit his palms as her tight hard nipples met the pads of his fingers. He could survive without her kiss, he told himself. He could survive without releasing inside her. It wouldn't kill him. Hell, other Breeds had gone without their mates for years before, and they had lived.

He would live as well.

But first, he would have to distract her. He would have to give her so much pleasure that she didn't realize the kiss wasn't there.

Bending, he put his arms behind her knees and her back, lifting her against his chest as he carried her quickly to the bedroom he had found earlier.

The bed was already turned down. She'd let someone know she was coming because the pantry as well as the refrigerator and bathroom were stocked with new items. Nothing had been used before.

Laying her on the bed, Creed moved to her feet and carefully pulled off her sneakers, then the soft cotton socks. Undressing her became one of the most sensual chores he had ever undertaken.

She arched to him as he pulled her jeans from her body. Free of those, she began to fumble with the buttons of her sweater.

He watched. Watched those graceful fingers release each button as he hurriedly tore his own clothes from his body, carefully laying a condom aside.

This would be agony. Agony and ecstasy. It would be the heights of rapture, and it would be the further depths of pain if what he'd heard was true.

And it would be worth it.

It would be worth every second of agony to feel her clenching and coming around his dick.

As she tossed her sweater aside, Creed tossed aside his own shirt.

Naked, so fucking hard each pulse of blood pounding through his cock was a pleasure so intense it was painful.

Sitting up in the bed, her hair falling around her face in sunlit and shadowed blonde waves, she looked like a damned temptress come to haunt his fantasies.

That was exactly what she was. His fantasy. That nameless woman he had dreamt of for years before Jonas had sent him to the Engalls estate.

She was his mate.

And she was reaching for him.

SIX

Arousal, that hunger, unsated desire, the desperate longings and pulse-pounding aches. It was the need for touch, the body so hypersensitive, each nerve ending rising in attention as pleasure became the focal point of reality.

It was also the need *to* touch, though.

Rising to her knees, she flattened her palms against the hard muscles of his abdomen, feeling them flex in response to her touch, heated, alive. At first glance, the hard, bronzed flesh seemed completely free of male hair. But beneath her sensitive hands, she felt the ultrasoft down, almost like a pelt, smooth, warm, invisible to the eye, but detectable to the skin.

Resting on her knees, the object of twelve months' obsession right before her eyes, completely naked, completely aroused, the hard length of his cock jutting forward, she couldn't help but compare it to her fantasies.

And the fantasies paled in comparison.

Nothing could have prepared her for the highly conditioned, fully aroused, steel-hard body of a male Breed in his prime.

Her fingers curled against the flexing abs, nails rasping against his flesh as she felt his muscles harden further beneath her touch. The head of his cock was sheened with moisture, engorged and flushed dark with extreme arousal.

Dragging her nails down his abs, she gloried in the hard male groan that met the caress as well as the visible throbbing in the heavy veins of the powerful, thick shaft.

As her hands moved down, caressing, stroking to his thighs, his fingers buried in her hair. Blunt male nails scraped across her scalp, sending trails of exquisite sensation tearing down her spine.

She needed to touch him, to taste him, to experience every sensual pleasure to be had in his arms. Every sensual, erotic touch, taste, and sound.

Her head lowered, her lips moving to his chest, her tongue licking over a hard, flat male nipple as she heard the smothered groan vibrate in his chest.

Part moan, part growl, the sound wrapped around her senses, stoked the sensations rising inside her as her teeth gripped the disk and she allowed her tongue to worry it with sharp little flicks.

The taste of male desire and a hint of cinnamon hit her senses hard and burned through her veins. Between her thighs, her clit throbbed and ached, the need for touch riding her like a fever as her hands moved to his heavy, muscled legs.

She felt as though she were growing drunk, intoxicated on the sheer wicked excitement. Fascination had followed her since the day she had met him, fantasy flowing through her mind as she fought to bring herself to relief when the need for his touch, his kiss, had grown out of control.

And now, he was here. So obviously aroused, his hands in her hair, the pads of his fingers rubbing against her scalp as she began to lick her way down his torso.

She had never touched a man as she was now touching Creed, with such freedom. There had always been hesitation, a sense of something just not quite right. The two men she had been with before had each been a disappointment, making her fear she would never realize the pleasure she sensed could be had in a man's touch.

In this man's touch.

In a Breed's arms.

A moan tore from her throat.

Her Breed. The human species that had been a fascination for her since the day they had revealed themselves, and tonight, she would claim one for her own.

Her lips moved down his abdomen, her tongue licked, stroked, until she came to the brutally hard length of his heavy cock.

One hand curved around the base of it, the feel of the heavy pulse beneath sending the blood crashing through her veins. Pulling her head back, she moved to lick, to taste the engorged head when she suddenly found herself pushed back to the bed, and a second later, rolled to her stomach as Creed came behind her.

"Oh God, Creed," she cried out, her back arching as his arm curved beneath her hips, jerking them up and back until he pulled her to her knees.

"Stay still." Hard legs gripped her thighs as she felt him moving behind her, one hand smoothing over the curve of her rear. "Just like that, Kita. So sweet and ready for me. Trusting me. Do you trust me, sweetheart?"

Did she trust him?

Only with her life.

"I trust you," she cried out as his finger eased between her thighs, pressing against the entrance to her pussy, easing inside as the calloused tip rasped against oversensitive nerve endings.

It was a fury of hunger. A craving. A need she didn't know how to bear as her hips jerked back, desperate for more.

"I need you," she demanded, her voice ragged now. "Please, Creed. Please need me."

She hadn't meant to sound so needy, so aching. She hadn't meant to beg, but the yearning inside her refused to remain silent. She had waited too long for this, waited too long for him. God, he had to ache just as deeply for her.

"I need you more than you know, Kita." He came over her, his lips pressing against her shoulder, the heat of him like a fire at her back as she felt the thick width of his cock slide along the slick folds of her pussy.

The pulsing flesh raked across her engorged clit, sent fire and ice rushing through her body as pleasure exploded at the back of her skull and sizzled through her brain.

With trembling fingers, she pushed her hand between her thighs, gripping the hard strength of his cock as the sound of his harsh growl rumbled at her back.

Her fingers stroked the length, lubricated by the heavy juices that eased from her pussy.

The muscles of her vagina convulsed as her womb tightened. His cock throbbed in her hand, and the need to have him inside her was like a fever she couldn't bear any longer.

A distant part of her realized that somehow, as he'd paused behind her, he'd donned a condom. For a second, confusion filled her mind. It was so rare for a Breed to be able to impregnate a woman. They were genetically coded against it. A few had defied that rule, but only a very few.

Then he was shifting, moving, following her grip as she tucked the thick head of his erection against the clenched, snug entrance to her body.

"I need you," she whispered, desperate for him now. "Oh God, Creed, I need you so desperately."

"Then take me, Kita," he groaned, his lips moving to her ear, a warm breath of air stroking over the tender shell a second before his rough cheek caressed it. "Take me how you need me, baby. Every inch."

Every inch. Every steel-hard inch pulsing against her pussy as she began to press backward, feeling the flared head slowly part the tender opening.

She was shaking, hard tremors racing through her body as she felt the entrance stretching, burning as she backed into his cock. Her head fell to the bed, pressing into the pillows, her fingers clenching into the blankets beneath her as she pushed back. Each thick, throbbing inch easing inside her made her feel taken, almost to the point of bruising, pleasure and pain combining until she was whimpering, smothered cries leaving her lips as he began to fill her.

"Kita," the growling whisper at her ear had her jerking, spiking pleasure raking through her body as the stretching burn amplified every touch of his chest against her back, his thighs gripping hers, his cock easing inside her. "Take me sweetheart. All of me. Push back, love. Fill yourself with me."

Her teeth clenched as her hips jerked back, burying him deeper inside her with a searing thrust.

Panting, crying out from the sensations as her body struggled to accept the iron erection pressing inside her, Kita fought to just breathe. To make sense of the clenching, searing sensations striking from her pussy to her womb only to echo with eruptions of near ecstasy throughout the rest of her body.

"More," she gasped, struggling to ease back. "Creed, please . . ."

"Take more of me, baby." It sounded as though he were forcing the words between his teeth, and she felt the warmth of his perspiration in a heated drop along her shoulder. "Take what you want, Kita. It's all yours, baby. As much as you want."

She wanted it all. She wanted to burn inside and out. She wanted to be taken by him, possessed, and flying through rapture as the agonizing pleasure building inside her released.

She wanted to see the sun, the flames she could feel licking at her flesh.

And she wanted his kiss. She could almost taste it. Cinnamon and a wicked brew of a storm infused with the ocean. Pure male. Pure iron-hard heat forging through her.

"Creed." She moaned his name again as her forehead dug into the pillow before her neck arched, pulling it back to rest against his shoulder as he braced himself behind her. "Fuck me. Please, I can't do it alone." She was to the point of sobbing now, the hunger tearing at her, building through her until she couldn't fight it. "Take me, Creed. Make me belong to you."

As though that request were all he needed, a savage growl sounded behind her as he jerked back, rising to his knees, his hands gripping her hips, and he forged, surged inside her to the hilt, burying his cock full length and more. She jerked at the hard entrance and shuddered, shook as her senses threatened to detonate at the extremity of the sensations.

There was no way to process it. No way to acclimate to the feel of him fully imbedded inside her before he began moving. Pulling back, the flared crest raking, rasping over exposed nerve endings before he was suddenly shafting forward once again and sending her reeling with the ecstatic preliminary explosions of release.

Except, release didn't come.

A scream tore from her throat as he jerked back again, a second later thrusting forward, fucking her with a driving rhythm she couldn't resist and had no intention of fighting. She could only accept. Only hold on for the ride as she felt the last threads of reality dissolve beneath the pleasure tearing through her.

The sound of his thighs slapping against hers, the feel of his perspiration against her back, the sound of his growls in the air, and the feel of the steely length of his cock taking her, possessing her. Oh God, he was owning her.

He was taking her outside herself with the excruciating pleasure and delightful agony. Blending sensations through her body, forcing them to melt together as his cock tunneled inside her, over and over again. It stroked, caressed hidden nerves endings she hadn't known her body possessed, and left her screaming, begging for release.

Each driving stroke was another painful pleasure, another step closer to the brilliant flames she could sense threatening to overtake her.

He was pushing her toward a plane she had never known. A

world where nothing existed but sensation, but the feel of his erection shafting, fucking inside her. There was nothing but sensation upon sensation, her clit swelling to a desperate point, her nipples burning as they rubbed against the sheet, her pussy blazing with pleasure.

She was riding a high she couldn't have known existed, and behind her, she could feel Creed tensing, feel the brutal sensations tightening through her, her womb clenching, her pussy gripping him tighter, milking his cock, fighting to hold him inside her, to achieve that final, all-consuming stroke that would throw her headlong into an abyss of sheer rapture.

It was there.

So close.

It was burning around her, filling her senses, drawing her closer. He fucked her harder, faster, his hands tightening on her hips until finally, with a scream of suddenly ecstatic fear, she felt it possess her.

Brutal, searing explosions began erupting through her body. Kita felt herself jerk beneath him, heard her strangled scream as her nails clawed at the blankets beneath her.

Her pussy throbbed, tightened, quivered with the sudden upheaval tearing through it. She heard him give a desperate, animalistic growl before burying his cock deep and hard inside her just as that final blaze of ecstasy tore through her mind.

She was aware of nothing but the sharp, all-consuming pleasure and Creed's arms surrounding her. Knew nothing but the brutal, enveloping heat that radiated in a conflagration of building explosions that finally left her shuddering, limp in his arms as they both collapsed to the bed.

It was exhausting.

It drained her to the point that she wondered if she would ever have the strength or the will to pull herself from him. It bound her to him, even more so than she'd realized she already was.

It was the reason she had run.

This was the reason she had made that desperate, racing escape from her father's home.

Not just because her father had betrayed her.

Not just because she didn't know if she could trust him any longer.

Because she hadn't known if she could trust herself. If she could keep from begging, just as she had ended up begging, for this.

For Creed Raines to tear through her senses, to burn past her reservations, and to steal the heart she knew, in that instant, she had saved for him.

SEVEN

Creed was in hell. Agony. His cock was so damned hard it felt as though it would split open. His balls were drawn beneath the heavy length of his shaft, and he swore his blood was on fire as it pumped through his body.

His release had drained him dry at first, rocking through his body and filling the condom. The lack of sensation against the underside, where the mating barb should have emerged, had kept that final release from triggering, though.

He knew the basics of mating heat. He and several other covert enforcers had been given only the sketchiest information just before leaving Sanctuary a year before.

He'd known, though, instinctually, of the mating heat; all Breeds did. It was the scent the mates shared, the sense of bonding that was a scent all its own. And the love.

The animal inside Creed had acknowledged it, and a part of him had longed for it since the first day he'd sensed it just after he'd arrived at Sanctuary.

The labs he'd been in hadn't been as monstrous as most. Once rescues had begun, the scientists, soldiers, and trainers there had worked with the Breeds to see to their safe release and transport to Sanctuary.

Not all the labs involved with the Genetics Council had subscribed to their methods of cruelty.

Lying in the bed with his own mate, Creed had come to understand why the mated Breeds he'd talked to had told him it was something that couldn't be denied.

The urge to mark her, to bite her delicate skin just above her shoulder and allow the mating hormone into her system there, the need to kiss her, to spill inside her, it was all part of the bonding and all a part of the overwhelming heat tearing through his senses now.

The agony was nothing compared to the sense of satisfaction and completion, though, as he sat, fully dressed, in the sheltered backyard of the small house Kita owned, holding her against him.

The overlarge lounger was thickly padded and wide enough to allow for both his much larger body and that of the woman stretched out between his spread thighs, her back against his chest, the long waves of her sunlit dark blonde hair cascading over his arm.

They had been there for hours, simply watching the sun rise until it was now beginning to warm the mountains that surrounded them and peek its golden trails of light into the shadowed grotto she'd created for a back deck.

"When did you buy the house?" he asked as she snuggled closer, the quilt he'd wrapped around her earlier falling off one bare shoulder before he tucked it back.

She was nice and warm, content and languorous as she lay against him.

"A few years ago." She sighed. "It took forever to figure out how to hide the purchase. My name isn't associated with it anywhere other than a paper signed between myself and a lawyer in Charleston. That seemed the simplest way."

"Why did you need it?"

She was right. Despite the thorough investigation the Breeds had done on her, this property hadn't come to light. They'd checked every friend, schoolmate, and even enemies she had, prying into every nook and cranny of her life to find even the smallest detail about her. And still, this had escaped them.

"I don't know why it was so important at the time." The note of bemusement in her voice couldn't be hidden, nor could the fact that now she wondered if she had somehow sensed what was coming.

The fact was, Creed was gaining a sense that Kita had known for years that her father was involved in something he shouldn't have been. Likely, from the first release of the news that the Breeds existed, Kita had been picking up on her father's subversion.

She was an intuitive little thing, there was no doubt. He imagined that once she got to know him well, there would be very little he could pull off without her sensing it.

"Tell me about you instead," she demanded softly. "All we've talked about the last four days has been me. I want to know more about you."

"Like what?" He stared into the fenced backyard wishing he could put off any questions about himself. He wouldn't lie to her, but he knew, at times, the truth was tricky.

"Like, what's it like at Sanctuary?" She tilted her head back against his arm as she shifted around to stare up at him. "I've read it's like an armed camp, and then reports it's one big orgy." She gave a low, light laugh. "Beth is certain it's the orgy. Though, if it is, she just lost her bet with Stacey."

Stacey was one of the girlfriends that came to the house often. A redheaded spitfire with more courage than good sense sometimes. Beth, on the other hand, was normally practical, though easygoing.

"And what does Stacey say it is?" he asked.

The amusement slowly filtered from her eyes. "An armed camp," she said sadly. "A place filled with tension and combat-ready at all times."

It was interesting to hear the two had bet at opposite ends of their character spectrum.

"Then they both lost." He gave her a smile he hoped would comfort the distress he saw in her gaze. It was one of the things he loved about her, he realized. Her compassion. A compassion neither her father nor her uncle possessed.

"Sanctuary is always prepared, it's secured. We have teams of enforcers that are constantly on guard, but, for the most part, it's more like a large community."

"Until it's attacked," she guessed.

Creed gave a short nod. "Until it's attacked. But we're trained for this Kita. We know how to react, and we know how to fight back."

"And those you've brought in who don't know how to fight?" she asked softly. "Your wives? What do they do, Creed?"

Did she want to be a Breed wife? There was a flash of hope and concern in her gaze, as though she had given the question a lot of thought but needed more in-depth information.

"They're protected," he promised her. "Every Breed in Sanctuary, whether it be male or female, feline, wolf, or coyote, dedicates his life to protecting the wives and children if an attack is launched." He lifted his hand and cupped her cheek as his thumb caressed her lower lip. "Love is something we dare never take for granted, Kita. Even those who haven't yet felt the fire of that emotion know that they long for it. They would give their lives to ensure that a Breed mate is completely protected."

"A mate," she whispered. "What does it take, Creed, to be a Breed's mate?"

She spoke against his thumb, her dark brown eyes becoming sensual, slumberous as her body softened further against him.

"Love. That's all it takes, Kita. The only difference is, Breeds love the first time, for all time. Just as our genetic cousins do." He was dying to kiss her. The hormone filled his mouth like a particularly spicy aphrodisiac, demanding he share. Until he kissed her, until he forced the hormone into her system, it would only grow worse.

God, if it became worse, he didn't know if he could bear it. It was an agony now. Like a brutal flame burning in his loins, threatening his self-control.

And it wasn't that he hadn't had her. They'd spent the past two days fucking like minks. She'd been exhausted when he'd carried her to the porch after fixing the decaf coffee he thanked God she drank. The caffeinated brew was like an accelerant to mating heat in both males and females. He didn't think he could bear to have anything intensify it. She wouldn't be safe with him if it became worse.

"Just love." Her head turned, her lips pressing to the bare flesh the unbuttoned portion of his shirt revealed. "What if your mate doesn't love for life, Creed? If they're human? Some humans are very fickle, you know."

His lips quirked at the reminder. Ah yes, humans could be fickle, as could Breeds in some instances. They weren't so different.

But the question she posed was damned tricky for him.

"There hasn't been a problem yet," was the only answer he could give her.

And apparently, it was the wrong one. Suspicion darkened her eyes. "Is there any truth to the tabloid stories about a mating hormone?" There was no fear in her gaze, just curiosity, suspicion.

"You know how the tabloids are, Kita," he tried to scoff, but went no further.

Creed refused to lie to his mate.

As a covert enforcer, he was used to lying. He had to lie to maintain whatever façade was required for the job. At times, even his name changed, his eye color, his hair color. At times, he'd wondered if he even knew who he was anymore. But that was before he'd walked into Kita's life.

"I know how they are," she admitted softly. "And I know you. You're avoiding my question, Creed. What are you not telling me?"

He almost smiled. As he'd said before, she was damned intuitive.

And it appeared she had paid more attention to him over the past year than he would have perhaps wished.

"There are differences with the Breeds," he finally admitted. "Things I'd prefer we discuss later."

He felt her tense. An air of hurt descended around her as her gaze took on a wounded look.

"Later as opposed to now in what way?" She was drawing away from him and he couldn't bear that.

The animal inside him was snarling in fury. First, he'd refused her the mating kiss more than once, then he'd sheathed his cock and prevented his body from locking inside her.

He was defying every natural instinct that his species lived and breathed for. Mating. The bonding of his life to another, the gift that would come to him only once, as far as the Breeds knew. And now, he was allowing her to distance herself, to pull away.

His arms tightened around her involuntarily, a part of his mind, his Breed senses, refusing to release her despite the fact that he knew it was best for both of them.

She stared back at him for long moments, her gaze a silent accusation.

"That's why you haven't kissed me again," she finally stated knowingly. "Because it does exist, and for whatever reason you've decided I'm not good enough for whatever your mating is?"

His eyes widened. "Have you fucking lost your mind?" Grating, filled with frustrated surprise, the question slipped past his lips.

"Have *you*?" Her eyes narrowed back at him, heavy, thick lashes shadowing her cheeks as brown ire sparked back at him. "Do you think I'm so easy to manipulate and control that I wouldn't notice you've not kissed me again? That despite the fact that conception only occurs with *mates*, you still use a condom. There are no STDs you can give me because Breeds are not susceptible to normal human diseases and viruses. Do you even fucking get a cold?" Her voice rose marginally.

She was angry. He could feel it in her, see it in the spark in her eyes.

"No, we don't." His head lowered until they were glaring at each other, nearly nose to nose now in a confrontation he hadn't expected. "No colds, no STDs, no fucking flu. Anything else?"

"Plenty," she snapped. "But as you're suddenly refusing to answer the important questions, then I'm only wasting my time." Her nose lifted as though she were offended by some smell. "And I do have this thing about wasting my time."

She moved to rise from him, to leave his arms, to deny him the warmth of her, the comfort, when mating heat was like a fatal wound destroying him from the inside out.

"Then you can waste a little more of it." Wrapping one arm around her, he lifted, turned, flipped the lever that completely lowered the back of the padded lounger before trapping her beneath his much larger body.

The chill of the fall air swirled around them as his hands gripped her wrists and pulled them above her head to clasp them with the fingers of one hand.

Straining against him, she glared back at him, frustration now anger as she attempted to drive her knee between his thighs, only to have him twist and smoothly maneuver his heavier thighs between hers, opening her to him as he snarled down at her in a warning growl.

It was a primal, desperate measure that slipped free of his control. The man and the animal trapped inside him warred, both savage in their determination to protect their mate in their way. To claim her as each felt she should be claimed.

It was the curse of any Breed. Those two halves suddenly in conflict, fighting for supremacy.

Rather than backing down in wariness, though, Kita bucked against him.

"I can't believe you dared to snarl at me like that," she raged

furiously, her features flushing, body stiffening, and a hint of feminine arrogance defining her expression. "I'm not one of your prissy
little Breed groupies to be frightened of those damned teeth, Creed
Raines. Find someone else to intimidate because you're so not getting away with attempting to intimidate me."

His cock was on fire. It hardened further, a feat he would have
considered impossible. It thickened further, his balls tighter, a lance
of pure agony tearing at his mind in his need to mate her. To mark
her. To claim her.

"You stubborn little minx," he snarled down at her as she bucked
against him, the soft, wet curls of her pussy pressing into his cock
as his hips bore down to hold her in place. "Stay still before you get
more than you even realize you're asking for."

"What? All of you?" She suddenly cried out. "Fuck you, Creed.
You can have all of me, but all you give in return is what you think
I might deserve? What little you want to allow me? You can go to
hell, because I'll be damned if I'll accept less than what belongs
to me."

He stilled. His muscles locked in place, holding her beneath him
effortlessly as surprise—fuck no, it was pure shock—had him staring down at her intently.

"Do I have all of you, Kita?" he growled back at her, knowing
he should be wary of the sudden primal quality in his voice. "Because it will require your very soul, Kita, to accept the animal you're
tempting."

She snorted at that, censure gleaming her eyes. "You're listening
to your own Breed press too closely, Creed. You're a man. A man
with a few added qualities and a hell of a lot more primal arrogance, but you still bleed. You still hurt and hope." Tears suddenly
filled her eyes. "You can still love, can't you?"

And there was the crux of Kita's fears. Staring back at her, Creed
sensed, scented, felt all the emotions tearing through her for the first

time. As though she had finally allowed a barrier of some sort between her and the world, between her and Creed, to slide open.

Kita loved.

She loved her father, and he wasn't the hero she wanted to see him as. But still, she loved him, even though Creed knew there were times she wondered whether her father returned her love.

She loved the sister that had disowned her family. She loved the mother she had lost and the friends that had deserted her when the press had revealed her father's duplicity against the Breeds.

And he knew now, she loved him.

"I love you, Kita." And he was damning her in the same sentence. Because he couldn't tell her what his soul held without giving her the truth, all of the truth, and all of the creature he truly was.

Part man, a primal animal, a creature that burned for her, that hurt clear to his spirit to give her the mating that would always mark her as his.

His.

She belonged to him, the same as he belonged to her.

Nature was gifting him with a strength far greater than the superb male body he had been created to have. She had given him more than the advanced instincts man had coded into his genetics. She was giving him the woman who would stoke the fires to fight, to protect. A woman who would ease the horrors of battle, who would soothe the desperation when darkness strengthened it.

Yet, at the same time, she was giving him his greatest weakness as well. A weakness that would pull him from covert duty to stay at her side. A weakness that would make him fear for the first time in his life. Creed had something far more important to fear than death. Now, fear of death would be a meager second to the fear of losing her.

Breeds didn't just mate for life. Couples mated for life. If he lost her, if she lost him, life would become a horrible, bleak existence he never wanted to face.

"Do you love me, Creed?" A small tear slipped from the corner of her eye. "If you love me, then you won't hide from me. You'll give me who you are, the same as I give it to you. Isn't that real love? You can't love me if you're willing to take from me the parts of you that make you a Breed."

He swallowed tightly. "And if those parts of me change you somehow?" he whispered, his teeth clenching as the demand to kiss her, to mate her, ripped at his senses, tearing at the control he was fighting so desperately to hold on to. "If I fear those changes will change that love to hate?"

She licked her lips. Soft, silken, a pink temptation he was dying to taste, her tongue licked over her lips. "Love isn't like that," she whispered roughly, the movement of her hips suddenly far more than an attempt to escape. "If even part of the tabloid stories are true, Creed, then it seems to me you'll only complete me." For a second, her eyes flickered with shadowed pain. "You have all of me now. Shouldn't I have the same from you?"

Complete her? He remembered when he had first come to the Engalls estate, hearing her confide to her friend Beth that she felt incomplete. That she felt as though a part of her were detached, distant, unable to reach out and find what it was she could feel missing.

He knew she was his mate. Knew she was his life. But he also knew his fear of turning that love to hate.

God knew, she was the part of his life that had been missing until the day he stared into the pure, sweet, chocolate depths of her gaze. From that moment, he had centered his entire being on drawing her to him, fascinating her, teasing her, encouraging the most minute emotional and sensual responses short of actually allowing her to touch him.

Because he knew once he touched her, holding back would be hell.

And he was in hell.

"Kiss me, Creed." She strained against him, tempting him, destroying him. "Unless you don't really want me?" For a second, fear flickered in her gaze.

"Not want you?" he groaned. "Kita. God. Sweetheart. For the past year, I've lived for you."

EIGHT

The kiss, when it came, she hadn't believed would be as good as the first. Surely it couldn't have been as good as she remembered the first.

But it was better.

If possible, it was hotter, wilder, more all-consuming than any kiss before it, even that first kiss he had given her four days before.

His lips parted hers, his tongue stroking inside, licking at hers, tempting her to lick back, to play, to tease in a sensual, wicked dance that combined lips and tongues in a manner far more wickedly erotic than she'd ever expected a kiss could be. So erotic it seriously should have been illegal.

Creed didn't just kiss her. He made love to her mouth.

His lips captured hers, pleasured them with sipping, licking kisses that spread a fire through her senses she couldn't control—didn't want to control.

He held her wrists easily above her head, restraining her gently as his free hand gripped her hips, holding her to him as his own hips shifted against the sensitive bundle of nerves between her thighs. Clasping his body with her knees, arching to him, rising against him, Kita felt the same brilliant conflagration exploding through her.

Cinnamon and sweet spice filled her taste buds. The fragrance, the flavor infused her senses, lending an additional sensuality to the caress.

Naked beneath him, vulnerable and aching, Kita hadn't known a moment's fear in his embrace. Each touch was delivered for her pleasure only. Bestowed with the greatest of care as the thin material of his shirt skimmed the tight buds of her nipples.

She wanted. She wanted him as she had never wanted anything in her life. The desperation traveling through her body was primal, instinctive. It was like a hunger she couldn't stop from raging through her system.

When his lips pulled from hers, Kita had to admit she well understood why he had attempted to warn her that it may be something she didn't want.

She could feel an almost unnatural heat rising inside her, a furious demand resonating throughout her body, crying out for more, for more than his kiss, more than the feel of his denim-covered cock against her pussy. She wanted all of him. His full possession. That blinding, overwhelming fullness that tore her past the bonds of reality and threw her into a shimmering world of release and ultimate satisfaction.

The heat, the demand, the need, was amplified. It wasn't unnatural. It was sharper, the sensations clearer, cleaner. It was like having a veil of restraint torn away, any fear, uncertainties, or natural hesitancies washed from the senses as pure hunger overtook it.

That was mating heat.

A sense of wonder rose inside her as his lips pulled from hers and traveled along her jaw, leaving the taste of him against her tongue, tempting her.

But it was only seconds later he returned.

Her lashes drifted as he paused above her, his breathing harsh, rapid. Dark gray eyes were nearly black, his lips swollen, cheeks flushed a dark brick red as his gaze centered on her lips.

She licked them slowly, teasingly.

"Let me taste you again, Creed." She strained against the hold he had on her. "Kiss me again. Do you know I dreamed of your kiss?"

"The perfect kiss," he answered.

Her eyes widened, lips parting to drag in more air, to ease the sudden restriction in her chest, the emotion, the arousal beating through her heart.

The perfect kiss.

That was what she had searched for. That kiss that fed the need, the arousal. That could soothe or could burn. That could bring ease or bring hunger.

"Creed's kiss." Her lips trembled, emotion nearly overwhelming her. "One more."

He shook his head slowly. "Not one more, Kita. A lifetime more."

This time, as his lips moved over hers, parted them, his tongue stroking inside, Kita took what she wanted. His taste. The pleasure to be found, the heat and the mark of the lion she'd believed could be no more than a rumor.

Her teeth nipped at his tongue; her tongue stroked over it. She suckled at each penetration of her mouth, glorying in the growl that rumbled in his chest each time the taste of him intensified against her tongue.

His kiss wasn't all he used to destroy her senses, though.

As one hand held her hands above her head, the other stroked her body. Caressing up her side, cupping her breast, his fingers toying with a nipple as she arched closer and strained to keep contact with his lips.

With the perfect kiss.

Their moans filled the air, swirling around their senses as heated flames licked at Kita's body.

It was exquisite. It was like being immersed in a world of pure sensuality and white hot pleasure. It whipped through her veins, tightened through her body, and had her gripping his hips with her knees as her body writhed against him.

The heated length of his cock throbbed beneath the denim,

pressing into her clit as she rubbed against it, tempting him, on the edge of begging him for the relief she was becoming desperate for.

He tore his lips from hers, gasping for breath, perspiration dotting his brow, a rivulet running from his shoulder as she lifted her head to catch it with her tongue.

The taste of male arousal and heated hunger exploded in her mouth. She moaned, her eyelids almost too heavy to keep open while her body vibrated with a languorous desperation she couldn't control.

"I want to touch you," she moaned as his fingers cupped her breast, lifted it, and his head descended to the hard tip of her nipple.

His tongue met the tight, hard bud first. Like a lash of pure electric sensation whipping over it, as she arched in a quick, reflexive jerk.

"Creed. Suck it," she demanded, suddenly so hungry for the feel of his mouth covering her that she couldn't bear it. "Oh God, Creed. I need your mouth . . ."

A cry tore from her lips as his lips surrounded it. Blistering, wicked. He sucked the bundle of nerve endings into his mouth, drawing it, his cheeks hollowing as his lashes lifted to stare back at her.

His tongue lashed at the tender tip, his teeth gripped. He worried the tiny point, sucked it, loved it until she was arching and begging, crying out for more as he growled above her.

He moved to the other, still holding her wrists above her head as he cupped the mound with his free hand and bent his head to it. He licked around the tip, licked over it. He sucked it inside, sending brutal slashes of pleasure racing from her nipple to her clit, clenching her womb and spilling heated moisture from between her thighs.

With another hard growl, a last firm lick, his head lifted once again, his gaze intent, savagely predatory as that adventurous free hand slid down her stomach.

"I can smell your sweet juices," he whispered as his fingers rasped over the tender flesh of her stomach. "I want to lick your pussy, baby. I'm going to eat you until all you can do is come for me. Until every thrust of my tongue up your tight pussy has you screaming, Kita. Begging for more."

She was shaking, watching in fascination as he began to lick a path of fire down her body, releasing her wrists, though she barely realized it, spreading her thighs wide and finally kneeling on the wood deck beneath the edge of the lounger.

The fingers of one hand smoothed through the slick folds as Kita whimpered in rising excitement.

"I dreamed of tasting you. Of kissing you here. Of feeling your tight little pussy rippling around my tongue, your clit swelling against it. That's what I'm going to have, Kita. I'm going to feel your pussy coming around my tongue."

His palms flattened on her thighs, pressing them farther apart as his head lowered, his heated breath caressing the intimate flesh a second before his tongue swiped through the saturated slit.

Kita had to watch. She couldn't help but watch. Watch as he devoured her pussy, licked around her clit, then slowly, oh so very slowly, sucked the swollen, tortured little knot of nerves into his mouth.

Kita tried to scream. Her upper body jerked, nearly rising from the lounger before his palm pressed against her upper stomach and pushed her back to the thick pad. Her hips arched, her feet sliding from the edge of the reclining chaise and lifting closer, pushing her clit further against him.

His tongue circled the swollen bud with flickering licks that had flashes of ecstasy nearly exploding inside her. His fingers parted the folds, two slipping inside her, rubbing, stroking in small thrusts until he was buried inside her and she swore she was dying from the pleasure.

Her hands gripped the pad of the chair above her. Her eyes closed, too heavy to remain open, but the sensations so much sharper, hotter from the lack of sight.

His fingers stretched the supersensitive tissue of her pussy. He thrust inside her, pulling back and pushing inside as he fucked her in controlled, easy penetrations that had her gasping from the pleasure.

His tongue tormented her clit. His lips closed around it, his mouth drew on it. She could feel sizzling pulses of electric sensation beginning to build inside her. Like sparks of lightning shattering the sky, each stroke, each thrust, each lick sent sparks of sensation tearing through her body.

It was so close. She could feel it. It was burning, tightening in her womb. The muscles of her vagina clamped down on his fingers as they pushed past with rasping thrusts. The hold his lips had on her clit was wicked, fiery, pulling each sensation through her clit before sending it racing hotter, harder through every nerve ending of her body.

She could hear herself calling out his name, begging. Her hips lifted and fell, grinding against his lips as she felt rapture continuing to build inside her.

She'd never known sensations like this. She'd always sensed they were there. Always sensed that the pleasure could be so much more, that the perfect kiss, the perfect touch, awaited her.

She had known Creed was there, somewhere. Sensed him. Felt him. Known life held so much more if she could only find it.

And she had found him. Or had he found her? But he was here now, his tongue lashing at the nerve-rich nubbin of her clit as his fingers pierced her pussy, fucking it with such slow, easy strokes that she could feel the heightened sensations building ever stronger.

Pleasure lashed at her.

Like bolts of quick-fire electricity zapping through her clitoris, her pussy, her womb, clenching, spasming through her until finally, with a desperate cry of broken control, she felt every nerve ending in her body rupture.

The orgasm exploded through her system in a rush of such ecstasy, such soul-binding pleasure, she felt as though a part of herself had flown free, straight into Creed's soul.

Her eyes flew open, her lips parting in a soundless scream as he gave a harsh groan, pulled his fingers out of her, and a second later pressed the thick crest of his cock against the tender, convulsing entrance to her cunt and gave a hard, heavy thrust.

Her feet dug into the wood of the deck, her hips arching from the padded lounge to force the thick flesh deeper, harder. The additional rush of sensation was like throwing gasoline to an already raging flame burning out of control, exploding into the night.

Opening her eyes, her gaze moved, mesmerized, to where he was working the hard stalk of his cock inside her body. The dark flesh, heavily veined and throbbing, shimmered with her juices as he pulled back.

Penetrating again, moving in further with the next thrust, he parted the folds, spreading her, finding nerve endings she was certain she hadn't felt the times he had used the condom.

He seemed harder, thicker, hotter. Almost bruising in its power and hardness, the engorged shaft forged inside as he straddled the lounge chair, his hands gripping her hips, her thighs lying over his, hips arched.

Her cunt still flexed and gripped in echoes of the orgasm she had barely survived and still, she could feel it building again. It was rising inside her with each thrust, with each burning, stretching penetration until with a final, hard stroke he was buried to the hilt.

Kita lifted her gaze.

He was throbbing inside her, so thick, so heavy she felt overfilled, overly possessed. Her inner flesh flexed and spasmed around the intruder, stroking it, milking it as she fought to catch her breath.

"When it happens," he said, his voice guttural, "when I come, love, don't be frightened." His chest was moving with harsh breaths, the effort to maintain his control obvious.

Kita shook her head. She had no idea what he was talking about. She had no intention of being frightened.

"Fuck me, Creed," she finally gasped when he didn't move. "Don't talk me to death."

His lashes drifted over his gaze for a moment. When they opened, his eyes had a dark, hungry look. Like a predator with its prey, determined now to enjoy every moment with it.

"Fuck you?" He moved back slow and easy as her back arched, her hands jerking from the cushion above her to latch on to the wrists holding her hips. "Oh, Kita, I've dreamed of showing you exactly how I can fuck you."

The next hard, blinding thrust set the pace. Her cries filled the sheltered deck and yard as her body strained at the hard slamming thrusts. The rasp of his cock over the nerve-laden inner flesh was agony and ecstasy.

She was being thrown into a world of pure sensation, and there was no escaping. She could feel every minute nerve ending as his cock burned across her inner flesh in a long, fierce stroke. Shafting inside her with powerful thrusts, he gripped her hips, holding her in place, forcing her to endure the brutal pleasure of it.

Her pussy gripped him, milked him. As each sensation tore across the other, she finally felt herself exploding, melting around him even as her cunt locked down on his shuttling cock and her release began to spill around the heavy length screwing inside her, making her wonder if she would ever recover her sanity.

Then, oh God. Her eyes jerked open as she felt it.

In that final thrust, he buried deep, gave a harsh groan, and she felt the heavy length of an added erection suddenly emerging from his cock, pressing inside her, fluttering with firm little strokes against that secret, hidden bundle of nerves just beneath her clit.

She died in his arms. There was no chance for fear to emerge. There was room for nothing but a rapture that stole each particle of her sanity and left her arched tight, her body straining, her gaze locked on his face.

His features were savage, a grimace of male ecstasy. His head was thrown back, his corded neck, his straining biceps, his abdomen flexing spasmodically as she felt each eruption of his semen blasting inside her. Branding her. Searing that delicate, so sensitive little area and sending her into another convulsive, shuddering orgasm that strung her tight, left her gasping and shuddering before she collapsed against the cushions as Creed came over her.

With small, furious beats, his cock went on releasing inside her as the hardened little extension continued to stimulate that aching bud, drawing sensation, forcing tiny explosions of pleasure through her even when she knew she was too exhausted to give more.

Until finally, Creed collapsed on top of her, sweating, his body heaving for breath. Limp with exhaustion, he managed to pull them both to their sides while remaining locked inside her.

Not that he had a choice, she realized distantly. He was literally locked inside her, the animalistic feline barb continuing to throb and jerk at intervals, drawing shattered cries from her lips.

Long, long minutes later, it finally began to ease, and at last, after what felt like eons, the searing little pulses of the extension stopped, allowing her body to settle into a satiation she knew couldn't be entirely natural.

Physically, emotionally, for the first time in her life, Kita felt at peace.

NINE

How much time had passed, Creed wasn't certain. His first indication of danger, though, was the hollow vibration of the small satellite flip phone he carried in the front pocket of his jeans.

He was moving immediately. Pulling himself from his exhausted mate, he jerked his jeans to his hips and gave a quick jerk to the zipper before quickly wrapping the blanket over Kita's body. Her eyes jerked open in surprise.

"Creed?"

There was fear in her eyes; he saw it. But after that first shocked exclamation of his name, she was moving. Even before he could help her from the chaise, she was on her feet and rather than asking questions, following him quickly into the house.

"We have trouble," he growled as he pulled her into the bedroom. "Hurry and dress. Jeans and sneakers." He was throwing jeans, a T-shirt, and a warm sweater from the closet as she pulled panties and socks from a dresser.

She didn't bother searching for a bra, he noticed. It wasn't required to survive.

She was dressed as he finished locating the small black leather weapons bag he had hidden in the back of her closet. Jerking it open, he quickly strapped on a handgun at his side and ankle, then within seconds had the powerful automatic rifle he carried with him, assembled and ready to fire.

Who the hell thought they could sneak up on him like this? In broad daylight?

It was either a moron or a man or Breed who thought he was better, smarter, and brighter than a lion Breed covert enforcer.

There was no mistaking the alarm still vibrating at his waist, though, a clear indication that someone was coming into the rear of the property Kita owned.

Another enforcer would have recognized the signs as well as the electronic traps laid and announced his presence. Jonas already suspected Kita was Creed's mate; he'd surely know better than to try such a stunt. Especially on Creed.

After pulling on a lightweight advanced-design jacket, Creed grabbed the extra one he carried with him and threw it to Kita with an order to put it on. He then slung the heavy leather pack of ammo over his back and the strap of the weapon over his shoulder.

Taking her hand as she jerked the jacket on, he was moving through the house toward the front door, his senses on alert, screaming in warning.

Behind him, he could sense Kita's fear, but overlaying it was the scent of her determination and her trust.

"Who knew you were here?" It was a question he should have asked days ago, damn it.

"No one. I just ran. I didn't tell anyone where I was going."

Moving quickly through the silent kitchen, he threw open the door to the garage and pulled her inside. The motorcycle was their best bet, not as protected as a vehicle, but . . .

He came to a hard stop.

They were there. Their scents were neutralized, blocked, expressions hard, eyes flat and filled with danger. And standing behind them was the specter of death that had haunted the Breeds for as long as they could remember.

"Uncle Phillip?" Uncertainty and rising fear filled Kita's voice as she stared at the much, much younger version of the uncle she had known.

Damn! Creed stared at the man, hiding his shock as he assessed how many decades the age regression had taken from Phillip Brandenmore. He looked as fit, as formidable as he had in his early forties, his face once again dark and roughly handsome, his brown eyes free of the dimness age had brought.

His dark brown hair was once again thick and sporting only a bit of gray at the temples, while his shoulders were broad, his chest muscular. As though his body hadn't forgotten its former shape, strength, and power, and had easily returned to it.

Kita moved to slip to his side before Creed tightened his fingers on her wrist in warning.

She stilled just that fast.

He could smell her fear, though, as well as her uncertainty.

Phillip Brandenmore smiled. Perfect, straight white teeth had replaced the aged, darkened ones Creed remembered from his last visit to Sanctuary, just after Brandenmore had been captured.

The shock Kita was feeling scented the air as Creed kept a careful eye on the men flanking Brandenmore and the weapons trained on Kita and himself. He paid especially close attention to the woman on his far right, knowing when he killed her, there would be hell to pay.

"Creed Raines, lion Breed enforcer," Brandenmore drawled as he moved in line with the mercenaries that had obviously broken him out of Sanctuary's cells. "Breed, you have balls to think you can kidnap my niece, fuck her, and not pay for it. She's too damned good for the likes of a fucking animal." His gaze flicked to Kita, and for a second, the smallest second, Creed could have sworn something painful, something filled with regret flickered in Brandenmore's eyes.

Could he get to his weapon in time? Could he throw Kita to the side and actually do any damage before they managed to hurt her?

His gaze went over the men once more. He shouldn't have felt disbelief at seeing them there, but damn if he had expected this. When he stared back at the woman, the commander these men followed, he was almost brought up short again by the small pendant she wore outside her T-shirt.

His attention returned to Brandenmore.

"What the hell are you doing here?" he growled, his fingers tightening once more on Kita's wrist to hold her in place.

"I came for my niece," he snapped. "Wyatt thinks he's so damned smart. So damned careful," he sneered. "I heard him, just as I heard his plans to turn Kita Claire into a fucking breeder for one of his Breeds. A Breed that had managed to gain her trust."

Kita stiffened, her harshly indrawn breath attesting to her shock, and he feared, her belief in what Brandenmore was saying or what she was seeing.

An uncle from the past, not the present. A man who now stared at her with reptilian eyes, a sneer on his lips when his attention turned to Creed.

A man whose hired guns were pointed in her direction.

KITA COULDN'T BELIEVE what she was seeing, what was happening around her. He looked like her uncle before she had even been born. This was the man who had stood so proudly in his sister's wedding pictures, the man who had held his newborn niece, his expression gentle and filled with love.

Her uncle wasn't this young, and it wasn't possible to turn back time, to return to youth no matter how much one might want to.

"Who are you?" she finally whispered. "You can't be Uncle Phillip. It's simply not possible."

But it was possible. She stared back at him as an odd smile tugged at his lips.

There was no warmth or compassion in this man. There was no

love, no gentleness as she had always seen in his face when her mother had been alive. There was none of the grief she had seen in his face when his beloved sister had died.

"Of course it can be," he said. "I must say, Kita Claire, I never expected this of you." He waved his hand to Creed as a look of distaste crossed his face. "Sleeping with the enemy, child? And one of a different species? I'm very disappointed."

Kita was terrified.

She shook her head. "I don't know you."

Desperation laced her voice, a plea that someone explain, rationalize, that they assure her this really wasn't the uncle she once loved so dearly.

He clicked his tongue, a mocking sound that raked across her senses and sent fear racing through her.

"Of course you do, child." He smiled back at her. "You just don't want to accept it. I've discovered the fountain of youth. The elixir of cures." Excitement lit his eyes. "I've searched for it all my life, Kita. I dreamed of finding it before your mother died. Before the cancer killed her. I could have saved her." For a moment, fanatical rage lit his eyes. "She could be alive today, young and whole, if I had found it sooner."

"It's destroyed his mind, Kita," Creed whispered softly.

"Shut up!" Phillip's furious scream made her flinch as her breath hitched painfully, fearfully. "You don't know what you're talking about. My mind isn't destroyed. Those Breed doctors are crazy themselves. I've tested it before!" Spittle gathered at his lips as Kita forced back her tears. "I know what I'm doing."

His attention turned back to Kita. "You would have thanked me later if this bastard hadn't mated you." He flung his hand toward Creed in a gesture of fury. "Son of a bitch had to go ruin it. You could have kept your youth, Kita, without having to fuck this animal."

Kita shook her head, terrified now.

"You haven't told her?" Phillip suddenly became amused, calm.

"Haven't you told her, Breed, how that hormone you've infected her with will stop her aging? How she'll remain young and beautiful, and you'll remain in your prime, strong and fully able to fuck her?" he sneered the last.

"Creed?" she whispered his name.

"Later, baby, I promise." It was only a breath of sound.

"Unfortunately, not later." Phillip gave a happy, satisfied little sigh as Kita watched him warily.

This was a monster standing in her uncle's skin.

"Let Kita go, Brandenmore," Creed stated, his voice dark, held tightly in control. "We'll deal with this, just between the two of us."

Phillip shook his head. "Sorry, Breed, I can't do that," he snapped. "She chose to mate an animal, now she can choose to submit to the tests I'll need." He glared back at them. "I may have found the fountain of youth, but it does need a few adjustments. As mates, you can help me make those adjustments." His gaze became harder as Kita slowly gripped Creed's arm in terror. "Unfortunately, you won't live past many of the experiments. But they should prove to be very helpful."

She knew the news reports had vilified her uncle and her father for using the Breeds as research subjects. For their cruelty, the deaths they had supposedly caused, the inhuman experiments and the drugs that had nearly killed several top-level members of the Breed community.

She held on to Creed, barely able to breathe, feeling the horrible sense of unreality become reality as she realized this truly wasn't the uncle who had spoiled her as a child, who had promised her he and her father would always protect her when they learned her mother had cancer.

Her uncle's head tilted as he saw the understanding dawn on her face. A frown marred his brow, and for just a second she thought, maybe, she glimpsed the beloved uncle he had once been.

"Mother loved you." Her breathing hitched, the accusation in her voice now filled with tears. "You lied to her."

His frown deepened as anger lit his gaze. "Never once did I lie to your mother," he gritted out. "She was like my own child. I raised her." He thumped his chest possessively. "I protected her."

"You swore to her you and my father would protect me," she cried furiously. "Look at you. What would she do if she saw you right now, Uncle Phillip? She would cry."

He had once stated nothing destroyed him more than to see his sister cry. As the words left her lips, she finally saw a flash of humanity in those cold, dead eyes.

He stared back at her, her brown irises shadowed, filled with agony as the tears she tried to hold back slipped free.

"Don't cry," he whispered.

"What have you done, Uncle Phillip?"

His expression twisted. "The fountain of youth, Kita." He looked around as though searching desperately for something. "I found it. The Breeds. They hold the fountain of youth." His gaze swung back to her, his fingers clenching at his side, his body tense now, ramrod straight, strong and young again. "You hold the fountain of youth," he whispered, his gaze, his expression shadowed with grief. "Why, Kita? Why did you let him touch you? You can't live without your liver, Kita. It creates . . ." He stopped.

His expression became frozen, his gaze laser sharp. "You'll have to die, just as he will."

"For the fountain of youth." Tears were rolling down her cheeks. "You stole my uncle for his youth." This wasn't her uncle Phillip any longer.

Beside her, she felt Creed tense, his fingers rubbing against her wrist to get her attention. He wanted something.

Again. He was scratching out the word on her arm.

Again. She followed each curve his nail made.

"Mother loved you. Do you remember?" Having grasped Creed's meaning, Kita said the one thing she now knew would distract her uncle. "She cried for you when she died."

The monster who had stolen her uncle's form swung his head away. His shoulders heaved, and then the world around her went to hell.

The lights in the garage suddenly burst, throwing them all into darkness as pieces of the fluorescent bulbs rained down on them.

Creed swung her around, pushed her beneath an old worktable she had never cleared out of the area, and suddenly, he was gone.

Laser fire and gunfire began ricocheting around her, blasting into walls as screams filled her senses. She knew that, if she survived, they would echo in her nightmares.

She couldn't see anything through the flashes of light. She had no idea where anyone was, who they were, or if Creed was even still alive.

"You bitch!"

Kita screamed as the table toppled over and a flash of light exploded through the room, revealing her uncle, his expression demonic, his eyes burning red, a second before everything went dark again.

TEN

Her father had saved her life. He just may have killed his brother-in-law.

Kita sat in the corner of the garage as Breed enforcers swarmed around the area, each consulting with Jonas Wyatt. Next to him stood the woman who had betrayed her uncle. Diane Broen. A mercenary her uncle had hired, but who, Kita learned, had already given her loyalty and the loyalty of her team to Jonas Wyatt.

Horace Engalls sat on an upended wooden box, his face in his hands, mourning the man who had betrayed them all.

When her uncle had disappeared, despite rumors of his death, Horace and Kita had assumed the Breeds had captured him. They had been right. He had been imprisoned in Virginia as the Breed scientists attempted to learn how he created the serum that began turning back his age. A serum he had injected into an infant child.

Kita was still in shock. Her uncle, her loving, doting uncle had done something that could potentially destroy an infant? He had let a baby go hungry. He had let her lie in her own waste without changing her diaper. He had attempted to kill her when he'd seen he couldn't escape with her.

For what?

For the fountain of youth. Because he believed Amber's reaction to the drug would answer the question of why the drug was killing him. Unfortunately, if it was going to answer anything, it wasn't doing so yet. Amber's body was only showing minute anomalies. Anomalies Kita hadn't yet been given details on.

"Kita." Behind her, Creed still held her.

He had caught her as her uncle fell, his blood spattering from a single gunshot wound to the shoulder, low, perhaps too close to his chest, inflicted by her father.

Her father had also been the reason the lights had blown.

As her uncle confronted Kita and Creed, Horace Engalls had done what he had always done best: he tinkered. This time, with the electric generator that fed the fluorescent lights in the garage.

As the lights went out, he had rushed in just in time to save Kita from the injection her uncle had been preparing to shove into her arm.

The one that would have destroyed her as it had destroyed him.

"I'm okay," she finally answered him.

The answers hadn't come quickly.

Kita felt as though they had been there for hours.

When the lights had been restored, Jonas Wyatt, a half dozen Breeds, Diane Broen, and the mercenary working with her were the only ones still standing.

Phillip Brandenmore and the other three mercenaries he had hired were dead.

"You're not okay." He was holding her against his chest, his hand at her head, and she was still crying.

Not as hard as she had been, but the tears didn't want to stop.

"Creed, I need your weapon." Diane loped over to them, a delicate hand extending, palm out, revealing a slash of scars emphasized by the blood on her hand. "Once the authorities arrive we don't want to blow your cover."

Creed handed it over as Kita lifted her gaze and saw the compassion in the other woman's expression.

Diane tucked the weapon into the back of her jeans, then hesitated before slowly hunching down in front of Kita. "Nightmares begin like this," Diane said softly, glancing up at Creed, then back to Kita. "Don't blame yourself, Ms. Engalls, and they won't be near as bad."

Kita could only shake her head as the other woman stood again and walked toward Jonas.

"Come on. Dealing with the authorities isn't something I'm in the mood for." Creed didn't give her a chance to answer; he picked her up in his arms and before she knew it, she knew she was holding on to him like the lifeline she needed, burying her face against his neck.

Minutes later, he sat down on the bed, his hand stroking her hair.

"I love you, Kita," he whispered. "I loved you before that first month was out, and I love you even more now. Give us a chance to work through this."

She shook her head.

"Don't make me beg." His voice was dark, tortured.

Lifting her head, she stared at him. "You don't have to beg, Creed," she whispered tearfully. "If you left me now, I don't know if I could handle it. Nothing seems real to me anymore except you. You are the only thing in my life in the past year that hasn't changed."

Surprise lit his gaze. "You didn't know I was a Breed."

"Didn't I?" She couldn't smile, even to comfort him. "I think a part of me did know. Subconsciously, I think I've always known. There's nothing to forgive. As long as you hold me. As long as you kiss me."

He kissed her. Gently. His lips parted hers, his tongue stroked, but in comfort rather than in heat, in love rather than in that loving lust they had shared before.

This was a kiss to warm, to comfort, to ease. It was a kiss to bind hearts and meld souls and build a foundation for the future on.

When his head lifted, she touched his jaw, and this time, she managed a smile.

"Uncle Phillip died a long time ago, didn't he?"

It was then her father entered the room. "He died the day your mother did."

Kita turned her head.

He stood there, his shoulders straight, the grief in his eyes and on his face as heavy as the weight she knew he carried on his shoulders.

"I was trying to protect you," he whispered.

"Your father is the one who has been feeding the Breeds information through the Engalls and Brandenmore companies for the past several years, though he remained anonymous until he contacted Jonas a few days ago," Creed informed her. "He knew I was a Breed, Kita. Just as he knew the horror your uncle was attempting to create."

Her father swallowed tightly. "For your mother. For you." He gave his head a hard shake. "I just wanted to protect you."

From the monsters of the world. Creed loosened his hold and helped Kita to her feet, rising as he watched father and daughter.

Horace Engalls moved slowly across the room, his face lined, heavy with the decision he'd been forced to make.

Even Creed hadn't been aware of what Engalls was doing until after the chaos in the garage. Only then had Jonas revealed the full measure of the other man's involvement and the information he held.

Bastard. Marriage sure as hell hadn't done anything to cure him of his manipulations.

"Kita." Horace paused in front of her. "I wanted you safe."

"You should have trusted me."

And Creed could do nothing but agree.

Horace nodded. "I should have. But the father manual didn't come with all the answers to the hard questions, sweetheart. It said follow your heart. And all I wanted to do was save you the knowledge of what your uncle was doing. Of how evil the world could be.

That's what fathers do for daughters, honey. Or at least, that's what they want to do. Just protect them."

Kita trembled, and Creed could sense her tears. But these weren't tears of anger or sadness; rather, they were tears of release, of reconciliation, and maybe even of joy.

"I love you, Daddy."

Father and daughter.

Creed stood back and gave Horace his moment. A chance to right any wrongs, to be the father, and for Kita to be the child.

Tomorrow would be time enough for him to claim his mate again.

Now, he gave the other man a nod and a smile. Now was the time to lay that foundation.

A foundation on which to build a life.

EPILOGUE

THREE WEEKS LATER

Tall, wide windows spilled brilliant light into the spacious bedroom of the Manhattan apartment Phillip Brandenmore had owned. A property his niece, Kita Claire Engalls, would soon possess once the courts ruled the missing owner as dead.

Once the authorities had arrived at the cabin after Brandenmore's attempt to kill Kita, her uncle had been transported back to Sanctuary, his mind almost broken. He'd been animalistic, incoherent growls and snarls leaving his lips as spittle gathered on his lips.

"I found it."

Creed turned from the impressive view of upper Manhattan as Kita all but whispered the words.

Her voice was filled with tears, the scent of her pain filling his senses and drawing him to her to stare at the files she had unlocked.

They had been stored, innocuously, on a hidden hard drive inserted into a digital video frame of family videos at Brandenmore's penthouse apartment.

Sitting in clear view on his desk, it was a device Creed knew for a fact had been checked.

"The hard drive was very cleverly hidden," she sighed tiredly as they stared at the files continuing to pop up on the computer the device was attached to. "It didn't show up with normal search parameters, or even those used to uncover hidden files. He was a genius." She rubbed at her face wearily. "I remembered the file when he was talking about Mother and the fountain of youth. I came into the office and surprised him days before Jonas captured him. He had the frame, and he was muttering about the fountain of youth. That was the second password."

Creed stared at the files. They hadn't even known there could be a second password.

"How did he hide it?" Creed stared at the proof that he had indeed hid it, in amazement.

"As I said, he was a genius." She gave a small shrug, though he felt the disillusionment that tore through her. "And he told me how to find it. He told me to always remember my mother the day I was born."

Minimizing the files, she pointed to the picture of her mother holding a newborn child. With a roll of her finger over the mouse pad the little arrow touched the very tip of the corner of the picture, and there, a thumbnail appeared. The mouse then moved to her mother's left eye.

"He told me I was the apple of my mother's eye." She clicked, and there, the message showed up, a request for the password. "Type in a password that has been found on any other file, and this is what you get." She typed in one of the more well known passwords the Breeds had uncovered.

A series of hidden files came up documenting the life and death of Kita's mother. Canceling those, she tried again.

"Type in the right password, Fountain of Youth, and you get the files you were looking for."

And there they were. Labeled by date as well as Breed. Hundreds of files hidden on a hard drive so minute it had been overlooked, because it had never been done before.

It was their last hope to learn what Brandenmore had done to the infant, Amber Broen. If the answers weren't here, then they faced a future of losing her, as they were losing Brandenmore, if the serum reacted the same as she became older.

He watched as she carefully copied each file to the epad Jonas had given him before disconnecting the frame and laying it carefully on top of the electronic pad used to connect enforcers with the bureau when needed.

Creed sent a carefully worded, encrypted message to Jonas to pick up the package, then lifted his mate from the computer and turned her to face him.

As he suspected, tears whispered down her cheeks. They were tears of regret, of acceptance. There was no longer any denial left inside her, no illusion of anything good left within her uncle.

"He loved you," Creed whispered. He was convinced of that. "Your uncle loved you and your mother, Kita. Loved you so much that the need to protect you from her fate drove him to the lengths he went to."

She nodded before laying her forehead against his chest, her breathing hitched from the sobs she tried to hold inside.

"There was no life more important to him than the life of the daughter his sister loved more than anything on this earth."

During one of the few coherent moments Brandenmore had had over the weeks, that information had come out. It was easy to kill, he had screamed, sobbed. Easy to torture, to maim and to destroy if it meant finding the secret of the fountain of youth. An elixir that halted aging, that cured all diseases, that could save his sister from death. And later, nothing had mattered but saving his niece from the same fate.

The experiments had begun the month Brandenmore had learned his sister had one of the few incurable cancers that still existed. Remission was possible, but the doctors had warned her family it would never last for long.

He'd accepted an offer the Genetics Council had made him that week and begun his research. For massive amounts of money he was given the Breeds needed, then the few mated couples he had been able to acquire. From there, it had snowballed and a monster had been born.

Then, he had learned he had the same cancer, years before his sister had died. Not the niece, but the brother was to be cursed with that fate. It had been more than Phillip Brandenmore could bear.

"He was selfish," she whispered. "A monster is born, Creed, they're not created. He was born a monster."

Unfortunately, Creed agreed with her.

The pain of realization was a strike of agony slashing at him as it tore through her.

As she lifted her head, his head bent, his lips slanting over hers, the need to replace that agony with pleasure driving him to kiss her with a strength and hunger he hadn't felt since that first kiss.

Her kiss flamed beneath his lips. Arching against him, she twined her arms around his neck, a low moan of need passing her lips as he picked her up in his arms and bore her back to the bed.

Her gown was removed easily. The soft cotton pants he wore pushed from his hips and down his legs with little thought to care.

Thick and heavy, his cock pressed against her lower stomach, throbbing, demanding the heat he sensed rising between her thighs.

Riding him as hard as the need for that pleasure was the need for her kiss though. Not just because of the mating heat that would intensify, or the pleasure he gained from that as well. It was a comfort mixed with a fiery hunger. It was an intimate dance of lips and tongues stroking against each other, loving, caressing as the taste of cinnamon and need filled both their senses.

Creed let his hands stroke up her back, then down. They feathered over her hips, returned to her spine, the sensitive pads experiencing the silken heat of her flesh as she moved against him, stroking fire over his dick as the warmth of her belly stroked across it.

Soft fingers stroked his neck, his shoulders as the kiss began to heat, to become hungrier, more intimate, more desperate.

Forcing his hands from the soft caresses he was delivering to her back, Creed lifted her gently and placed her in the bed before coming over her, a growl vibrating in his chest as he slid between her thighs, pressing them wide with his knees as his lips covered hers once again.

He wanted so much. He wanted every taste of her, each soft inch of flesh stroked with his tongue.

The need rolling furiously within him wouldn't allow that time. Later perhaps, he thought as his lips moved down her neck, laying a trail of kisses along the slender column as he moved inexorably to the swollen rise of her breasts.

Tight, hard nipples drew him. The taste of them, a banquet of sweet heat as he rolled one against his tongue before pulling it into his mouth.

Human instincts were urging him to hurry, to bury the hard length of his cock inside her, feel the ecstasy of tight, heated flesh enclosing it, milking it with hungry, convulsive strokes. There was another part though. A deep, primal instinct that demanded he reinforce the life commitment his heart, his very soul, had made to her.

As his lips traveled down her body, his tongue peeked out to lick at sensitive flesh, the hunger to hear her cries of need echoing around him driving him to touch her, to taste her in the most intimate of ways.

His tongue stroked over the silken curls surrounding her swollen clit, his fingers parting the moisture-laden folds as her hips arched to him.

Fucking her was the most pleasure he had ever known in his life, but he was learning, discovering other pleasures, other ways to amplify that pleasure with each touch against her flesh.

As he lowered his head, his tongue slid up the narrow slit, flicking against the snug entrance and teasing her with the promise to stretch that sweet flesh soon.

His cock pulsed with burning hunger at the thought of working inside her, nearly obliterating any other need from his mind.

That guiding instinct remained steadfast instead.

To pleasure her.

To ensure she knew, forever, to the depths of her heart and soul that no other man could ever pleasure her, could ever stroke her or satisfy her or fulfill the emotional needs he felt inside her.

Emotion that had begun as fascination, then as attraction, and was only now easing into a fully developed devotion, a love that could span the decades they could have together.

It was a love he was determined to encourage. A love the animal inside him seemed to understand, to crave, and was determined to encourage.

He would argue with her, push her, challenge her. He would never allow what they had to become boring, stale, or predictable. The animal instincts inside him would always know which way to turn.

The man would always know how to whisper the words; the animal would understand how to ensure them.

As his tongue pressed into the tight center of her flexing pussy, a growl rumbled in his chest at the rain-sweet taste of her. The slide of silken juices and the sound of her rising moans beginning to fill his senses.

This was what he had longed for.

Her hands buried in his hair, fingers clenching in the strands as she fought to hold him in place as the pleasure began to tighten inside her. The slide of her heated moisture caressed his tongue as he fucked it inside her, tasting her, building her pleasure, determined to lock her soul to his as her release exploded.

Seconds before she could melt into that oblivion he came over her, the throbbing, sensitive crest of his cock pressing against her, a growl escaping his lips as his head bent to her shoulder and the man he was lost himself to the animal as it rose inside him.

KITA CRIED OUT in a pleasure so exquisite she swore she couldn't bear it.

Her lashes drifted open as she felt the head of his cock begging to press inside her as his teeth pressed against the curve of her shoulder, beneath her neck.

She knew what was coming. She hadn't carried his mark, despite the fact that mating heat had been driving them insane for weeks.

Merinus Tyler and her sister-in-law, Sherra, had told her what to expect when it came, but nothing could have prepared her for it.

His teeth raked over her flesh as he began to work the thickly engorged crest of his erection inside her. Tight, hard thrusts that forged a path of burning flames through her pussy, stretching the tender tissue, exposing nerve endings that screamed into life as the broad head parted them and the thick shaft caressed them.

Aching, desperate sensations began to pulse through her vagina. A deep-seated torturous response that silently demanded more. Always more. Harder, stronger, deeper.

She felt taken, possessed, and still, it wasn't enough. She needed more.

"Creed," she gasped his name as she felt the next thrust, powerful and fierce bury the heavy flesh in to the hilt.

Her legs lifted, wrapped around his hips. Her head arched back, grinding into the pillows as her hips lifted, demanding more.

"Yes, Kita," he groaned. "Press up, baby. Give me that sweet pussy. Every tight inch."

He was buried until he could go no farther before he pulled

back and thrust in again, his hips shifting, plunging as he began to fuck her with hard lunges that sent a cry tearing past her lips.

This was life, and it was living.

The brutal ache building in her vagina had her writhing beneath him, her pussy tightening further, that ache coiling around her clit as she felt her womb tightening, an agony of pleasure beginning to burn, to ignite. The snug walls of her pussy milked the hard flesh thrusting inside her, sucking at him, stroking, drawing him deeper as each thrust became harder, faster, lightning striking over her clit, burying to her womb until it ignited a release that had her screaming his name as rapture began to lance through every nerve ending in her body.

She felt his teeth sink home, the fact that he had broken the skin barely registering as she was swept away by sensations so brilliant, so exquisite there was no thought, no memory, no sense of self.

There was only them. His cock flexing and pulsing inside her as he began to come, the feel of the thick, heated extension protruding from beneath his cock to lock him inside her, to stroke against a hidden bundle of nerves that only had her exploding again, harder, brighter, than ever before.

She was crying his name, strangled sounds that she doubted made sense as she was carried away on a wave of pure, blinding sensation.

She swore she felt not just his body, but something more. She felt him, wrapped around her soul, protecting her, his strength cushioning her heart should she need to find solace.

She felt him holding her inside. Felt him bound to her as she had never been bound to another.

In that moment, Kita felt him become her mate.

"I love you." Barely coherent, the words were torn from her lips. "Creed, I love you . . ."

And that love was answered.

A whisper at her ear as his teeth lifted from her flesh.

"My soul," he groaned, shuddering in his release. "Sweet God, Kita, you're my soul."

And his lips covered hers again. His tongue took her mouth, his moan fed hers.

A kiss as sweet as it was demanding. As binding as it was primal. It was the kiss that dreams were made of . . .

31901050284761